Contributors: Kevin J. Anderson, Paul Danner, Patricia A. Jackson, Duane Maxwell, Steve Miller, Tom Moldvay, Timothy S. O'Brien, Angela Phillips, Eric S. Trautmann and Daniel Wallace

Editing: Steve Miller • **Proofreading:** Jen Seiden

Graphics: Richard Hawran

Cover and Title Page Illustration: Lucasfilm Ltd. • **Cover Design and Graphics:** Tim Bobko

Interior Illustrations: Tim Bobko, Kathy Burdette, Mike Chen, Joe Corroney, David Day, Brandon McKinney, Doug Shuler and Will Warren

Special Thanks To: Allan Kausch, Julia Russo, and Sue Rostoni of Lucasfilm Licensing; Richard Hawran, Jeff Kent, Peter Schweighofer, Paul Sudlow and Eric S. Trautmann of West End Games; Timothy Zahn, Sonja Miller, Louis J. Prosperi, Elaine Cunningham, Jeff Grubb, Charlene Newcomb, Tish Pahl, Jeff Menges and Will Warren

Publisher: **Daniel Scott Palter** • Associate Publisher/Treasurer: **Denise Palter**
Associate Publisher: **Richard Hawran** • Editors: **Fred Jandt, Steve Miller, Jen Seiden, Peter Schweighofer, George Strayton, Paul Sudlow, Eric S. Trautmann**
Graphic Artists: **Tim Bobko, Thomas ONeill, Brian Schomburg**
Sales Director: **Jeff Kent** • Sales Assistant: **Timothy S. O'Brien**
Licensing Manager: **Ron Seiden** • Warehouse Manager: **Ed Hill**
Accounting: **Karen Bayly, Mary Galant, Wendy Lord**

E-Mail

Editorial: WEGEdit@aol.com **Art: WestEndArt@aol.com**
Sales: WEGSales@aol.com

Published by: West End Games • RR 3 Box 2345 • Honesdale, PA 18431

®, TM and © 1997 Lucasfilm Ltd. (LFL). All Rights Reserved. Trademarks of LFL used by West End Games under authorization.

STAR WARS®

Vol. 1, Issue 15 November, 1997

Adventure JOURNAL

In This Issue

Special Section: Scoundrels

ONE DIE,

INFINITE POSSIBILITIES...

D6™

A Customizable Roleplaying Game

WEST END GAMES®

Now creating a game system is as easy as creating a character!

This revolutionary plug-and-play game system allows you to customiz
every aspect of your game, from character generation to combat an
magic. Each time you fill out new Game and Character Creation Tem
plates you've got a new game system specially designed for your gam
world! It's as simple as that.

TM & © 1996 West End Games. All Rights Reserved.

STAR WARS
SOURCEFILE

Alien Encounters

The SHARD

By Stephen Kenson

Illustrated by Kathy Burdette

"Welcome home, sir," Enthree said as his master entered his quarters on board the Star Destroyer Thunder. Commander Tobal Siy was not a happy man. Even a droid could see that plainly. That meant that N–3PO could see it better than most. The protocol droid had served as his personal assistant and valet for several years and knew his moods and manner well. "May I get anything for you?"

Siy loosened the collar of his gray uniform. "No, Enthree." He paused, massaged his forehead with one hand, and sighed heavily. "On second thought, bring me some water and a dose of something to take care of this headache."

The droid shuffled off to comply with his master's request while Siy collapsed into one of the room's padded chairs. Enthree returned quickly with a glass and a pair of white tablets.

"If I may ask, sir," the droid ventured as Siy swallowed the pills, "are you ill or in need of medical attention?" Commander Siy took

another sip of his drink, letting the warmth of it soothe him before he answered.

"No. Just another futile day of chasing Rebel smugglers through the sector, Enthree. They are like ghosts. Somehow they evade our every effort to catch them; probe droids, TIE fighter sweeps, sensor scans, orbital bombardments, nothing we try seems to have any effect. If we get word of a Rebel supply depot or base, it's always abandoned before we can get there." Siy stopped and forced himself to unclench his jaw and take another sip of water.

"I'm sure that you will catch the Rebels in time, sir," Enthree said in as hopeful a tone as a droid could manage.

"There is only one way that the Rebels could possibly be one step ahead of us all of the time," Siy mused, speaking more to himself than the droid. "They must have a spy on board."

"A spy!" Enthree squeaked. "On this ship? But, sir! That's impossible!"

Siy took another sip of his drink and said in an irritated tone, "I know that. I've had security tightened three times. There are no signs of any infiltration in our personnel. There are no listening devices, no unusual transmissions. No signs of a Rebel spy, but the Rebels are getting information somehow." A wave of fatigue swept over Siy, and he set his glass down on the nearby table and leaned back in his chair.

"Perhaps you should rest, sir," came Enthree's voice from what seemed like very far away. Siy felt like he was drifting off into sleep even as the droid spoke. "That's right, sleep and take your mind from your concerns. There is nothing to worry about. You should be feeling quite relaxed by now." Commander Siy made a small noise and nodded his head a bit.

"Good," the protocol droid said, its unblinking yellow eyes fixed on the Commander. "Now tell me, Commander, about the latest efforts to find the Rebel smugglers and the security measures you've taken to find any spies on board." Commander Siy licked his lips a bit and began to ramble in a quiet voice about a new plan to place Imperial spies in the ranks of the local smuggling community in an effort to locate those smugglers who were aiding the Rebellion. He provided the names of the Imperial agents and talked about efforts to identify any foreign elements on board the *Thunder* that might be indications of a Rebel infiltration. The protocol droid listened carefully to Siy's every word.

"That's very good, Commander," the droid said in a soft and

calming tone. "Now, go to sleep and forget all about our little talk. You will wake up in an hour or so feeling quite rested and confident that your plans will allow you to locate the Rebels." Siy settled back into the chair cushions and promptly fell asleep. Enthree watched the Commander for a few moments until his breathing fell into a steady and even pattern. Then the droid picked up the water glass and dropped it into the waste-reclamation unit.

Enthree shuffled to the small maintenance closet in the back of the commander's quarters where the droid was supposed to spend its time recharging when necessary. The door of the closet slid closed with a faint hiss and Enthree opened a panel that concealed a small, but complex set of circuits and wires. The droid manipulated control studs on its own shoulders and chest and opened its chest panel to reveal the usual array of circuitry that made up the innards of a 3PO model protocol droid.

This layer of mechanics was likewise lifted away to reveal a glimmering crystal, nearly the length of the droid's torso, embedded among the mechanisms and wires inside Enthree's body. The droid swiftly and efficiently hooked up connections from the open panel to ports around the crystal, which pulsed and flickered with its own inner light. Once all of the connections were in place, Enthree began dictating a report that would help its Rebel allies avoid Imperial capture for another day and, perhaps, bring the Rebellion one step closer to victory against the Empire.

The Shards

The Shards are a unique non–humanoid species allied with the Rebellion and the New Republic against the Empire. The unique physiology and abilities of the Shards make them an unexpected surprise for anyone who considers droids to be just a part of the background of the galaxy.

Appearance and Biology: The Shard are a silicone-based life form. They are 30 to 40 centimeters in length, up to 10 centimeters in diameter, and appear like irregularly faceted and roughly cylindrical crystals. The silicate structure of the Shard makes up the molecular "circuitry" of their brains. Faint energy pulses can be seen glimmering inside their body. Various chemical impurities give the translucent crystal of the Shards different colors, and those familiar with their homeworld can tell which region the Shard originated in. Each Shard also has a unique electromagnetic "signature" that others of its race can recognize.

The Shards developed on the planet Orax, a world known for its beautiful rock and mineral formations and natural hot springs. They form from an interaction between the ion-charged atmosphere of the planet and the natural crystals and mineral–rich water, "growing" energy-sensitive crystalline lattices in clusters along the rocks near the numerous hot springs.

Each Shard is a discrete entity made up of a block of crystalline "circuitry." When the Shard has reached its full size and "adult" energy signature, the accretion of crystal begins to produce a new Shard. A large colony contains hundreds or even thousands of individual Shards.

Some of these Shard clusters can grow to enormous size, towering like giant trees formed from multi-colored crystal. Shards are immobile all of their lives, and some of the oldest Shard clusters have existed for several millennia. Over time, natural erosion causes some Shards to dissolve back into the environment they came from, but otherwise Shards live for thousands of standard years.

The size of a cluster is of minor importance, since the Shards are able to sense and produce electromagnetic charges. This network of electromagnetism, conducted by the ionization of Orax's atmosphere, allows the Shards to form a single group–mind. This electromagnetic communication also allows the Shards to interact directly with computers of all kinds as well as sense transmissions and electrical pulses from technological equipment. This electromagnetic "vision" is the Shard's sole means of perceiving the world. They have no sense of hearing, touch, taste or smell.

Temperament: Shards tend to be thoughtful, logical and introspective by nature, able to think and process information with computer-like speed and accuracy. They tend to be calm and reasonable at all times, and many species find Shards rather cold and emotionless.

Many Shards also have a childlike curiosity about the world

around them; they want to see other worlds, meet new species and travel. The thirst for knowledge seems to be a driving force for them. These are the Shards most likely to take advantage of the new opportunities open to them to leave their home world.

Many "wandering" Shards have become intoxicated with the experiences of movement and the ability to see the world around through their droid vehicles' sensors. Many Shards consider this a perverse lifestyle and a "corruption" of their culture, while others believe that the experiences of these wanderers only enhance the greater whole of the race when they are brought back into the group–mind once again.

History and Culture: Orax is an Outer Rim world first discovered a little more than a century before the fall of the Old Republic. When scouts first came upon the world, it was thought to be uninhabited and a survey of the planet revealed rich deposits of many different minerals suitable for mining. Mining operations on the planet all fell victim to a series of mysterious equipment failures that endangered the miners and threatened to make operations unprofitable.

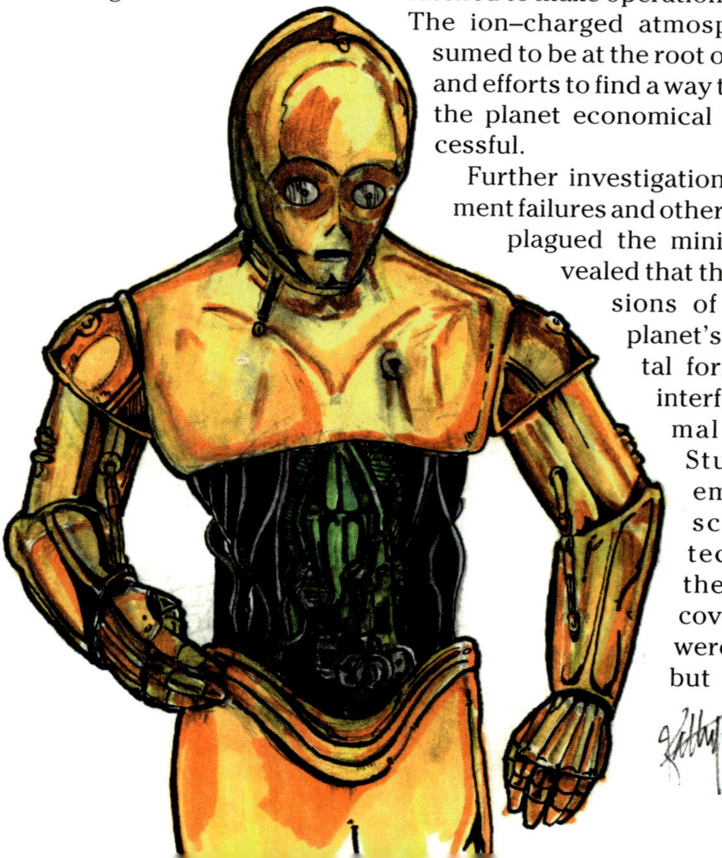

The ion–charged atmosphere was assumed to be at the root of the problems and efforts to find a way to make mining the planet economical were not successful.

Further investigation of the equipment failures and other problems that plagued the mining colony revealed that the energy emissions of some of the planet's natural crystal formations were interfering with normal operations. Studying the emissions, the scientists and technicians of the colony discovered that they were not random, but specific program instructions being fed into the affected systems. Eventually, Republic technicians created a translator that converted the Shard energy pulses into speech and back again, allowing the Shards to learn to communicate directly.

While the Shards had initially been confused and frightened by the sudden discovery of an existence outside of their own collective, and then angered by the damage being done to their world by the miners, they quickly came to realize that the people of the Republic had been as unaware of the Shards as they had been of the Republic. Much information was exchanged between the Shards and the visitors. The crystalline entities were intrigued by all they learned about the galaxy. They came to thirst for more information, but they were also uncertain about becoming part of the greater galactic civilization. Part of the trouble was the fact that the Shards could only be told about the Republic, but couldn't see any of it for themselves.

A solution was provided by the Shards' unique ability to control computers. Republic technicians developed a droid–control interface that took advantage of the Shards' abilities. Several Shards were voluntarily disconnected from their growth-rocks and placed inside droid bodies, giving the crystals mobility and sensory input for the first time, allowing them to become Orax's "ambassadors" to the outside world.

Dozens of Shards left Orax to travel the galaxy. All they learned would then be transferred to the group-mind when they returned, allowing the Shards to better decide if their destiny lay with joining the Republic or in further isolation. The crystalline creatures weren't in much of a hurry, their decision would come only after decades of careful consideration and information gathering. Unfortunately, they never really got the chance.

When the New Order inherited the reins of power, the Shard "ambassadors" were cut off from their home world. Many were killed, while others went into hiding masquerading as ordinary droids. Aggressive mining of Orax's mineral resources began with"machines" that the Shards could not interfere with — slave labor. The crystal entities watched helplessly as their world was looted and Shard colonies were destroyed. A few of the "wandering" Shards made attempts to return to their world, but none succeeded, since the Empire kept all droids away from Orax.

Some Shards decided to ally themselves with the Rebellion as a means of freeing their home world from the domination of the Empire. With their ability to naturally affect computers and their droid guises allowing them to go many places undetected, the Shards became valuable spies and covert agents of the Rebellion. Very few Rebels even knew of the existence of the Shards or their abilities.

After the defeat of the Empire at the Battle of Endor, mining operations on Orax ceased, but the ecology of the planet was devastated, and the survival of the Shards as a race was threatened. Eventually, the New Republic became aware of the plight of the Shards by some of the remaining Shard wanderers and made efforts to re–establish diplomatic relations, providing new droid technology and ecological aid to the Shards in exchange for limited mineral rights on Orax.

Politics: All political decisions among the Shards are decided by general consensus of the group–mind. Shards love nothing more than a good debate, so Shard politics move unbearably slow by the standards of other, more time-bound species of the galaxy. The Shards might take a century or more to come to an important decision, which is why Orax has yet to join the New Republic, despite their dislike for the Empire and their need for Republic aid to rebuild their world. The Shards are gaining some understanding of the concept of limited time, brought back from the wanderers, but it is a *slow* learning process.

Technology Level: The Shards have no "technology" as such, but they are nonetheless some of the finest technicians ever encountered by the Rebel Alliance and the New Republic. The Shards have an intuitive understanding of computers and electronics of all kinds, allowing them to interact with and repair such things with amazing speed and accuracy. Shard wanderers and those on Orax who have encountered the technology of the galactic civilization have managed to learn its innermost workings in a matter of days, enough to allow them to control and influence the technology using their energy transmissions.

Trade and Technology: Access to technology—especially droids—is the basis for the Shards' relations with the rest of the galaxy. They trade mining–rights on Orax for the opportunities to access Republic computer systems and databases as well as gain droids that the Shards can control and, sometimes, use as vehicles to leave Orax and explore the galaxy. Since the defeat of the Empire, the Shards are conservative in their negotiations over mineral rights on their planet. They still recall the ravages of the Empire and are not willing to place their world in further ecological danger. However, their world does host several successful mining operations and have many others looking to set up shop on Orax.

In the Galaxy: The experience of living apart from the Shard group–mind has proven too terrifying for most Shards, who prefer to remain as they are, but some members of the race have taken to space in their robotic "vehicles," becoming valuable technicians and programmers for the New Republic. The surviving Shards who took an active part in the Rebellion continue to be the strongest proponents of their race joining the New Republic.

Gamemaster Notes: Shard characters provide a way of including "droids that aren't really droids" in the campaign, as well as providing "droid" characters that have a bit more free will and autonomy that ordinary droids. Gamemasters should work with the player of a Shard character to design an appropriate droid body using the droids given in the *Star Wars* rulebook as a guideline. All of the skills of the droid are provided by the Shard "driving" it. Shard characters with more than one droid body should be quite rare, and the gamemaster will want to limit the abilities of any droid body so they are not too powerful. Shards, especially those operating during the period of the Rebellion, prefer to inhabit droids that are more common and likely to go unnoticed, liked 3PO and R2 units. Their goal was to remain undetected by the Empire, so they avoided droid–bodies that were likely to get them in trouble, like assassin droids.

Personality Notes: Shards are highly rational and logical creatures with a strong streak of distrust for organic creatures like those who devastated their home-world. Most Shards are incredibly patient and tend to spend a great deal of time thinking. They are slow-moving by the standards of most other species, taking their time to reach a decision, although Shards disconnected from the group-mind seem to be able to make up their minds much faster.

Suggested Skills: *Computer programming/repair* and *droid programming* are practically required for Shards (although some very inexperienced Shards make do with their natural *Technical* ability). Shard wanders will also want to have *droid repair* so they can fix any

Stephen Kenson

damage to their droid bodies when necessary. Sessile Shards tend to learn many *Knowledge* skills, while wanderers might pick up virtually any skill although they seem most comfortable with other *Technical* skills.

Shards

Attribute Dice: 12D
DEXTERITY 0D*
KNOWLEDGE 2D/5D
MECHANICAL 2D/4D
PERCEPTION 2D/4D
STRENGTH 0D*
TECHNICAL 3D/6D
*** see below**

Special Skills

Computer Mind: Shards have an instinctive understanding of computers and droid brains and gain +1D with the *computer programming/repair* and *droid programming* skills as well as any other skill that involves computer programming or operation such as *astrogation* or *security* (versus computerized locks and devices). Shards can interact directly with comlink–equipped computers using their telecommunication ability.

Telecommunication: Shards can emit and receive electromagentic transmissions as a means of communication. This allows them to detect any operating technological device or droid within 100 meters with an easy *Perception* roll. Their signals can reach out to about one kilometer individually, but are enough to reach anywhere on their home world when the Shard is part of the group–mind. Shard transmissions can be picked up on standard comlinks and other devices tuned to detect them. Shards can also affect droids equipped with restraining bolts as if they had a control wand by making a moderate *technical* or *droid programming* roll.

Story Factors

Sessile: Shards are incapable of movement on their own. They have no natural *Dexterity* or *Strength* dice. They can learn *Dexterity* or *Strength* based skills and use them in conjunction with a droid body, if the body is capable of performing that skill. They can only move inside a droid "vehicle" or by being carried by a droid or another creature. In their natural state, Shards also have no senses apart from their electromagnetic sense.

Fragile: Shards have no *Strength* attribute dice and gain only 1D to resist damage in their natural state. A damage result that kills a Shard shatters its body into fragments. Normal medical treatment is ineffective on Shards, they must heal naturally unless they can be returned to Orax to receive treatment in the mineral hot-springs on the planet. Force abilities such as accelerate *healing* and *transfer Force* do affect Shards, as they are still living creatures.

Move: 0 or by the droid body the Shard controls.
Size: 30–40 centimeters.

Adventure Ideas

Escort: The player characters are chosen for the unusual job of escorting a droid to a hidden Rebel base. The Empire is searching for a Rebel spy that has escaped with important information, but they are unaware that the spy is actually a Shard using the droid as a vehicle. The Imperials are likely to overlook the droid, and believe the player characters to be the spies if they catch up to them. If the circumstances become serious enough, the Shard will reveal its presence and use its unique abilities to help the characters out of tight spots.

Return to Orax: A Shard who is a friend of the player characters (perhaps the same Shard introduced in the suggested adventure above) is gravely injured and will die unless returned to the mineral-rich pools on Orax. Unfortunately, Orax is under Imperial control and travel to and from the mining world is restricted. Rebel characters have to find a way to reach the Shard home world undetected long enough for them to make their way through the ionized storms and harsh wilderness of the planet to reach one of the Shard colonies that can heal their injured comrade. Then they have to get off the planet without being detected or captured by Imperial forces. The mission is complicated by a Shard cluster on Orax that is debating the possibility of collaboration with the Empire as a means of ending the destruction of their world. The Rebels will have to find a way to convince the Shards not to turn them in to the Imperial garrison on the planet.

Author's Note: This story takes place between my novels *Jedi Search* and *Dark Apprentice*. It describes the first encounter between Luke Skywalker and the Jedi historian/singer Tionne, who will become one of his most important trainees. The background on Exis Station also ties in with my forthcoming *Tales of the Jedi* comic series from Dark Horse, "The Redemption of Ulic," and Rebecca Moesta's third Junior Jedi novel, *Kenobi's Blade*. Of course, I hope it stands alone as its own story, too.

FIRESTORM

By Kevin J. Anderson

Illustrations by Doug Shuler

The world of Ossus had once been the greatest center of Jedi learning—a magnificent library that contained knowledge of the Force and the history of a thousand generations of defenders of the Old Republic. Scrolls and dataplaques contained their legends and songs, their triumphs and tragedies. Ossus had been filled with fountains and statues, beautiful pavilions of embroidered fabric, fluted columns of milk–stone, courtyards with mosaics of flagstones and tile, wind chimes of crystal and gold. . . .

Now, though, it was merely a tomb, a blasted dark scar, its glory obliterated by fiery violence.

Tionne climbed down the ramp of her ship, the *Lore Seeker*—an obsolete, quirky craft almost as old as the ruins themselves—and just stood still as she absorbed all the echoing memories around her. Her mother–of–pearl eyes widened, and her silvery hair blew about in the dead wind. She let her imagination swirl with stories that might have been told by ghosts, epic ballads the Jedi would have sung—if Ossus had not been incinerated when ten stars exploded in the Cron Drift four thousand years before, during the height of the Sith War.

Overhead, filling the sky like a brilliant stain, was the incandescent gas of the Cron Drift, now a funeral pyre for this once–magnificent information center.

Venturing away from her vessel, Tionne saw glassy, hardened puddles around the remains of cyclopean statues and pillars slumped from the raging shockwave that had struck this world. Her silvery hair blew about her elfin face in the dead wind. She could smell the burnt aftereffects that still clung to the breeze like shadows.

As she walked, the broken stones and rubble crunched under her small feet. The sight overwhelmed her and a tear at the magnitude of the loss hovered on the edge of her quicksilver eyes. She stumbled ahead, not knowing where to start.

A few fast–moving, lizard–like creatures skittered to shelter. So, Ossus wasn't entirely dead. Small lifeforms often managed to survive, no matter how great the devastation. Four millennia has passed, and the radiation levels had dropped to below immediately lethal amounts, although Tionne might still suffer illness if she stayed here long. She certainly couldn't remain long enough to uncover all the secrets hidden in the rubble.

Her glittering eyes scanned the debris, and she walked to where two pillars held up a reinforced, ornate arch that had miraculously survived the holocaust. She wondered how many long–lost answers might be buried here, how much more information about Jedi history she could find beneath the broken stones. Learning everything about the great Jedi Knights had been Tionne's driving quest all of her life, and Ossus was a huge treasure trove.

The Empire had frowned on remembering Jedi legends, on idolizing the great defenders of the Old Republic... on keeping the flame alive. Before she was born, the Jedi had been slaughtered, all but wiped out. Tionne had lived on a drab Imperial world, Rindao, a training station and outpost near the Outer Rim. Though her people did not support the Empire, they had not resisted outright when the stormtroopers came to take over, and thus their civilization had not been punished.

In Tionne's uninteresting childhood she had sought refuge in the ancient stories. Her old grandmother had an archaic two–sided stringed instrument, and she would sing legends of the Jedi, heroic stories about Nomi Sunrider, her daughter Vima, and other champions of the Force who had fought and perhaps perished during the Great Sith War.

But one night the Imperial commander had found the old woman telling such stories. The stormtroopers had hauled Tionne's grandmother out into the town square and executed her with their blaster rifles, cutting her down for implying that the olden–days were more heroic than the Empire's current glory.

Young Tionne had been devastated. Before the stormtroopers could ransack her grandmother's house, she broke in through a back window and took away the stringed musical instrument, the only memento she wanted.

Quietly, as she wandered the spacelanes on her quest, Tionne had taught her fingers the mysteries of the strings, stretching her voice with the secret songs the old woman had played for her. Now, though, the Emperor was dead, and his New Order had fallen more than six years ago. With the Empire and its repressive restrictions gone, Tionne had let herself be swallowed by her search for Jedi knowledge and lore.

The New Republic had occupied Coruscant, and Tionne had just heard the wonderful news that Luke Skywalker—perhaps the sole remaining Jedi Knight—had taken it upon himself to train the Jedi again, to bring about a new brotherhood of protectors.

Bending down to the scorched rubble, Tionne moved aside a fallen cluster of flagstones and found in the shadows beneath a small statue of what must have once been a Jedi Master. The figure was a short, unimposing alien with a sloping, rounded head and exposed teeth. She wondered if it could have been the renowned scholar Jedi Master Odan–Urr, who had fought even earlier, in the Great Hyperspace War against the original Sith Empire, and had then lived for a thousand years as the keeper of the library on Ossus.

Smiling, feeling her heart swell with pride, Tionne cradled the small statue, saw its carbonized and glassy surface layers where the heat of an exploding star had crisped it. She took the figure, astonished to be actually touching a piece of Jedi history.

No doubt if she spent the rest of her life combing through the debris on Ossus, Tionne could find more clues, more information, more vital tidbits of history. The Empire had declared Ossus off–limits, fearing other seekers might discover too much knowledge of the Jedi—but now, perhaps, the New Republic could devote its time to a real excavation, with crews of scientists and historians who wanted to recreate the golden age of the Jedi Knights.

Tionne turned back toward her battered and creaking ship. She had found the statue of Odan–Urr; that would be enough for now. But she would continue her quest until she knew all there was to know about the Jedi Knights.

Yavin 4 was an emerald moon orbiting a huge, pastel gas giant—the site of one of the galaxy's greatest battles, home of a former Rebel base. Soon, it would become a training center for new Jedi.

As he fought his way through the tangled foliage, Luke Skywalker thought that the sheer tenacity of the primeval jungle would prove an even more difficult foe than the Empire itself. Beside him, Artoo–Detoo followed the path Luke chose, grinding his tractor wheels through the underbrush.

Finally, Luke stood at the ruins of the Great Massassi Temple, its stone steps ravaged by time and the forces of nature... as well as Imperial bombardment after the destruction of the first Death Star. If this moon had been good enough to shelter Princess Leia and her freedom fighters, he thought, it would be good enough for a place of Jedi learning.

Luke had already found two candidates in his Jedi search, and they had accompanied him here to Yavin 4. Streen, the eccentric old hermit who had lived on Bespin, was a gas prospector who searched the skies for valuable upwellings of tibanna gas. Streen had an affinity for the winds, an ability to sense when a storm might happen. Luke had tested him and found an untapped potential for using the Force—Streen would be an ideal Jedi candidate, though the old man had been reluctant to leave his peaceful and quiet life. After arriving on the uninhabited jungle moon, he seemed much more content that he could find solitude again.

Luke's other new trainee, Gantoris, had wild black hair and a beard, accentuating his fiery eyes and grim temperament. His personality had been forged by living on the hellish colony world of Eol Sha, where a close moon caused tidal chaos, seismic upheavals and volcanic eruptions. With his untrained echoes of the Force, Gantoris had experienced nightmares about a powerful, dark man who meant to lead him down a road to destruction. Gantoris had thought Luke fit that premonition and had tried to kill him. But Luke had survived. Eventually, Gantoris had come with the Jedi Master in order to be trained in the Force.

Clearing away the overwhelming jungle and repairing the crumbling temple ruins seemed an insurmountable task. Luke smiled as the thought came to him. Yoda could probably have done it all single–handedly. Luke and two hard–working trainees could accomplish it well enough.

The three men began the hard work of stripping out regrown weeds. Luke ignited his lightsaber and began hacking away at the underbrush while Gantoris and Streen cleared fallen rocks and swept away dirt. Artoo helped where he could, extending his tiny cutting saw and attacking fibrous creepers.

"Glamorous work for a Jedi Knight," Gantoris muttered, tossing a dusty load of stones aside. "I could get a better job as a maintenance worker."

"You're not a Jedi Knight," Streen said. "You're just a Jedi trainee."

Luke stacked the torn underbrush in a clearing outside the main pyramid, while Artoo buzzed along, dragging a sledge filled with other forest debris. In the middle of the clearing, Luke used his igniter to set the mound of dead foliage on fire. The heaped pile of burning brands reminded him of his father's funeral pyre on Endor, how Luke had set the fearsome black uniform ablaze.

For months, he had been keeping himself busy with the menial tasks of setting up his Jedi academy—because it troubled him too much to deal with the larger issues. Luke Skywalker didn't know *how* to train Jedi Knights; he didn't have enough knowledge about the ancient warriors, what they had studied, who they had been. Obi–Wan Kenobi and Yoda had begun his instruction, but that had been cut tragically short. Luke now had to discover his own way, and he also needed to find other students.

He did have the Jedi Holocron, which Leia had taken from the resurrected Emperor a year earlier, and he had the library from the

Chuunthor, the wrecked Jedi ship he had found in the wilds on Dathomir. It would be enough. Luke vowed to work as hard as he could, to gain knowledge every chance he could so that he might enhance his own training.

The Jedi Knights would be reborn, but it would be a long and hard struggle.

Tionne went from spaceport bar to trading station to backwater outpost, living by her wits and her skills. She secured jobs in cantinas where she could use the stringed musical instrument she had taken from her grandmother on Rindao. She could sing Jedi ballads and disseminate her passion for the drama of history—folktales of how Gav and Jori Daragon had sparked the Hyperspace War, or the early training of Vodo Siosk–Baas, or how the Twi'lek Jedi Tott Doneeta had been horribly burned while single–handedly fighting a heat storm to defend a small cliff city on Ryloth.

She was paid little in credits, but plenty in food and lodging, so she could continue her search. Her main goal in hanging out at such

rough establishments was to ask her questions, ply the traders and smugglers into giving her clues about lost Jedi history.

Whenever she had completed her repertoire of Jedi ballads, Tionne would ask if any members of her audience had other stories to tell. Many times this simply encouraged some of the drunken male customers to try to lure her to the private chambers in their starships, but Tionne could sense when they were telling the truth, when to signal for the bar bouncers to get them away from her.

One night, after her show in an all–species restaurant near one of Ord Mantell's many spaceports, she received a message from a rodent–like alien named Fonterrat, a down–on–his–luck scavenger. Normally Tionne would have been suspicious: creatures of all different species had attempted to take advantage of her. She sensed though, that Fonterrat simply wished to make a deal, and as she sat down across the table from him, she noticed he was eating the cheapest item on the menu and did not offer to buy her a drink.

"This information about the old Jedi Knights—" Fonterrat said in a squeaking voice. He had large ears and a pointed face, and close–set eyes like black beads under a furry brow ridge. "How much is it worth?"

Tionne regarded him calmly, her pale skin flushing slightly. "I don't know. How much is it worth?" she said. "I have some credits, but not enough to make you rich." With one gesture of her delicate, pale hands, she indicated the seedy restaurant. "Would I be working here if I had that kind of money?"

Fonterrat fiddled with his hands, fast–moving fingers playing with a napkin wipe. He sniffled. "I'm a scavenger," he said. "I need to make money for the things I find. Someday, I'll stumble across something that'll make me rich and famous . . . but right now I'm just trying to get by."

Tionne could sense his sincerity, could see that he wasn't trying to scam her. "Tell me what you found," she said. "I'll be fair. I'll pay you what I can."

"It's an ancient city in space," he said. "Exis Station. It's been abandoned for centuries."

"Exis Station!" Tionne leaned forward, widening her mother–of–pearl eyes with sudden interest. "That was the site of one of the greatest Jedi convocations in history! Nomi Sunrider herself called together the Jedi Knights a decade after the Great Sith War."

Fonterrat did not appear interested in the details "So . . . is that worth something to you? I could tell you its location. You can search the wreck yourself for any artifacts, though bear in mind that it's been empty for a long time. Damaged by solar flares."

"Yes, I'll pay." She scanned her own accounts, determining just how much she could give to this man and still buy enough fuel to get the *Lore Seeker* to Exis Station. The amount she came up with was distressingly low.

"But it might be better if you don't go there," Fonterrat said, twitching his nose.

She sat up, alarmed. "You give me the location, then tell me not to go? Why?"

"Because Exis Station is at an unstable star," he said. "Teedio. It's entered an active phase, with increasing flares. Over centuries the drag from solar wind has pulled the city closer and closer to the flares. Radiation levels on board have been lethal for some time now. You'll risk your own life if you go there. All of Exis Station is going to plunge into the sun before long."

"I don't care," she said. "I'm still going."

She reached out her credit pad and punched up a number. "That's all I have," she said. "Give me the location."

Fonterrat looked at it in dismay, but he didn't seem to have any choice either. "All right—I need the credits, even as few as these." He gave her a chip with navicomputer coordinates embedded in it. "Good luck. I thought the information was worth more that that." He stood up, hanging his head.

Tionne said, "Wait. If you go to the New Republic government and give this information to Luke Skywalker, he may also be interested. He'll pay you much more than I can. He's trying to found a new order of Jedi Knights."

"New Republic!" Fonterrat squawked. "I'm a smuggler. I have a thousand arrest warrants from different systems. I don't dare set foot near the law."

Tionne crossed her thin arms over her chest. "You're a scavenger and a smuggler—you must have *some* connections that you could use to get this information to him. Trust me, Luke Skywalker will make sure you get paid. From what I've heard of his exploits, he's a man of his word."

Fonterrat groaned, but already she could see his dark little eyes flicking back and forth, racing through possibilities of how he could use his smuggler's knowledge to surreptitiously send the message to Skywalker.

He left. Tionne quickly gathered her belongings and raced off to her ship. If Fonterrat was right, and the solar flare storm was growing worse each day, she didn't have much time to search Exis Station.

The bonfire in the clearing had burned out, leaving only a broad swath of ash in front of the Great Temple. It made a nice landing area, and the *Millennium Falcon* set down with a hiss of repulsorjets and a cloud of crunched charcoal.

Luke hurried outside the ancient pyramid with Streen and Gantoris at his side. Han Solo extended the landing ramp of his modified light freighter, and Chewbacca roared loudly as he strode down onto the blackened clearing. Han stepped into the blackened cinders and kicked them roughly with his boot.

"Good to see you, Han!" Luke waved. "We need some extra muscle for our work here."

Chewie groaned and looked down at his own hairy arms. Han laughed and shook his head, tugging down his dark vest. "Not me, buddy. I just brought you some supplies. Your sister wants me to make sure you get all the equipment you need." Han looked around

and sniffed the burnt air. "This is like a wilderness outing."

Luke shrugged. "A Jedi Knight knows how to cope." Artoo rolled up beside him and whistled.

With a laugh, Han clapped Luke on the shoulder. "Sure, kid. But if you're trying to convince new recruits to stay here, you should roll out the red–carpet treatment, not warn them about how much they'll have to suffer."

"I'll find the new recruits, somehow," Luke said.

Han pursed his lips. "You know, you should test that kid Kyp Durron—the one I rescued from the spice mines of Kessel. He's so talented I'm sure he's using the Force somehow, but he doesn't know what he's doing."

Luke laughed. "Sure, Han. I'll test him anytime you want to bring him here. I need new candidates. In fact, I've also got to go back to Dathomir where I can talk to Teneniel Djo and some of the other Force–wielding witches there. Somebody might be willing to come here—red carpet or no red carpet."

Han opened the *Falcon*'s cargo bays. He and Chewie worked with Luke, Gantoris and Streen to remove new power generators, air circulation systems, and food–preparation units.

"Leia doesn't know this, but I've got them programmed for some good, greasy Corellian sausages," Han said, cracking open a crate to flash the control panel on a food–prep unit. "But if you'd prefer something more bland, you can program in plenty of other dishes using raw materials from the jungles right here."

Luke smiled calmly. "We'll get by, Han."

Han brushed a hand across his forehead to smear perspiration aside. "Don't you even sweat anymore, kid?"

"Not unless I have to."

When they were finished unloading and setting up, Chewie went back to checking out the preflight systems on the *Falcon*, while Artoo downloaded a summary of all the Holonet reports that had backlogged since their arrival here. "Duty calls," Han said. "Back to Coruscant."

But instead of heading back for his ship, Han Solo hunkered next to Luke on the second level of the Massassi pyramid. He found a reasonably comfortable spot on one of the moss–covered stone blocks and dangled his boots over the side, rapping his heels against the time–smoothed stone.

"I got a strange message from another smuggler," he said. "A scavenger named Fonterrat. Strictly small–time, thinks he's in more trouble than he really is, keeps a low profile. But he passed along a message that you might be interested in some information he has. An ancient space city called Exis Station. He says a great Jedi convention or something took place there."

"A convocation," Luke said. "Yes. Exis Station. I've heard of it, but I don't know much about the place."

"Well, he gave me the coordinates, warned that the station itself was in danger. He's heard you're a fair man and hopes you'll pay him for the information." Han raised his eyebrows. "Me, I think it's a scam."

Luke shook his head. "No, it's real, if the coordinates are correct. Pay him what it's worth. Take it out of my credit accounts."

Han seemed alarmed. "Luke, you can't just go trusting people like that. There are more con artists and—"

"Pay him," Luke said. "If it really is Exis Station, I need to go there. Maybe it can help me with my quest."

"If you say so, kid," Han said, disbelieving. Chewie signalled on the comlink and roared that the *Falcon* was ready for departure. Han swung himself down off the mossy block and climbed down the crumbling stairs toward the *Falcon*.

"If you need anything, just call me," Han said.

"I will, Han."

Luke watched the disc–like shape of the *Millennium Falcon* take off from the burned landing clearing, then disappear into the sky. After a moment of concentration, he hurried to his newly established quarters inside the dank pyramid. There, among his personal belongings, he kept the pearly white cube of the glowing Jedi Holocron, an artifact filled with untapped knowledge of the old Jedi Knights.

He took out the ancient object and held it in front of him, caressing its sides. This had once belonged to the Emperor Palpatine, but Luke had retrieved it after he had saved Leia.

In his final confrontation with the resurrected Emperor, Luke had almost become lost to the dark side. But that terrible ordeal had finally cast him through so much anguish and mental fire that it had tempered him, taught him to ascend beyond a mere Jedi Knight to the point where others called him a Master.

But Luke still felt so small, so untrained. Even here, alone in the ancient Massassi temples, he felt intimidated at his self–appointed task of bringing back the Jedi Knights. Who was *he* to do such a thing? It would take him a lifetime even to begin learning how to train others, but he knew it had to be done.

As a young Rebel pilot, he had come earlier to these empty temples. At the time he'd been barely touched by Obi–Wan Kenobi, just started in his path along the Force. He had known little then, understood nothing about how the Force affected all things. Young farmboy Luke had sensed nothing back then... but now that he had more years of practice, more training, and more pain, he felt the ancient Massassi ruins somewhat oppressive, mysterious. They seemed to hold secrets, a dark presence buried deep in the cores of the stones. A coldness he could not explain.

But he could not run from it. Yavin 4 was a place that would foster the rebirth of the Jedi.

Luke looked down at the Holocron, touched its side, and called forth the holographic gatekeeper. The image of Bodo Baas, a small shrunken alien, arose before him, wispy, shimmering. Luke said, "Show me Exis Station. Tell me what I need to know."

The Holocron grew brighter and the image of a giant city in space filled the air in front of him. Luke looked with awe upon the great abandoned metropolis, its sprawling turrets and modules, its starports, its domes, its cargo holds.

And he knew he had to go there.

When Tionne arrived at Exis Station, the sight took her breath away.

She trimmed the solar sails on her *Lore Seeker* and cruised closer to the sprawling city in space, orbiting high and looking down on the plane of the metal–walled settlement. The station had once been a metropolis, a bustling spaceport, a rendezvous point for traders, diplomats and Jedi Knights.

As the system's sun Teedio became unstable, Exis Station had taken advantage of what could have been viewed as a disaster: ion miners and solar–flare skimmers operated in a boom–town during the time when Teedio provided fast energy resources that ambitious risk–takers in the Old Republic could exploit. But when conditions grew too dangerous, the entire city had been abandoned—left to hang empty in space for centuries.

But Tionne hoped it wasn't entirely empty.

As she looped above the north pole of the flattened central hub, she studied the numerous other pods and modules extending like the spokes of a wheel. The modules were of varying sizes and shapes, tacked on as the station grew asymmetrically. The structure had kind of a beautiful chaos, sizes and shapes and materials all spread out in a glistening array.

But Exis Station hung canted on its axis, knocked off kilter by centuries of pummeling by heated flares. Uneven temperature shifts had gradually worked their damage upon the station.

The sun itself looked like an angry red eye, its surface roiling and bubbling. Flares swept out like tidal waves, prominences gushing upward in geysers of plasma. Sunspots stood out like open sores on the stellar surface. Teedio's heavy radiation bathed Exis Station, pounding through its shielding, blistering its hull plates. Obviously, the place wouldn't last long.

She had her work cut out for her.

During the evacuation of Ossus, the Jedi had had enough forewarning of the supernova shockwave that they whisked away a few of the greatest artifacts, the most precious history texts. They were taken to Exis Station to form a temporary library, a place where they would be safe. It was also here that Nomi Sunrider had declared her legendary convocation, where the surviving Jedi from the Sith War had discussed the reshaping of the Republic.

Tionne could not ignore the potential of such a place. She had to see it, had to set foot on board and walk the corridors that had once been a precious Jedi library—before solar flares engulfed the city in space and obliterated it for all time.

In the *Lore Seeker*, she transmitted a signal, hoping that the automated systems onboard the station hadn't been shorted out by the blasting radiation or the effects of time. She was pleased to receive an archaic recognition signal that operated one of the main docking ports currently on the shadow side of the rotating station.

Tionne folded several of her solar sails to prevent them from damage in the blasting force of the nearby solar wind. She drifted her ship around into the station's shadow. The docking bay doors creaked open automatically, as if glad to welcome one of their first visitors in a thousand years.

Of course, Tionne realized, the scavenger Fonterrat had come here, but she hoped he hadn't known what to look for. The information was what she valued, not jewels or mundane treasures.

The *Lore Seeker* drifted into Exis Station and landed as the doors sealed behind her. As a precaution, she ingested a dose of radiation–protection drug and wore shielded clothing. That would give her a little extra time to explore.

Jumping down from her ship, Tionne set off in a hurry. Exis Station had very little time left.

With Artoo–Detoo loaded into his X–wing socket, Luke Skywalker took off from the jungle moon of Yavin 4, soaring above the treetops and leaving the stark temple ruins behind. He maneuvered away from the orange gas giant into interplanetary space, heading toward his insertion point into hyperspace. He had an important place to see. "Set course for the Teedio system, Artoo," Luke said. "We're on our way to Exis Station."

Later, when they emerged from a numbingly long flight through hyperspace, Luke squinted through the cockpit windows as the star system snapped into view around him.

At high speed, they headed straight into a river of stellar fire.

Even as Luke reacted with Jedi reflexes, Artoo squealed in mechanical alarm. Luke banked and rolled, roaring the X–wing away from the giant solar flare that slapped across their path like the licking tongue of a krayt dragon. The g–forces smashed him to the right, but he did not relent until the X–wing had followed a sharp hyperbola path to safety.

Luke felt a strange, twisting agony in his gut as another explosion occurred deep in the unsettled sun, and a flaming belch of ionized gases spewed out from the chromosphere.

The Force was in all things, Obi–Wan Kenobi had said, and Luke could feel the pain, the anguish, of this prematurely dying star.

"Not a good way to start our visit," he said. Artoo shrilled in agreement. "Recalibrate the instruments and we'll proceed with a bit more caution."

Exis Station was huge, glimmering under the boiling bath of solar radiation. The wrecked starport was rotating, trying to maintain some semblance of its original artificial gravity, although it was cockeyed and off balance. Its precession, like a gyroscope's, was enough to bring the station erratically closer to the stellar inferno.

Luke studied it from a distance, taking in every detail. "Find us a docking port, Artoo," he said as he raced toward the beleaguered station. "This place is in real trouble."

Artoo transmitted to the ancient systems on Exis Station and received a warning in response. "I don't care if the last functional docking bay *is* about to rotate into the sunlight," Luke said. "Let's land in there and get to protection before the bay heats up."

The X–wing swooped around in a tight maneuver, just as if Luke were fighting Imperial ships again. On his approach he noticed engine ports dotting the ring of Exis Station—orbital adjustment jets and all–axis thrusters used in times past to stabilize the space city. Once the danger had grown too severe, though, no one had remained to keep Exis at a safe distance.

The docking bay doors opened sluggishly, and Luke easily slipped his X–wing between them, anxious to get inside. The relentless patch of sunlight crept like a flame across the outer hull of Exis Station, but Luke managed to land the X–wing and close the groaning bay doors before the direct glare struck that sector of the abandoned starport.

As safety levels rose to nominal, Luke swung out of the cockpit, ducking under the raised X–wing canopy. As he turned, using the Force to levitate Artoo up and out of his socket, Luke saw another ship deep inside the cargo bay: an antique vessel with an exotic configuration that used hyperdrives, in–system jets, as well as triangular reflective solar sail panels for slow cruising in–system.

At first he thought it was an antique, abandoned along with Exis Station. But he sensed that the craft was warm, recently landed... another visitor.

"Somebody else is here, Artoo."

The little droid bleeped in affirmation, though he could provide no information as to the make or ownership of the strange vessel.

"Whoever they are, let's hope they're planning on getting out of here soon," Luke said. "Come on, let's take a quick tour and see what we can salvage before it's too late."

Artoo trundled after him as Luke strode into the dark and stuffy chambers of the long–abandoned station.

Small and wiry, Tionne jogged along the metal passageways with a light step. She hurried down the corridors that curved off, vanishing into the distance under the flickering light of intermittently functioning glowpanels. Some of the electronics had been ripped out, scavenged by people such as Fonterrat. She ducked low to avoid a dangling ceiling plate, dodged around the hulk of a broken old–model worker droid.

The air smelled sour, old, dusty. The silence hung like a shroud, interrupted only by distant clunks and groans as the station trembled from Teedio's fiery onslaught. A background hiss like static crackled against some of the outer wall plates, the rain of high–energy particles showering out from the solar storm.

She kept exploring. Many chambers were barricaded with frozen security systems or piled debris. Several of the locked habitation modules for non–air–breathers had been blasted away into space, leaving only sealed space doors and the ripped connectors from where they had been jettisoned. Tionne knew that each of these modules had been added one at a time during the growth of the station; she supposed that some of the more valuable modules may have been stolen wholesale from the hulk of Exis Station.

The corridors seemed to be leading her toward a central area, and she followed her hunches, absorbing details with her eager eyes. Finally, she came out into an airy promenade and stopped short in astonishment as her last footsteps echoed several times in the enclosed chamber.

The ceiling dome gleamed with triangular and diamond shaped

transparasteel windowplates that illuminated the broad open area with glittering colors. Pulsations of electric light sizzled through from the flare star to dapple the deckplates. Faded emblems and family glyphs were etched onto the walls alongside archaic symbols. The enclosed area seemed like a cathedral, a meeting place... possibly the site of a great convocation.

Tionne recognized the inset alcoves right away, repositories for thick crystalline memory plaques, an ancient information–storage device. Unfortunately, few people could read data from such ancient technology anymore, and so the scavengers had not bothered to take the plaques. Leaving them for her!

Tionne studied the Exis archives with absolute delight. She picked up one plaque after another, studying the etched summaries, ancient speeches, the philosophy of ancient Jedi Knights, reminiscences of dying masters who had lived for hundreds upon hundreds of years. She felt breathless, and her hands trembled. A wealth of knowledge! She had been searching all her life for a treasure such as this.

But now Exis Station rumbled beneath her, its deckplates groaning as the furious sun continued to pummel it with intensive flares, doing final damage. Tionne could feel the station barely holding itself together. She had to take these crystalline plaques, as many as she could carry, and rush back to her ship. She would stay until the last moment, but she had to rescue as much as she could. She couldn't bear for this all to be destroyed.

She gathered plaque after plaque, tucking the thick crystal sheets under her arms, wishing she had brought something more efficient to carry them. Her throat was dry, and she breathed fast as she worked.

Tionne stopped dead cold, though, as she pulled out one of the plaques and saw by the markings that it contained a recording of the actual speech by Nomi Sunrider, given at the great convocation of Jedi Knights.

Tionne's fingers went numb as she gripped the plaque. Nomi Sunrider herself! She held in her hands the actual words, the images! She could see how the legendary Jedi hero moved and spoke and gestured. Her heart felt huge in her chest.

Then she sensed as much as heard someone coming, and spun about in time to see a man accompanied by an astromech droid. She instantly recognized Luke Skywalker, hero of the Rebellion, from all the images she had seen. He had come here at last. He had received

Kevin J. Anderson

her message from Fonterrat after all!

"Who are you? What are you doing here?" Luke said. "Don't you know it's dangerous? This station is breaking up."

Before she could answer him, though, an explosion ripped through Exis Station, ringing against the hull like a gong. The shockwave rocked the station, throwing Tionne off her feet. She dropped the data plaques all around her. One of the crystals shattered, but the others remained intact. The astromech droid squealed as it rolled across the deckplates. Tionne was filled with admiration when saw how Skywalker managed to keep his balance, using Jedi abilities to remain on his feet.

"Artoo, find a data terminal!" he shouted. "Jack in and figure out what that was, how great the damage is." He hurried over to Tionne and bent down. "Are you all right? What are you doing here?"

She scrambled on the floor trying to retrieve the data plaques she had held in her arms. "I'm Tionne. I sent a message for you to come here. I thought—" She gasped, trying to catch her breath as she clutched the data plaques against her chest. "I thought, since you were training Jedi, you'd want to come here and find the Jedi history."

"But this whole station is breaking up," Luke said. "We'd better get off as soon as we can."

"Then help me carry some of these plaques." Tionne handed him several from her stack, then grabbed more from the archive. She looked sadly at the shattered data plaque on the floor, then held the others more tightly. At least she had saved Nomi Sunrider's speech.

Artoo hooted mournfully from the wall station as he tried to adapt his circuits to the archaic electronics of Exis Station. Overhead, the ceiling thrummed, as if barely maintaining its integrity against the scorching flares. Luke went over to the little droid and saw the readout. "I take it that was your ship in the docking bay," he said over his shoulder.

"Yes," Tionne answered. "I named it the *Lore Seeker*."

"Well, it's not going anywhere now—and neither is my X–wing. One of the stabilizing engines ignited in the firestorm, and the explosion tore out the door circuitry. Our ships are trapped, and because that section is now under the full solar radiation, we can't even go inside to begin repairs. We have to wait until Exis Station rotates the docking bay back into shadow."

Tionne steadied herself as the adrenaline of fear sped her senses, made all the colors brighter, the metal gleam. She listened to the groaning sound of one of the hull plates. "If the station lasts that long," she said.

Luke began to say something, then the ceiling gave a strange creaking noise. He looked up, flashing his eyes. With a hissing snap, one of the triangular colored–transparasteel panels split from its moldings after thousands of years of strain.

In the explosive decompression, Tionne's ears popped. Her silvery hair flew about her head in a breeze as the ages–old station air squealed out through the small opening.

"Quick!" Luke said, grabbing her arm and accidentally dropping several of the data plaques. "We've got to seal ourselves behind a bulkhead somewhere."

Artoo–Detoo bleeped and spun about on his wheels. Luke gestured for Tionne to follow him back the way he had come, a corridor she had not explored. He took charge immediately, but he didn't seem to know exactly where he was going. As the escaping air roared behind her, she ran after him, cradling the precious crystal plaques, wishing she could go back and grab another handful, but the sudden change in stress points on the hull of Exis Station had bent and cracked another of the transparisteel windows. Soon, this entire chamber would be uninhabitable, exposed to space.

She raced after the Jedi Master, her slender feet skittering on the deckplates. They turned down another side passage where the corridor curved off from the main Jedi library and museum toward the external habitation modules. Luke stopped short in front of a double–sealed airlock door that bore several brilliant markings. Tionne thought she recognized the writing, the language from the Old Republic, an archaic Jedi script.

Artoo–Detoo stopped at the intersection of a corridor and twittered to himself as he extended his data connector and accessed another control panel on the wall.

Luke Skywalker ignored the droid and ran to the double doors. "If this mechanism still operates," he said. "We can seal ourselves in here, wherever it goes." His fingers flew over the buttons as if instinctively knowing how to operate the ancient machinery.

Tionne, though, felt a sudden chill as she labored to translate the old writing. Dropping her load of artifacts, she threw herself forward, yelling, "No!" just as Luke succeeded in opening the airlock.

Clawlike tendrils of high–pressure greenish–yellow mist sprayed from the crack as the door groaned open. Luke staggered back, coughing, unable to breathe.

Tionne knocked him out of the way and lunged for the control panel, pounding buttons. She had no idea how to work the system, but she needed to seal the door shut again. The poisonous gas continued to escape. She held her breath, but her eyes burned, blurring her vision. Tears shimmered across her mother–of–pearl irises, but still Tionne fumbled with the system. Finally, with a screech of poorly lubricated gears, the door slammed shut again.

Luke staggered back against the wall and slumped down, coughing, trying to catch his breath from the fumes he had inhaled.

Artoo–Detoo squealed with triumph, bleeped and flashed his lights. At the corridor intersection, another set of bulkheads came down from the ceiling, closing off the passage from the decompression on the other side. Tionne and Luke were safe from the broken windows in the library now, and the station's own air–recirculation systems rapidly drained the poisonous gas Luke Skywalker had inadvertently let into the corridors.

Luke used all his remaining strength to catch his breath again. He looked over where Artoo stood wobbling victoriously. "Thanks, Artoo. You thought faster than we did."

Tionne looked at Luke angrily. "That was one of the chlorine–breather's habitation modules! High–pressurized poisonous gas. If we had run in there, we'd both be dead in an instant," she said, shaking her head. "You're a Jedi Master—can't you read Old Republic script?"

Luke shook his head sheepishly. "I haven't finished those studies yet." He took a deep breath and controlled himself from coughing again. "In fact, I haven't found a teacher who could show me yet."

Then Tionne heard rumbling, groaning alarms. Amber lights flashed around the double airlock. With an explosive roar, the chlorine-breather's habitation module blasted free of its pinnings and launched away from Exis Station, ejected in an emergency release.

"Looks like I did more than just seal the door again," she said. "I disengaged the entire module from the station." Tionne blinked her eyes in astonishment. "It must have been prepped for removal. I just went through the final steps."

The large habitation module thumped away, shoving itself from the main ring directly toward the churning sun—and its doom. Tionne could feel the station lurch and move off kilter and start to spin away from Teedio and its flares.

"I think you helped," Luke said, standing up, his eyes bright. "Simple physics. When you pushed that large module away, it pushed against the station, shoving us in the other direction. You may have bought us a little time."

"Not very much," Tionne said. She held the historical plaques next to her, wondering if she would get out of here alive so that she could watch them, see the entire speech Nomi Sunrider had made, and contribute to the New Republic's knowledge of its most precious history.

Luke Skywalker stood up with an odd gleam in his eye. "What you did gave me an idea," he said. "Let's get to the central control hub. Exis Station may still be just functional enough for what we need to do."

The central control hub of Exis Station was dark and musty, all of the glowpanels shut down when the station had been mothballed and evacuated. But Luke found the automated systems to slide aside the thick window coverings that shielded the viewing ports all around the control station. The heavy coverings scraped aside in corroded tracks to reveal the filtered dazzle of Teedio's corona.

Artoo trundled up to the main stations and let out a mournful whistle as he inspected the old computers. After checking, Luke found that many of the antique computers had shut down, or their circuits had been scrambled so much by stray radiation that their sentient memory banks were either senile or insane.

"Get to the controls and do what you can, Artoo," he said, scanning the panels. "Tionne, you might need to help me translate some of this script." He gave her a wry smile. "I don't want to make another stupid mistake."

"That'll be a first step," the silvery–haired woman said, flashing her eerie quicksilver eyes at him. She seemed to be having trouble dealing with him as a person. At first she had seemed in awe of him, a Jedi about whom she had heard so much. Now she showed a bit of disappointment accepting him as a simple human as well. "Once we know what the controls mean, we need to get them functioning again."

Luke stood by her side as she analyzed the faded labels and etched words on the control decks. He ran testing routines and checked the mechanisms. He hoped a few of the stabilizing rockets could still sputter and provide enough thrust to move Exis Station away from the firestorm danger zone... at least until the docking port rotated into shadow again, where Luke could work on the inoperable bay doors to free his X–wing and Tionne's solar–sail ship.

Tionne managed to call up a diagram that showed the station and its position. She identified the habitation modules studded around its expansion spokes. The docking module holding both of their ships had passed beyond the high point of the sun's flood, but it still had a long way to go before it fell into the relative safety of shadow.

Now one of the larger alien habitation modules broiled under the heat. If Luke correctly interpreted what the computer said, this module was filled with water for sea–dwelling creatures.

Luke looked up as he felt a wrench in his chest again, a sudden violent outpouring from the sun. He looked up to see the blistering red giant smoldering, regurgitating, and spraying an enormous prominence into space like a hose of fire. The dense plasma shot toward them in the largest inundation ever.

Tionne saw it too. "We can't survive that. Exis Station is going to be incinerated."

Luke dove back to the sluggish controls, frantically trying to get the station rockets functioning again. Most of them remained off–line, but he powered up three on the sunward side so he could give the abandoned hulk another push away. Exis Station wobbled, still slowly drifting from when Tionne had ejected the chlorine–gas pod. But that small nudge had not been enough to give them sufficient

velocity and the deadly blast of solar fire was hurtling toward them with incredible speed.

"These rockets are the only ones that work," he said. "I'm gonna fire full thrusters. Maybe they'll give enough of a push to get ourselves far enough away to survive." He swallowed hard. "But you'd better hold on."

He pushed the buttons, waiting for the thrust. But the control indicators went red as two engines failed. Then an explosion shuddered through the station.

"Two more fuel pods just exploded." Tionne looked at the readouts and then at him. He expected to see more fear in her eyes, but instead her face hardened. "We're dead in space, and there's nothing we can do about it."

"I'm not giving up," Luke said. "We just have to understand how this place works."

He went to the controls again and called up the diagram showing the habitation module filled with water. It was now under the harshest glare of the sun; the skin on its hull must be turning cherry–red by now. Stability alarms flickered on. The diagnostic panels and the station integrity would never hold once the firestorm's peak reached them.

"Artoo, find the emergency cargo doors on this water bay!" he shouted.

"What for?" Tionne asked.

"We don't have time!" Luke said. The little droid was already twittering, scanning the controls, coaxing unreliable computers to give up one bit of information. Finally, the codes appeared, and Luke punched the emergency override, opening the double–layered outer cargo doors to space—exposing the huge volume of ocean to the blazing flare.

Thousands of tons of seawater evaporated in the incandescent heat and deadly vacuum, blasting and blasting. Luke grabbed one of the nearby chairs as the entire station shuddered and then began to accelerate outward. The water continued to gush out like a rocket engine, pushing Exis Station farther and farther away from the sun.

"That's giving us enough velocity!" Tionne said.

"Let's just hope there's enough water," Luke answered.

Exis Station picked up speed and continued to move. The incredible solar flare surged toward them, but it seemed to fall behind as they drew away from it. The abandoned city groaned and shuddered, barely holding itself together.

Luke continued punching the controls and finally managed to get a single one of the station–keeping engines to function. The small rocket added its thrust to the dwindling evaporating roar of the escaping ocean.

Tionne said with weary sadness, "No doubt that module was filled with well–preserved artifacts."

"At least we'*re* well preserved now," Luke said.

The snake–like tongue of the solar flare reached its peak and began to loop backward toward the sun, drawn by Teedio's gravity and magnetic fields, falling away from them.

"Now Exis Station should be safe," Tionne said, "for a few hundred more years, at least."

Luke smiled at her. "That's plenty of time to come back and look around all you want."

Fallen into shadow once again, the docking bay rapidly cooled enough that Luke, Tionne, and Artoo could safely reenter it. Light–footed, Tionne hurried back to the *Lore Seeker* to make certain that none of its ancient and delicate systems had been damaged.

While Artoo went to run diagnostics on the X–wing with his diagnostics, Luke inspected the automatic controls that opened the huge docking bay doors. The explosion that had ruptured the stabilizing thrusters had also fused the computer guidance connections. With a grim look on his face, he drew his lightsaber and switched it on. The pulsing yellow–green energy blade sizzled in the enclosed chamber.

"We'll just have to do it manually," Luke said as he slashed through the computer control cables. The mechanism sparked and slumped into dormancy. Now it would be a simple effort to trigger open the sealed doors.

Unable to stop herself, Tionne turned to stare at the Jedi blade, marveling at it. Her mother–of–pearl eyes widened, and her small mouth hung open in astonishment.

When he saw her fascination, Luke held up his lightsaber in salute. "You never told me why you came here, Tionne," he said. "Why did you send that message that I was to come here?"

"Because you're a Jedi," she said. "I know you intend to train other Jedi Knights, and I felt you should know whatever knowledge is stored here on the station." She held up the data plaques she had rescued.

"I couldn't agree more," Luke said. "My background in Jedi history lacks quite a bit."

Tionne inserted one of the data plaques into her antique reader. "Watch this, for instance. If you intend to teach new Jedi Knights, you must know their history, what other Jedi did."

A small, flickering holographic image of a young, driven–looking woman shimmered up from the player. She was slender, dressed in archaic clothes; her hair was tucked back, serviceable but not styled. She would have had a soft and lovely face, but tragedies seemed to have hardened her, added lines to her expression.

"Together, we have suffered a great disaster, and now comes a time for healing," she said.

"That is Nomi Sunrider," Tionne whispered. "One of the greatest of all Jedi Knights. This is a speech she gave here on Exis Station, during the Jedi convocation."

Luke listened raptly as Nomi continued. "War has spanned the galaxy, but now it is over. We can never forget the dead—but we must also not forget the future. We must trust in the Force. As long as there are Jedi Knights, there is hope."

Nomi continued, but Luke felt his mind reeling. "Those words are thousands of years old," he said, "but they still have a lot of relevance today."

"History always has relevance to the present," Tionne said. She swallowed hard and looked up at him. "I understand that you have a Holocron which is also filled with stories."

Luke nodded. "True. But that doesn't explain *your* interest."

"I've always been fascinated by the Jedi," she said with an uncomfortable shrug. "The stories, the legends, I've been collecting them all my life. It was like a compulsion for me. I know many of the songs, the ballads, as much history as I could gather, though the Empire has destroyed many of the records."

Luke looked at her with deeper interest. "Do you think you could share some of it? Would you be willing to come to Yavin 4 while I set up my Jedi academy? You can perhaps tell me where I'm going wrong, point me in directions that I should know. Otherwise, I'd have to spend years gathering the same knowledge that you've already found."

Tionne stood up straight, swelled with joy. Then she calmed

herself and stood with squared shoulders, her chin held high. "I would be honored, Master Luke Skywalker."

"Who knows," Luke said, "you may even have a bit of Jedi potential yourself."

"That's too much to hope for," Tionne said. Her words were quiet, a whisper barely mouthed. "But you would never find a more dedicated student."

When they heard the ships approach, Gantoris and Streen came out of the shaded temple, looking up into the hazy midday sky. They saw the silvery shapes of not only Luke Skywalker's X-wing but another strange craft as well.

The orange sphere of Yavin dominated the horizon, shimmering pastel oranges like the cataract-filled eye of a giant The incoming ships passed in front of the planet. Streen marveled at the silhouetted shape of the other ship, an ancient craft with large triangular sails.

"For the wind," he said. "The solar wind."

Gantoris looked sidelong at him. "Master Skywalker's probably found another student."

They went to meet the two craft as they touched down on the bonfire-scorched landing clearing in front of the Great Temple. Luke popped open the canopy of his X-wing and climbed out, looking toward Tionne's ship. The slender, silver-haired woman stepped gracefully down the metal rungs of the boarding ladder and stared up at the weathered stone ziggurats in amazement. She then looked at Streen and Gantoris.

"This is Tionne," Luke said. "She's already studied more Jedi lore and history than anybody I've ever met, so I thought she'd better come to Yavin 4."

"Is she going to train with us as well?" Streen asked.

Luke gave a secretive smile and glanced sidelong at Tionne. "Yes, I think so. I tested her on the flight to Yavin. She has an affinity for the Force, and I could use plenty of help in my own teaching."

Tionne smiled, breathless in her own excitement. "Soon, Master Skywalker, I hope there will be plenty of other new Jedi Knights who can start making new history for all of us to tell."

Together, they walked into the cool shade of the Great Temple.

Kevin J. Anderson

Roleplaying Game Statistics

Tionne

Type: Minstrel
DEXTERITY 2D+2
Blaster 3D+1, dodge 4D, pick pocket 3D+2, running 4D
KNOWLEDGE 4D
Alien species 5D, business 4D+1, cultures 4D+1, languages 4D+1, planetary systems 4D+2, scholar: folklore 5D+2, scholar: Holocron 5D, scholar: Jedi history 6D, streetwise 5D+1, survival 4D+2, value 5D
MECHANICAL 3D+1
Archaic starship piloting 4D+1, beast riding 4D, musical instrument operation: double viol 6D, repulsorlift operation 4D+2, sensors 4D, space transports 4D+1, swoop operation 4D
PERCEPTION 4D
Bargain 5D+1, con 5D, gambling 4D+2, persuasion 5D, persuasion: storytelling 6D, search 4D+2, sneak 5D
STRENGTH 2D
Brawling 3D, climbing/jumping 3D+1, swimming 4D
TECHNICAL 2D
Blaster repair 3D, computer programming/repair 3D, droid programming 3D, first aid 4D, musical instrument repair: stringed instruments 4D+2
This character is Force-sensitive
Force Points: 2
Character Points: 10
Move: 10
Equipment: Blaster pistol (4D), double viol, datapad, the Lore Seeker
Note: Tionne's skill in piloting archaic starships was not reflected in the game information and description of her in *The Jedi Academy Sourcebook*. Gamemasters who wish to continue to use the space transport piloting skill to describe her ability to pilot ships may do so, or they may opt to use the archaic starship piloting skill added to her skill list in this description. (This modification is official errata.)

Capsule: Tionne is a young scholar whose principal passion is for knowledge, particularly that concerning the Jedi. She learned much of what she knows from her grandmother, who passed her knowledge to Tionne through stories rather than in written form. Tionne's talent as a storyteller and musician have enabled her to continue her grandmother's tradition as she passes on her discoveries to others through story and song, keeping alive the histories of a nobler time. Charming, graceful, and light of spirit, Tionne brings a smile to the faces of all but the most hardened of beings.

She wanders the galaxy in her ship, the *Lore Seeker,* a remnant of less dangerous times, seeking information on the Jedi of the Old Republic and sharing what she learns in frontier cantinas and trade stations. She avoids systems still under the influence of Imperial authorities, which keeps her from the more populous worlds, but she makes enough in the smaller systems to keep her ship running properly and continue her search for the histories of a bygone era.

She considers what she has found on Exis Station to be the greatest collection of Jedi lore she has ever seen, particularly the data plaque containing Nomi Sunrider's speech to the Convocation. But even that discovery may dim in comparison to what she has discovered about herself when she met the Jedi Master Luke Skywalker.

The Lore Seeker

Craft: Hyrotil *Jemlaat*-class in-system sail yacht
Type: Modified sail yacht
Scale: Starfighter
Length: 22 meters
Skill: Archaic starship piloting
Crew: 1
Crew Skill: See Tionne
Passengers: 4
Cargo Capacity: 20 metric tons
Consumables: 2 months
Hyperdrive Multiplier: x3
Hyperdrive Backup: x15
Nav Computer: Yes
Maneuverability: 1D
Space: 4 (sublight engines); 2–3 (sails)
Atmosphere: 280; 800 kmh
Hull: 3D
Shields: 1D
Sensors:
Passive: 10/0D
Scan: 20/1D
Search: 40/2D
Focus: 2/3D
Weapons:
1 Laser Cannon
Fire Arc: Front
Crew: 1
Skill: Starship gunnery
Fire Control: 2D
Space Range: 1–3/12/25
Atmosphere Range: 100-300m/1.2km/2.5km
Damage: 4D

Capsule: The Lore Seeker reflects her current captain well. The aging ship combines modern practicality with the romance and grace of a bygone era. When the Lore Seeker arrives in port, old trader captains sigh wistfully as they remember the days of their youth, and even busy port authorities take a moment to admire the sleek ship nestled among the squat, blocky freighters.

The original ship was designed by Hyrotil Engineering as an in–system pleasure yacht. It had sublight engines capable of a slow maneuver in cases of emergency, but its principal means of propulsion came from its maneuverable solar sails. These sails could rotate relative to the position of the nearest stellar mass, and the sails' sensitive radiation collectors enabled captains to pilot the ship in all but the outermost reaches of a system. Particularly adept pilots could thread their way through systems in which several stars were located, trimming their sails just so to maximize the thrust provided by one star while minimizing that of another. Hyrotil even produced a sails–only variant of the *Jemlaat* for the sailship race circuit, but, sadly, the sport has nearly died in the wake of the dissolution of the Old Republic and the rise of the Empire.

Tionne's Lore Seeker has been modernized from its original design. At the expense of cargo area and crew and passenger quarters, the ship has a small hyperdrive engine and an upgraded sublight engine. In addition, Tionne has placed a single laser cannon in the nose of the ship to give the ship some defense against pirates and protection against asteroids. The sensors have also been modernized, but not upgraded. The shield generator will not work while the sails are extended, as they break up shield integrity. It takes about one minute to retract the sails, and about half that to extend them.

Tionne has taken steps to ensure that the ship maintains as much of its original appearance as possible. With the exception of the laser cannon, a regrettable necessity, the modifications she has made to the *Lore Seeker* have not appreciably altered the look the original ships had. Collectors have offered Tionne a handsome sum for the *Lore Seeker*, but she views the graceful old ship as her home now, and she could not bear to part with it.

Game information created by Duane Maxwell, based on material by Kevin J. Anderson and Paul Sudlow.

SPECIAL MILITARY UNIT INTELLIGENCE UPDATE

By Timothy O'Brien

Illustrations by Joe Corroney

From: Captain Zgorth'sth, Department of Threat Assessment

To: Admiral Ackbar, General Rieekan, General Cracken, General Madine, Admiral Drayson, General Antilles, Senator Bel Iblis.

Re: Special Unit Threat Assessment

cc: General Dodonna (ret.), Admiral Tallon (ret.), Marshal Starkiller (ret.).

Sirs,

The Threat Assessment Office has established its offices and the staff is assessing threats from Imperial and other unfriendly and neutral military assets. This report focuses on an assortment of special units, in most cases updating their status from older Alliance reports. These units saw a good deal of action in the fighting following the Emperor's death—this report updates their status as of the latest available intelligence reports.

Asset Tracking continues to follow these units. Recommendations are included.

For those who have not yet been introduced to Threat Assessment: this office was created shortly after the re-establishment of the New Republic on Coruscant after the second defeat of the Emperor. The office is expected to detect early warning signs of Imperial activity, such as the generally ignored re–allocation and re–assignment of Imperial forces and supplies to the Deep Core, which were attributed at the time to Imperial incompetence. This office replaces the Alliance Security Task Force, which had atrophied during the drive on the Core Worlds to the point that logistical analysis was being ignored.

In Service,
Capt. Zgorth'sth, Threat Assessment

Entry Formats

Type/Unit Level/Size: Unit designation (armor, infantry, aggressor squadron, etc.)/How the unit fits into its order of battle/Size.
CO: Commanding Officer
Base: Base of operations, planet, sector, region.
Mission: The basic mission the unit typically engages in.
Affiliations: The unit's political organization and military alliances.
Zone of Operations: Area in which the unit typically operates (continental to regional).
Success Rate/Threat: Odds the unit will succeed in a given mission/Threat to New Republic military, assuming parity.

Ailon Nova Guard

Type/Unit Level/Size: Planetary Military
CO: High Marshall of Ailon
Base: Ailon System, Inner Rim
Mission: Any
Affiliations: Formerly the Empire, currently independent
Zone of Operations: Galaxy
Success Rate/Threat: NA/High

The Ailon Nova Guard is an ancient military service with 13,000 years of history and tradition. The Ailon people are militaristic, devoted, and highly focused on professional military service. Soldiering has a deep religious meaning to the Ailon, and all able-bodied Ailon serve at least a five year term in the Guard. The history of the Nova Guard is far too lengthy to go into here. (Interested parties should consult reports filed by Major Arhul Hextrophon and Professor Tem Eliss. Those with access to the central database on Coruscant will find a great deal of information on the Ailon Guard in the research performed by Professor Obo Rin; readers should be aware, however, that Rin was a researcher working under the direct supervision of COMPNOR officers. Much of his work is tainted by the New Order's racist agenda.)

For thousands of years, the Guard was allied to the Republic and served in its defense with honor. With the coming of the Empire, the Guard's activity was sharply curtailed and largely restricted to ceremonial duties, except on occasions when Imperial Central Command needed cannon fodder to soften up tough positions (which led to a few embarrassments when the Nova Guard overran opposition before the Imperial military could act). The non–human Ailon were largely forced into inactive peace for a generation. The Empire realized that eliminating the Guard, so Central Command simply left it "in reserve."

During this period, the annual Ailon Military Ceremonies became the primary focus for the Nova Guard. The Guard honed its skills, upgraded its equipment, observed the martial traditions of other species, staged full war–games, and waited.

This turned out to be a grand strategic disaster for the Empire. The high reproduction rate of the Ailon allowed the Nova Guard regiments to fill to capacity, and in time new regiments were created simply to train the burgeoning youth. By the time of Palpatine's death, the Ailon had a huge, well–trained, dedicated—if largely inexperienced—military. Central Command was racist enough to keep the Ailon out of the majority of the post–Endor war, and when it became clear to the Ailon Marshallate that the Empire was losing, they swore allegiance to the New Republic.

The resulting campaign wiped the Imperial forces from a score of

worlds. Whole regiments gained first battle–honors, and the abundant units shook out their less qualified troopers and officers. After assisting in the removal of Imperial troops from the Inner Rim region, the Nova Guard petitioned to aid efforts to liberate the Mid-Rim. The resulting influx of Nova Guard troops to the Mid–Rim liberation campaigns may finalize the long war over the area. These troops make up blooded regiments, tempered and fierce. The Nova Guard is likely at an all–time high, in terms of both quality and quantity.

Projection: After the Empire is finally defeated, the Nova Guard will in all likelihood remain loyal to the legitimate government, as long as that government remains strong and in control. The Ailon regard strength and fitness as a mandate to rule. If the New Republic were to suddenly demonstrate critical weakness or ineptitude, the Nova Guard would likely allow it to suffer the fate of the weak. At the same time, the Ailon are honorable and eager to contribute to the preservation of the overall strength of the New Republic.

Recommendation: The Nova Guard should be allowed to serve the New Republic in the front lines whenever possible, and be honored for that service. Their relish of military service is deeply inculcated and would require massive social engineering to replace. This is unfeasible and undesirable. If peace ultimately reigns in our galaxy, the Ailon will be happy to serve as guardians, so long as they are allowed to actively serve.

Typical Nova Guard. *All stats 3D except: Dexterity 4D, blaster: blaster pistol 6D, blaster: blaster rifle 6D, brawling parry 8D, dodge 6D+2, melee combat 6D, melee parry 6D, Knowledge 2D, intimidation 6D, Strength 3D+2, brawling 7D+2, climbing/jumping 6D+2, Technical 2D+1.* Move 11. Nova Guard armor (+1D to head and torso, -1D Dexterity and related skills), helmet comlink, blaster rifle (5D) vibrobayonette (STR+2D+2). Character points: 0-5.

Churhee's Riflemen

Type/Unit Level/Size: Mercenary Scout Company
CO: Maydla Churhee
Base: Turcan III
Mission: Hot Combat Scouting
Affiliations: New Republic and friendly governments
Zone of Operations: Sarin and Parmel Sectors, Outer Rim Territories
Success Rate/Threat: 81%/Low

Churhee's Riflemen was originally a low–profile operation mercenary unit, specializing in scouting and harassment missions. The unit was modeled after the standard, fully augmented Imperial scout company, with each trooper in the line squads qualified as sharpshooters. This made the unit a powerful and mobile light infantry force, with the ability to cover and defend large areas with low risk. Vlaydm Churhee, the unit's founder, primarily contracted to the Empire, and was well paid for his elite unit. The Riflemen would rip at the flanks and rear of enemy forces, and stage nasty bait–and–trap actions, slow enemy advances and retreats, and tie up a large number of enemy patrols.

Churhee was not a particularly loyal mercenary, and often breached contracts and switched sides if offered enough credits: this may have been what killed him at Y'Trella, where Imperial forces failed to provide adequate backup. Churhee's behavior may have fostered an attitude that the Riflemen were expendable. The Riflemen lost many of their number on the Y'Trella mission and have resented the Empire since.

In the months that followed, Maydla Churhee, Vlaydm's widow, brought the Riflemen back from their defeat. Thereafter, the Riflemen took anti–Imperial contracts only, cheap, and allied itself with

the Alliance. This pushed the Riflemen onto Parmel Sector's Moff Tallis' "wanted" list, and he eventually dedicated a whole Naval line to backing up battlegroup operations on Turcan III, where the Riflemen had spent weeks snarling Imperial operations against local Alliance ground forces. The Riflemen suffered 50% casualties in the final action on Turcan III. The survivors were evacuated by the final Alliance transport offworld.

The Riflemen had a formidable reputation in Parmel and Sarin Sectors before Turcan III; now they were legendary. Their ranks were quickly replenished. Maydla Churhee signed on with the Alliance with a long–term contract. The Riflemen stayed dedicated until the contract terms were filled: the Emperor's death.

The Riflemen continued to work for the Provisional Government that was established in the years following the Battle of Endor. The propaganda value of having Churhee's Riflemen fighting for the New Republic was tremendous, and the Riflemen are credited with helping push the Imperials out of Parmel a full year ahead of time.

As the New Republic was being formally established on Coruscant, the Riflemen once again began to hiring themselves out as a mercenary scout company. Their fearsome reputation allows them to charge a very high fee, particularly high for a unit that avoids main combat. Maydla Churhee seems to have learned from her husband's demise and has adopted a contract fulfillment policy, no longer allowing the Riflemen to be bought out by a higher bidder. They are currently based on Turcan III, the world where they fought their greatest battle.

Projection: Churhee's Riflemen are no longer considered an overt threat. They are unlikely to enter into contracts with employers directly opposing the New Republic. The Riflemen will likely find their future contracts in local brush wars and corporate fringe wars.

Recommendation: The Riflemen are worth their high fee, and should be kept on retainer for future needs.

Typical member of Churhee's Riflemen. *All stats 3D except: Blaster: blaster pistol 6D+2, blaster: blaster rifle 8D+2, dodge 5D, grenade 4D, melee combat 4D+2, melee parry 4D+2, planetary systems 5D, survival 5D, hover vehicle operation 4D, repulsorlift operation 4D, walker operation 3D+2, hide 5D, search 7D+2, sneak 5D, stamina 5D, computer programming/repair 4D, demolition 4D, first aid 4D.* Move 10. Comlink, macrobinoculars, survival kit (tempshelter, long–range comlink, rations, molecord rope, magnetic grapplers), blaster rifle (5D) heavy blaster pistol (5D+2), blast helmet and blast vest (+1D to head and torso from physical damage, +1 energy), knife (STR+1D), uniform. Character points: 0–5.

First Sun Mobile Regiment

Type/Unit Level/Size: Mercenary Mobile Infantry Regiment
CO: General Maska Zural
Base: Mobile
Mission: Search, Locate, Annihilate
Affiliations: Empire, other totalitarian governments
Zone of Operations: Mid-Rim
Success Rate/Threat: 99%/High

The First Sun Mobile Regiment was, at its height, one of the largest, most powerful mercenary units in known galactic history. This was achieved by the patronage of the Empire, architects of the largest military in galactic history.

First Sun was wholly an Imperial tool, although the corporate officers, General Zural, and the command staff believed otherwise. First Sun took only about 18% of its contracts from non–Imperial agencies and over 65% directly from the Imperial Army.

To facilitate smooth integration and operational utility, the regiment was equipped like a fully augmented Imperial repulsorlift regiment. Even the Empire had little need for such a large mercenary company, and tended to hire units in battalions rather than the regiment as a whole.

The regiment assisted in a dozen invasion and suppressions, and specialized in SLAMs (Search, Locate, Annihilate Missions), operations devoted to region–wide eliminations of all production assets. The regiment excelled at these assignments and hired only the worst sociopathic thugs to carry them out. Several notable atrocities were committed or compounded by First Sun troopers.

A few months prior to the Battle of Endor, an entire First Sun company was executed by Moff Nile Owen of the Rayter sector for violating interrogation protocol (specifically, slaughtering all troops in a Rebel outpost instead of taking prisoners for interrogation). Afterward, First Sun began to distance itself from the Empire. Imperial contract prices went up, and bond–fees were assessed for the first time. Imperial High Command was unamused, and Imperial contracts dried up. Deprived of

primary income, the regiment suddenly shrank, as whole units left First Sun's employ. This process finished almost immediately before the Battle of Endor.

Post–Endor, First Sun found itself a lean, veteran mercenary force with a galaxy of new customers as the Empire fractured. The regiment currently wanders from contract to contract, working for Imperial, corporate, or system–state employers as fortune dictates. In the earliest days of the New Republic, the regiment approached the fledgling government, and offered itself at a discount (to avenge itself against the Empire), but was turned away for its history. SLAMs remain their preferred missions, but the call for such wanton destruction has largely vanished. Although the modern regiment has whittled away, down to two repulsorlift battalions and an armor company, it remains a formidable fighting force.

The unit repulsorlifts use hoverscouts and landspeeders with dismountable repeating blasters. The armor unit uses a combination of KAAC Freerunners, Light Assault Vehicles, and a section of Firehawk repulsortanks.

Projection: The First Sun Mobile Regiment will hopefully become a victim of galactic peace. The Imperial Civil War has cooled off, the Empire–Republic War has largely come to an end, and the assorted local brush wars and corporate "policing actions" can only sustain this expensive unit for so long. The regiment is likely to reduce to a battalion, or perhaps simply disband.

Recommendation: The corporate officers and command staff, most especially General Zural, should be sought out, located, and arrested for crimes against the galaxy. First Sun's crimes must not be forgotten. As many First Sun troopers as possible should face the justice that befell the worst of the Imperial military. This will be very difficult to achieve, since First Sun wields considerable firepower and experience, but should not be beyond the abilities of the New Republic Special Forces.

Typical First Sun Trooper. All stats 3D except: *Blaster: blaster pistol 5D, blaster: blaster rifle 7D+2, dodge 5D, grenade 5D, melee combat 4D+2, melee parry 4D+2, vehicle blasters 6D+2, planetary systems 5D, streetwise 4D, survival 5D, ground vehicle operation 4D, hover vehicle operation 4D, repulsorlift operation 4D, walker operation 3D+2, hide 5D, search 7D+2, sneak 5D, stamina 5D, computer programming/repair 4D, demolition 6D, first aid 4D, security 4D*. Move 10. Comlink, datapad, glow rod, macrobinoculars, 2 medpacs, survival kit (tempshelter, long-range comlink, rations, molecord rope, magnetic grapplers), blaster rifle (5D) blaster pistol (4D), 3 fragmentation grenades (5D), blast helmet and blast vest (+1D to head and torso from physical damage, +1 energy). Character points: 0-5.

Hoverscout. Speeder, maneuverability 1D, move 70;200 kmh, body strength 3D. Weapons: 1 Heavy Blaster Cannon (fire control 1D, 50-250/750/1.5km, damage 6D), 1 Laser Cannon (fire control 1D, 50-100/200/500, damage 2D), Concussion Missile Launcher (fire control 2D, 50-500/1.5/3 km, damage 4D).

KAAC Freerunner. Speeder, maneuverability 1D, move 105; 300 kmh, body strength 3D, shields 1D. Weapons: 2 Anti-Vehicle Laser Cannon (fire-linked) (fire control 1D, 50-400/900/2km, damage 5D), 2 Anti-Infantry Blaster Batteries (fire control 2D, 50-300/800/1.5 km, damage 3D+2).

Imperial Hammers Elite Armor Unit

Type/Unit Level/Size: Imperial Vanguard Armor Regiment, plus supporting units.

CO: Colonel Zel Johans

Adventure Idea

A New Republic Special Forces strike force (the player characters) is assembled to capture First Sun's current command base, on Zin Taal, a remote Outer Rim world. Intelligence says the base was established in the last three weeks and the Regiment is likely to remain for at least another month before relocating. They are given orbital-images of the base-camp with patrol patterns and lookout posts indicated, and shown the best lines of approach.

The journey to Zin Taal is uneventful. The SpecForce is dropped in a manner appropriate to their specialty, and makes their way to the camp to secure it.

Unfortunately, something happens to complicate the mission; exactly what is up to the gamemaster. Perhaps the drop–shuttle is detected, or maybe an attack by natives put the base on high alert. Maybe the base is on the move again, either to a fresh contract or because the mission was leaked or just because the general is jumpy. The complication shouldn't be so bad that the mission automatically fails, but it should give a good chance of bloodying the force's nose.

Base: Brintooin
Mission: Front line armored assault
Affiliations: Select Imperial remnants
Zone of Operations: Throughout Imperial Space
Success Rate/Threat: 99%/Very High

Founded around the end of the Clone Wars from Old Republic armor units, the "Hammers" Elite Armor Unit became the core of the Army of the Republic's repulsortank armor and premiere unit. While many other army units languished in the torpor of the Old Republic's collapse, the Hammers remained at a high state of professionalism and readiness, even as the regiment's support withered under the post–Clone Wars stand–down.

With the coming of the Empire, the unit found itself the core and model of Imperial armor units. Even as the Imperial AT–AT rose in importance, the Hammers success rate prevented conventional armor from disappearing from the order of battle. The Hammers gained support and filled out to full regimental strength. As resistance to the Empire began to grow, and increasingly became military, the Hammers were often called on to suppress local uprising and revolt, often by well–equipped planetary defense forces. The regiment landed on world after world, usually in the first or second landing wave, and often staying only long enough to crack resistance and defeat the primary local armor units. The Hammers racked up the highest number of landings and engagements of any armor unit in the Empire.

The unit's only major defeat, in the Hitak mountains on Turak IV, actually improved its reputation. Two entire battalions fell to Alliance assaults, while the Hammers virtually annihilated the Rebel units. This was a pivotal battle in the early Rebellion, demonstrating once and for all that Alliance forces should not engage in conventional war with Imperial units; although officially a victory for the Alliance, it cost a vast amount in lives and material, and broke the back of Allied resistance in that sector for years. The Hitak campaign had been intended to strike a ringing blow and rallying victory for the Alliance: instead, it became a propaganda victory for the Empire.

The Hammers had previously been considered a valuable, but expendable unit. Now the Imperial Central Command reassessed the remaining Hammer battalion to be crucial to suppression efforts, and issued an order requiring first–class priority for Hammer requests for fire support, material and troops. The order came too late for the regimental commander, Colonel Johans, who never trusted his superiors again.

The unit functioned at battalion level for over two years while a new repulsortank design lumbered through its phases, intended to replace the functional but aging *Firehawk* repulsortank. In the meantime, the Hammers racked up a score of victories. Shortly after the Hammers were instrumental in finally suppressing the Yatir, the indigenous species of the planet Absit, Johans was promoted to high colonel and the Hammers were recalled to Brintooin to train and build up to regimental strength. Although now above regimental command rank, Johans remained at the head of the Hammers, and orchestrated the reinvigoration of the elite armored regiment. Requests for transfer to the Hammers poured in from across the Empire. Weeks of tests and trials were required to pare the applicants down to the cream of the crop, the finest armor troopers the Empire had. The standing Hammers battalion was reduced by 10%, as Johans put his own troopers to scrutiny.

Johans intended to place the Hammers regiment at the heart of a armored battlegroup. Never again would the Hammers have to rely on rear-echelon command decisions. The proposed battlegroup would have the firepower, mobility and support of three standard regiments dedicated to supporting the Hammers. Those troopers who scored 99% in the Hammers tryouts (100% being the admission qualification) were transferred to the battlegroup High Colonel Johans was forming. Brintooin Base became a center for armored warfare training, and specially selected tank crews were transferred there for training by Hammer elites.

While engaged in this reorganization and retraining, the Hammers missed its chance at a great victory: the destruction of the Alliance base on Hoth. The victory went instead to Johans' newest rival, General Maximilian Veers, who used AT–ATs to destroy the Alliance shield generators. Veers' triumph was incomplete, however; due to the slow speed of the AT–ATs, several transports escaped before the shield generator could be destroyed, and the entire command core of the Alliance escaped along with a substantial amount of material and nearly a full wing of starfighters. The Alliance had snatched survival from the jaws of defeat. Johans, on reading the after–action reports, declared that if he had been there, the Alliance would have been irrevokably shattered. Analysis performed both by Imperial and Alliance experts at the time support his opinion: the faster *Imperial* repulsortanks would have been largely immune to Alliance firepower, unaffected by the tactics used on the AT–ATs, and able to destroy the shield generators in roughly one–third the time Veers took.

Even as the Hammers were placed back on the active–duty roster, the Emperor was killed at Endor, a fleet of Star Destroyers routed, and the Empire began to crack at its seams. The Hammer regiment was quickly rushed off-planet to add weight to the crackdowns that followed. The support regiments were transferred to other theaters, the battlegroup was never used as a cohesive unit, and the Hammers found themselves being treated like disposable pawns once again.

The Hammers continued to win victories, but this only padded the campaigns being lost. As the Empire fragmented, the Hammers found themselves fighting Imperial troops, including enemy Walkers. Alliances shifted, broke and melded, and after many months of fighting, the Hammer regiment, pride of the Empire, found itself in battle against what had been one of its own support regiments. This event spurred Johans into the political decision he had avoided for months. After ordering the support unit to his side, he exited the battlefield, and recalled all Hammer affiliated units, and invited any Imperial commanders interested, to Brintooin. Many commanders broke ranks and joined Johans.

Analysts believe Johans intended to wait out the fighting and join a side with a legitimate claim to inherit the Empire, as shown by circumstance. The units rested, repaired their tanks and other equipment and trained. Weeks turned into months. Meanwhile, the Alliance of Free Planets began to defeat the little empires one by one. The Alliance successfully drove a campaign home against Coruscant, the ancient seat of galactic power, and established itself as the New Republic.

Grand Admiral Thrawn arrived on the scene, and Colonel Johans watched with interest. His successes demonstrated great ability, and Johans soon allied himself to the alien. Thrawn's campaign was primarily naval, and the Hammers were only used for one operation in this period. Johans' disappointment at Thrawn's assassination must have been tremendous. Still, Johans was now allied with the loose confederation Thrawn left in his wake.

Within a half–year, the Emperor (or something claiming to be the Emperor) returned. Johans did not jump at the chance to enter the service of this being, but remained attentive for orders. They never came, as the Emperor–creature seemed more concerned with superweapons than superior units. The threat of a reforged Empire swiftly passed with the destruction of this being. (For more information, consult reports filed by Commander Luke Skywalker (ret.) and Princess Leia Organa Solo.)

Colonel Johans has survived the three most catastrophic armed conflicts of recent history, and continues to occupy Brintooin without incident. Johans has not promoted himself to General, Moff, Governor, or Warlord, and commands a frighteningly effective armored unit consisting of four fully augmented Hammer battalions, half an artillery regiment, a fully equipped garrison, and a planetary economy to fuel such a military. The Hammers lack adequate infantry support, and haven't had stormtrooper support since retiring to Brintooin.

Brintooin itself is a world of plains, deserts, marshes, scrub, scattered woods, and other flatlands—ideal terrain for armored combat (the reason it was selected as the baseworld for the Hammers). Intelligence indicates the planetary shields and defenses are strong enough to withstand a full siege with attendant all–out assaults. The 100–million strong human population exists under Imperial rule—not Imperial rule as it was known to billions of sentients throughout the galaxy, but Imperial rule closely resembling the ideals propagated by COMPNOR. Life is somewhat restricted, but overall the population is loyal to the Empire as personified by Colonel Johans. The population credits Johans and the presence of the Hammers with keeping war away from Brintooin and is likely to whole–heartedly resist New Republic invasion or military intervention. The planet is administrated by Imperial

Governor Thalkuss, but his position is reliant on support of the planetary hero, Johans. Further, many of the planets inhabitants rely on the Hammers for their livelihoods: the Hammers have an entire factory complex dedicated to repulsortank manufacture, and have a staff of engineers working on improving their tank's design.

Projection: Unless forced by circumstances to another course of action, Johans is likely to remain on Brintooin, isolated and untouchable. Although currently loosely allied with other Imperial surviving governments, the rollback and collapse of Imperial space is slowly eliminating his ability to transport his troops—Johans relies on his allies to provide transport. Currently, the Hammers are unable to move more than one battalion at a time without outside aid. If ultimately isolated, Johans may become approachable.

Johans has, so far, not offered his tanks for mercenary hire, and is unlikely to do so. He must not be allowed to find himself in a position where this is necessary. He has also been most discriminating about aligning himself with other Imperial holdouts (notably rejecting Warlord Zsinj's attempts to bully and bribe him into accepting his command).

Recommendation: Allow Colonel Johans to remain in place on Brintooin. Although his units provide considerable support to other Imperial strongholds, their threat is greater if confronted than if sidestepped. The population of Brintooin is not under notable oppression, and in time, a diplomatic solution and absorption should become viable. A military confrontation would likely be disastrous. If absolutely necessary, a coordinated assault following infiltration and sabotage of the planetary shields should be able to destroy the Hammers, but this would require Brintooin to be occupied for an extended period.

Hammer *Imperial*-class Repulsortank. Speeder, maneuverability 1D+2, move 140;400 kmh, body strength 4D+2. Weapons: heavy laser cannon (fire control 2D+2, 200–1km/3km/5km, damage 6D), medium laser cannon (fire control 1D+1, 50-200/500/1km, damage 3D+2).

Typical Imperial Army Hammer Trooper. All stats 2D except: *Blaster 5D+2, blaster: repeating blaster 6D+2, blaster artillery 4D+2, brawling parry 3D+2, dodge 4D+2, grenade 4D+2, melee combat 3D+2, melee parry 3D+2, running 3D+2, vehicle blasters 7D+1, intimidation 3D, streetwise 3D, survival 4D, communications 4D+2, ground vehicle operation 4D+2, hover vehicle operation 4D+2, repulsorlift operation*

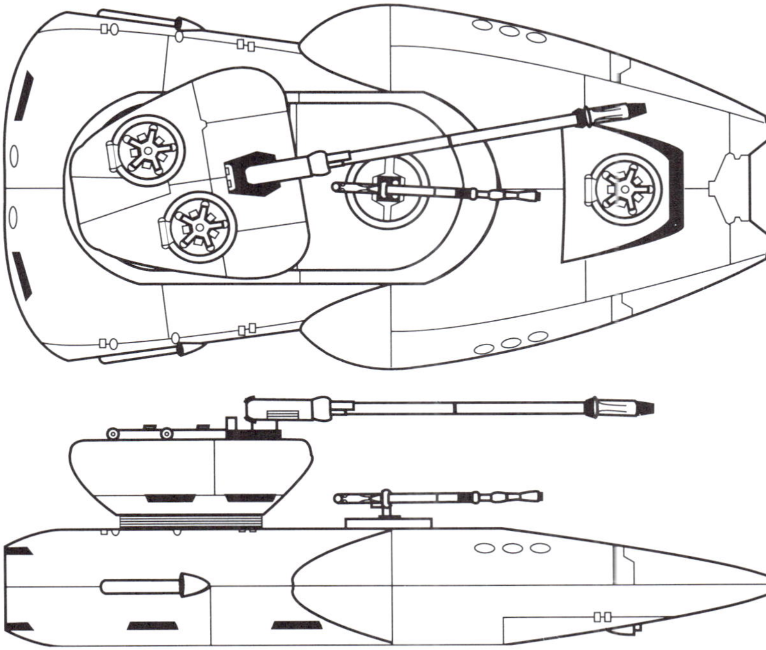

Imperial-class Repulsor Tank Mark II

5D+2, command 3D+1, hide 3D+1, search 3D+1, sneak 3D+1, brawling 4D+1, climbing/jumping 4D+1, stamina 4D+1, armor repair 3D, blaster repair 3D, first aid 3D+2, ground vehicle repair 3D, hover vehicle repair 3D, repulsorlift repair 3D. Move 10. Blaster rifle (5D) or light repeating blaster (6D), field armor and helmet (+1D physical +2 energy), grenades (5D), helmet comlink, survival gear, utility belt with supplies. Character points: 0–3.

Laramus Base Irregulars

Type/Unit Level/Size: Ragtag Partisan Band
CO: Tagg Pierce
Base: Mobile
Mission: Suicide operations
Affiliations: New Republic
Zone of Operations: Parmic Sector
Success Rate/Threat: 90%/Moderate

The Laramus Base Irregulars were originally a loosely organized quasi–Alliance company–sized force with a habit of finding or creating trouble for themselves, their allies, and their enemies. They have developed, over the past few years, into a pseudo–military, New Republic–allied company with a habit of succeeding, or at least surviving. Although they are known to have a high success rate with impossible missions, they have paid for that success in blood. In the past five years, the Irregulars have experienced a 96% turnover rate, with over 50% fatalities.

The Irregulars were created by former Lieutenant Tagg Pierce after his ejection from the Alliance military for gross insubordination (a difficult honor to achieve in the early days of the Rebel Alliance). Pierce probably intended to prove his methods and points with the unit, and, despite the horrific casualty rate suffered among his troops, continues to be self–righteous in his command and pathologically contemptuous toward line officers. The Irregulars have always been a gathering point for highly able mavericks, eager to flout convention and fly in the face of prudence. Alliance pilots were known for foolish brashness and bravado—the Irregulars are almost insanely brash.

Mobile since Laramus Base was destroyed by Imperial forces, the Irregulars wander from theater to theater. In the modern galaxy, the Irregulars are primarily used by New Republic forces as a predator–paw. Although Pierce remains utterly spiteful of High Command officers, he can be persuaded to commit his Irregulars to crucial, impossible missions. Pierce's brilliant but erratic genius generally pulls the unit, or remains, through. The Irregulars consider any mission achieved a success, regardless of casualties.

Although the structure of the unit is necessarily plastic, it generally consists of six infantry platoons and two heavy weapons platoons.

Projection: The Irregulars will likely convert to mercenary work as the Empire crumbles away to nothing. There is a small chance the unit will vanish, but this sort of warrior band (I am loathe to call them soldiers) attracts people like Pierce: ferocious, able and haughty. There is an equally small chance the unit will turn to outlaw–fringe work, but only if Pierce finds the blaster bolt with his name on it.

Recommendation: The Irregulars should be used as they currently are. If they do convert to mercenaries, they should be kept on retainer (if possible) and carefully tracked. In the event New Republic

forces oppose the Irregulars in combat, their neutralization should be given high priority: they are too dangerous to be ignored.

Typical Laramus Base Irregular. All stats are 3D except: *Blaster 7D+1, dodge 5D, grenade 3D+1, intimidation 5D, planetary systems 5D+1, streetwise 3D+1, survival 4D+2, con 3D+1, hide 6D, search 6D, sneak 7D, brawling 5D, climbing/jumping 4D*. Move 10. Equipment varies from mission to mission. Most soldiers are equipped with a heavy blaster pistol (5D) and little else. New supplies are scavenged from targets. Character points: 2–15.

Mantis Syndicate

Type/Unit Level/Size: "Bounty Hunter Guild"/Private Military/Battalion and smaller
CO: Lady Marina Mantis
Base: Santarine
Mission: High-risk special operations
Affiliations: Independent
Zone of Operations: Sarin Sector, Outer Rim Territories
Success Rate/Threat: 85%/High

The "bounty hunter guild" known as the Mantis Syndicate is, a private army/security force of special operatives, until recently under retainer to High Lord Jaris Affric. The Syndicate specializes in collecting bounties on groups of people andcan field up to a partial battalion of bounty hunters. These hunters operate in small groups of four to eight.

Not particularly subtle, Mantis Syndicate operatives were frequently employed to capture or otherwise eliminate criminal organizations, pirate gangs, and Alliance units operating in Sarin Sector, especially those groups whose operations ran counter to Lord Affric's interests. As Affric controlled several corporate and criminal interests, had considerable hereditary holdings in Sarin sector, and was the Imperial governor of Santarine, there were quite a number of such groups, and Affric issued bounties in each guise.

Mantis also hired out small units, up to company size (three to five squads) for other bounties. The Mantis hunters were generally looked on by other guilds as a mercenary unit, but were tolerated as a guild with a specialty in acquiring large groups. The squads are made up of highly trained specialists, and resemble special operations units.

As the war in Sarin Sector heated up, Mantis found itself being used for Affric's special military operations, both in special operations and in regular combat. During this period, it clashed with Churhee's Riflemen (in an attempt to capture Maydla Churhee), and against Alliance regular troops. When the war began to go badly, Affric began to accumulate debt to Mantis. This was only briefly tolerated, then Lady Mantis pulled her hunters out. Affric howled in protest, then cannily switched sides to the newly declared New Republic. Affric has lost a great deal of power and influence, but remains free.

Lady Mantis, deprived of much of her income, has been forced to hire Mantis hunters out much more widely than before, and for somewhat lower fees. The local New Republic sector government has hired Mantis hunters for certain jobs (including retrieval of wanted Imperials), and is satisfied with the guild's ability, professionalism and political disinterest. However, there is ample evidence that Lady Mantis' personnel is available for whomever has the money to pay for their services.

Projection: Lady Mantis is amoral and mercenary, and likely to hire her hunters out to whoever can pay her price. Lord Affric wasn't very concerned with legality, but Mantis will conform to her employer's wishes—as long as the hunters are monitored, they will likely obey New Republic law.

Recommendation: Retain the Mantis Syndicate as a source of trained unit–hunters.

Typical Mantis Syndicate Hunter. All stats 2D except: *Blaster 4D+2, dodge 4D+1, grenade 4D, melee combat 4D+2, melee parry 3D+2, cultures 3D, streetwise 3D+2, survival 3D+1, Perception 3D+1, investigation 4D+1, search 3D+2, sneak 4D, Strength 3D, brawling 4D, demolitions 2D+2, security 2D+1.* Move: 10. Blast vest (+1D physical, +1 energy), heavy blaster pistol (5D), blaster rifle (5D), hold–out blaster (3D), grenade (5D), vibroknife (STR+3D).

Mercenary Guild of Coyn

Type/Unit Level/Size: Mercenary Guild, about 800,000 warriors unevenly divided among 30 Kroyn'Tra (army–equivalent units)
CO: King Im'Toral XV
Base: Coyn, Elrood Sector
Mission: Front line battle, security, special operations
Affiliations: Independent
Zone of Operations: Throughout the Inner and Mid–Rim
Success Rate/Threat: 89%/Low

The huge Mercenary Guild of Coyn employs approximately 1% of Coyn's population at any given time, and generates a huge portion of the planetary income, while serving to release cultural pressures among this warrior people. Coynite society is centered on a warrior ideal, but the planet has been united under their En'Tra (king-master) for thousands of years. This would lead to an unending series of civil wars if the Coynites were unable to hire themselves out to aliens and fight in their wars.

Even at the height of the Old Republic's peace, Coynites were always able to find some local trouble to fight in, or at least a truce to guard. The honorable Coynites have always hired their units to legal entities—governments, noble houses, or corporations. In a few cases, they have been willing to work for potentially legal entities, like one side of a civil war, but only if convinced that the potential employer is honorable and has a legitimate claim to authority.

For years, this meant that the major client for the Coynites was the Empire. The Empire was usually unwilling to employ aliens, and preferred not to allow large standing armies, but considered the situation economical; it was cheaper to hire Coynites to soften targets and die in battle for the glory of the Empire (the Empire claimed the credit for victory, and laid blame for defeat on "unreliable alien units") than to conquer their world, with its millions of fierce warriors and modern defenses.

The Coynites did not recognize the Alliance as legitimate under their honor-code, but did accept the declared New Republic as a legal entity. The Mercenary Guild promptly made itself available to both the New Republic and the Imperial factions. As the war became more confused and Republic forces pushed back Imperial occupations, Imperial atrocities and dishonors became known to the En'Tra. After a short debate among his nobles, the En'Tra refused to allow Coynites serve the Empire, now considering it dishonorable.

Currently, the Guild leases a large Kroyn'Tra, some 75,000 Coynite warriors, to New Republic service. Coynite mercenaries also serve a dozen system–states and corporations throughout the Mid–Rim region.

Projection: The Guild is politically neutral and will remain a loyal contractor unless the New Republic behaves in a dishonorable fashion. The Guild is also willing to hire on with our honorable enemies. This is to be expected.

Recommendation: Maintain the lease on the Kroyn'Tra. In the event a Coynite unit is hired by an enemy of the New Republic, NRI should attempt to uncover evidence of behavior the Coynite consider repulsive; cowardice in particular. The Coynites are extremely ethnocentric, and although they don't hold aliens strictly to their code, they refuse to deal with cowards.

Typical Coynite Warrior. *Dexterity 3D, blaster 5D, brawling parry 4D, melee combat 5D, Knowledge 1D, survival 4D, Mechanical 1D, Perception 2D, Strength 5D, brawling 6D+2, Technical 1D*. Move 10. Blaster rifle (5D), Coynite battle armor (+2D to all attacks), coyn'skar polearm (STR+2D, blade; STR+2, hook). Character points: 1–4.

Natori Association

Type/Unit Level/Size: Mercenary Training Academy and Unit
CO: Unknown
Base: Sperin, Palaquin system, Bajic sector
Mission: Military Training and Shock Combat
Affiliations: Ororo Transportation
Zone of Operations: Throughout Outer Rim Territories
Success Rate/Threat: 75%/Moderate

The Natori Association began primarily as a mercenary training organization, teaching combat skills primarily to non–humans. Many of the graduates then pay for their training with a hitch in the Natori Shock Troops (those who paid up front usually find good wages in other units). Natori training focuses on using a species' natural abilities and cultural traits to the utmost advantage. Wookiees, for example, are usually trained as forest troops, and Duros are trained for space combat. Species from heavy gravity worlds are favored for front line close combat (they tend to be very strong and dense), while species from water worlds usually make excellent amphibious troops, even if they can't breath in water.

Natori has a long term security contract with Ororo Transportation, and is thought to have connections with assorted shady groups. They provide a number of corporations and known criminal organizations with security troopers, but also hire troops out to local governments. Natori seems to be trying to legitimatize itself as a special security and training corporation.

One long–standing mystery who is actually in charge of Natori. Repeated efforts to identify the CO of Natori have met with failure. Much of the company is apparently held by Malakin Enterprises—which some members of New Republic Intelligence believe is secretly controlled by Hutt crimelords—but several successful infiltrations of Natori has brought us no closer to discovering who is in charge of the organizations day–to–day operations.

Projection: Natori is a stable entity and likely to remain so. It has too much raw firepower at its disposal to be overtly threatened, and too many shady connections to be covertly attacked. It may find itself on the wrong end of a criminal investigation, but that's a standard hazard for such groups.

Recommendation: The best trainers at Natori might be tempted away from them for a high enough salary. This should be attempted.

Typical Natori Association Trooper. *Dexterity 2D+2, blaster 4D+2, brawling parry 4D+2, dodge 4D+1, melee combat 4D+1, melee parry 3D+2, Knowledge 2D, survival 2D+1, Mechanical 2D, starfighter piloting 2D+2, Perception 2D+1, hide 3D, search 2D+2, sneak 3D+1, Strength 2D, brawling 4D+2, stamina 3D, swimming 2D+1, Technical 2D.* Move: 10. Blaster pistol (4D), vibroblade (STR+2D).

Ragnar Syndicate

Type/Unit Level/Size: Bounty Hunter Guild/Mercenary Clearinghouse
CO: Reshton Severindas
Base: Ragnar VIII
Mission: No overall mission profile
Affiliations: Empire, criminal
Zone of Operations: Outer Rim Territories
Success Rate/Threat: NA/Moderate

The Ragnar Syndicate, which claims to be a bounty hunter guild (most other guilds do not recognize it as such), maintains connections to bounty hunters, mercenaries, assassins, and assorted freelance paramilitary experts and consultants. The assets at their

disposal are too varied to be easily summed up. The Empire, Black Sun, the Hutt families, smaller criminal organizations, ruthless corporations, and other groups needing a predator–paw have been known to hire Ragnar–retained agents.

The Ragnar Syndicate is not a military unit itself, however. It simply serves as an arrangement service for those wishing to hire experts in a field.

Projection: The Ragnar Syndicate is a thorn in the New Republic's side, and will likely remain so. The Imperial warlords have used Ragnar as a source of hire specialized assistance, and future enemies are likely to as well.

Recommendation: The Ragnar Syndicate should be eliminated. It remains too valuable a resource for the opponents of the New Republic. Ragnar VIII is remote and defendable and need not fear casual attempts at military action. The easiest way to remove Ragnar may be to post bounties on Ragnar "hunters." The bounty hunter guilds would love an excuse to harass what they consider a blot on their profession.

Scimitar "White Death" Assault Wing

Type/Unit Level/Size: Special TIE Bomber Wing
CO: Captain Tomax Bren, Wing Commander
Base: ISD *Retribution*, mobile with Qeimat fleet
Mission: Precision and Support Bombing
Affiliations: Last known affiliation: Grand Admiral Thrawn
Zone of Operations: Imperial Space
Success Rate/Threat: 99%/Very High

Originally created as a stopgap measure from six bomber squadrons to target Alliance emplacements in the Hook Nebula, the Scimitar assault wing, consisting largely of the then–new TIE Bomber, was an impressive success. Captain Bren used the bombers to great effect in the Hook Nebula campaign, effectively countering early Alliance inroads against the vital resource and manufacturing worlds. The Scimitar wing, nicknamed "White Death," was eventually credited a major factor in defeating the Alliance in that sector, despite wide local support. The success rate of the Scimitar wing is likely the only reason Captain Bren's disregard of Imperial Central Command's initial guidelines on TIE Bomber deployment was ignored.

In the Hook Nebula campaign, the ISD *Retribution* was devoted primarily to assist in the Scimitar's assault mission, subordinating an entire Star Destroyer to what is generally considered a support element. This was only one more example of Bren's unorthodox methods, and was tolerated in the face of his record.

After the subjugation of the Hook Nebula sector, Bren filed his post–campaign reports. He included recommendations for the still relatively new TIE Bomber, for reconfiguration of TIE wings to reflect mission and theater, and called for correction of a few flaws in the TIE Bomber design. He advocated a carrier–based fleet, predicted that the starfighter was ascendant, and suggested that future Star Destroyer models devote more room to TIE hangars. Furthermore, the TIE Bomber was too slow and unmaneuverable for Bren's tastes, although admittedly still an improvement over the older TIE/gt model. Bren admired the bomber's flexible payload capacity, but wished for a less prominent profile than the twin-pod design. Also, the bomber had to rely too much on escorts, and filling the wing with escort TIEs restricted the wing's bombing potential. Bren recommended shielding and armor upgrades for a proposed TIE Bomber Mark 2.

Bren also filed complete reports of his most effective tactics, from the Vertical Swoop to the Coordinated Bombing–Landing. These tactics were generally disseminated to TIE wings, but gained little hold in Navy wings. Army wings took to Bren's tactics almost immediately, though, as they dealt with planetside gravity well problems the Army routinely encountered.

Although highly successful, the Scimitar wing was not widely copied by other fleets. Many of Bren's tactics gained general acceptance, and Bren evaded the court martial that awaits most attempts to alter Imperial doctrine. An investigation was launched, and vigorously prosecuted, but the wing was ultimately left unaltered and under Bren's command. Outsiders commented that Bren had traded his career for his wing, but his confidants knew that that was exactly what Bren wanted: to fly and serve the Empire in the field.

The Scimitar wing itself was reassigned to a series of assault missions, none as demanding as the Hook Nebula campaign. Bren's career languished, although he was politically safe as long as he continued to be successful in his campaigns.

The death of the Emperor and resultant roll–back required a new mission: instead of covering landing invasion forces the Scimitar wing now provided interference for evacuating ground troops. In time, the Empire dwindled to a quarter of its former size. The Scimitar wing, often held in reserve and considered too valuable to squander on less than crucial missions, survived as much from inaction as skill or luck. The return of Grand Admiral Thrawn changed that.

Captain Bren was among the first commanders picked by Thrawn to counterattack the New Republic. Thrawn knew of Bren's innovative work with the TIE Bomber, and had read his Hook Nebula reports, including his critique of Bomber design, tactics, strategy, and doctrine. After a short period of planning and consultation, Thrawn ordered the creation of a new TIE model—the Scimitar Assault Bomber, to Captain Bren's specifications. Much of the design had been in the planning stages for years (most of the Sienar designers had listened to and agreed with Bren from the beginning), and production began in only a few weeks.

The newly equipped Scimitar Wing became a valuable asset to Thrawn's campaign against the New Republic. Several new bomber wings were commissioned in the short period of Thrawn's rule. The Scimitar Wing itself was instrumental in the assault on Mrisst, and the Scimitar Bombers was quickly integrated into Imperial military doctrine. Thrawn used the Scimitars for highly effective pinpoint attacks on shield generators and other critical planetary defenses.

Thrawn's death left the Scimitar Wing with Captain Pallaeon's command. Ignored by the resurrected Emperor, the original Scimitar Wing has found itself an elite unit with no mission, a timid central command, and without adequate supply support. Meanwhile, the Scimitar Bomber assault wings created under Thrawn continue to add power to Imperial military might, although they are

steadily dwindling in numbers as supply centers and manufacturing facilities revolt or are liberated by the New Republic.

Projection: Captain Bren has always been a loyal Imperialist maverick, and is unlikely to tolerate the isolation fate has imposed on his wing. When, under what circumstances, and to whom the Scimitar Wing will defect remains to be seen.

Recommendation: Ideally, Bren should be induced to retire his unit. This is highly unlikely, though, as he and his men have always been highly politically reliable to the New Order. It may be necessary, therefor, to eliminate the wing, perhaps by drawing it into an assault mission, and destroying it with high–speed starfighters. While risky, the wing does generally operate as a whole unit—properly laid and executed, the entire wing might be crippled or eliminated in one stroke.

TIE Scimitar Assault Bomber. Starfighter, *missile weapons 5D, starship gunnery 4D, starship piloting 5D, starship shields 3D.* Maneuverability 2D+1, space 9, atmosphere 295, hull 5D, shields 1D+2, Weapons: 2 Laser Cannons (fire control 2D, damage 4D), Concussion Missiles (16 carried) (fire control 3D+2, damage 9D).

Typical Scimitar Wing Pilot. All stats 3D except: *Blaster 4D+2, brawling parry 4D+2, dodge 4D+2, survival 3D, communications 5D+2, starfighter piloting 5D, starfighter piloting: Scimitar Bombers 7D, starship gunnery 6D, command 5D+1, search 4D+1, brawling 4D+2, climbing/jumping 3D+2, stamina 4D+1, computer programming/repair 4D+1, first aid 4D+2, starfighter repair 5D.* Move 10. Navigational computer linkup helmet (internal comlink, +1 to sensors), high gravity stress flight suit with life support equipment, one week emergency rations, blaster pistol (4D). Character points: 0–4.

Timothy O'Brien

m'Yalfor'ac Order

Type/Unit Level/Size: Planetary Military Order (about 700,000 troops)
CO: Colonel Quaal Tavier Catharius
Base: Guiteica
Mission: Republic Opposition
Affiliations: None known
Zone of Operations: Kadok Region
Success Rate/Threat: 50%/Moderate

The m'Yalfor'ac Order is a native military service of the planet Guiteica, home of the Bitthævrian species. Bitthævrians are naturally and culturally inclined to use direct conflict to resolve disputes. This has led to a warrior ethos and intense dislike of aliens who use diplomacy, political process or indirect methods. Two generations ago, this led to a military confrontation between the Order and the Old Republic. This short war was settled by the efforts of a band of Jedi, who used their powers to the Republic's advantage. The Republic and Jedi were therefore condemned by the Order and declared perpetual enemies of the Bitthævrian people.

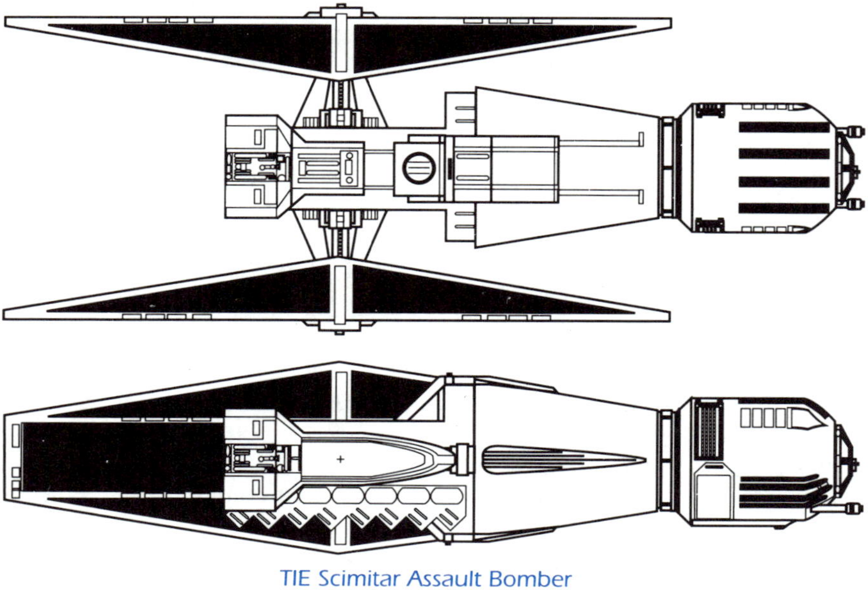

TIE Scimitar Assault Bomber

This was regarded as a formality by the Old Republic, since the Bitthævrians rarely ventured offworld and lacked the military technology to be a real threat. When the Empire took control, it continued the policy of ignoring Guiteica, an isolated world with few allies. Even though the Order condemned the Empire as immoral, Guiteica wasn't thought to be worth the effort of pacifying, especially when the Order publicly rebuffed Alliance efforts at recruitment. The only reason to venture to the tertiary Kadok system at all was for Guiteica's mineral deposits, notably the rich veins of Bal'ta'ran crystals. Guiteica would have eventually been conquered by the Empire, simply because resistance was intolerable, but ongoing conflict with the Alliance delayed the final destruction of the Order. In the meantime, the Order traded Bal'ta'ran crystals for second–hand military gear in an attempt to acquire the technological backing to make themselves a modern military power.

In the post–Imperial world, the Order continues to hang onto it's old bitterness. It loudly reviles the New Republic and officiously claims a large section of space outside the Tertiary Kadok system, although it lacks colonies or outposts to support the claim. It has occasionally made itself a pest in local Kadok Region politics, but otherwise seems ineffective. Intelligence reports suggest that the Order's purchased military hardware is two to three generations out of date—AT–PTs, outdated M91 light walkers, and a few pre–TIE era Toscan 8–Q and C–73 Tracker starfighters. The Order recently bought some KAAC Freerunners, a significant upgrade of their armor force. Although the Guiteica Militia (the Order makes up 80% of the Militia) boasts an army of 700,000 troops (a huge 9% of the population), these are largely part-time warriors. The standing Order numbers closer to 70,000, still a formidable force.

Projection: Oddly enough for a warrior people, the Bitthævrians seem to have little interest in extra–system conquest. They hold the Empire in disdain and are unlikely to ally with them. If a non–Imperial, anti–Republic ally arose, the Order would almost certainly be eager to align itself with them, but there are few species willing to deal with the headstrong Bitthaevrians.

Recommendation: Avoid the Order as much as possible. The New Republic has no vital interests on Guiteica and can buy Bal'ta'ran crystals on the market. A ban or heavy tariff on military hardware intended for Guiteica may be desirable to keep them from gaining enough military equipment to create an appetite for conquest.

It is highly unlikely that the Order poses a serious threat to the New Republic. Its weaponry and tactics are outdated, and although they could present a formidable third–class military force, mainly via sheer numbers, the New Republic forces should easily be able to counter the Order if necessary.

Typical m'Yalfor'ac Order Trooper. *Dexterity 2D+1, blaster 3D, dodge 2D+2, Knowledge 2D, Mechanical 2D, walker operation 2D+1, repulsorlift operation 2D+2, Perception 3D, Strength 2D+1, brawling 3D, stamina 3D+1, Technical 1D+1, walker repair 2D+2.* Move: 9. Blaster carbine (5D), Dematoil morning star (STR+1D)

Report ends. Further updates pending.

ISB Intercepts

By Eric S. Trautmann

Welcome to another installment of "ISB Intercepts" where West End Games writers and editors answer reader questions about the *Star Wars* roleplaying game.

This issue's "ISB Intercepts" is by Eric S. Trautmann, one of the co–designers of *The Star Wars Roleplaying Game, Revised and Expanded* and author of the forthcoming *X–Wing: Rogue Squadron Sourcebook*.

This column marks the beginning of a new policy for "ISB Intercepts"—we are awarding a $10.00 gift certificate to people who submit questions that are used in the article. These gift certificates are good for orders placed directly to West End only; they are not redeemable through other mail–order companies or retailers. (Only one gift certificate per person will be awarded, and West End reserves the right to edit letters for space and grammar.)

Letters may be addressed to:

ISB Intercepts
c/o West End Games
RR3, Box 2345
Honesdale, Pa 18341

or may be e-mailed to us at:

WEGEdit@aol.com

(E-mail submissions should include "ISB Intercepts" in the "Subject" or "Regarding" box.)

Please include your full name and address on the letter (though names and addresses will be withheld upon request; gift certificates will still be awarded if your name and address are withheld).

And now, without further delay....

Q: If a character has claws, could they roll their *melee parry* skill instead of *brawling parry* when fighting unarmed?

—Robert Nemergut, Ohio.

A: No. In this case, since the claws themselves are probably not used to block an attack (instead a hand or arm is used to parry), *brawling parry* is the more appropriate skill. Claws are not defensive weapons; they are "designed" for slashing and cutting attacks.

Q: I play a Coynite bounty hunter with a *Strength* of 4D+2. When using a sat'skar (a Coynite sword) which does *Strength+3D+1* damage, do I roll 8D or 7D+3?

—Robert Nemergut, Ohio.

A: In cases like this, the "pips" are not cumulative; a total of +3 does not equal 1D. Your Coynite bounty hunter would roll 7D+3 to determine the damage his sat'skar inflicts.

Q: When a larger vessel is hit by a smaller one, does the scale die modifier of the larger vessel apply to both the shield roll and the hull roll? For example, against a starfighter–scale proton torpedo (9D damage) would a Star Destroyer resist at 22D (7D hull + 6D capital-scale hull modifier + shields 3D + 6D capital-scale shields modifier)?

—Ruben A. Reyes, New York.

A: Yes, which gives you a fairly accurate

idea of how difficult a Star Destroyer is to defeat. Bear in mind that it usually takes a squadron of X–wings or other starfighters (all targeting the same spot on the Star Destroyer's shields) to penetrate the capital ship's defenses. Witness the Super Star Destroyer *Executor* in *Return of the Jedi*, which was well–nigh invulnerable until a lucky shot took out the vessel's bridge deflectors. Starfighters can take out capital ships, but it takes tremendous luck and skill and most of the attacking fighter pilots won't be returning from the battle.

Q: Does West End/Lucasfilm suggest that Starlog's *Star Wars Technical Journal of the Planet Tatooine*'s version of the *Millennium Falcon* is more accurate than the version in the *Star Wars Sourcebook*?

—Ruben A. Reyes, New York.

A: The version of the *Millennium Falcon* blueprints that appeared in the *Star Wars Sourcebook* was in print several years before the Starlog version. Any West End references to the *Falcon* rely on the *Star Wars Sourcebook* blueprints, not the Starlog version. However, Han Solo modified the *Falcon* repeatedly during his smuggling career; the excellent Starlog blueprints represent one of the stages of these modifications.

Q: In the "ISB Intercepts" section of the February 1996 issue of the *Journal*, one of the questions asked was about possible alternatives to the X-wing for the Brash Pilot template. Upon seeing this, one of my players became obsessed with the idea of getting his hands on an Assault Gunboat from the "TIE Fighter" computer game. I was wondering If you could provide me with the *Star Wars Roleplaying Game* stats on an assault gunboat.

—Jerry L. Hullander, Tennessee.

A: The following stats (extrapolated from *TIE Fighter: The Official Strategy Guide* by Rusel DeMaria, David Wessman, and David Maxwell) should suffice:

Imperial Assault Gunboat

Craft: Alpha Class Xg–1 Star Wing
Type: Assault fighter/gunboat
Scale: Starfighter
Length: 15 meters
Skill: Starfighter piloting: assault gunboat
Crew: 1
Cargo Capacity: 100 kilograms

Consumables: Three days
Maneuverability: 2D
Space: 8
Atmosphere: 365; 1,050 kmh
Hull: 4D+1
Shields: 2D+2
Sensors:
Passive: 20/0D
Scan: 35/1D
Search: 50/2D
Focus: 3/2D+2
Weapons:
Two Taim & Bak KX5 Laser Cannons (single or fire-linked)
Fire Arc: Front
Skill: Starship gunnery
Fire Control: 2D
Space Range: 1–3/12/25
Atmosphere Range: 100–300/1.2/2.5 km
Damage: 3D+2
Two Borstel NK–3 Ion Cannons (single or fire-linked)
Fire Arc: Front
Skill: Starship gunnery
Fire Control: 2D
Space Range: 1–3/7/36
Atmosphere Range: 100–300/700/3.6 km
Damage: 3D+2
Two SFS M–s–3 Concussion Missile Launchers (8 missiles each)
Fire Arc: Front
Skill: Starship gunnery
Fire Control: 3D
Space Range: 1/3/7
Atmosphere Range: 50–100/300/700
Damage: 9D

Q: What are the difficulty numbers for building a lightsaber?

—Norman R. Hensley, Ohio.

A: The *Tales of the Jedi Companion* describes lightsaber construction:

"To construct a lightsaber from its component parts requires a successful *lightsaber repair* roll against a Very Difficult difficulty. Decrease the difficulty by one level for each extra month spent building the saber, to a minimum of Easy."

See page 142 of *Tales of the Jedi Companion* for additional modifications and a more detailed lightsaber construction description

Q: On the cover of *The Kathol Outback*, the first supplement for the *DarkStryder Campaign*, there is something my friends and I didn't understand. In the bottom left corner of the cover is a starfighter that looks similar to an X-wing. We looked through the book and couldn't find anything else about the ship. What type

of ship is it?

—Patrick Ryan Roach, California.

A: The fighter is a variant Z–95 Headhunter. Essentially it is a design prototype used to test the S–foil system that eventually was incorporated into the Incom T–65 X–wing; in effect, it is a Z–95 fuselage with X-wing S–foils. In game terms, it is little different than a standard Z–95.

Q: I'm a big fan of several comic books and novels based on the Star Wars universe (including *Dark Empire II, X–wing: Rogue Squadron, Darksaber, Dark Lords of the Sith,* and *The Sith War.*) Are there any sourcebooks for these series in the works?

—Jean–Francois Beauchemin, Quebec.

A: There are no plans to produce *Dark Empire II, Dark Lords of the Sith* and *Sith War* tie–ins. There are only a handful of "new" characters, equipment, locations and so on to talk about in *Dark Empire II* so it is difficult to produce an entire sourcebook on the material. As to the *Tales of the Jedi* material, Lucasfilm has requested we not produce tie-in material to *Dark Lords of the Sith* and *The Sith War* (so, although literally hundreds of readers have asked for follow–up releases, the *Tales of the Jedi* line is effectively shelved). An *X-wing: Rogue Squadron* sourcebook will be out this winter (written by myself, with a new short story by Mike Stackpole). However, in July we released *Cracken's Threat Dossier*, a mega–sourcebook covering *The Courtship of Princess Leia, The Black Fleet Crisis* and *The Corellian Trilogy* novels. If *Cracken's Threat Dossier* does well, expect to see more volumes in the future, covering some of the more recent novels and comics.

Q: Are there any more storehouses like Mount Tantiss from *The Thrawn Trilogy Sourcebook*? If there are, can you give any information on where they are located?

—Dale Harper, Michigan.

A: There is no definitive information on other treasure troves like Mount Tantiss. However, Timothy Zahn believes that the Mount Tantiss facility was the Emperor's main storehouse. While he may have had other smaller "trophy rooms," none of them were comparable to Mount Tantiss. This is borne out by the fact that the cloaking device, Spaarti cylinders, and Luke's hand and lightsaber—all extremely important devices or relics—were all stored here,

Eric S. Trautmann

implying that the Emperor favored Mount Tantiss over any other facilities he may have used. These lesser facilities could have been located anywhere, from antechambers hidden in the bowels of Coruscant to remote asteroids in the Outer Rim Territories. The implication that there are more storage areas was included in *The Thrawn Trilogy Sourcebook* as a potential scenario hook for imaginative gamemasters.

Q: Are there stats for the Falleen from *Shadows of the Empire*?

—Jeremiah Hatcher, Tennessee.

A: Yes. Stats for the Falleen appeared in the *Shadows of the Empire Sourcebook* by Peter Schweighofer. For a more detailed description of the Faleen, see pages 95–97 of the *Shadows of the Empire Sourcebook*. The basic stats are as follows:

Falleen

Attribute Dice: 13D
DEXTERITY 2D/4D
KNOWLEDGE 2D/4D+2
MECHANICAL 2D/4D
PERCEPTION 2D+1/4D+2
STRENGTH 2D+2/4D+2
TECHNICAL 2D/4D
Special Abilities:
Attraction Pheromones: Exuding special pheromones and changing skin color to affect others gives Falleen a +1D bonus to their *persuasion* skill, with an additional +1D for each hour of continuous preparation and meditation to enhance their effects—the bonus may total no more than +3D for any one skill attempt and the attempt must be made within one hour of completing meditation.
Amphibious: Faleen can "breathe" water for up to 12 hours. They receive +1D to any *swimming* skill rolls.
Story Factors:
Rare: Falleen are rarely seen throughout the galaxy since an Imperial blockade in their system severely limited travel to and from their homeworld.
Move: 9/12
Size: 1.7–2.4 meters tall

Q: Is there a font I can purchase for my computer that contains the "aurebesh" alphabet from *Star Wars Gamemaster Screen, Revised and Expanded* and other West End products?

—Anthony Marino, New York.

A: There is no officially sanctioned version of the aurebesh available; West End Games does not have the rights to produce *Star Wars* material of any kind for computers.

Q: I've been killing myself trying to find out the names and commanders of the Super Star Destroyers. I know Lord Vader was in charge of the *Executor* and Warlord Zsinj was in command of the *Iron Fist*. What were the other ships?

—Noel C. Jackson, USS Essex.

A: Not all of the Super Star Destroyers have been named. The *Executor* was under Lord Vader until it was destroyed at Endor. The *Lusankya*—under Ysanne Isard's command—was destroyed at Thyferra. The *Guardian*, commanded by Admiral Gaen Drommel, is detailed in *Wanted by Cracken*. Warlord Zsinj's *Iron Fist* was destroyed by Han Solo. Finally, there is a Super Star Destroyer, the *Allegiance*, though her commander remains unknown; the *Allegiance*—along with another unnamed Super Star Destroyer of apparently unique design—was destroyed in the *Dark Empire* comic book series.

However, according to Mike Stackpole (author of the *X–Wing: Rogue Squadron* novels and comics): "…the number of Star Destroyers listed in the *Imperial Sourcebook* [may be out of date.] Cross-referencing the *Executor* entry in the [*Guide to the Star Wars Universe* by Bill Slavicsek] would indicate that the number of four Super Star Destroyers (SSDs) was current as of the Battle of Yavin. Simple math suggests an output of roughly four SSDs per year from just after Yavin to Endor, or roughly *sixteen* possible SSDs completed just before the Empire fell."

Laughter After Dark

By Patricia A. Jackson

Illustrations by Mike Chen

Bowing his head to the blower jets, Thaddeus Ross stood in the darkened cubicle as the biting cold of the Najib rain evaporated from his closely cropped blond hair. Still damp from his brief excursion through the storm, his collar was hot from the torrid blasts of air gusting over him and he flinched slightly. As the doorway opened, admitting him into the innermost room of Reuther's Wetdock, he raised his head and proceeded inside.

In no mood for a confrontation, the Corellian swept the length of his rain duster away from his right hip, exposing the wicked profile of his Caelli–Merced heavy blaster, which was slung low in its holster. There were few patrons to take note of the smuggler or his pistol as he walked into the deserted bar. He fumbled through his pockets for a credit, squinting against a cloudy smog of stale liquor and spice smoke. As he fingered the thin coin against his palm, he briefly made eye contact with Reuther, the Najib bartender, who greeted him with a slight nod and a look of bemused concern.

Ross continued to the back of the establishment, pausing in the far right corner at the sound slug machine. The dilapidated music box had seen better years. Its bubbled, glass dome was dingy from layers of dust and caked with accumulated smoke particles. Dented and scuffed by careless drunkards or brawlers, the antiquated entertainment unit was supported by a sawed-off metal piece where one of its support struts had been broken off. Inside the thin plasteel dome, a collection of sound slugs and mini–holovids were displayed in the selector, waiting for an interested party to program a request.

Ross dropped the credit piece into the corroded slot and pressed his selection. After a moment of low humming and static, the holo–projector dimly lit the area above the inverted projector tube, producing the svelte image of a Twi'lek woman. She was dressed in a scarlet gown that accentuated her hips and slender torso. Between a staggered line of brilliant glass buttons, her mahogany skin showed through in places, exposing smooth sections of her shapely body from bare shoulder to thigh.

With full, pouting lips, the seductive image beckoned to him with a subtle nod. "*Used to be that darkness frightened me so; used to be I spent my life chasing the sun.*"

Ross swallowed the lump in his throat and turned away from the holo–phantom. The Corellian sat down at a nearby table and closed his eyes, enduring the insistent protest of his tense muscles.

"*I know all too well the fear of night... but with you, there is only laughter... laughter after dark.*"

Carrying an intricately carved bottle and a glass, Reuther shuffled over to Ross' table. Dressed in a stained work tunic and apron, the bartender dragged a seat over the scuffed floor of his bar and sat down. Despite the depth of the shadows, his eyes flashed with inner brilliance, bringing a spark of optimism to the tavern's lonely back corner. Coarse, white hairs were tightly braided against his skull, joining into a single, thick braid that ran the length of his back. He cleared his throat, pushing the glass across the table toward the smuggler. "How long have we known each other, Ross? Seven, maybe eight years?"

Lethargically, as if in a trance, Ross pulled the stopper from the bottle and smelled the pungent aroma of the liquid inside. "About seven years, I guess," he replied softly.

"A man gets to know his friends, especially a partner, over that many years." Reuther sniffed disdainfully, wiping at the wide bridge of his nose. "I know you better than you think I do."

"I'm not in the mood for a psychiatric evaluation, Reuther. Get on with it."

Reuther sat back in his chair, thoughtfully rubbing the stubble maturing at his chin. "What's gotten into you, boy? I could set my ordering catalogs by you. Once a year, and only once a year, I order this Twi'lek t'ssolok," he pointed to the sculpted container, "and guaranteed within two or three days, you show up at my doorstep, looking like Death's first mate just took a shot at you." The Najib snorted, leaning over the edge of the table. "You come in here, play that same song. You drink until you can't see straight. Then you leave without a word about what's ailing you. I'm no head fixer, Ross, never claimed to be. But I'm the next best thing." Reuther took the bottle from Ross and poured a generous portion into the waiting glass.

"*I've often dreamed of a perfect world,*" the song continued, "*in clear amber and white light.*"

Ross sipped pensively from the glass, wincing at the bittersweet aftertaste. "I never told you about my little side adventures with Trep Winterrs, did I?"

"You've mentioned Trep a few times."

"Have I ever mention Saahir? Saahir Ru'luv?"

Reuther slowly turned to the music box, then back to the smuggler with a glimmer of mischief in his eyes. 'The singer? You knew her?"

"About seven years ago, shortly before I met you, Trep and I found ourselves on the wrong side of an Elomin protection scam that went all wrong..."

The shot slammed through his blast vest. Ross gasped as the point–blank discharge forced the air out of his lungs. Though disoriented, he pulled the trigger of his blaster rifle, firing into the Elomin assassin. The reptilian was thrown back several meters, blast scores smoking from its chest and abdomen. Muscles recoiling involuntarily, the Elomin returned fire randomly at its aggressor.

Several subsequent shots were absorbed by the vest; but Ross felt the bruising concussion of each one. He gritted his teeth as his body finally hit the hard, polished floors of the embassy lobby. Numb from the initial blast, he opened his eyes and stared at the light rod swinging precariously above him, wondering when the final moment, the last breath would come. “Ross?” he heard the concern in his partner’s voice.

Trep Winterrs brushed the long black hair over his shoulder as he entered Ross’ field of vision and stooped down to look over the fallen smuggler. His handsome features were buried beneath layers of sweat and grime. He shook his head as a wide grin spread across his face. “I can’t believe you took that hit for me.”

“What was I suppose to do?” Ross had hoped for a snarl, but his retort was more of a groan. He struggled inwardly, desperately holding on to the last shattered fragments of consciousness. He rolled to one side in a frantic attempt to get up, but failed. “Stand there and watch him shoot you in the back?”

Trep took the blaster rifle from Ross and checked its power cell. “The deal’s gone sour, buddy. The old ambassador is growing cold as we speak. I’m not going to let the same happen to you. Can you shoot?”

“I’ll manage.” Ross squeezed his eyes shut as the pain washed over him. He forced his body to react and respond as Trep helped him to his feet.

Ducking a blast from the far corridor, Trep turned so Ross could return fire. The blast ricocheted off the polished sheen of the wall and brought down one of the intruders. “Whole thing’s falling apart,” Trep complained. He pulled Ross tightly against his back and crouched over, carrying the smuggler’s full weight.

Ross struggled to keep his eyes open. “Whose idea was it to put a Gamorrean in charge of a diplomatic security team?”

“Ishenn had promise. Besides, if you weren’t going to do it, and I wasn’t going to do it, who was? That little Chadra–Fan with the patch over his eye?”

Explosions sounded from farther inside the embassy building, scattering debris into the deserted streets of Elos, one of several capital cities littering the surface of the Elomin homeworld. A siren blared in the distance, a warning that reinforcements were on the way. In a hurry to vanish before any questions could be asked, Trep scurried over to an abandoned landspeeder and gently laid Ross inside the passenger seat. “Hold on, buddy,” he said, hopping over Ross and into the driver’s seat.

Trep tore loose the guidance assembly and quickly gathered the connecting wires and plugs. Ross watched from what seemed like a great distance. "The red wire first," he slurred, slumped against the back of the seat. "Always the red wire first."

The smuggler rewired the red filament as Ross instructed. Startled as the spark flew from the connection, he gunned the throttle, bringing the cold engine to life. Under his guidance, the landspeeder lurched forward onto the streets, swinging wide as a troop carrier swerved onto the boulevard. Trep threw the steering bar to the side and managed to control the landspeeder through the 180–degree turn. He made a hasty retreat, revving the engine as they sped into the spaceport docking pads just outside the perimeter of the embassy yards.

The landspeeder bucked as Trep hurdled the partition, which cut off the exterior flight docks from the inner holding bays. Ross could see the outline of his ship, the *Kierra*, resting just beyond the main port building. Despite his failing vision, he could clearly see the yellow sentry lights flashing beneath the ship, signaling that the freighter's preservation systems were functional.

"Ross?" He gently pulled the smuggler against the seat. "Ross, stay with me. You hear?"

"I'm not going anywhere." A numbing chill settled over him; but Ross was too exhausted to tremble against it. He shrugged indifferently and allowed himself to silently fade into the oblivion of unconsciousness.

"Kierra, open the hatch!"

"It *is* open," the droid replied. "Why? Are you expecting a visitor?"

Ross swallowed the dryness in his mouth and struggled to sit up. The familiar sights of his personal cabin swam around him in a blur. A searing pain shot through his body, making the sweat break out against his feverish skin. Falling back into the cot, he closed his eyes, composing himself and the muddle of his disconnected memories.

There was a slight hum of electronics as the droid intelligence trapped within Ross' ship—and who was named for the freighter—refocused the optical lens over his bed and began taking sensor readings. "Ross," she said, panic creeping into her voice, "your heart rate and blood pressure are dangerously low. Some vital signs aren't even showing up! Trep, do something! His critical systems are failing!"

Ross managed a short, painful snort of laughter. "I'm not going anywhere, darling. Don't you worry about that." Even though he was quite still, he felt sore and bruised throughout his being and took a deep, cautious breath to quiet his racing heart. "Kierra, if you use your hydraulic sensors to test my vital signs, I'll come out on the verge of dying every time. They're not sensitive enough."

"I know, but I feel so helpless." The feisty droid's manner was subdued with concern, striking a soft chord in the smuggler's heart. "Just lie still, okay? Trep's coming."

"Well I'll be a Kowakian monkey's uncle! He's alive!" Trep swaggered into the cabin, grinning broadly.

"Where are we?"

"You know, I was really worried about you. I don't know a thing about first aid, Rosco."

"I said, where are we, Trep?"

Trep wiped his hands on his work tunic and grinned even wider, purposely holding back the information. "You should have seen your face when that blast went through your vest."

Grabbing Trep by the sleeve, Ross clenched his teeth against the pain and yanked the smuggler against the side of the bunk. "I'll ask you one more time! Where are we?"

Trep easily dislodged the smuggler's hand. "You're home, buddy. Corellia. Dock 52."

"Dock 52!" The reference raced through his mind "The private mooring dock for the Orange Lady Tavern?"

"Your memory's not bad for a man who's been technically dead for five days."

"Dead? Five days!" The room started to spin and Ross once again teetered on the edge of unconsciousness. He closed his eyes and fell back against the bunk.

Trep called out, "Saahir! Saahir, I think he's slipping back into it."

"Saahir?" Ross whispered the name, feeling his heartbeat quicken as his mind reeled with the emotional complications associated with it. For a moment, his body settled into a warm, secure cradle of love, happiness and a sense of belonging, but as the sensation matured, it was darkened with the burden of commitments unkept, separation, and loneliness.

Ross struggled back to lucidity, as he heard a gentle metallic clinking, which echoed in the room. The chime momentarily stopped and in a frustrated moment of rage, he panicked, falling back into the darkness. When he felt the gentle touch of her fingertips against his chin, Ross opened his eyes, staring up at the Twi'lek woman who smiled down at him from a long forgotten pedestal.

"How you feeling, hero?" Her mouth curled into an almost menacing smile as she gently plucked at a tuft of his hair.

Ross took her hand to assure himself that this was no phantom. "I don't know. Why don't you tell me?" He sat up slowly on one elbow and caressed one of her smooth cheeks.

Saahir was wearing a brown, tapered–down waistcoat, her favorite outer apparel, and a low–cut white blouse that showed at the sleeves, accentuating her slender arms. Black leggings revealed every curve of her legs and hips. In the placid illumination of the cabin lights, her head tentacles were a mysterious black hue, rather than the swarthy earth brown of her face.

"Doesn't take you long to get in the mood, does it?" she teased, bring his attention back to her face. "You know, Ross," she held up a large silver ring that encircled the middle finger of her left hand, "my magic potions are guaranteed to be successful, but there's a price."

"You poisoned me?" Ross cried. He remembered that the ring hid a small needle for injecting an unsuspecting host with t'ssolok extract, a dangerous paralyzing poison that was always fatal with-

out the necessary antidote.

"Somebody had to slow you down," Saahir replied, pouring an odd blue solution into a cup. "You were swiftly on your way to Otherspace, flyboy. You were on your way out for good." She sat back and smiled, holding the cup in her hand. "I couldn't allow that to happen. At least not without saying goodbye."

She put the cup to his lips, raising his head slightly, and allowed him to drink a mixed variant of the antidote. "You know, Ross, once you've fallen under one of my spells, you're mine, body and soul, forever." The Twi'lek set the empty glass aside, smiling sadly. "If only that were true, huh?"

"Can you handle him alone, or should I stay?" Trep crossed his arms over his chest, leaning against the hull wall.

"Erbus has a menu waiting for you in the kitchen," Saahir said. "I suggest you take advantage of it before he gets busy. I'm doing a show tonight, and the place is sure to be packed wall to wall."

As Trep left them alone, Ross carefully managed to put an arm behind his head. "So you're still singing?"

"That and saving your sorry choobies. The two things I do best." Saahir pulled the medical kit closer to the side of the bed and leaned over him, checking the damp dressing over the blaster wound. "That bandage needs changing." She gently pulled at the tape, pausing briefly as the smuggler flinched beneath her slight touch. "Would you look at yourself?" she teased. "Stop being a baby and hold still."

Ross closed his eyes and tried to focus on something else, besides the chest hairs the Twi'lek was forcefully removing with the medi–tape. Unable to bare the slow prick of each hair as it was ripped from the skin, he winced dramatically. "You know, you could go a little slower and really get back at me for all those years."

"Or I could just make one quick twist." Saahir pulled the tape off in one sudden motion. "And get back at you anyway." She glared at him as he opened his eyes. With a coy smirk, she checked the wound, pleased with its progress. "I know my opinion won't matter much to you," she carefully packed a new bandage around the injury, "but I think you should stay in bed for a few more days." The Twi'lek pulled the blanket over his chest and shoulders and stood up, slinging the med pack over her shoulder. "I'll be back by morning."

"Back?" Ross grabbed her by the wrist. He winced sharply as the motion caused pain to shoot through him. "Back from where?"

"Ross, lay still," Saahir scolded, gently pushing him down. She pursed her lips, shaking her head sternly. "It's a little late for you to start acting like a husband, don't you think?"

"I didn't mean it that way," Ross countered. "It's just," he avoided her cold eyes, "we just got here and now you're rushing off."

Cocking her head to one side, Saahir smiled, showing an even row of white teeth. "Well, if you must know, flyboy, I have a business venture waiting for me offworld."

"Who's flying?"

"Me, of course. Since I don't have my own in–home flight jock, I've had to make do myself."

"You? Since when did you start flying cargo?"

"I haven't. This'll be my first, but because of the schedule it couldn't be helped." Her lips were drawn down in a subtle pout.

Sucked in by the expression, Ross felt a pang of guilt, complicated with a twinge of jealousy. "What's the cargo?"

"The less you know the better."

"Oh, one of those. I get it." He stared up at her, gently caressing her long fingers. "Look, Saahir, I owe you one and—"

"You'll fly it for me?" she asked, cautiously curving the pitch in her voice.

"I didn't say that. I said I owed you one."

"So that means you'll fly the shipment for me, right?" Saahir began playfully rubbing the hairs on the back and sides of his neck. She watched in delight as the smuggler squirmed, blushing from the attention.

"You know I hate it when you do that."

"Liar," she whispered in a husky voice. "You love it, always did."

Growling against the warmth spread through his body, Ross clenched his teeth. "How much?"

"I can guarantee you five thousand credits up front." Saahir intensified her efforts. "There may be more, depending on your role."

"What do you mean, 'depending on my role?'"

"We can talk about that later." Before he could protest, the Twi'lek frowned, examining his forehead. "Oh, look here. I missed a scratch." She bent over and gently kissed him on the forehead. "And here's another." She kissed him above his right eye.

"Okay, okay. I'll do it." Holding her slender waist, he smiled as he pulled her down onto the cot. "Now give it to me straight, doc. Will

I make it?"

"Don't worry." Saahir took off her jacket as he unbuttoned her blouse. "Under my care, flyboy, you're certain to make a full recovery."

"Saahir?"

Ross raised his head from the pillow, smelling Saahir's perfume. His back was against the hull wall, allowing enough space for another body beside him; but the Twi'lek was not there and the blankets were cold. She had been gone for some time. "Saahir?" he called again. Thinking her absence might be an overdue game of hide and seek, he held onto the top bunk support and stood up, holding his injured side.

Ross found a pair of pants and a shirt, pressed and folded over the back of his cabin chair. Stiff from the shock of his wound and the extended bedstay, the Corellian dressed himself, carefully pulling his boots over his feet and ankles. Zipping the back of the leather tops, he straightened his flattened blond locks and stared into the darkened corridor. The fragrance of her perfume was everywhere, on his skin, his clothes, even in the passage, making it difficult to tell whether she had recently been there. However, there was a stale ambiance to the scent that suggested the singer was long gone from this area of the ship.

Stepping through the narrow bulkhead into the flight cabin, Ross quickly glanced around the cockpit for some sure sign of the Twi'lek. He found none. Beside him, curled up beneath his flight jacket and a blanket, Trep Winterrs was sound asleep at the navigator's station, oblivious to his presence. Ross grinned, leaving the exhausted smuggler to his sleep, and moved over to the main command console. "Kierra, did Saahir leave the ship?" He keyed up the display monitors, scanning miscellaneous reports on his freighter's current functional status. "Kierra," he raised his voice. "Is Saahir still aboard with us?"

"Yes and no," came the curt reply.

Stung by the unexpected acridity in the droid's voice, Ross leaned into the acceleration chair, glaring into one of her optical orbs. "What do you mean yes and no?"

"You asked two questions. I gave you two answers," Kierra said smugly. "Yes, she left the ship. No, she's not on board."

Though Kierra had a tendency to be combative and difficult, Ross knew that there was a cherished common bond between them. Puzzled by the droid's peculiar behavior, he slowly filtered through the caustic verve in her voice and picked up on the jealousy behind it. Drawn back to the events of the previous night, he hung his head as a warm flush spread over his cheeks and neck. "Kierra, about last night," he began pensively, realizing the droid had seen and overheard the entire affair. "I didn't mean for you to see— I mean—" He threw his hands up, exasperated by a need to explain himself. "I wasn't thinking clearly. I'd never intentionally hurt—" Ross cut himself short, struggling with a justification for his actions. "Kierra?"

"It's been hard, you know," Kierra said at last, her speakers barely audible in the quiet of the cabin. "We haven't known each other very long, and I suspect it will take a lot more adjustment, for both of us." A sigh registered over the static of the receiver. "I understand, Thadd, really I do. I haven't exactly been the best companion for you, especially over the last few months." The sigh grew into a slight sniffle, reverberating through the channel. "And then there are my mood swings, my emotional outbursts, my hydraulic bloating, and weight gain. It all takes its toll, Thadd, in ways you couldn't begin to imagine. And of course, I can't give you that physical satis—"

"Will you stop it!" Ross snapped, seeing through the droid's dramatics. Hearing a snort and a chuckle from behind him, Ross turned on Winterrs. "And that goes for you too. Always humoring her."

Sluggishly shifting in the acceleration chair, Trep grinned impishly. "Hey, don't take it out on me, Rosco. You're the one who put the smug in the word smuggler." He rolled his eyes with mock indigence. "Courting two gorgeous ladies at the same time. You know the old saying, buddy. If it's got a good set of hips or servomotors, you're going to have trouble with it." Winterrs tossed a datapad to the vexed smuggler.

"What's this?"

"That clue you've been looking for. Saahir gave it to me before she blasted off. Coordinates, contacts, passcodes, the whole works."

Ross briefly scanned the information as it scrolled across the screen. "The Aurea system. That's not too far away."

"Only a half hour in hyperspace." Trep stood up and stretched, his joints cracking and popping along the length of his lean body. "We set down at Merich's Bend, on the far side of Aurea's third moon. That's where we take on the cargo."

"Well," Ross said with a grin. He started flipping flight switches and toggles, powering up the *Kierra's* ion drives. "We can't keep the lady waiting. Kierra, contact Traffic Control and ask for take–off clearance."

Ross waited until the vent of pressurized hydraulic steam dissipated before he reached under the strut cuff to reattach the hose. Ducking under the faulty valve, he burned his fingertips attempting to reseal the conduit. He swore a vehement Corellian oath and quickly donned his gloves, managing to secure the damaged unit. The support strut dropped down from the hull and locked its dock boot against the mooring floor. Smuggler's sense tingling with suspicion, he cautiously popped the restraint on his holster, propping the heavy blaster at his side. Then with feigned interest in the strut, he watched from aside as the port steward and a crew of seven men approached him from the port terminal.

"Are you Ross?" the head crewman asked. A heavily built man, he was dressed in orange and gray cargo fatigues, fitted with a work belt of tools that barely managed to support his ample stomach and bulk.

"Maybe." Ross leaned against a structure integrity rod, cocking his hip slightly to display the lifted blaster. "Who wants to know?"

The older man grinned sardonically. "There's no need for that, Captain Ross. My name is Hante." Glancing over his shoulder, he nodded to one of the crewmen behind him. The rangy youth advanced on the freighter. "The tower instructed us to bring on the cargo as soon as you arrived."

The necessary passcodes were sufficient to ease Ross' suspicions, but before he could alert Winterrs, one of the crewmen was moving up the ramp and into the ship. "Bad idea," he heard Trep saying in the corridor. "I didn't hear you ask nicely." A moment later, the crewman reappeared on the ramp with Trep's blaster pointed directly at his nose. Ross hung his head and laughed quietly.

"Keep moving," Trep growled, pressing the muzzle against the frightened loader's nose. At the bottom of the ramp, he paused to initialize the hatch, closing and securing the entrance to the ship.

Ross activated his comlink with a smile. "194?"

"I read you, Ross."

"Kierra, is the inner bay corridor secure?"

"That's what you wanted."

"Open the cargo bay doors for the gentlemen."

Hante signaled to his crew and watched on as a repulsorlift cart was backed into the freighter's opening cargo doors. As his men assembled themselves along the edges of the carrier, he turned his attention back to Ross, holding his hand out to the smuggler. "I was told to give you these as soon as you arrived on the planet."

Ross took the small, silver strips from him, glancing over the decal and inscription. "Tickets?"

"Lady Saahir is giving a performance at Merich's Bend. Standing room only, I understand." Hante paused to acknowledge a wave from one of his men. "If you hurry, you might be able to catch the last few minutes of the show."

"I might just do that." Ross felt Trep's shadow fall in across his shoulders and started toward the hangar doors.

A late afternoon storm had left the city of Ifeoma shrouded in night mists and showers. Outside in the deserted streets, the music from Merich's Bend Tavern caused a slight vibration in the multitude of puddles left behind in the wake of the storm. Ross grinned, anxious to be reunited with Saahir.

"At least one of us has something to smile about," Trep complained. Hands thrust deeply in his jacket pockets, he glanced about the streets as if expecting trouble.

"What's eating you?"

"Something stinks about this deal, Ross. Did you see the way those guys lined up at the cargo ramp? Military style cargo outfits use that formation, highly trained military cargo units. I don't like it."

"So they're using a military technique. A lot of spaceports have gone in for that sort of efficiency thing."

"You don't understand. I can smell a Rebel from half a kilometer away, and I tell you, Ross, this place stinks. I think Saahir's up to one of her tricks."

Ross shrugged off his partner's concerns, ignoring his own nagging suspicion. He stepped through the double doors of the tavern and was engulfed in a resonating pulse of music and background noise. From the density of bodies and smoke in the front room, he realized that Hante was not exaggerating about the crowd and found himself shouldering his way through the packed audience.

Shifting around a flock of enthralled Ithorians, Ross threw a quick glance toward the center stage. He smiled as Saahir's costume glittered in the bombardment of the spotlights. As her voice died away in time to the music, she turned to a sharply dressed human man with close–cropped hair standing at the side of the stage and blew him a kiss. Ross paused, fighting a sudden rush of jealousy. Ignoring Trep's playful tug at his sleeve, he stood still, watching as the man walked onto the stage and handed Saahir a large bouquet of some sort of exotic flowers. While the act did not at first seem out of order, Saahir's reaction sent chills down Ross' spine.

As Ross watched in horror, the beaming Twi'lek wrapped her slender arms around the stranger and kissed him. It was not a playful, teasing kiss that she had used to woo him during one such performance, long ago. It was not the kiss of friendship, new or cherished. It was a passionate display, the way she used to kiss him, the way she used to hold him during their three–year affair. It was the way she had held and kissed him last night, suggesting intimacy with this stranger.

A peculiar lump rose in his throat. His hand flew to his blaster as he moved through the crowd.

"No, you don't," Trep grunted, grabbing Ross by the sleeve and hauling him back. "Beat it," he gestured at three Jawas who were sitting in a center aisle booth. The diminutive creatures scurried into the crowd. "You look like you could use a drink." Trep sat Ross down in a chair and waved for the waitress.

"I'm not thirsty." Ross allowed the raw emotion to wash over him, instilling life to his rage. He glared at Saahir, willing the Twi'lek to look toward him. In a moment, she did, but the glance was fleeting. Recognizing him in the front room, she turned back to the human at her side and tapped him on the shoulder, pointing in the direction where Ross and Trep were sitting. He nodded to a nearby companion and then followed her off the stage.

"You made it!" Saahir gushed. With her arms intertwined around the human's waist, she hesitated at the edge of the table, flinching slightly under Ross' fierce glare. Throwing her head back in defi-

ance, the Twi'lek flared her nostrils, as if daring the smuggler to question her relationship with the human at her side. "Juri, this is Captain Thaddeus Ross and his partner, Trep Winterrs." Glaring at Ross, she leaned close to the pair and whispered, barely audible over the noises of the crowd, "Boys, this is Juri Marbra, my fiancee."

Trep groaned, cautiously putting his hand over Ross' blaster to prevent the unthinkable.

Saahir sat down as Marbra pulled the chair out for her. "Stop looking at me like that!" she hissed, keeping her voice in low tones so as not to attract undue attention.

"How should I look at you?" Ross growled. "After three years together, I never," he slammed his fist against the table top, "*never* had you figured for a Rebel sympathizer!"

"Don't even try and deny it, pretty boy," Trep said evenly. "You've got it written all over your face."

"You didn't tell him?" Marbra whispered in Saahir's ear.

"I decided not to," Saahir replied, not being so discreet. "As you can see, it would have complicated things."

"I can't believe you'd involve me in this, knowing how I feel about lost causes."

"And what do you consider a lost cause, Captain Ross?" Marbra asked, his voice sharp with the experience of giving commands.

Ross glared at Saahir, responding to the question without any need for words. He was rewarded by a glimmer of tears that swelled in her eyes.

"Sooner or later, we all get involved," Marbra commented. "There's no such thing as a disinterested bystander these days."

"Aren't there?"

"Most of them are dead." Marbra looked uncomfortable as he glanced from Ross to Saahir, then back to Ross. Then the practiced, neutral expression of a military man returned to his face. "Shall we check on our cargo?"

As the first tears rolled down her cheeks, Saahir rose. "I have to change," she whispered, deftly wiping at her eyes. Kissing Marbra once on the forehead, she turned back to stare at Ross and then quickly withdrew to the safety of the shadows.

Leaving Trep to guard his back, Ross stormed out of the bar, leading them with long, angry strides. The lump in his throat was expanding, giving way to emotions that he would rather have avoided. Ross locked his hand against the cool heel of his blaster, ready for a confrontation as he passed through the spaceport doors and into the main bay area. Angry at Saahir's betrayal and at being an unwitting pawn for the Rebel Alliance, he was prepared to take on anyone who challenged him.

Feigning disinterest, a trio of armed security guards kept vigil a few docks away from the *Kierra*. As separate groups—the cargo crew, the guards, the custom wardens—the Rebels might fool even the most suspicious Imperial official; but seen as a whole, they could not fool him. Ross realized that they all sported the same slick, military cut and precision-team manners, insuring his smuggler's sense that they were all part of the elaborate scheme. The fact that they knew more than he did only served to further infuriate him.

In an attempt to rattle their cool disposition, he walked directly to the back of his freighter and moved into the cargo bay, where several stacks of crates had been loaded. Staring into the scandoc on a few of the boxes, he did not recognize the coding and blinked in horror as the scandoc suddenly shifted, mutating and degrading before his eyes. "Can you make this out?"

"Don't need to read the doc to know what's in the box, Rosco," Trep snorted. Kneeling beside the crate, he pointed to the affixed Imperial seal. "This is the mark of an Imperial Munitions sector chief."

"Guns? Ammo?"

"Guns, ammo, and then some according to the docket." Trep grinned, leaning against the box. "All the stuff that makes war fun."

"Wish I could share your view," Marbra said evenly, eyeing Trep. Then targeting Ross under his critical gaze, he nodded to his men, dismissing them from the area. "You know," his voice echoed in the spacious compartment, "you were quite hard on Saahir. It wasn't necessary."

Ross straightened abruptly, balling his hands into fists. Trep stood between him and the Rebel, prepared to keep some semblance of peace. "And just where do you think she spent last night? While you were collecting your cargo—"

"She was with you." Marbra smiled with unexpected pleasure, amused by the Corellian's surprise. "Saahir is a woman, a beautiful woman of worldly means, Captain Ross. But you see, I love her, and because I love her, I don't expect her to change overnight. It took her years to learn how to survive this deviant lifestyle, and it will take years for her to outgrow and forget it. And I'm prepared to wait and aid her in any way possible. Besides, you needed her and she needed you for our cargo. She only did what she had to in order to assure your cooperation. But if you still want cash payment," Marbra pulled a credit voucher from his breast pocket, "I can accommodate you."

"You're a dead man!" Ross screamed, fighting to break away from Trep's grasp.

"Ross!" Trep bellowed. "I don't know what you were expecting, buddy. Same old Saahir, turning tricks for the upper–class masses. Get a grip." Managing to keep the Corellian in check, Trep inspected the voucher. "It's 10,000 creds." He showed it to Ross, hoping the sight of riches would entice the smuggler to behave.

Ross ignored the money, wrestling with a frantic urge to draw his blaster and fire on the Rebel leader. "What's the deal?"

"Our backs are to the wall, Captain Ross," Marbra began. "The people we've secured these weapons for are in trouble. We'll need a seasoned pilot and skilled guns to reach them. Saahir assures me we can rely on your skills alone." He grinned at Trep. "But a renegade from the Imperial Army will be more than welcomed, even helpful."

Trep straightened his flight jacket, cocking an eyebrow at Marbra. "With the extra money, that's 2,500 a piece for the muscle."

"What if I said it wasn't enough?"

"What?" Trep gasped. "Ross, you get three times—"

Marbra pulled one more chit from his pocket. "Would an additional 5,000 credits secure your services?"

Ross nodded to Trep to receive the chit. Then turning his back on Marbra, he stepped through the corridor bulkhead. "Come on, let's get this over with."

Staring at the accumulation of dirt and dead skin beneath his fingernails, Ross used the edge of his knife to clean out the debris. He leaned against the cushioned back of the control chair, blowing away bits of grime as they surfaced. Folding the knife back into position, he tucked it inside his pocket and sighed, rubbing the tension from his forehead. Above him, somewhere along the perimeter of the hidden Rebel base, an explosion sounded. A shadow moved into the doorway, and the smuggler sat up, staring in that direction. "What took you so long?"

"I had to slip by the sentries." Trep's face was dark with disappointment. "All they had was this t'ssolok." He pulled the carved bottle from his coat, shaking the viscous blue liquid inside the container until it thinned against the sides of the glass. "The cook says the good stuff is locked away in the officers' quarters. Wouldn't that figure?" He sat down across from Ross, straddling another control chair. "A poor man can't get a decent swig of the good stuff nowadays. Doesn't matter whose army it is." He sniffed disdainfully at the bitter smelling t'ssolok. "Are we really going to drink this?"

Ross snatched the bottle from him. "Have you got something better to do?"

"Yeah, but it's at least 50 light years from this place." A distant explosion sent a shock wave through the deserted station room. "And a whole lot quieter." He watched as Ross took a swallow from the bottle, then boldly took one himself. "Hey, this isn't bad." His eyes abruptly began to water and twitch in response to the caustic flavor that burned his lips and tongue. Trep gasped as the liquor inflamed his throat, sending spicy fumes through his nostrils.

"It's not the flavor you have to worry about," Ross said with a grin, taking the bottle from Trep's trembling hands. "It's the aftertaste that kicks."

Another explosion rocked the control room, shifting the ceiling supports. The lights flickered. "Whew," Trep said hoarsely, massaging his throat. "That was a close one."

"Doesn't sound like Saahir's Rebel friends are doing too well." Ross threw his head back for another swallow, closing his eyes as the rich flavor assailed his senses.

"They're not." Saahir stood in the doorway, the graceful curves of her slender body were a dark silhouette against the brighter lights in the corridor.

"Maybe they need a little morale booster," Ross said. "Why don't you get on the comm and hum a few patriotic bars for them. That'll get their blood going." He laughed softly and glanced at Trep to share his cold humor, but the smuggler was having nothing to do with it.

"What about our little shipment of munitions?" Trep asked soberly. "Surely that evened the odds a little."

"What use are 500 rifles with only 100 men to utilize them?"

"It's been done. Where's Marbra?"

"Out there. With his men," she whispered, tears in her voice. "I'm on my way to join him now. I stopped by hoping you might come with me."

"You can count me out," Ross sneered. "I'm not going anywhere for anyone." He propped his legs up on the console, bracing his head and neck against his hands. "I've done more than my share already."

"That's what I figured you would say." Saahir moved farther into the room, crossing her hands behind her back as she stood over Ross, gazing down at him. "There's an old Twi'lek saying: *It's easier to forgive an enemy than it is to forgive a friend who betrays you.* I hurt you, Ross. I know that and I think that I shall regret it for the rest of my life." She turned away from him, a sheen of tears on her cheeks. At the doorway, the Twi'lek paused, looking back at him. "I only hope that one day, you'll look back at all the good things that happened between us and you'll find it in your heart to forgive me."

Trep took a deep breath, staring at her as she lingered in the doorway. "Ross?"

"Shut up, Winterrs. I'm not buying it." Ross took another swallow of the t'ssolok, angry over the weakness Saahir always managed to trigger in him. He felt the sharp sting of the liquor washing away any remorse he might feel for denying her.

"Clear skies, Ross," Saahir said softly and stepped into the corridor.

Trep watched the Twi'lek slip beyond his view. "Ross?"

"I said, shut up, Trep!"

A violent explosion and secondary concussions struck abruptly with enough force to knock both men out of their seats. Rolling under the console, they watched in horror as the ceiling barricades folded under the blast, allowing the interior walls to crack and fall in from the aftershocks. Dust particles and evaporated debris engulfed by the heat of the explosion, belched through the doorway and into the control room. Unlike previous explosions, this one was accompanied by blaster fire in the corridor, reverberating in the hallway.

That familiar, strangling lump again came to Ross' throat. "Saahir!" he bellowed. Digging himself clear of the debris, he staggered over the wreckage of the room, hearing Trep scrambling behind him. At the doorway, voices created a shallow well of echoes and interference, interspersed with the static of comlink discharges that were shouting orders. A trio of Rebel troopers ran past the doorway, firing haphazardly down the obscured corridor, into billowing clouds of white dust. One of them was hit by return fire and crumpled to the ruined garrison floor. The distinctive shapes of stormtrooper armor began to become visible in the haze.

Ross drew his blaster and jumped into the hallway, firing randomly at the stormtroopers converging on their position. "Saahir!" he screamed, standing over her mangled body. "Trep!"

"I'm with you, partner!" Wrapping the sling of the Imperial blast rifle around his forearm, Trep fired into the gallery of stormtroopers. His first several shots made a permanent impression on the Imperial soldiers' advancement team. Eyeing Saahir on the floor beside Ross, he nodded to the weary freedom fighters, who had paused to regroup behind them. "Get her out of here, Ross. We're right behind you!"

Taking Saahir's light weight into his arms, Ross choked at the severity of the injuries caused by shrapnel from the blast. He cradled her against him and sprinted into the corridor beyond the control room, hearing Trep shout orders to the two surviving Rebels.

"You and you, want to live? Come with me and do exactly as I do!"

Blaster fire rang out behind him, marked by wild catcalls from his partner, Ross continued his desperate run to the end of the corridor. The explosion had ripped the pressurized doors from the inner channel, leaving a darkened portal into the cold night air. As he wrestled his way through the mangled metal doors, he heard the click of blasters at his back and turned, blinded by a battery of brilliant lights.

"Hold your fire! It's Lady Saahir and her smuggler friend!"

Shielding his eyes from the glare, Ross yielded to the tug at his sleeve as a gray-haired squadron leader led him hurriedly away from the door. "My partner's on his way with two of your men," Ross said.

The two Rebels appeared at the doorway, slipping through the wreckage. One of them was on his stomach, laying suppressive fire down the corridor as Trep followed on their heels. "That's it, boys. From left to right, then change the pattern. They won't know what hit them!"

The sergeant activated a dim light source inside the abandoned med-shelter and swiftly cleared a table for Ross to comfortably position the injured Twi'lek. "Our reinforcements are folding, son. There isn't much time. You can stay here with her; but we're going to need every pair of hands we can find in order to hold them off

until the evacuation teams arrive."

"If I don't stay, she'll die!" Ross screamed. Staring into Saahir's bloody face, he tightened his grip on her hands, as if holding her fragile life in his fingertips. "Where's the medic?"

"Dead."

"Dead? Is there anybody—"

"The only chance of medical help died when he died." The sergeant's features softened. "I can't promise you anything, son. But there might be a medical frigate in orbit on the far side of the planet." He pointed to the night skies overhead. A squadron of X-wings streaked by, firing on targets at the opposite end of the shattered base. "That's where those fighters just came from. The Imperials have a stranglehold on us and we're evacuating the entire base, but reinforcements can't get through to us for another hour, maybe two. If you have a ship—"

"Trep!" Ross yelled.

"I'm on it!" He vanished into the darkness outside the shelter.

"Where's he—"

"He's going for my ship," Ross said. "It's hidden in a cavern not far from here."

The sergeant nodded, waving the soldiers out of the tent. "We'll hold them off as long as we can, son. You stay with her now. I'll see if one of my men can locate that frigate." The Rebel left him, alone in the dark with Saahir.

"Ross?"

It was barely a whisper, but he heard it. Holding the Twi'lek's trembling fingers, tightly, Ross leaned over her. "I'm here. I'm here," was all he could bring himself to say.

"It's so cold."

Ross took off his jacket and quickly covered her. He scanned the shelter for a blanket, and snatched one from a nearby table. The bloody fabric swirled through the air, and the stiffened corpse of Commander Marbra was uncovered. Aghast, the smuggler threw the blanket back over the body, shielding it from the Saahir's view, and then hurried back to her side. "Better?" he asked, tucking the collar under her chin. He used a damp towel to wipe the debris and scorched skin from around her eyes.

"I can't see anything."

"Flashburns, that's all. You'll be fine in a day or so." He bit his lip to suppress the rush of emotion.

"It scares me." She flinched abruptly as the blaster fire beyond

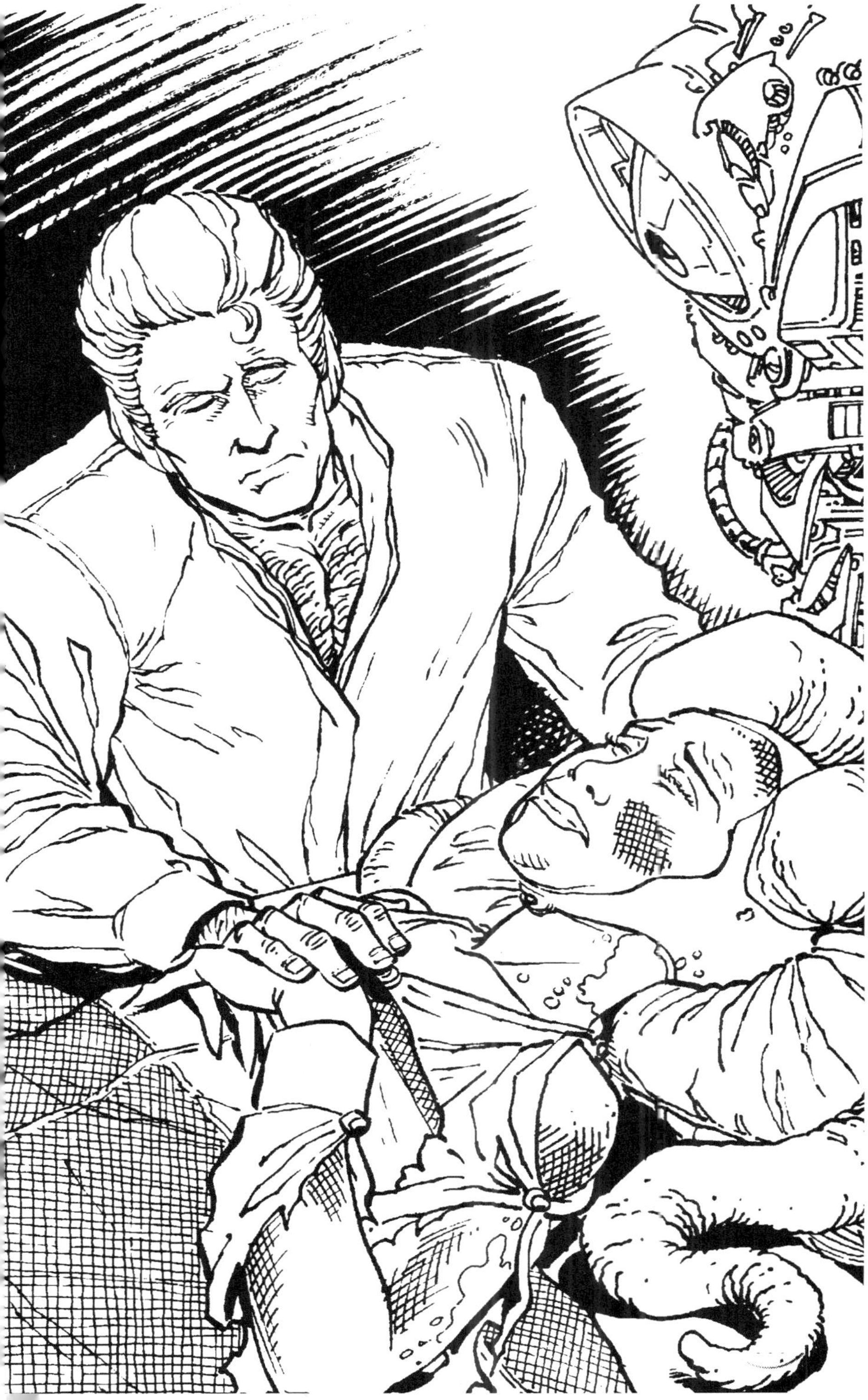

them intensified, marked by the dying screams of someone caught in the exchange. "It's so dark."

"It's okay," Ross whispered. "I'm still here." He gently held her, keeping his face close beside her so that she could feel him.

"Ross, how do you do it?"

Ross frowned, puzzled by her inquiry. "Do what?"

"You're never afraid, never scared." Saahir trembled suddenly, reaching out for him. "How do you do it?"

Exasperated for lack of an answer, he smiled down at her, caressing her cheeks and forehead. "I just don't think about it. Which is exactly what you should be doing. Not thinking about. Trep's going to be here any minute, and we're going to get you to that medical frigate."

Saahir tightened her grip on his hands, sensing the warmth of him slipping away from her fingertips. "I'm so scared, so scared." She swallowed convulsively. "I deserve this. After what I've done to you, I deserve this."

"No, no one deserves—"

"But I hurt you," she sobbed, rubbing his hand against her cheek. "I hurt you; and that's the last thing I'd ever want to do, Ross. You've got to believe me."

"I believe you." He squeezed both her hands, feeling the Twi'lek groping for the sensation of touch.

"I've always loved you, Ross. Always. You weren't like any of the others. I really loved you; but I could never bring myself to believe that you could love me the same way — until I saw how it hurt you when I introduced Juri as my fiancee." Lips trembling, Saahir turned her face toward him, tears falling to the sides of her swollen face. "I was so sorry, so sorry." Her eyes went suddenly blank, expressionless, and still. A disturbing quietude settled over her body.

"Saahir!" Ross cried with mounting panic. "Saahir, please!"

The Twi'lek gasped softly and suddenly, her chest rising and falling in shallow rhythm. "Do you remember Isamu, that little moon in the Birjis system?" Her voice was barely audible. "You didn't believe me when I told you the trees made love there every night. But then you saw it for yourself, didn't you? You saw it."

Ross bowed his head against the cradle of her neck, fighting back the sting of tears. Nodding softly against her, he whispered, "I saw it."

"I didn't tell you it was simply a trick of shadows. On Isamu, the trees grow in pairs and at night time, they look like lovers kissing under the moonlight." Moving with the slow, easy grace she was known for, Saahir pulled her hand from Ross and twisted the ring from her finger. She slid the cold band onto his little finger and smiled.

"What are you—" Ross ignored the warm swell of tears at his eyes. "Saahir, no."

"I want you to go back there, Ross, back to Isamu in that grove we discovered. I want you to go back there, and I want you to forgive me for all the hurtful things I've done." Her eyes were glassy jewels in the dimness and as each moment passed, the brilliance faded from them.

"But I do forgive you!"

"I want you to go there with someone special to you."

"There is no one else, Saahir. No one!"

Saahir convulsed suddenly in a fit of wracking pain. She began to sing. "Used to be that darkness frightened me so. Used to be I spent my life chasing the sun. I know too well the fear of the night. With you, there was only laughter, laughter after dark." She laughed softly.

Ross grinned, believing that she was rallying against her injuries. "What are you laughing at?"

"There's no truth to that song, Ross. There is no laughter after dark... only silence."

In the stagnant, stale atmosphere of Reuther's Wetdock, Ross leaned against the sloped back of his chair, shielding his emotions in the comfort of the shadows. Shoving away the empty t'ssolok bottle, he stared into the peculiar crystal, feeling as clear and hollow as the sculpted glass. To still the trembling in his lips and chin, the smugger wiped anxiously at the corners of his mouth, sighing as the reality of seven haunted years sank deeply into his disquieted spirit. "She died," he croaked. "Right there in my arms. And there wasn't a thing I could do."

Reuther swallowed the last of his t'ssolok, wishing the biting aftertaste of the fermented liquor could dislodge the lump growing in the back of his throat. "That's a hard vector to reckon with, Ross. Never knew you were carrying that kind of cargo with you. A burden like that would kill a normal man." He nodded, swallowing a moment of his own pain. "I know how you feel. When the Empire started colonizing this sector, my people took it upon themselves to fight back. To show the invading *igaluus* that we were not a race to be trifled with." He pursed his lips thoughtfully, crossing his legs under the table. "I lost my wife, my three daughters, and my spirit to the retribution that followed our insolence." Reuther stared into the Corellian's eyes, strumming his fingers lightly against the table. "You need to go back to that moon, Ross."

Ross flinched slightly. "How do you know I haven't been there all ready?"

"Because you haven't forgiven her. Or yourself. If you had, you wouldn't be here. You'd be up there under the moonlight. Until you go, you'll never fully recover."

Staring at his hands, Ross took a deep breath. "Did you ever recover?" he asked, thinking about Reuther's family.

"Why do you think I own a bar? As long as I have customers," he nodded to a trio of Rodians who walked through the doors, "I don't have to worry about my problems." The Najib saluted the smuggler before he excused himself from the table.

Ross rubbed thoughtfully at the growth of beard at his chin, listening to the harsh rasp beneath his fingertips. He stood up and tossed a few credits onto the table and started walking toward the door. At the entrance, he paused briefly to glance at Reuther, smiling despite himself as the bartender winked at him from across the way. Pulling his collar snugly against his neck, he stepped out into the deserted streets and pressed the comlink against his cheek. "194."

"Reading you, Ross. What's up?"

"Set a course for the Birjis system. For Isamu." He moved through the spaceport to the exterior lot behind the main bay, walking with a smooth fluidity induced by the effect of the t'ssolok.

"What are we going to do when we get there?" Kierra asked.

Ross paused to glance over his shoulder into the sky. The rains had stopped, leaving a light glaze of freshness and newness over the spaceport grounds and buildings. Beyond the dense mantle of storm clouds, he could see the dawn breaking, fighting its way through the upper levels of darkness to dispel the night's shadows.

"Ross," Kierra whined, "what are we going to do on Isamu?"

Ross walked up the ramp, cueing the keypad and hatch to close. "We're going to lay a few souls to rest."

A chilling autumn wind blew in from the high country, disturbing a thin layer of cooling mist from the surface of the mountain lake. Ross felt the gentle fingers of the breeze moving through his blond spikes and smiled as his body shivered in the grip of cold. After a seven–year hibernation from living, full living, it was comforting to experience the sensations of the world again.

Surrounded by the intertwined shadows of Mu trees, he grinned as the shadows about him and a mixture of the blue light being cast by Isamu's primary made it appear as if a dozen or more lovers had gathered with him on the shores of the lake to celebrate that most cherished of all emotions. Folding his arm behind his head, Ross stared into the black expanse of the atmosphere, indulging himself by counting all the stars in one sector of the night sky.

"Ross, why didn't you ever tell me about this place?"

Sensing an annoyed tenor in the droid intelligence's voice, Ross begrudgingly sat up on his elbows. "Don't worry, Kierra, we're not staying long."

"Oh no, no, no. I don't mind it. It's sort of romantic Makes me feel like, like..."

Ross glanced over his shoulder to where the YT–1300 stood on an extended outcrop of rock. "Like what, Kierra?"

"Like," an embarrassed giggle translated over the comlink, "like singing."

Ross smiled, sinking back into the late season growth of grass. "Knock yourself out, darling." After a few moments, a soft humming could be heard. He recognized the first few bars of Saahir's song, "Laughter After Dark." He pulled a leather cord from around his neck and broke the knot as he took the metallic ring from the end. It was warm from being so close to his skin.

Cupping the band in his hand, he again folded his hands behind his head and sighed as a quiet peace stole over him. Nearby, the light cast by the rising planet spotlighted a lone Mu tree. Disease or natural disaster had withered away its twin and it stood alone on the edge of the lake shore, surrounded by joined couples. No worse for its loss, the tree was the only one in the immediate area to boast several branches full of late autumn blossoms.

Ross closed his eyes, listening to the melody of Kierra's voice and that of the wind. He envisioned the Mu tree behind his lids, still growing, without a partner, still surviving, and fell soundly into a well–deserved, peaceful sleep.

Roleplaying Game Statistics

Thaddeus Ross

Type: Ex–bounty hunter and smuggler
DEXTERITY 3D
Blaster 7D, dodge 5D+2, grenade 4D, melee combat 4D+2, melee parry 3D+2, running 4D
KNOWLEDGE 3D
Alien species 6D, languages 5D, planetary systems 6D+2, streetwise 4D+2, survival 4D, value 4D
MECHANICAL 3D+1
Astrogation 6D, beast riding 4D, space transports 6D, space transports: YT–1300 transports 8D+2, starship gunnery 6D, starship shields 5D
PERCEPTION 3D
Command 5D+2, investigation 5D+2, search 3D+2, sensors 6D, sneak 3D+1
STRENGTH 3D
Brawling 6D, climbing/jumping 3D+1, lifting 3D+1
TECHNICAL 2D+2
Blaster repair 4D, starship repair 6D+2
Special Abilities:
Investigation: Gains +2 when his investigations involve any Imperial business.
Force Points: 2
Character Points: 10
Move: 10
Equipment: Caelli–Merced heavy blaster (5D), comlink

Capsule: Thaddeus Ross is a handsome, easygoing spirit who comes from a long line of smugglers. A non–traditionalist, he broke free of the family legacy and became a bounty hunter. However, the novelty quickly wore off and he returned to the family tradition of smuggling.

Ross is cynical and self–righteous and easily provoked by senseless violence. His past relationship with family and people close to him is as mysterious as the smuggler himself, who is an intensely private individual, except among his closest friends

Patricia A. Jackson

TREP WINTERRS

Type: Outlaw and smuggler
DEXTERITY 3D
Blaster 5D+1, brawl parry 5D, dodge 5D, melee combat 4D, running 4D+1
KNOWLEDGE 3D
Alien species 5D, intimidation 5D+1, languages 4D, planetary systems 5D, streetwise 5D, willpower 5D+2

MECHANICAL 3D
Astrogation 6D+2, beast riding 5D, sensors 4D+2, space transports 6D+2, starship gunnery 5D+1, starship shields 5D, swoop operation 6D
PERCEPTION 3D
Bargain 4D, command 4D+1, con 3D, gambling 3D+1, persuasion 4D
STRENGTH 3D
Brawling 5D+2, climbing/jumping 4D, stamina 5D+1, swimming 3D+1
TECHNICAL 3D
Blaster repair 4D+1, droid repair 3D+1, respulsorlift repair 3D+1, security 4D, starfighter repair 3D+1

This character is Force-sensitive.
Force Points: 1
Dark Side Points: 2
Character Points: 15
Move: 10
Equipment: Heavy blaster pistol (5D), comlink

Capsule: Trep Winterrs is a laid back, amiable sort, who has a tendency to blend in with a crowd. Despite his good looks and sense of humor, he has a fatal mind set that keeps him moving from one dangerous thrill to the next. To those closest to him, the smuggler's reckless antics are a serious cause for concern, particularly when their lives are on the line. However, the soft-spoken, yet intimidating outlaw has never been known to leave a friend in a bad spot.

Winterrs' ability to out-maneuver and out-think Imperial strategies is a talent that brings the smuggler under fire with potential employers, who suspect that he is an Imperial infiltration agent working the space lanes in search of smugglers or Rebel spies. Because his appearance on the criminal underground was so sudden, many have tried to trace the smuggler's origins and have come up short of information into his past. Many prominent crime syndicates have inquired about his history, but Winterrs remains tight–lipped about his personal life and is rarely seen without the company of his closest associate, Thadd Ross.

Kierra (the personality)

Type: Droid intelligence/sidekick
DEXTERITY 0D
KNOWLEDGE 3D
Alien species 6D, cultures 6D+1, languages 7D, planetary systems 7D+2, technology 7D
MECHANICAL 3D
Astrogation 7D+2, communications 8D+2, sensors 8D, starship gunnery 6D, starship shields 7D+1
PERCEPTION 3D
Bargain 5D, con 4D+1, gambling 4D, investigation 4D, investigation: bounty hunting law enforcement 7D+1
STRENGTH 0D
TECHNICAL 3D
Computer program/repair 7D, droid programming 7D, droid repair 6D+2, security 8D, starship repair 7D, starship wpn repair 6D+1
Special Abilities:
(see ship stats)
Character Points: 7
Move: (see ship stats)

Capsule: How and why Kierra got into the onboard systems of the light freighter are not known. However, it is certain that she either was trapped inside the ship or hidden there, sometime after the construction of the freighter. While inspecting the ship, Ross accidently awakened her and thus began a long partnership with the eccentric droid. While Kierra can manipulate certain ship functions like sensors and communications, she had to learn astrogation, shields and gunnery from her human mentor. She is continually learning new functions by way of self–programming and additional input from Ross.

Her uncanny ability to imitate human behavior is disarming to strangers and has been heavily influenced by Thaddeus Ross and prolonged contact with other intelligent (often eccentric) species.

The Kierra

Craft: Modified Corellian Engineering YT–1300 Transport
Type: Modified light freighter
Scale: Starfighter
Length: 26.7 meters
Skill: Space transports: YT–1300 transport
Crew: 2, gunners: 1; skeleton 1/+15
Passengers: 10
Cargo Capacity: 135 metric tons; 55 cubic meters
Consumables: 3 months
Cost: Not for sale
Hyperdrive Multiplier: x1
Hyperdrive Backup: x10
Nav Computer: Yes
Maneuverability: 2D+2
Space: 4
Atmosphere: 260; 750 kmp
Hull: 4D
Shields: 2D+2

Sensors:
Passive: 15/0D
Scan: 30/1D
Search: 50/3D
Focus: 2/4D
Weapons:
One Double Laser Cannon
Fire Arc: Front
Skill: Starship Gunnery
Fire Control: 2D+2
Space Range: 1-3/12/25
Atmosphere Range: 100-300m/1.2km/2.5km
Damage: 4D+2
One Laser Cannon
Fire Arc: Turret
Crew: 1 (or auto)
Skill: Starship gunnery
Fire Control: 2D+2
Space Range: 1-3/12/25
Atmosphere Range: 100-300m/1.2km/2.5km
Damage: 4D+2

Scoundrels

"My name's Kels Turkhorn, and I'm a professional thief. I hear you've been looking for someone to hook up with?

"Hey, I'm not ashamed of what I do for a living. At least I'm honest about being a thief, unlike the Imps who couch their extortion rackets in terms of tariffs and fees. Oh, and then there's the Rebels who steal everything from credits to starships in the name of freedom. And neither side cares whether their marks can afford to replace the stuff they're stealing. I only steal from those who have too many credits to begin with.

"A few months ago, I met a thief named Cavv. He summed up our profession nicely: 'Kels, if you steal a girl's man, you'll get your eyes clawed out. If you lift a man's credit voucher, you'll get tossed in the local detention block. If you steal something really big, however, you ll be a folk hero and you'll get a medal pinned on you. It's a strange line of work, we're in.'

"Every pro is looking for that 'big score.' We're not shifty and lazy and stupid like many would have you believe... at least not those of us who are *good* thieves.

"The outfit I'm currently with is looking for its first big score. Perhaps you'd like to join us? Here, let's go over here, and I'll introduce you to the boss. You heard of Tasariq? No? Well, there's a fortune to be made there. We've got a fail–proof plan. All we need is a little start–up capital...."

The Great Herdship Heist

By Daniel Wallace

Illustrations by Will Warren

Fifteen seconds. That was all the time Lyle Lippstroot had remaining in his misbegotten life.

He'd woken up twenty–one minutes ago in his rented living quarters, splashed a double handful of tepid water on his face, and draped himself in a loose–fitting Froffli smock. Vop, that greasy Rodian tyrant, had transmitted a new series of figures during the night. In his fifteen years as Vop's bookkeeper, Lippstroot had covered the loanshark's tracks, buried any number of illegal deals, and kept suspicious Imperial investigators vainly chasing their tails. In that time, he had grown to detest the way Vop the Usurer constantly reeked of cheap *raava*. And the depraved spinehead had never, not *once*, said thank you.

Lippstroot had picked up the waiting datapad, scanned the new numbers, and established a neural link within moments. His

SoroSuub 221 cyber–interface, wrapping around the back of his skull like a broken halo, was still formidable, even after two decades of continuous use. A toothless Snivvian had once told Lippstroot that long-term cyborg implants made their bearers into unfeeling automatons, but he had bitterly scoffed. The SoroSuub band had not dulled the pain of a lost love, or buried the shame of his vile and petty career, or broken his addiction to *lesai*. The two-kilogram headpiece did allow him to maintain a direct link with Vop's mainframe and process numbers at blinding speed, and, at the moment, it was telling him he was in trouble.

His band now contained a Bartokk program–trap. Someone had sliced into the original transaction array and imbedded a new bit of coding. When Lippstroot had linked to the datapad, the virus downloaded into his headband and executed itself.

Within a millisecond, he identified the malignancy. Within two, he realized there was little hope. The Bartokk program–trap had last been used in a coup assassination on Turkana, and, as always, had proven fatal. The virus would create an overload spiral in his interface band and wipe his neural pathways clean in fifteen seconds. The only possible solution was to remove the system from his cranium, manually.

Fourteen seconds.

He reached up and flipped the outer locks. His left index finger drew back the durasteel release tab, drawing out a small square of sixteen grounding dots.

Eleven seconds.

He tapped a simple four-digit code into the dots and was met with a low, guttural buzz. *Blast it! How could I have miskeyed that sequence?!*

Nine seconds.

He re–entered the code, heard a welcome high–pitched tone, and waited until the three faint clicks indicated a dermal release.

Five seconds.

He punched the "retract" control, hearing a wet slurp as the deepest neural jacks withdrew from his cerebellum and retreated into their metallic housing.

One second.

With a hiss of equalized pressure, he slid the SoroSuub 221 slightly forward, preparing to lift the device off his head and heave it onto the stained carpet—

Lyle Lippstroot pitched forward, crashing into the low end table and sending three sealed disks of lesai sailing through the fetid air. He uttered a brief squeal, and was silent.

Dead.

"Down! Down–down–down!"

Kels drew the macrobinoculars away from her sweat-streaked face and squinted across the desert hardpan at the squat Tynnan demolitions expert. He had straightened up from the blast mine and was sprinting back towards her position as fast as his stumpy legs would carry him. He had a wide-eyed, desperate look on his furry, buck-toothed face. *"Down!"*

The human girl ran back four paces to their recently dug slit trench and dove in headfirst. A moment later, the Tynnan leapt in beside her, mashing the fingers of the her exposed hand with his left knee and clapping two webbed paws over his ears.

A deafening explosion rocked the desert. A scorching shockwave rolled over their heads, followed by a pelting rain of dirt and fire-blackened sand. The Tynnan let out a long, slow whistle through his front buckteeth, brushing dust from his sleek brown pelt. "Close call, hey?" He squinted up at Kels.

Kels glared back. "Dawson, for pity's sake, I thought you were an expert. Why'd it blow up early?"

The Tynnan ignored the insult and flipped down the ocular enhancer that helped compensate for his species' inherently poor eyesight. "Let's go have a look, shall we?" He vaulted the trench wall and began loping out towards the fresh blast crater.

Kels sighed. It had been three months since she'd agreed to apprentice herself to this motley band of robbers—one human, one Sluissi, and this scatterbrained Tynnan. She was the youngest of the group by far, but was becoming increasingly certain that these self-styled "master thieves" were learning more from her than she was from them. Their last attempt at grand larceny had resulted in a messy shootout with a Sector Ranger patrol boat, stranding them in the Kamar badlands until they could make repairs to their ship, an old bulk freighter that looked like a pregnant bantha. To take advantage of the downtime, Dawson had insisted on dragging her out to a dry lake bed to test an eclectic sampler of safe-cracking explosives.

In the breast pocket of her coveralls, her comlink vibrated. She removed it, cupped it to her ear briefly, then shouted across the sand to her furry comrade. "Move your tail, Dawson! Noone wants us back at the ship."

Cecil Noone slid out on the repulsor sled from beneath his vessel, as Kels and Dawson trudged up to it. Sweat and engine grease streaked the dark skin of his face. He raised his grease-coated right hand and the laser welder he held in it, in a casual greeting.

"How's the *Borogove*, boss?" Dawson asked, nodding at hyperdrive components scattered on the desert floor around the carbon-scored freighter.

"Not as bad as she looks. Once I get her guts put back in, we'll be ready to leave this hotbox." Noone wiped his dripping brow with the back of his forearm, the only part that wasn't smeared with lube. "Just in time too. Get aboard. Sonax will fill you in."

Kels led the way, stomping up the extended ramp into the welcome shade of the *Borogove*'s belly. She slid the detonator satchel from her shoulder and tossed it onto her bunk with a clatter, drawing an annoyed hiss from the Sluissi hunched over the main data terminal.

"Careful!" the slender alien spat, rearing up on her thick muscular tail. Sluissi had two arms, but their bodies ended in a single tapering snakelike appendage. "Thossse are explosssivesss!"

"Not without arming pins, they're not," Kels countered. "Right, Dawson?"

The Tynnan wrinkled his whiskered nose. "She's right, Sonax. But just the same, Kels, don't toss 'em around. These are sensitive pieces of work, and if you rattle 'em too much they could misfire or not go off at all." He cleared his throat. "Like you saw just thirty minutes ago."

Kels rolled her eyes. "Anyway. Sonax, what's up?"

The gray serpent slithered forward and coiled into a sitting position. Most of the Sluissi Kels had encountered in her life were an easygoing, methodical lot, but Sonax was distant, high–strung, and easily irritated. Kels found it hard to like her. "Guttu the Hutt," Sonax explained in her sibilant Basic. "He transssmitted on our private cipher this morning. He claims to have a job for usss."

Kels' mouth drew into a tight line. One of the things she'd learned about these thieves, besides the fact that they weren't nearly as competent as they pretended, was that they were deeply in hock to Guttu. Though the Hutt was only a mid-level crime boss on Nar Shaddaa, when he struck up a tune, this group danced.

"A loanshark'sss bookkeeper hasss been killed," Sonax continued. "The asssasssins placed a program-trap in his cranial interface." Unconsciously, she lifted one hand to touch the metal band running beneath her saggital crest. The BioTech AI^6 allowed her to work as the group's computer expert and data slicer, but Kels suspected the assassination news apparently hit a little too close to home.

"The hit—did Guttu do it?" Kels asked.

"I doubt it. Not his ssstyle."

"What does it have to do with us? What is this job?"

"I don't know. Guttu sssaid he'll have the details for us when we arrive at Nar Shaddaa."

"So when are we leaving?" Dawson spoke up.

"Now."

Noone stood at the entrance to Guttu the Hutt's private penthouse villa, tugging at the hem of his ill–fitting jacket. The highest permacrete pinnacles of Nar Shaddaa's vertical city stretched into the rarefied air of the upper atmosphere. Noone blew out a frosty breath.

The *Borogove* had dropped into the system an hour ago, just in time to make Guttu's rendezvous. As the leader of his little larceny league, it was his duty to report to his Hutt creditor and accept whatever assignment the slug had cooked up for them this time. Hopefully, it would pay enough to get them out of the red with Guttu and leave a little extra for workday worries like food and fuel. Realistically, he knew they'd be lucky if all four of them evaded arrest and cheated death once again. One day, possibly quite soon, Lady Fate would deal the Demise card. And, with his recent string of luck, it'd probably come from the bottom of the deck.

He punched the entry bell again and drew the black shimmersilk cape over his shoulders. Beside him, Kels gave a brief sniff. Noone looked her way and raised one eyebrow challengingly.

"Do you always dig out your finest attire when going to visit a Hutt?" The snicker had spread into a wide grin.

"Guttu practically owns us," Noone replied. "I'll fill you in on the backstory some day, but let's just say a good impression can't hurt."

The grin faded, replaced by an expression of detached amusement. "Maybe so. But that style went out of fashion ten years ago, when I was a kid. Even in the Outer Rim."

Noone stifled an annoyed grunt. The girl was good, very good. She was an excellent pickpocket, a brilliant con artist, could fight well in a pinch, and had the potential to be a better card shark than he was. They certainly needed her skills. She just wasn't much of a team player. Not yet.

With a heavy groan, the golden-filigreed double doors swung ponderously inwards. Beyond, nearly filling the dim hallway with his formidable bulk, a six–legged Sludir stamped his left forefoot and beckoned with a humming force pike.

"My master will see you now."

"Noone! You inept, worthless sack of gravel–maggots!" Guttu's voice boomed through the narrow confines of his audience chamber.

Thank the Fates, he's in a good mood, thought Noone. He threw both hands out from his body in an exuberant gesture and approached the reclining Hutt. "Magnificent Guttu!" he responded in Huttese. "Benevolent benefactor and paternal pat—"

"That's far enough." Guttu halted him with a wave of his bloated hand. Large even for a Hutt, each year Guttu looked less like a sentient creature and more like a pasty lump of uncooked dough. He frequently boasted that he hadn't moved under his own power in 150 years.

At the moment, the Hutt was sucking on the roasted foreleg of some ill-fated herd animal. The meter–long slab shimmered wetly in the soft lighting as it emerged from his cavernous mouth. Noone glanced around the audience chamber. The rancid smell was still the same, as were the ostentatious tapestries and the absurdly thick–piled carpeting. The stilt–legged spotted bird, ruffling its wings and littering the rug with mangy feathers, was one bizarre addition. Cocking its tiny head, the creature scanned the floor for scraps or vermin.

Guttu leaned forward, peering intently at Noone's unannounced companion. "Who's the shadow?" he rumbled. His hover–chair whined as its repulsorlifts compensated for the shift in weight.

Noone nodded. "My apologies. Kels, the Great Guttu. Kels is the latest addition to my merry troupe. She's only apprenticing right now, but I think you'll agree that her talents make us more formidable than ever. She masterminded the firefacet crystal heist on Druckenwell, nabbed the four crowns of—"

"You're wondering why I summoned you." Guttu was clearly uninterested in Kels' resume, which Noone assumed was mostly fictitious. The thief put on his most attentive face.

"Two days ago a human was murdered. He was the bookkeeper of a Rodian loanshark named Vop the Usurer — a minor functionary for an inferior criminal. I care nothing for either of them." Guttu cleared his throat, a low, wet gurgle. "But the murder was orchestrated by my repellent rival, Ritinki the Bimm."

"The *Bimm*?" Kels said incredulously, seemingly oblivious to Noone's waggling *shut up* gesture. "You're saying one of those little pacifists is a crime boss?"

Guttu's laugh burst forth like a thunderclap. "Ah, humans!" he roared. "So pestilently common, yet so culturally ignorant. There are exceptions to every rule, my dear. Take myself, for instance," he continued, inunciating every word carefully as though he was speaking to an unruly child. "Hutts have an unjust reputation as cruel, selfish hedonists and shameless gluttons. Yet, you need only take one look at me to realize that is not true." As if on cue, he released a seismic belch.

"Er... yes, of course." Kels said hesitantly.

Guttu beamed at her, then turned his gaze back to Noone. "Ritinki and Vop plan to hold an amicable 'meeting of the minds' aboard the Ithorian herdship *Song of the Clouds* the night after next. I've learned that Vop plans to use the meeting as an opportunity to secretly purchase a sealed lockbox from the Ithorians. The money has already changed hands. The bookkeeper was to slip away after dinner and pick up the goods."

"But now he's dead," Noone commented.

"Precisely. Ritinki also got wind of the plan. He bumped off Vop's bookkeeper in a wretched, underhanded fashion and inserted his own duplicate in his place. And Vop, that wall–eyed fool, is none the wiser!" Guttu's flabby frame shook with laughter.

"So Ritinki's duplicate picks up the box and delivers it to his master, not Vop," Noone speculated. "What is he, a clone?"

"Bah. Not even Jabba could grow a clone. Most likely a surgical alteration, but Ritinki could have sprung for a holo–shroud. It doesn't matter, because it's not going to work." Guttu's eyes narrowed to golden slits. "You're going to steal the box before he gets there."

Noone swallowed. He expected things to end up here.

"Don't let me down, Cecil Noone. The vrblthers are hungry this season, and I know a band of thieves who'd make an exquisite four–course meal."

"You don't say," Noone muttered, feeling as though he was sinking several centimeters into the carpeting.

Guttu forced the rack of oily meat into his cavernous mouth, then slid it back out again. "Forgive me. I have forgotten the duties of a host. Please, have some roba." With stumpy fingers, he pulled loose a chunk of milk–white fat and held it out, as if he were giving his pet nashtah a special treat. Noone stepped forward and accepted the quivering lump.

Guttu tore another scrap from the slab and idly tossed it into the far corner, where it rolled beneath a gaudy wall–hanging depicting the Third Battle of Vontor. The spotted avian squawked hungrily. With a flurry of feathers it pounced on the tidbit.

Noone squeezed the piece of roba experimentally with his

fingertips. It glistened damply with grease and Hutt saliva. "So," he said, "what are the details of the meeting? And the herdship's arrival time? Also—" He silenced himself as he looked up. Guttu was glaring at him sternly. Drawing a deep breath, Noone popped the pungent chunk of gristle in his mouth and smiled through clenched teeth. Guttu smiled back.

"Quammo will give you a datapad on the way out. Now, if you'll excuse me, I must begin my evening repast. You will return in two days with the lockbox."

Noone turned to leave, but Kels had one more question. "The box—what's in it?"

"My dear," Guttu said and chuckled. "I have no idea. But if it inspires this degree of backstabbing in two of my competitors, I want it."

Kels placed one hand against the bulkhead for support as the overloaded shuttle rose shakily from the landing pad. Dishes rattled, and one of the waist-high catering carts bumped painfully against her knees. She smoothed down her clean white uniform and glanced across the passenger cabin at Noone, who was securely strapped to his padded seat and clad in a spotless linen uniform similar to hers. He flashed a quick smile of reassurance.

She shifted her gaze to the window beside Noone's head and watched the blinking towers of Nar Shaddaa slip from view as the shuttle pilot began a slow banking turn. The bruised surface of Nal Hutta, the moon's swollen primary, was just beginning to rise above the jagged ferrocrete horizon.

It was a day and a half since their meeting with Guttu. When Kels and Noone had returned to the *Borogove*, both Dawson and Sonax had howled with outrage at the enormity of the task and the short time in which to prepare for it in.

"Two days!" Dawson had fumed, his beady eyes scanning the scrolling readout on Guttu's datapad. "Two days to get aboard *this*," he thrust the pad in their direction, revealing a schematic of a colossal, saucer-shaped Ithorian herdship, "and steal their precious box? Did that diseased slug realize that they're sealing off all space traffic to keep the meeting private? Not one trader, buying agent, or botanist is going to be permitted to dock with the herdship until after the meeting. Not one."

"Vops and Ritinki both know rivals might try knocking them off during the meet," Noone had commented. "They probably don't trust each other, either, which means each of them is going to bring his own personal army of security thugs. Add to this the fact that each of them is planning to walk off the ship with this mysterious lockbox, and we can expect that herdship to indeed be sealed as tight as a drum. We're not dealing with fools here."

Sonax had waved slightly from side to side, one of her characteristic tics indicating nervous energy or bottled-up frustration. "So how do we get inssside?"

After six hours of dead–end suggestions ranging from the conventional (posing as a maintenance team) to the ridiculous (wrapping themselves in camo–netting and hoping the Ithorians would bring them aboard as strange new bioforms for the herdship's zoo), it was the dinner that finally inspired a workable plan.

Sonax had dug up a subspace call the *Song of the Clouds* had routed through system communications satellite 355–D. The party was being catered.

Not surprisingly, there wasn't much call for caterers on Nar Shaddaa. Most of the moon's inhabitants were destitute vagrants, uncultured smugglers, or decadent Hutt overlords like Guttu. Estimable Epicures was on the verge of closing its doors forever when the *Song of the Clouds*' transmission came over the comm. The request had thrown the two-month old company into a state of panic.

Estimable Epicures had a staff of twelve, down from eighteen after a Hutt suffering from indigestion launched six of their chefs into a nearby nebula. This job would put the fledgling company on the welcome path to solvency, but in order to handle an event that large, they had needed to double their workforce in twenty–four hours.

Frantic calls had gone out to the private kitchens kept by the oldest Hutt clans, apologizing for the short notice but begging to hire anyone with culinary experience for a temporary job. Three dozen beings expressed interest; only seven actually showed up at Estimable Epicures the following morning. The new arrivals were given cursory background checks, issued clean white uniforms, and put to work preparing the evening's entrees and loading them onto three rented shuttles. Thanks to some simple computer slicing on Sonax's part, two of the new faces belonged to Noone and Kels.

The shuttle's engines wheezed sickly as the ungainly vessel

cleared the atmosphere and slid beneath the drifting, burned-out hulk of a *Marauder*-class corvette. The space around Nar Shaddaa was littered with battered wrecks like this, Kels knew. She hoped the pilot had the good sense to shunt extra throttle energy into the particle shields.

The shuttle dipped sharply to avoid the slowly spinning torus of an abandoned turbolaser housing, causing the acceleration compensator to shudder and gasp. Through the pitted canopy visible just beyond the back of the pilot's chair, their destination came into view.

The *Song of the Clouds* was an awe–inspiring sight—a titanic bronze disc nearly a kilometer in diameter. Its edge was dotted with docking bays and airlocks, while its hub boasted a soaring transparisteel dome covering arboretums and manicured water-gardens. Like most herdships, the *Song* traveled the galaxy's hyperlanes selling rare and unusual merchandise to any and all comers. As a rule, the ladle–necked Ithorians thrived on interaction with other species. A herdship being hired out to host an exclusive private conference was unprecedented.

Their craft fell into position behind the other two catering shuttles and followed their exhaust trails to the nearest hangar. The pulsing blue rectangle indicating an atmosphere containment field grew in size. As the pilot made preparations for landing, a voice piped up at Kels' elbow.

"And how long have you worked in Tagta's kitchen?" The voice was irritatingly high-pitched, with a primly cultured accent. "We're a tight–knit bunch around here, and I don't remember seeing *your* faces before."

Kels looked over at the speaker, a short, stout human with a preposterously pointed mustache. He and his companions, two meek, golden–skinned humanoids of a species Kels had never encountered before, had arrived with the temporary help this morning. It wasn't clear whether he suspected something, or was merely being friendly. Quickly, she recalled their cover story. "I doubt you would have. We were transferred to Tagta's Winter Palace two weeks ago. Our master is currently visiting his permanent home on Nar Hekka, so we decided to make a few extra credits."

The shuttle settled in the bay with a rattle and a thump. The rear loading doors hissed open.

"Ah. Well, you had better hope he never finds out," the little man sniffed. "I've heard Tagta can be quite inflexible."

"We can take care of ourselves, got it?" Kels snapped, unbuckling her shoulder restraints. She had no desire to chitchat with an overinquisitive cook.

The man exhaled suddenly and noisily, as if he'd been punched in his ample gut. "Well!" His two companions were already pushing carts down the aft ramp. He whirled to follow them. "Just stay out of my way, *amateur*," he called haughtily over his shoulder. "I trained under the great chef Porcellus himself."

"Prima donna," Kels muttered under her breath, shaking her head contemptuously.

Noone gave her an expectant look and placed both hands against a metal handcart labeled CHARBOTE ROOT IN GUMBAH PUDDING. "It's showtime."

They wheeled the cart across the open hangar bay and into the winding corridors leading to the main atrium. Noone gradually slowed his pace until the group in front disappeared around a bend, then abruptly veered down a side passage and from there into a maintenance alcove. Kels popped the cart's corner latches, swinging open the side panel. Instead of gumbah pudding, the pushcart contained much less appetizing fare. One Tynnan and one Sluissi, horribly cramped.

Kels knelt and leaned forward. "Having fun?" she whispered with a grin.

Dawson growled. Sonax's shoulder was pressed against his ear, her elbow digging in his eye. He, in turn, had both feet wedged against the thinnest part of her tail. He clasped the detonator satchel against his chest protectively. "Oh, yes," he grunted. "Help us out of here, funny girl."

Dawson and Sonax stood perfectly still in the waste-reclamation chamber as the knot of Ithorians moved past in the adjoining corridor. Dawson waited until the sounds of burbling conversation had faded, counted five more beats, and palmed the door open. Stepping back into the hallway, he consulted his datapad for the tenth time since the two of them had headed off together.

Sonax slithered up beside him. "Give me that!" she demanded, reaching for the pad.

"Not a chance," the Tynnan countered, holding the device just out of arm's reach. "You'll just get us lost."

"We *are* lossst!" Sonax hissed, as they continued down the passage. "We have to be back in the food cart, *with* the contents of the lockbox, before the dinner party ends. If you just give it to me, I can download the entire map into my interface band."

"And leave you in charge? Sonax, you'd become captivated by some mathematical singularity and—" Dawson stopped in his tracks, shifting his eyes from the datapad to the looming blast doors in front of them and back again, before finally looking over at Sonax. "And we're here."

The cargo hold on the *Song of the Clouds* encompassed nearly a quarter of the aft section, running just below the hyperdrive motivator and one deck above the sublight engine banks. According to Guttu's information, the lockbox was being stored deep behind these reinforced blast doors, in a shielded vault surrounded by an array of security alarms and a phalanx of armed guards. The direct approach would never work.

The duo retreated around the last corner they had turned, lest they be caught flat-footed if the blast doors suddenly rumbled open. Dawson pointed at the ceiling. "Access tunnels, right?"

Sonax shook her crested head, the pale lighting glinting off her interface band. "The tunnels will surely be wired," she said. "I can bypass the alarms by accessing the *Ssong's*ss mainframe, but the blocks would be noticed by any alert

Ithorian operator. And I am sure they have one."

Dawson looked worried. "So what—"

"So we make sure he doesss not *remain* alert. Hand me my box."

The Tynnan rummaged through his duffel bag and pulled out rectangular gray case about the size of a drinking glass. He handed it to Sonax.

"Boossst. Quickly."

Grimacing, Dawson dropped to both knees as Sonax flowed onto his back and shoulders. With a grunt, he staggered to his feet. Sonax wrapped her tail tightly around his chest for support.

Sonax popped the ceiling panel and slid it out of the way. "Hold ssstill!" she whispered down at her prop, and poked her head inside. The dim access passageway ran straight for perhaps ten meters, then split into three separate branches. Perfect. Resting both elbows against the edge to brace herself against Dawson's drunken tottering, the sinuous alien slid the cover off the small gray box. A hundred angry red myrmins seethed inside, their jaw pincers twitching greedily for an enemy to gnaw to pieces. Sonax dumped the box, sending the insectoid army boiling into the shadows. Rapidly, she ducked back out and replaced the overhead square.

Dawson sighed with relief as Sonax slid from his shoulders and back to the floor. "That will trigger every alarm they have up there," she told the panting Tynnan. "Meanwhile, we take the low road."

She was already removing the lower deck plate.

"Loolalekkipaa soookii–pa esoopili?" The Khil glowered at Noone angrily, whistling through his hullepi and stabbing one finger against the metal tray. "Hooodoffi dip–dip?"

Noone stared back apprehensively. He could speak five languages fluently, and could bluff his way through a dozen more, but he couldn't decipher a word of the shrill argot warbled by this feeler–faced alien. Maybe he was out of practice. Or maybe the Khil was drunk.

Trying to guess his customer's intent by intonation and body posture, Noone raised his serving tray and rotated it a quarter–turn. "If you don't care for the fleek–eel, sir, I also have canapes of

poached icefish, dusted with—"

"*Goohilli*!" The Khil pounded his fist against the tray, sending several butter-basted land shrimp onto the floor. He slapped two clawed hands together in an elaborate and probably obscene gesture, and stalked off into the milling crowd. Noone exhaled with relief as he bent to retrieve the fallen appetizers.

So far, things seemed to be going well. Before their arrival in the domed conservatory at the herdship's heart, all the caterers had been thoroughly scanned for weapons or explosives, and all gastronomic delicacies had been sampled by an unhappy-looking pair of food tasters. The party was apparently running behind schedule, and their foreman barked orders while they uncovered the hors d'oeuvres, lit the flame pots, stirred the soup, and uncorked the Corellian brandy. The rich aromas mixed with the sweet scent of vesuvague leaves and donar flowers.

The main serving table, a mammoth wooden slab with seating for one hundred, sat directly beneath the apex of the transparent dome. At the head of the table were two carved chairs, so large they might more accurately be termed thrones. Side by side, they awaited the guests of honor. Neither seat was larger, more intricately detailed, or closer to the table than the other—clearly, appearances were key to this negotiation. To the left of the table, a large area had been cleared for the guests' mixing and mingling. At the periphery, just in front of the moss-draped treeline and meandering garden paths, Noone and the rest had arranged an irregular semicircle of catering carts.

The guests had arrived *en masse* a short time ago. Ritinki the Bimm and Vop the Rodian each had scores of underlings, hangers–on, and bootlickers in his entourage, and every one of them seemed to relish the welcome sight of an open bar. The atmosphere was becoming increasingly, earsplittingly raucous, as a sea of staggering beings downed various intoxicants and fought to shout each other down. At the moment, neither of the crime bosses had made an appearance.

Noone caught the flash of a bright white jacket through the press of bodies. Squeezing between two well-dressed Twi'leks engaged in a passionate debate over shockball scores, Kels sidled up to him.

"How goes the war?" he shouted in her ear.

Kels smiled slightly, lifted her right fist up to her shoulder, and spread her fingers slightly, showing him the distinctive outline of a Sif–Uwana certified credit voucher. The hand dropped inside her jacket and reappeared an instant later, empty.

"You *lifted* that? Off the Twi'leks?" Without turning his head, he shifted his eyes towards the two aliens, fearing the worst. They were still swapping bellicose insults, their head–tails gesticulating wildly. And clearly oblivious to their immediate surroundings. The tightness in his chest eased, but it was replaced by anger. He thrust a warning finger in the girl's face. "No more of that. Or you're off the team." He leaned closer. "We can't take the cart back if we're both shot dead. Understand?"

At this point in the scam, it was all up to Sonax and Dawson. All he and Kels could do was play out their assigned roles throughout dinner, scrape the leftovers off the flatware, retrieve the pudding cart from the side alcove where they'd left it, and load it back aboard the return shuttle. With any luck, it would be just as cumbersome as it was when they'd unloaded it, with the weight of two stowaways and the extra ten kilograms of a metal lockbox. He glanced around at the revelers. Hopefully, none of them was especially hoping for a cold dish of gumbah pudding.

Noone swiveled his head in a casual scan of the room, and the tiny device rubbed against the skin of his neck. They were spending too much time talking together. "We'd better split up," he said. "Just remember what I said about pinching. We're good little waiters, nothing more." He forced a hard expression on his face. "How much is the voucher made out for, anyway?"

Kels opened her eyes wide as she stepped back into the crowd. She held up one hand, fingers splayed, as if waving goodbye to a friendly coworker. Now Noone couldn't stop the smile from reaching his lips and breaking into a full grin. *Five thousand! Teach her some discipline, and she's going to make us the most successful thieves in the sector.*

The throbbing hum of the security field was quite distinct, now that they knew to listen for it. But the field was imperceptible on all visual wavelengths, and Dawson, clambering forward on all fours, had banged his head straight into it. He now sat back, grumbling and rubbing the singed spot in his fur.

Sonax leaned her head closer, almost but not quite touching the force barrier. She tapped the edge of her portable luma against it experimentally. It spat and crackled with taut energy. They weren't going to force their way past this.

Closing both eyes and drawing a deep breath, Sonax accessed her cybernetic band. The action was automatic, almost unconscious, but as always she felt a welcome surge of warmth and pleasure. This inner world was secure and comfortable, its silicon pathways as familiar as the crowded confines of Sluis Van Habitation Sphere D, where she'd lived as a child with her father and sisters.

In her mind's eye, an option matrix popped into view, its branching tunnels spreading out beneath it in brilliant streaks of green and red. She selected the two hundred thirty–second shaft on the fourteenth tier. Her consciousness shot into the tube, following it through dizzying drops and turns to its termination point, where an interlocking gridwork of fine mesh squares, rotating slowly in opposite directions, blocked all access. Sonax *nudged* the first grid into alignment, then the second, then the third. She slid through one of the myriad pinprick holes, emerging in a whirring, buzzing amphitheater whose lines stretched off into infinity. Number packets and strings of coding whizzed by as illuminated blurs, in a chaotic, clamorous jumble of sound and sensation. She had entered the *Song of the Cloud*'s mainframe.

Moments after she and Dawson had started worming their way through the lower maintenance tunnel, they'd come upon a miniature data terminal, just as she'd expected. It was a simple device, suited for diagnostic checks only, but it had a direct link to the main computer — a single subdirectory only, for the sole purpose of pulling repair logs. Using a cable jack, one end plugged into the data port and the other to her headband, Sonax sliced out of the directory and into the main drive. She disabled any latent intruder alarms in maintenance crawlway B43, then located the remote signal code and copied it.

The *Song's* remote signal code allowed datapads and other portable equipment to remain linked to the mainframe without being physically connected via a wire, jack, or scomp-link. This convenience was a standard feature on most large starships. After unhooking the cable, she wound it up and handed it back to Dawson. By duping the signal, Sonax could connect to the ship's systems at any time, so long as she remained on board. Just as she was doing now.

The cacophony of the *Song's* mainframe would have overwhelmed a purely organic mind incapable of perceiving its underlying structure. To a cyborg like Sonax, it was beautiful, a breathtaking masterpiece of intricate architecture. Dropping into position behind a pulsing data stream, she followed its wake through two virus filters and a password lock, coming up short against a towering bulwark representing Security Operations.

The virtual wall was studded with the rectangular protrusions of subdirectories; she moved into the slot at the intersection of column Mern-Krill and row 3135—Security Countermeasures. At her gentle prompt, numbers flew by at blinding speed, but she knew what they needed, would recognize it when—*there*! The control command for containment field 776, crawlway B43.

A faint blue link soared off from the control command, heading off along another silicon pathway. If power were cut, the energy barrier would collapse, but a reflexive signal along this link would trigger an alert signal on some Ithorian tech's station. They might be too distracted by the myrmin infestation to notice, but it was better to be safe than sorry.

Sonax *pushed* the delicate link slightly, not enough to snap it (which could cause a menacing self–diagnostic program to burst into this sector), but enough to insert a temporary patch buffer. Turning back to the indistinct dark smudge representing the security field command, she shifted the numbers into a new, powerless alignment. As the blurred coding began to slow and cool, Sonax began retracing her steps back to the stable matrices of her own neural network.

She opened her eyes. Dawson was still rubbing the top of his head. The entire operation had taken less than one second of real time.

Beside her, the energy barrier sizzled, sparked with a thousand strobing dots of light, gave off one alarmingly bright flash, and vanished. Sonax reached up with her luma again. This time, her arm passed easily through the junction and into the corridor beyond.

Dawson nodded appreciatively. "Excellent, Sonax, excellent. Great work."

Sonax was already advancing, snaking forward on her powerful tail. She found it much easier to move through the narrow passage than her two-legged Tynnan compatriot did.

"Quickly," she said. "We don't have much time."

The R'alla mineral water gurgled as Kels poured it into the Veubg's glass. She over–filled the glass, and the overflow splashed onto the white tablecloth, forming a spreading dark blotch. The Veubg seemed not to notice. Kels headed back towards the ring of carts, her heavy ceramic pitcher wet with quivering beads of condensation.

Things had settled down a bit since dinner had been started. Most of the guests were arranged around the heavy wooden table, the hearty mugruebe stew beginning to take the edge off their inebriated high. Ritinki and Vop had made their appearances, from opposite sides of the courtyard, immediately after the others had taken their seats. They had settled into the vacant thrones at the head of the table, their personal bodyguards standing at their sides and casting suspicious glances in each others' directions.

Kels twisted the spigot and held the pitcher underneath to catch the cold stream of bubbling mineral spirits. The tap was slower than she would have liked, and she glanced back towards the table. Vop, his green snout waggling, was speaking fervently to his disinterested rival. Ritinki appeared intent on to be brushing lint specks off his yellow cravat. The Bimm was so short his feet dangled far above the floor. Neither of the two had touched their food.

She also noted that there was no sign of the cyborg bookkeeper. The man was Ritinki's duplicate agent, but in order to maintain his cover, he should have appeared in Vop's entourage by now.

Kels checked the water level in her container—not quite full—as another server moved up behind her. She turned her head. It was one of the golden–skinned humanoids they'd ridden up with in the shuttle—stoop–shouldered, pot–bellied, weak–kneed, with downcast eyes that wouldn't meet her face. He and his twin had been bowing and fawning obsequiously since the first guests had arrived. Their compatriot, the pudgy, mustachioed egotist she'd snapped at earlier, was flitting from one place setting to the next like a witless moon moth dancing about a glow rod. He was clearly in his element.

The cool, swirling water finally reached the rim. She shut off the tap with her free hand, and turned back towards the table. "It's all yours, golden boy." The alien bobbed his head and stared at the floor. "Ma' thanks, ma' thanks," he breathed in a rapt whisper. Kels' lip twisted up in a contemptuous sneer. She hated rubbing elbows with snobs and submissives. The sooner this charade was over with, the better.

Overhead, the clear dome offered a spectacular view of the local constellations, countless stars circled by worlds whose inhabitants were surely having a better time than she was. Kels wrenched her neck, vainly trying to kill a persistent itch caused by the stiff collar of her uniform, and continued filling the water glasses where she'd left off. The monotony was killing her. Something had better happen soon.

The actinic glare from the tip of the fusion cutter grew brighter as metal began to superheat and vaporize. Dawson reached up with his left paw and tapped the side of his ocular enhancer, simultaneously darkening both lenses and increasing magnification by two hundred percent.

The cutting tool traced a burning white line down the side of the bulkhead. Dawson paused, then continued the incision by striking off at a perpendicular angle. Sweat beaded on his black nose. With steady hands, he proceeded through two more ninety-degree turns, switching off the fusion cutter when he'd returned to his starting point.

This is it, he thought. *It took longer than we expected, but we made it.* He secured a magnetic handle in the center of the square, which glowed a dull red as the severed metal cooled. *Right here*—he placed one paw on the handle and grasped it firmly—*right behind this bulkhead, is the vault where they're keeping the lockbox.* With a yank and a grunt, the square of metal came free from the wall. Behind it was more featureless gray alloy—the exterior of the safe. Dawson searched through his duffel bag.

He looked at his companion. Sonax sat motionless against the side of the crawlway, her arms crossed and her body bent so severely her head almost touched the floor. He knew the trance–like state meant that she was deep in a cyber–link, scanning for any silent alarms he might inadvertently trigger, but he still suppressed an involuntary shudder. She looked dead.

The brownish putty felt pliant and clammy in his palm. He tore loose four small wads, rolled them into balls, and pressed them solidly against the vault at the four corners outlined by the quadrangular hole. Into each pellet, he would insert a minute quantity of nergon–14.

And then, he thought with pleasure, *we'll see what this vault is really made of.*

Trouble. That's what Noone thought the continued absence of the bookkeeper meant. He'd expected the man to appear as part of Vop's retinue, and excuse himself at the conclusion of dinner to pick up the box that Vop had previously paid for. At least that was what Guttu had *told* them to expect. Noone should have learned by now that nothing ever went according to plan.

Noone once again scanned the alien faces seated around the table. Nothing. He gritted his teeth. Perhaps Vop had discovered that his trusted advisor was now a treacherous double, and had had the man executed. Noone didn't care one way or the other about the bookkeeper's fate, but such an action would mean Vop was likely to make other arrangements to secure his prize. The box could have been moved to another vault, or transferred to deep storage for pickup at a later date.

Guttu didn't like failure. Noone envisioned several vivid scenarios in which he was dragged down to the deepest bowels of Nar Shaddaa and thrown to a pit of starved vrblthers. In all of them, his suffering lasted less than ten seconds—which was the only good thing he envision about his future prospects at this point.

He shook himself out of it. There was no sense in brooding. There were dozens of likely reasons for the bookkeeper's non–appearance, and none of them had anything to do with a botched robbery attempt. Nevertheless, he was becoming worried for his team's safety.

Theoretically, Noone could contact Sonax and Dawson whenever he chose. Clipped to the inside of his starched collar, just behind the stylized double–Esk logo of Estimable Epicures, was a military–style comlink. The gadget had been scrounged from a Rebel Alliance field pack Dawson had picked up on the black market and could purportedly cut through any jamming field. It was keyed to transmit directly into Sonax's headband, and she could respond on the same frequency. Before going in, they'd agreed not to use it unless absolutely necessary—there was no way of telling whether the signal would be detected by the *Song's* internal sensors.

Kels walked up beside him, each hand supporting a garnished plate of grilled crupa breast. "Left side," she whispered. "Twenty meters."

He turned his head in the direction indicated. There, emerging from the sheltering treeline surrounding the decorative garden terraces, was the bookkeeper.

He was a nondescript human, middle–aged, of average height and weight. The silver ends of his cybernetic interface were plainly visible on either side of his bald head. Noone squinted intently, but couldn't see any indication that the image was a holo–shroud projection. This meant nothing, of course—only the cheapest chop–jobs left a telltale blur, and Ritinki obviously had credits to burn. His instincts told him it was likely an expensive surgical alteration. Having never met the original bookkeeper, he'd have to assume that this was a perfect copy.

The man strode forward confidently, stopping beside Vop's chair and standing at attention, both hands clasped behind his back. The Rodian tilted his snout to gaze up at his employee with bulbous, expressionless eyes. His antennae dipped in casual acknowledgment, then he turned back to Ritinki and resumed his hooting conversation. Noone wasn't an expert on Rodian mannerisms, but unless Vop was an exceptionally good actor, he'd been completely taken in by the duplicate.

A few of the more gluttonous guests leaned back in their seats, already pushing forward plates littered with heaps of picked–clean crupa bones. Other waiters moved forward to remove them. The bookkeeper would be leaving soon, Noone estimated. He hoped Dawson and Sonax were working fast.

"Three... two... one..."

Sonax winced.

The report sounded like a muffled blaster shot. There was less noise than Sonax had expected, but there was considerably more smoke. Dawson scrambled into the acrid haze and disappeared around the bend. Sonax stirred to follow.

The nergon charges had torn a ragged hole in the side of the vault. She prayed the Tynnan hadn't grievously miscalculated and destroyed the vault's contents as well.

Only Dawson's hindquarters were visible in the corridor. His torso was thrust through the blackened gash and his arms were flapping madly, as he squirmed and twisted. Sonax coughed uncomfortably and waited.

After a long, anxious moment, Dawson slowly withdrew his head. He sank to the floor of the crawlway, blinking at her stupidly.

"It's empty."

Noone was about to join the dish collectors when he saw the bookkeeper's head turn slightly. Noone followed his eyes—the man was staring straight at Ritinki. The Bimm looked up, and they locked gazes for an instant. The human gave a barely perceptible nod, and Ritinki gave a concealed head bob in return. The clandestine exchange took a fraction of a second.

Noone's blood turned to ice. He prided himself on his ability to read subtle gestures, nervous tics and hidden signals. It was a skill that had proven invaluable in countless games of high-stakes sabacc. And he would bet the *Borogove* that that little interchange had meant only one thing: Mission Accomplished.

He pressed two fingers firmly against his collar, activating the hidden comlink. "Sonax," he murmured in a hushed tone.

Kels saw the movement, and leaned close. "What are you *doing*?" she whispered.

"We're too late," he shot back. "The bookkeeper wasn't moving after dinner after all—he's already been and gone. By now, that lockbox is safely stowed aboard Ritinki's personal ship." He gave a tight scowl. "It's over." Lowering his head, he muttered into the comlink again. "Sonax?"

His answer was an abrupt burst of crackling static. After a moment of garbled nonsense, the signal locked onto the correct frequency. "—oon— th— —sss —onax. Go ahead."

"Pull out. The box isn't there."

"We know. We're at the vault now."

"Get back to the cart," he ordered. "The box is out of reach now. Guttu will just have to accept that."

There was a pause. "Noone, Dawssson says the box is probably on the Bimm's vesssel. If so, I have the herdssship's arrival logs and know where it isss docked—"

"No, blast it! You can't board it. We don't have a plan, and we don't have time. Get back to—"

"But Guttu—"

"Damn Guttu! I'm not going to risk you two on a suicide run for a box. Now get back before—" A squeal of angry feedback drowned him out. Disgustedly, he switched off the comlink.

"Think they'll head back?" Kels inquired.

He glared at her. "Of course they will. Even *I* think Dawson and Sonax are a little odd sometimes. But neither one of them is stupid."

Dawson stood in the airlock, struggling to keep his breathing under control. *Can't back out now*, he reminded himself. Cold fear lay coiled in his stomach, threatening to bubble up into his brain. He forced it down again, and slowly, meditatively, exhaled. The sound echoed noisily in the claustrophobic confines of his vacsuit.

Ritinki's personal ship, the *Asaari Wind*, had docked at an exterior airlock instead of landing in one of the open hangar bays. When they'd discovered this fact, he'd cursed out loud. The only way into the yacht's interior was through the airlock's circular hatch, and the hatch was guarded by a pair of snorting, drooling, vicious–looking Gamorreans. The swinish aliens were too stupid to bribe, and any attempt at a con was likely to get you neatly halved by a vibroaxe. Sonax had been ready to give up, until Dawson had a flash of insight. Both berths on either side of the *Asaari Wind* were unoccupied.

They'd broken into this airlock, one slip over, which was vacant save for a maintenance locker and a row of dangling Ithorian vacsuits. With a great deal of effort, Dawson had donned one of the oversized suits, hitching up the baggy fabric and cinching it with engine tape around the elbows, knees, and waist. Sonax, however, was another matter. The serpentine Sluissi could not fit into any of the bipedal suits without an amputation or a miracle. After a short but heated argument, she'd agreed to climb into an equipment sled that he sealed behind her. She was curled up in there now and likely hating every minute of it. Dawson didn't feel much better himself.

The tiny light next to the outer hatch winked from green to red, indicating the chamber had reached total vacuum. With one bulky, long-fingered glove, he pushed down the manual release lever. The round hatch ground sluggishly upward, revealing an ever–widening slice of star–speckled blackness. His breath quickened involuntarily. Moving quickly before he could change his mind, he stepped to the edge of the airlock and shoved off.

He had only drifted a few meters when the tether around his waist extended fully, stopping him with an abrupt jerk. Puzzled, he twisted his head around inside the elongated hammerhead helmet. The equipment sled, secured to the other end of the tether, was still resting on the airlock deck, held firmly in place by the *Song of the Cloud's* artificial gravity.

If the suit had allowed it, Dawson would have slapped his forehead in disgust. *Idiot*, he thought. *You should have pushed it out first.* He considered reeling himself in and starting over. *No, wait. Maybe I can still pull it loose.*

He looked down at the rectangular control panel on the suit's left forearm. Like any standard zero–gee vacsuit, this one was equipped with maneuvering jets located just beneath each shoulder, positioned out from the body so they could be aimed in any direction. After an extremely unpleasant bout with vertigo nearly six years ago, he'd avoided space walks like a hive virus. Still, it shouldn't be too hard to figure out.

The illuminated buttons were unusually large, built for awkward gloved fingers. He frowned as he scrutinized the spidery Ithorian script. "This one," he muttered.

A chime sounded in his helmet speaker as he depressed the button. With a hiss of escaping gas, the back jets shuddered to life. He jerked forward slightly, but was again halted by the anchored tether.

Dawson punched the control square twice more, hearing a successively higher-pitched tone each time. The hissing in his ears grew louder and the pull at his waist tightened as the jets doubled in strength. He craned his neck to look backwards. The tether quivered with tension. The equipment sled moved forward, scraping along the deck plates for about five centimeters, then stopped.

He turned back towards his suit controls, both jets still blasting at full force. *Well, this is a bust.* He searched the arm panel for the shutoff button. Looks like *I'll have to go back inside and shove her out the old-fashioned way.*

He suddenly lurched forward as if shot from a cannon. White stars burned brightly on every side, while the glittering gridwork of Nar Shaddaa, banded by a thin limb of faint blue atmosphere, appeared kilometers beneath his booted feet. His surging stomach fought to keep pace with his brain, which was racing at light speed.

His first thought—that the tether had snapped—was dispelled by a worried glance over his shoulder. He was towing the sled through open space. But the forceful tugging at his waist, coupled with the rapidly shrinking circle of the open airlock hatch, could only mean one thing. He was accelerating, and rapidly. Cursing, he stabbed repeatedly at his forearm, hoping to hit the cut switch.

Instead, he keyed for a hard left turn. The power of the leftmost jet was cut by half, shunting the extra force into the gas stream spewing from the right nozzle. Dawson whipped around in a tight arc, stars streaking past his faceplate in crazy bright stripes. The attached equipment sled swung around to follow and he found himself spinning out of control—metallic sled and spacesuited biped twirling around on opposite sides of an invisible pivot point like partners in a Sarkan ballet. The burnished bronze expanse of the herdship's edge suddenly obscured the striated stars, then vanished just as suddenly as Dawson spun into another gut-wrenching rotation. Clenching his teeth in near-panic, he fumbled wildly for the attitude controls. Through sheer luck, he managed to cut power to both jets.

With no atmospheric friction he continued to spin, but at least he was no longer accelerating. Pushed forward in his suit by the invisible hand of centrifugal force, Dawson raised his left arm as close as the faceplate would allow and studied the delicate lettering intently. With new confidence and no small measure of relief, he pressed the keys that would cause him to make a gentle right turn.

Dawson emerged from the violent gyrations as the left nozzle slowly bled off speed. He switched off power and breathlessly surveyed his surroundings. Pulse pounding, his fluttering heart forced a roaring stream of blood through his ears. Any moment now, the adrenaline would belatedly kick in.

Thankfully, he hadn't drifted as far from the airlock as he'd feared. There, not more than one hundred meters away, was Ritinki's ship, its slender nose plugged solidly into the adjoining airlock. The sleek lines of the space yacht were blemished by the barrels of heavy turbolasers and ion cannons. Dawson made a quick scan of the hull, identified his target area, and carefully jetted forward.

He stretched both arms out wide as he watched his destination grow larger through the distended faceplate. Built for Ithorian eyes, it distorted objects in his peripheral field of vision—a minor irritant. He concentrated on his breathing, and chuckled ruefully as he thought of his near–disastrous lesson in zero–gee maneuvering.

"Now I remember why I don't do this," he said out loud. "Wonder what Sonax thought of that." He laughed again, louder this time.

The *Asaari Wind* drew so close he could pick out the mynock sucker-marks on its slate-gray hull. He was approaching too quickly. He needed to reverse the jets slightly and slow to a crawl, or he'd smash into a wall of plasteel with enough force to snap a bone—or worse, breach his suit.

Dawson waited until he had glided just a bit farther, then swiveled both jets forward and released a light stream of compressed air. His speed dropped marginally. He held the button down harder. *A little more—*

Dawson gasped as a massive weight struck him squarely across the shoulders and lower back. His spine shrieked in agony as every nerve ending came alive with sharp, prickling pain. The next instant he slammed into the *Wind*'s hull, and the air was forced from his lungs and his vision to clouded with blotchy dark spots.

It was, like so many things, obvious in hindsight. The equipment sled, on a flexible tether, hadn't slowed when he'd applied the brakes to the vacsuit's momentum. Obeying the simplest laws of inertia, it had continued on a straight line until it encountered the nearest obstacle: him. And his suit jets. His carelessness had finally done him in, Dawson thought grimly. And worse, he'd doomed Sonax as well.

Both maneuvering jets appeared to be crushed beyond repair—neither responded to his frantic taps on the darkened instrument panel. The hull slid by beneath him as his gloved fingers vainly scrabbled for purchase on the welded edges of the armor plating. He would reach the aft end of the ship in a matter of seconds. Without suit power, he'd continue sailing out towards Nar Shaddaa, towed by the sled all the way. Dimly, he wondered if he would suffocate from lack of air before burning up upon planetary reentry.

He snagged a tenuous hold on the concave edge of an external sensor dish, lost it, and continued his slide. The rear sublight engine bank rushed up at him. Beyond it, empty space yawned. *Well, this is it. Won't even get to hear Noone say "I told you so"*

Something hard-edged and solid caught him in his right side just below the ribcage. As his body twisted around the obstruction, Dawson caught a glimpse of the pointed tip of a subspace signal antenna. Flailing both arms like a drowning man, he snagged the slim spire and hugged it to his chest like a lover. The sled continued to coast, reaching the end of its tether and threatening to pull him loose. Dawson squeezed his eyes shut and held on until the tugging subsided.

It was nearly a minute before he had regained the courage to open one eye. The stars were still where he'd left them. He slowly unclasped his arms. With the determined, precise movements of a climber free–scaling the glaciers of Toola, he inched several meters forward and down to what he'd tentatively identified as the ventral engine room. Nervous exhaustion started creeping into his muscles. Soon, his hands would start shaking. *That's enough excitement for one day*, he thought.

The fusion cutter was secured to the front of his vacsuit with a silvery X of engine tape. He ripped it free. *From here on out, we're doing it by the book.* Igniting the cutter with a soundless burst of plasma, he started slicing through the hull.

The sugar beignets had vanished, the ryshcate pans held only crumbs, and the blicci–flavored ices were melting to mush. Dessert had gone rather well, Kels thought, despite the minor panic when the catering foreman had been unable to locate the cart of gumbah pudding. Ever the professional, he'd pressed on anyhow, but the perplexed look on his face had been the highlight of Kels' evening so far.

Well, that and the boosted credit voucher. She smiled. Even though the Tynnan and the Sluissi had missed nabbing the lockbox, the evening hadn't been a total waste. Around her, Noone and the other workers glided to and fro, removing empty plates and filling small crystal glasses with thick, cloyingly sweet liqueurs. Kels chose not to join them. She needed a break.

The pompous little man from the shuttle strutted by her, bouncing daintily on the balls of his feet. He clasped a bottle of Gruvian Tovash in his soft hands. Kels decided a snort of derision would be wasted on the overstuffed buffoon, and lazily scanned for his two docile chums. Both aliens also held bottles of Tovash and, like their friend, were heading for the catering carts nearest the table. *Odd*, she thought languidly. *Gruvian Tovash isn't a traditional after–dinner drink.*

There was a rustle of movement at the head of the table and an interested buzz from the rest of the room. Ritinki and Vop, their discussions concluded, were rising to exchange the ritual handclasp that would formally conclude the evening's festivities. Two silent bodyguards pulled the ornate chairs back from the table with a heavy scrape. Slowly, with great ceremony, the lanky Rodian and undersized Bimm walked between the chairs and ascended the raised dais immediately behind them. As they turned to look out on their assembled entourages, four burly security goons filed in front to form a formidable protective barrier. One appeared particularly alert, but Kels figured that was probably because of the way his eyes seemed to bulge within his face that appeared to have been ravaged by fire at some point. Ritinki cleared his throat to speak. "Gentlebeings—"

Out of the corner of her eye, Kels caught a sudden flash of movement. Before she could turn her head fully, a thick plume of oily blue smoke boiled up from one of the carts with an angry hiss. She blinked as the billowing cloud stung her eyes and coughed spasmodically. A voice shouted, "Fire!" Through the growing haze, she noticed that two other carts were similarly smoldering.

Several of the guests overturned their chairs in their haste to reach the exit. Kels dropped into a crouch, danger senses instantly alert. She doubted this was a coincidence. If it wasn't, the perpetrators would have to strike immediately. She whipped her head towards the dais. The four guards had formed an impenetrable bulwark around their charges, their eyes intently scanning the crowd.

Except for the rightmost man. He was, incredibly, staring down at the silver pin ornamenting his black tunic. Staring dumbly, and opening his mouth to speak—

Kels eyes snapped into focus. That wasn't a decorative pin. It was a serving fork that cleanly pierced the narrow gap between the man's fourth and fifth ribs.

The man's mouth opened wider. A trickle of blood beaded on his lower lip. With a slow motion that put Kels in mind of someone moving in zero–gee, he began to pitch forward—a movement counterbalanced by the backwards tumble of the gruesomely disfigured thug to his right. Scarface let out a gurgling moan, both hands tightly clutching his throat. Protruding from between his stained fingers was the handle of a carving knife.

The third goon stared goggle–eyed as his companions fell; the fourth went for his blaster. A flash of silver caught him in his left ear; he went down with a heavy thump. Simultaneously, the remaining guard drew his weapon from beneath his jacket and peppered the crowd indiscriminately with blaster bolts. Cries of pain and panic rang through the hall as the crowd continued its frenzied surge for the exits. Kels heard a crash of shattering dishes as if someone had knocked over a fully laden cart. A snorting Saurton, eyes wide, came barreling directly at her in a mad, panicked dash. She got out of the way.

The fourth and final projectile, a broiling skewer with a small gobbet of meat still embedded on its blackened shaft, impacted the randomly firing blaster just above the trigger guard. The weapon exploded spectacularly, and its bearer went down with a stifled shriek. This time, Kels tracked the missile to its source, and gasped in astonishment.

There, grasping another piece of cutlery and cocking his arm back for a deadly throw at the fleeing figures of Vop and Ritinki, was the chef. The silly, pompous little fool she'd sneered at in the shuttlecraft. All traces of his previous demeanor had vanished. Above his wax–tipped mustache burned the alert, pitiless eyes of a professional assassin.

Before he could complete his throw, two great gouts of blaster fire erupted from behind him, streaking on either side of his body towards the dais. The golden-skins, standing behind an overturned cart, were firing heavy blaster rifles with the cool expertise of hired killers. At their feet was an open weapons locker.

A blaster bolt caught Vop in the back, and he fell to the floor, tumbling and rolling as his momentum continued to carry him forward even as life fled his body. Ritinki scampered to the far edge of the dais and leapt behind it, narrowly beating out a hail of super–heated plasma bolts.

This was too much. Keeping her head down, Kels started backing away slowly, carefully stepping over the shattered crockery and puddled wine. The blue–tinged haze was beginning to clear. With any luck, she'd make it back to the treeline without incident, and from there, it was a short sprint down the garden path to the exit. She looked around quickly. Where the *stang* was Noone?

"Get down!" Noone's forearm hooked across her chest and see was thrown roughly to the ground. She twisted as she fell, hoping to get free, but he landed on top of her. A blaster bolt whined through the air where her head had been a heartbeat before.

"Thanks," she gulped.

He motioned to the periphery of the clearing. Several of the party guests now had sidearms out. They had obviously been additional security. They had their sidearms out now, and were trying to catch the assassins in a flanking maneuver. Unfortunately, Kels and Noone were in the crossfire.

Lethal darts of plasma traced a sizzling web above their heads. One of the goldskins was down, but the two surviving killers retreated behind a makeshift barrier of metal carts and wooden chairs. They were evenly spitting their fire between the encircling thugs and Ritinki, their remaining target. From her vantage point on the atrium floor, Kels could see the tiny Bimm cowering behind the blaster–chewed lip of the dais. His men had the executioners greatly outnumbered, but after seeing their lethal skills in action, Kels still put Ritinki's survival odds at ten to one.

Over the din, Noone shouted in her ear. "Some party, huh?"

Kels barked a bitter laugh. "You're a master of understatement. Did you see it coming?"

"Not at all," he replied. "Kid, I think we've stumbled into the middle of a mob hit!"

A poorly aimed shot tore a jagged furrow into the ground near their huddled forms. By unspoken agreement, they both started squirming on their bellies out of the immediate line of fire.

"Where in the galaxy did they dig up those blaster rifles?" Noone grunted.

"Smuggler–style weapons locker," Kels answered. "Sensor shielded beyond reason. Looks like we weren't the only ones to think of stowing something in a cart." On her elbows, she wormed her way past a dead Nimbanel. "What I don't understand is where the smoke diversion came from."

Noone nodded. "I think I can help you out there. Gruvian Tovash, when mixed with ryll spice, reacts in a rather alarming fashion. And there was plenty of both substances in use here tonight."

Kels shook her head in disbelief. "A mob hit. Just your luck. Who do you suppose is behind it?"

"Not Guttu, that's for sure. He only wants the box." He pursed his lips as two more bodyguards fell, blaster–wounds smoking in their chests. The "chef" and the surviving golden–skinned humanoid were still firing doggedly. "Those characters are experts. And experts don't come cheap. We're looking at a major Hutt player here. Durga, possibly, or maybe even Jabba himself."

Kels looked across the floor at Ritinki. The Bimm was still crouched in the protective umbra of the raised dais. Sprawled a short distance away was the crimson–perforated body of his phoney cyborg bookkeeper.

Persistent barrages of incoming blaster fire prevented the cringing Bimm from moving out of his isolated shelter. As Kels watched, he slowly withdrew a long, metallic object from beneath his patterned waistcoat.

"Watch your head," she warned Noone. "Looks like Ritinki's finally getting a blaster out." She looked again. "No, hold on. It's not a blaster. Some kind of electronic control, I think."

The Bimm tapped a key sequence into the face of the device, then reached into another pocket and removed an emergency breathing mask. Snapping an oxygen cartridge into its base, he slipped the mask over his mouth and nose.

"Gas!" Noone shouted. "He must be planning to flood the room with nerve gas. Kid, we need to get out here *now*."

Kels looked at the crisscrossing tangle of deadly bolts that laced the charged air of the atrium. The bright streaks burned afterimages on her retina. "Easier said than done."

As they'd expected, the *Asaari Wind* was deserted. Dawson cautiously padded through the empty corridors, Sonax gliding sullenly at his side.

"You said you knew what you were doing," she spat. The out–of–control banging of the equipment sled during their zero–gee hop had raised several welts on her smooth gray skin.

"For the hundredth time, I'm sorry," he pleaded. "Physics isn't exactly my strongest suit. And anyway, I got us here, didn't I?"

She hissed through her peglike teeth. "Barely. And now you've got to get us back the same way."

A sour expression crossed Dawson's face. After cutting an access hole into the small, sealed engine chamber, he had hastily patched the breach before throwing open the chamber door. With pressure equalized, he'd shed the ruined Ithorian suit and freed Sonax.

But with Gamorreans standing guard outside the docking hatch, they had no choice but to leave in the same manner they'd arrived. Dawson had located a replacement human–sized vacsuit from the *Wind*'s supply closet—a little large, but it would do. He'd desperately hoped to find a Sluissi suit, but once again Sonax was out of luck. He thanked the Fates that the equipment sled was still intact.

An indicator light on Sonax's cyborg band flashed red as she accessed her internal chrono. "We're running out of time. Find the box and let'sss go."

Dawson's footfalls echoed down the passage. "Let's see. If I were a wealthy, underhanded Bimm crimelord with a ruthless streak and a taste for expensive starships, where would I put it?"

He started to raise one paw to his chin theatrically, but halted in mid–motion. "Do you hear that?" His pointed ears twitched.

Sonax cocked her head. The faint buzz Dawson had heard doubled and tripled in strength. The sonorous thrumming was now unmistakable. A moment later, the deckplates began to vibrate.

The ship was powering up.

Sonax and Dawson looked at each other—one accusatory, one apologetic. Dawson found his voice first. "Uh oh."

Kels gritted her teeth. A mad sprint through the fire zone would be suicide. If Ritinki had donned the oxygen mask so he could engulf the area with poison fumes as Noone kept insisting, they were doomed.

She scanned the room one last time. They had little choice. Noone was already crouching into a sprinter's start, preparing to make break for it. He looked over at her reassuringly. "Ready? One. Two—"

"Wait!" she shouted, grabbing his arm. He followed her gaze, staring straight up at the apex of the dome overhead. An oblong patch of shimmering stars was no longer visible. In its place was an indistinct dark blotch, evenly dotted with blinking red lights.

They looked like starship running lights. And they were getting closer.

Noone swallowed. "I don't think that was a nerve–gas controller after all. Find something heavy and hang on to it!"

The lights grew brighter. The dark shape grew larger.

And, with a deafening crack of shattered transparisteel, the *Asaari Wind* crashed through the skylight. Thousands of jagged glassine shards rushed out through the gaping hole as the escaping atmosphere vented into space. Kels desperately wrapped both arms around a heavy Andoan wine–cask.

The two assassins, caught almost directly beneath the breach, were swept up in the smoky vortex along with assorted chairs, carts, and spent blaster cartridges. Limbs flailing, the white-jacketed chef bounced hard against the hull of the *Asaari Wind*—holding steady amid the maelstrom—and continued out into cold blackness, head bent back at an unnatural angle. The goldskin squeezed the trigger of his rifle until the bitter end, spraying the room with blaster fire even as space's vacuum sucked him inexorably to a swift and painful death. The surviving security personnel dove desperately back to the treeline for something to cling to. Some succeeded, others were sucked screaming into the void.

Kels turned her head towards the dais, away from the stinging grit of onrushing dirt and debris. Ritinki, bracing himself against the platform's edge, held one hand squarely over his breathing mask as the atmosphere continued its rush into space. Kels' anchoring barrel slipped across the floor, its weight no longer enough to withstand the terrifying gale.

And then, miraculously, the movement stopped. A shimmering force field snapped into place across the underbelly of the dome to plug the ragged break. The violent turbulence ceased, and small bits of loose wreckage began raining back to the floor. Kels gasped in the thin air and shakily stood up.

A transparent dome was a rather vulnerable structure to place at the heart of a spacegoing vessel. The *Song of the Clouds* must naturally have an emergency system that lets the central computer to seal off the dome with an atmosphere containment field in the event of a canopy breach. But what had taken so long, Kels wondered. There should be a sensor dish at the lip of the dome that instantly triggered the field at a sudden drop in atmospheric pressure.

She scanned the rim of the dome, and found her answer—and immediately wished she hadn't. The sensor dish she had expected to see had apparently been struck by a stray blaster bolt. The housing was a twisted, black mess with melted components dangling from it.

Noone staggered weakly over to Kels. He pointed to the sensor box Kels had already spotted. "We've still got to go," he croaked. "That's not going to hold long. The shunting chips are probably fused and are going to overload any minute."

As if on cue, a shower of sparks erupted from the damaged sensor.

Kels glanced at Ritinki, who tapped a command into what she now recognized as a beckoncall—a ship's remote control. The *Asaari Wind*, hovering five meters above the ground, suddenly dropped like a rock, landing on the ponderous wooden dinner table and crushing it to splinters. The Bimm grimaced and punched another button. The *Wind* bobbed up a meter on its repulsorlifts, rotating in a slight circle as the boarding ramp gracefully extended. With surprising quickness, Ritinki rounded the dais and sprinted across open ground for the hatch—

Only to be knocked flat on his back as the ship's ventral turbolaser blasted a bantha-sized crater near his feet.

The cockpit viewports swung into view as the *Wind* continued its slow turn. Kels couldn't believe his eyes. Through the tinted glass, waving both arms excitedly and mouthing something inaudible, was Dawson.

Noone pulled Kels to her feet. "Come on," he wheezed.

They ran for the shadowy rectangle of the yacht's welcoming ramp, past the still body of Ritinki the Bimm. *Stunned insensible by the shockwave*, Kels guessed when she didn't see any lacerations or burns on the body. She reached the edge of the ramp as her knees buckled with fatigue. Gasping, she fell to her hands and knees on the cold metal. Noone moved ahead of her, fighting the wind caused by cabin pressure venting through the open hatch

The field control box overhead let out a piercing whine and burst into a cascading sparks. Kels looked up. The emergency energy shield flickered feebly, and vanished.

The room exploded in a thunderous roar, as space tried once again to claim its tenuous gasses. Still hovering, the starship bucked roughly in the tempest, and Kels found herself slipping off the side of the ramp. As her fingers desperately sought purchase, they squeaked across the polished surface. Then a gray hand firmly grabbed her left wrist.

Kels looked up. Sonax grimaced down at her. The Sluissi's tail was wrapped securely around the ramp's left support piston. With a whiplike jerk, she pulled them both inside as the ramp started to raise.

And, buoyed by the rushing atmosphere, the *Asaari Wind* climbed for the stars.

The lockbox rested in Noone's lap, glinting dully in the bright track lighting of the yacht's passenger cabin. He tapped the silvery sheen with one knuckle experimentally. "Dawson, you're *sure* you disabled the anti–tamper safeguards." It was not a question.

The Tynnan looked up from his reclining position on the floor near Noone's padded acceleration couch. "Boss, I went over it a hundred times. It's safe. I guarantee it." Noone still looked dubious. "What's the matter, don't you trust me?"

Noone snorted. "Now's not the time to ask *that* question, my furry friend." He was still a bit angry over Sonax and Dawson's failure to obey his recall order, but this was a band of thieves, not a crack stormtrooper regiment. Besides, he'd been in this business long enough to know you didn't argue with success.

Through the starboard porthole, wispy strands of luminescent vapor swirled past in mindbending kaleidoscopic patterns. They had flown their stolen starship into the vast radioactive nebula near Nal Hutta—not far enough so that they might lose their way in there, but deep enough to discourage pursuit.

He sighed heavily. "Well, here goes. You all might want to take a few steps back in case it blows up in my face." Dawson rolled his eyes. Kels and Sonax actually moved a half step closer, so as not to miss the unveiling.

With a muted click, Noone released the locking clips with a twist of both thumbs. Putting gentle pressure on the ribbed metal siding, he cautiously lifted the hinged top. Four heads clustered together for a clean view of the contents.

"It'sss—" Sonax began.

"It's a *gun*," interrupted Kels.

"Huh," muttered a clearly nonplussed Dawson.

Snugly ensconced in a shock–resistant foam casing, the two halves of the black weapon—barrel and stock—crawled with external wiring and electrical relays. When properly fitted together, it would be about the size and heft of a blaster rifle.

Noone removed the stock carefully. "Some powerful people are very interested in this, people." He handed the stock section to Kels, then offered the barrel to Dawson. "Any idea what it is?"

They sat in study for a moment. A soothing hum of static reverberated through the room, as irradiated gasses washed against the energy shields.

Dawson finally hazarded a guess. "An Imperial prototype weapon of some kind? It seems equipped to shoot electromagnetic waves, but I don't really know what that would be good for."

Kels looked up with wide eyes. "It's a Gun of Command."

Everyone turned to stare at her. "A *what*?" said Noone.

She held the stock out towards them. At its base was a short line of tiny, machine-stamped lettering in an unfamiliar script. "That's Hapan. It identifies this as a product of the Royal Armaments Guild of Charubah."

She knows Hapan, Noone thought. *Another surprise*. "Kid, the Hapes Cluster has been sealed off from the galaxy for three thousand years. I've never even heard of—"

"The Gun of Command fires a magnetic burst strong enough to temporarily scramble the brain of even the strongest foot soldier," Kels continued. "It turns beings into weak-minded morons who follow any order they're given, no matter how outrageous. Simply put, it's irresistible."

Noone leaned back heavily in his seat. "I see. I think I'm beginning to see why Ritinki and Vop were so interested in this little box."

Kels nodded. "There's no limit to what an ambitious and scruple-free crimelord could accomplish with a fully functional Gun of Command."

"In that case," Noone grinned broadly and laced his fingers behind his head, "we don't want Guttu's greasy paws on the trigger."

Dawson's mouth opened in astonishment. "Boss, what you're saying is—"

"What I'm saying," he interrupted, "is blast Guttu out the airlock. There are plenty of groups out there who'd pay an emperor's ransom for this gadget. The Corporate Sector Authority, the Rebel Alliance, the Empire—"

Sonax uttered a hiss that was low and full of menace. Her hatred of the Empire ran deep, and all of them knew it. Noone held up his hands. "Okay, maybe not the Imps. But we're sitting on a crysopaz mine here, and I'm not about to voluntarily turn the deed over to that stinking Hutt."

"But what about the *Borogove*?" Dawson wailed

Noone made a sweeping gesture that encompassed the expansive passenger cabin. "I rather like our new accommodations, myself. Comfy chairs, greel–wood paneling, and a galley selection to kill for. We've always dreamed of making a big heist. Well, my friends, this is it."

"But Ritinki—"

"The Bimm is dead," Noone said, getting to his feet and heading down the arching corridor towards the cockpit. "Nobody left in that room could possibly have survived."

He reached the helm and settled into the pilot's seat. "This ship is ours now," he said, flipping the startup switches. "But if you really miss that old rattletrap all that much, Dawson, you're welcome to come back here sometime and try to break her out of impound."

Sonax glided into a seat behind him and took up her customary navigator's position. Hands dancing across the control board, Noone brought them out of the enshrouding nebula. The varicolored gasses parted like a curtain. With a triumphant whoop, he threw the overmuscled space yacht into a tight barrel roll.

"Hang on tight, folks," he shouted exuberantly. "We've got a fortune to make."

The starlines shivered, and the *Asaari Wind* vanished into hyperspace.

Roleplaying Game Statistics

■ Cecil Noone

Type: Thief Band Leader
DEXTERITY 3D
Blaster pistol 5D+1, brawling parry 5D, dodge 4D+1
KNOWLEDGE 4D
Alien species 6D, cultures 5D+1, languages 7D, planetary systems 4D+2, streetwise 7D, value 6D
MECHANICAL 2D
Space transports 5D
PERCEPTION 3D+2
Bargain 5D+2, con 6D, gambling 6D+1, gambling: sabacc 7D
STRENGTH 2D+1
Brawling 4D
TECHNICAL 3D
Space transports repair 5D
Character Points: 13
Move: 10
Equipment: Blaster pistol (4D), shielded comlink, sabacc deck

Capsule: Cecil Noone grew up as the privileged son of wealthy idealists, crusaders in the insurgent movement known as Freedom's Sons. Their piety and political rhetoric eventually became too much for Noone to swallow; at the age of thirteen, he stole a decommissioned Freedom's Sons' courier ship and naively tried to sell it to a gang of shipjackers on Byblos. The chuckling thieves took the vessel and all his pocket cash, in exchange for letting him live.

Noone survived on the streets of Byblos through petty theft and con games. He graduated from simple smash–and–grab thievery to fleecing rich tourists in rigged sabacc games on Atzerri and Ixtlar. Over the decades, he started taking on associates and accepting commissions from the shadowy world of organized crime. Noone's career has not been what most would describe as successful—heists or scams that go off without a hitch are inevitably countered with catastrophic failures. Though he would argue the fact vociferously, his small organization has never made it out of the minor leagues. Still, neither Noone nor anyone who works with him has yet to apprehended, no matter how badly a job is botched.

Kels Turkhorn

Type: Young Pickpocket
DEXTERITY 4D
Blaster: hold-out blaster 5D, dodge 5D, melee combat: vibro–shiv 5D, pickpocket 7D, running 5D+2
KNOWLEDGE 3D
Cultures: Hapan cluster 3D+2, languages 4D, streetwise 5D+1, value 5D
MECHANICAL 2D+1
PERCEPTION 3D+2
Con 5D, hide 5D+1, sneak 6D
STRENGTH 2D
Brawling: martial arts 5D, climbing/jumping 5D+1
TECHNICAL 3D
Character Points: 10
Move: 10
Equipment: Hold-out blaster (3D), vibro–shiv in boot (STR+1D+2), comlink

Capsule: Kels has spoken very little of her past since joining up with Noone's group three months ago, and nobody has pressed her for details. This is a good thing, since she has no desire to discuss the bitter string of betrayals, deceits, and exploitation that comprise her seventeen years of life.

In dizzying succession, Kels has moved from abandoned waif to galley slave on a pirate raider, to a member of Noone's outfit, with dozens of disreputable stopovers in between. She is an extremely competent thief for her age, and is smart enough to know that she doesn't know everything. Kels is tough and self–reliant, and keeps her true emotions hidden behind a wall of detached sarcasm.

Daniel Wallace

Hass Sonax

Type: Sluissi Cyborg
DEXTERITY 2D
Dodge 2D+2
KNOWLEDGE 3D
Business 4D,
planetary systems 5D
MECHANICAL 2D
Astrogation 4D+1
PERCEPTION 2D+2
Forgery 5D
STRENGTH 2D+1
TECHNICAL 5D
Capital ship repair 4D+1, computer programming/repair 7D, droid programming 5D, security 6D+2
Special Abilities:
Borg Construct: Increases computer programming/repair reflected in stats above. Increases any Knowledge or Technical skill by +1D. Can hold three knowledge cartridges, with a maximum of 6D worth of additional information.
Character Points: 11
Move: 9
Equipment: BioTech borg construct AJ^6, several knowledge cartridges

Capsule: The daughter of dockworkers, Hass Sonax was forced to learn the art of starship repair at an early age in order to support her struggling family. She and her five sisters worked twelve–hour shifts at the Sluis Van stardocks, until a visiting Imperial Star Destroyer announced two temporary maintenance positions. Eager for adventure and cash, Sonax and her sister Resh signed on. They were treated as slaves, and quickly became disillusioned by the Imperial military's contempt for aliens. Later, when a faulty fusion coil caused a spectacular blowout and a thirty–six hour mission delay, the ship's captain strode into the tech room and had Resh executed on the spot. Sick with shock, Sonax jumped ship when the war vessel reached the Roon system. She drifted between planets and jobs, eventually accepting a cyborg headband while working as an accountant on Kelrodo-Ai.

Sonax tends to be irritable and withdrawn; apparently from the dehumanizing borg implant, the memory of her sister's death, or some combination of both.

Dawson

Type: Tynnan Demolitions Expert
DEXTERITY 2D+2
Dodge 4D, grenade 5D+2, missile weapons: grenade launcher 6D
KNOWLEDGE 2D+1
Survival 5D
MECHANICAL 3D
Space transports 4D+1
PERCEPTION 4D
Search 4D+1
STRENGTH 2D
Stamina 5D, swimming 9D
TECHNICAL 3D+2
Demolitions 7D, security 6D+1, space transports repair 4D
Special Abilities:
Low Temperatures: Tynnans are native to near-frigid waters and suffer no penalties when in extreme cold temperatures (equal to or above -50 degrees Celsius).
Swimming: Tynnans are excellent swimmers and can hold their breath for as many minutes as their stamina die code.
Character Points: 12
Move: 6 (walking); 11 (swimming)
Equipment: Ocular enhancer (+1D to Search), detonator satchel, set of safecracking tools, datapad

Capsule: On the wealthy, state–run world of Tynna, no one has to work if they don't want to. Dawson didn't. A coterie of successful uncles tried to interest the young Tynnan in the stock market, but Dawson spent the first eighteen years of his life playing water–wall and finding new, fun ways to blow things up. Then the congratulatory message came over the comm—the Tynnan government, traditionally selected by lottery, had a vacancy, and Dawson had "won" the honor of filling the position. Horrified at facing a lifetime in community meetings and orbital platform control legislation, Dawson fled the planet. He hasn't been back in ten years.

Dawson's ability to make things explode has been appreciated by a number of underworld clients since, but he has stayed loyally with Noone for the last four years. Dawson can be impulsive, single-minded, and even oblivious to his surroundings, but he knows his craft well. He is quite fond of Sonax, despite their frequent personality clashes.

Daniel Wallace

Song of the Clouds

Craft: Brathflen Corporation's Manollium-class Herdship
Type: Ithorian herdship
Scale: Capital
Length: 980 meters
Skill: Capital ship piloting: Herdship
Crew: 800, gunners: 24, skeleton 375/+5
Crew Skill: Capital ship gunnery 3D, capital ship piloting 3D, capital ship shields 4D, sensors 3D+2
Passengers: 1,050
Cargo Capacity: 500,000 metric tons
Consumables: 1 month
Hyperdrive Multiplier: x4
Hyperdrive Backup: x14
Nav Computer: Yes
Maneuverability: +1
Space: 1
Hull: 4D
Shields: 4D
Sensors:
Passive: 40/0D
Scan: 60/1D
Search: 100/2D
Focus: 3/2D+1
Weapons:
10 Ion Cannons
Fire Arc: 3 front, 2 left, 2 right, 3 rear
Crew: 2
Skill: Capital ship gunnery
Fire Control: 1D
Space Range: 1–10/25/50
Damage: 3D
2 Tractor Beam Projectors
Fire Arc: 1 left, 1 right
Crew: 2
Skill: Capital ship gunnery
Fire Control: 2D
Space Range: 1–5/15/30
Damage: 5D

Capsule: Ithorian herdships are mobile bazaars, roaming the hyperlanes and attracting merchants, traders, and collectors. The *Song of the Clouds* features a vast cargo hold, a trader's plaza, and a garden/arboretum beneath a clear transparisteel dome. In keeping with the Ithorian reverence for life of all kinds, the *Song*'s defenses consist of heavy shielding and ion cannons designed to incapacitate, rather than destroy, enemy craft.

Asaari Wind

Craft: Modified SoroSuub Luxury 3000
Type: Private Space Yacht
Scale: Starfighter
Length: 50 meters
Skill: Space transports: SoroSuub Luxury 3000
Crew: 2, gunners: 3, skeleton: 1/+10
Passengers: 10
Cargo Capacity: 70 metric tons
Consumables: 1 month
Hyperdrive Multiplier: x1
Hyperdrive Backup: x5
Nav Computer: Yes
Maneuverability: 1D
Space: 7
Atmosphere: 350; 1,000 kmh
Hull: 3D
Shields: 3D
Sensors:
Passive: 25/D
Scan: 50/D
Search: 75/2D=2
Focus: 3/3D
Weapons:
2 Light Laser Cannons (fire–linked)
Fire Arc: Front
Skill: Starship gunnery
Fire Control: 2D
Space Range: 1–5/10/17
Atmosphere Range: 100–500/1/1.7 km
Damage: 4D
2 Medium Ion Cannons (fire–linked)
Fire Arc: Front
Skill: Starship gunnery
Fire Control: 2D
Space Range: 1–3/7/36
Atmosphere Range: 100–300/700/3.6km
Damage: 6D
2 Heavy Laser Cannons
Fire Arc: Turret
Crew: 1
Skill: Starship gunnery
Fire Control: 2D
Space Range: 1–3/12/25
Atmosphere Range: 100/1.2km/2.5km
Damage: 5D
1 Turbolaser
Fire Arc: Rear
Crew: 1
Skill: Capital ship gunnery
Fire Control: 3D
Space Range: 3–15/35/75
Atmosphere Range: 300–1.5km/3.5km/7.5km
Damage: 7D

Capsule: Ritinki the Bimm, a ruthless crimelord who was at the center of several successful protection rackets and extortion rings purchased the *Asaari Wind* directly from SoroSuub just as work was completed on it in the shipyard. He wanted a vessel that was free of unpleasant legacies left by former owners, such as ill–considered upgrades or tracking devices hidden in the ship's systems by Imperial or Sector Ranger infiltrators.

Ritinki has nonetheless had several major modifications performed on the *Asaari Wind*. The ship is a rather unique combination between a pleasure craft and a small combat starship, with speed, maneuverability, and weapons compliments far exceeding the standards expected from personal yachts.

The weapons of the *Asaari Wind* include forward–mounted, linked laser and ion cannons that can be fired from the ship's bridge, two turreted laser cannons, and a rear–mounted turbolaser installed where most yacht's feature an open platform for passengers to enjoy the out–of–doors while on–planet. The hull and shields have also been upgraded from the standard. Finally, the primary and secondary hyperdrives on the vessel, as well as the ion engines and repulsorlifts have all been replaced with units typically found on larger ships, or with top–of–the–line Sienar Fleet Systems drives. Ritinki also installed a slave circuit to start the ship by remote. Once the engines have been warmed up, an auto–pilot guides the ship to his current location, using the ignition command as a homing signal. (This feature only works when used with a transmitter designed exclusively for Ritinki by a moonlighting Industrial Automaton engineer.)

Unlike many starship owners he attempt to push their vessel beyond its specifications, Ritinki has been very careful to make sure that none of the modifications to the *Asaari Wind* are stable and will never burn out themselves or other components of the ship's systems.

While he wanted to give his yacht teeth, Ritinki did not want to sacrifice any of its luxury. The ship's five cabins are spacious and equipped with lush double bunks and soft glow-lamps. The ship features exotic wood–paneling throughout, except on the bridge and in the galley. The galley includes a Gourmet Food Master 500 and ample stores for fresh food. The upper deck features an observation lounge with plenty of comfortable couches and a jet–stream meditation pool. Although the external observation platform has been replaced with a turbolaser pod, the lounge still affords travelers with a breathtaking view of the starry vistas of realspace, or the hypnotic swirls of hyperspace.

Hapan Gun of Command

Model: Charubah Industries Gun of Command
Type: Neural–Effect Blaster
Scale: Character
Skill: Blaster: Gun of Command
Ammo: 6
Cost: 17,500
Availability: 4, R or X
Fire Rate: 1
Range: 3–7/ 25/50
Damage: 5D, Special (see below)
Game Notes: A successful hit with the Hapan Gun of Command lowers the target's ability to resist orders from the wielder of the weapon The target uses his *willpower* skill against the Gun of Command's damage dice instead of *Strength*. Use the chart below to determine the Gun of Command's effects.

If the target's *willpower* falls to 0D or below, the character enters a trance–like state and will automatically accept any command from the wielder of the weapon, within reason. If an order is issued that will cause immediate harm to the target (such as commanding him to jump off a cliff), the target will "snap" out of the trance, voiding the effects of the Gun of Command completely.

Damage Roll ≥ *Willpower*	
0–3	-1D to target's *willpower* for 1 round.
4–8	-1D to target's *willpower* for 1D rounds.
9–12	-2D to target's *willpower* for 2D minutes.
13–15	-2D to target's *willpower* for 2D hours.
16+	-3D to target's *willpower* for 3D hours.

Capsule: The Gun of Command was designed by the technologically advanced society of Charuba in the Hapes Cluster. The idea behind the device was to disarm criminals by ordering them to drop their weapons rather than shooting them with a destructive energy weapon.

In the end, however, the Gun of Command was prohibitively expensive, and outfitting every law enforcement team with one would have easily bankrupted many regional governments.

A Gun of Command is rare in the Hapes Cluster, and the existence of these devices is unknown by virtually all other peoples of the galaxy.

Game information created by Daniel Wallace, Steve Miller, and Eric S. Trautmann.

TASARIQ
THE CRYSTAL PLANET

By Tom Moldvay and Steve Miller

Illustrated by Jeff Menges — Maps by Tim Bobko

"Tasariq: The Crystal Planet" is a source article for the *Star Wars Roleplaying Game*. It includes all the information game masters need to incorporate this new planetary system, with its unique native species and culture, into an ongoing campaign—or use as the starting point of an all–new, Tasariq based campaign.

The designers have attempted to make Tasariq a place where most types of adventures can be fit in. It is a rough frontier world within reach of the Core systems; the Empire's presence here is growing, and the Alliance has yet to establish any real presence in the system; smuggler's are doing their utmost to evade Imperial tariffs; and a handful of corporations are starting to establish firm presences here. The planet's surface is a barren wilderness with a poisonous atmosphere, while craters dotting the planet are packed with cities, smuggler's hide–outs, and camps of miners looking to make their fortunes through rich strikes of highly sought–after tasar crystals.

Tasariq is described in this article as it existed in the years between the events of *A New Hope* and *The Empire Strikes Back*; the Rebel Alliance is growing in strength, the Empire is at its mightiest, and the Jedi Knights are but a dim memory. The Empire's influence might grow stronger here, or a few dedicated individuals might sway the world to the side of the Alliance.

System Datafile Entry

System: Tasar
Star: Gyrlat (yellow)
Orbital Bodies:

Name	Planet Type	Moons
Arganu	searing ball	0
Tasariq	terrestrial	1
Deadbelt	asteroid belt	0
Trenal	gas giant	14

The Tasar system is located in the Inner Rim, but was not deemed worthy of exploration or colonization until the final decades of the Old Republic; the system was too far from standard shipping lanes, and long-range scans indicated that only one world could support life, and that it was barely fit at that.

Near the end of the Clone Wars, the first detailed survey of the system was conducted by an Old Republic Admiral looking for a suitable location for a hidden shipyard. The hope was that new, untapped, rich mineral resources would be discovered. The hope was in vain.

Arganu, the system's innermost planet was discovered to have rich mineral deposits but the intense radiation and heat from the star made mining those resources impractical.

Tasariq, the only planet capable of supporting humanoid life—and barely able at that—had been subjected to intense meteor bombardment at some time in the distant past. The world had far too few mineral resources to support a shipyard. However, it was found to be the source of an amazingly beautiful type of crystal that so far has not been found anywhere else in the galaxy. The native sentient species believes to this day that these crystals hold mystical powers that improve the health of mind and body. While less advanced technologically than many civilized species of the galaxy, the Tasari in general do not suffer from xenophobia or a reluctance to be part of the galactic civilization. They welcome off–worlders on Tasariq and undertook several large construction projects soon after their initial contact with the Old Republic to encourage spacefarers and traders to come to their world. The world is orbited by a moon comprised of solid ice.

Tasariq's atmosphere is Type III on the planet's surface, but a number of factors have combined to produce Type I atmosphere at the bottom of large craters in which the Tasari civilization is centered.

Deadbelt is a massive asteroid field that rings the system. Scans indicate that it might at one time have been the system's third planet, although the natives claim that it is merely a small portion of a meteor swarm that swept through the system millennia ago. While many of the asteroids are large enough to construct facilities upon, once again there were not enough minerals to suit the Admiral's purpose.

The outermost world is a gas giant with 14 moons and an elaborate ring system. One of the moons is capable of supporting humanoid life, but the local flora and fauna is so ferocious that the trouble to develop the moon for settlement has thus far outweighed the need to do so. Plans to develop the system were abandoned for good.

Tasariq is a quaint, backwater system with friendly natives. They do not have interstellar flight technology of their own.

System Datafile Addendum/Update: In recent years, a minor industry has sprung up around the mining and exporting of "tasar crystals," a rare mineral resource found only on Tasariq. These crystals have no apparent practical application, but many races find them ascetically pleasing and they are gaining in popularity as parts of jewelry. The indigenous alien population encourage and support this development. They remain a friendly, simple–minded and primitive people, despite ongoing efforts to educate them and bring them up to a cultural level that matches the rest of the civilized aliens of the Empire

The Imperial Ministry of Tourism has issued a travel advisory in regards to Tasariq. While Tasariq City, Elikann Crater, and the Tasari ceremonial capitol—Barimoq Crater—are listed in their catalogue of "Wonders of the Galaxy," they warn that the mining activity on the world has attracted a rougher element than was seen on the world in the past. Those who travel to Tasariq are urged to beware of thieves and con artists. The local Ministry of Tourism branch office maintains a list of bonded guides and bodyguards who, for reasonable fees, can insure safe and pleasurable visits to all of Tasariq's important sites.

Tom Moldvay and Steve Miller

Tasariq World Summary

Tasariq

Type: Terrestrial crater bottoms; inhospitable surface
Temperature: Temperate crater bottoms; hot and cool extremes on surface
Atmosphere: Type I in crater bottoms ranging to Type III on surface
Hydrosphere: Moderate in inhabited craters; dry on surface
Gravity: Standard
Terrain: Barren desert surface with habitable crater system
Length of Day: 25 standard hours
Length of Year: 372 local days
Sapient Species: Humans, Iotrans, Sullustans, Tasari (N)
Starports: 1 Stellar class (Tasariq City), 2 Standard class (Barimoq Crater and Elikann Crater)
Population: 74 million native; 100,000 non–native
Planet Function: Mining, tourism; native agriculture and developing manufacturing
Government: Imperial governor; native eldership councils
Tech Level: Space (around starports only), industrial merging into atomic in native cities
Major Exports: Minerals (Tasar crystals)
Major Imports: High technology, luxury goods

Tasariq is an Inner Rim planet situated far from the usual trade routes. According to native legends, it was once an idyllic world, a temperate planet covered with plains and rolling hills. The native Tasari, small hairless bipeds with scaly skin, had developed Atomic Age–level technology and were just beginning to explore the other worlds of their system. Then disaster struck. A meteor shower of unprecedented proportion swept through the system. Tasariq was almost shattered, and Tasari society was thrown back to the stone age. Even worse, the planetary ecosystem was permanently altered. The atmosphere became heavily contaminated with light gases that were released from beneath the planet's surface by the impacts of meteors.

However, the very craters born from the destruction of Tasari civilization and Tasariq's ecosystem also turned out to be the salvation of sentient life on the planet. The largest craters were several kilometers deep. Rivers emptied into them to form lakes, and the water plus the lower altitude yielded a higher percentage of oxygen, making the atmosphere in the craters breathable by humanoids. On the planet surface, the percentage of lighter gases is so great that most beings can only survive if they wear breath masks.

Tasari civilization is now focused in the deep craters. At the very bottom are lakes and lowlands that can be irrigated to grow crops. The Tasari build their cities into the sides of the craters, burrowing into the earth. Over the centuries, the Tasari have continued their digging, creating a complex web of underground tunnels that unites the scattered crater–cities.

Tasariq and the Republic

Tasariq was explored by survey teams near the end of the Clone Wars. The natives were immediate and firm supporters of the Old Republic, and did all they could to encourage off–worlders to bring their wondrous new technologies to Tasariq. For millennia, the Tasari have passed down many tales of how their species stood on the threshold of traveling to the stars when the great disaster happened. It has become a collective dream of the Tasari to someday travel to the stars and the arrival of the Old Republic survey teams was the way to fulfillment of that dream.

The Tasari as a people were so excited about becoming part of a greater Galactic civilization that the world was a granted full membership in the Republic within a few years of the establishment of formal relations. To encourage trade and investments, Elikann Crater was donated as a settlement for off–worlders, while the Tasari volunteered much of the labor used in building the artificial island that holds Tasariq City spaceport was built on an artificial island in a large crater. As the natives became better versed in the technology of the Galactic civilization, they assisted in the construction of three underground rapid–transit tube connecting Tasariq City, Elikann Crater, and the Tasari ceremonial capitol, Barimoq Crater. This transit system is now one of the cornerstones of both business and tourism activity on the planet.

Tasariq Under the Empire

Despite the intentions and best efforts of the Tasari, their world remains a distant backwater planet, too remote from commercial space lanes to merit development. Very few major corporations have any interest in developing Tasariq as a market so the system is likely to remain obscure for decades to come.

Since Tasariq first entered the Old Republic the planet has enjoyed a modest tourist industry. Tasari cliff–side cities are marvels of ingenuity, and monuments of the Tasari's ancient culture—long–abandoned temples and the shattered remains of surface cities—are scattered across the planet In recent years, however, Tasariq has evolved into a market exporting a unique commodity: tasar crystals.

Tasar crystals were formed as a result of the meteoric bombardment. The intense heat of meteor passage through the atmosphere, the high pressure of impact, and decades of planet–wide volcanic activity following the deadly rain from space combined in a unique way to create exceptionally beautiful crystals of vibrant colors. Tasar crystals cannot be duplicated artificially and so far nothing like them has been discovered anywhere else in the galaxy.

The Tasari believe that tasar crystals promote healing and good health, and all carry at least one tasar crystal as a good luck charm. Many Tasari even claim that the tasar crystals induce telepathy and other psychic powers in their owners. Most off–worlders dismiss such claims as baseless superstition, but it is hard for even the most ardent skeptic to deny that some tasar crystals have a noticeable soothing effect, as if they radiated peace and tranquility.

One thing is undeniable, however. Tasar crystals are among some of the most beautiful items in the galaxy. Tasar crystals come in a variety of colors and sizes. The colors are bright and vibrant, and the sizes vary from a few millimeters to as much as three meters in length and width. Some crystals have several colors blending into each other or swirled together. The more colors in a crystal, the greater its value. The famous Rainbow Labyrinth crystal sold for 50 million credits. Even a small tasar crystal can sell for thousands of credits.

As word of the beauty of tasar crystals has spread throughout the Core sectors, they have become highly sought–after items. For generations, the Tasari have been mining tasar crystals as they constructed their cities in the crater walls. Each family has been handing down ever–growing hoards of the crystals to successive generations. The majority of Tasari are now pooling their family crystals, selling them to free traders who transport them to gem dealers in the Core to fund technological development on their world. They have also opened an Imperial–accredited university and pay high salaries to off–world instructors so they can gain the technical know–how to build and maintain the technology.

The Tasari are not the only ones who are engaging in the export of tasar crystals. An ever–growing number of off–worlders are finding their way to Tasariq, lured by the promise of making a fortune by mining tasar crystals.

The world of Tasariq does not offer easy wealth, however. The craters inhabited by Tasari have long since been mined out. To find new tasar crystal deposits, it is necessary to risk the harsh conditions of the surface, or to scale the sides of as–of–yet unexplored craters.

As independent miners comb the surface and craters for crystals, new settlements are created, particularly in areas where crystals are discovered. Initially, these settlements are merely collections of pressure tents and temporary shelters for the heavy mining equipment. If it is a rich discovery of crystals, particularly in a crater, than efforts are undertaken to make the settlement more permanent; rivers are diverted and vegetation is cultivated to insure a breathable atmosphere, and prefab buildings are brought in and raised. Most of the construction for these off–worlder settlements (called "boom–towns") is performed by TranStar Construction, one of the few interstellar companies to have invested significant manpower and resources into Tasariq.

The boom–towns quickly fill with cantinas, gambling dens, and other less savory entertainments designed to part highly paid workers from their credits and miners from their crystals. These diversions naturally attract a share of criminals, and the boom–towns can occasionally become dangerous places for the unwary. While violent criminals present threats, con artists also look for victims in the boom–towns. In ancient times, the Tasari viewed the tasar crystals as "gifts from the gods," and they built temples in their

honor. It is rumored that there are lost temples, hidden in remote craters or deep inside the earth, filled with choice Tasar crystals. "Maps" to these lost temples can be bought at any mining camp.

The Tasari encourage the growth of boom–towns, for even after the crystals run out, and a boom–town is abandoned almost as quickly as it sprang up, the crater remains livable. The Tasari then have another place on their world that can be exploited for tourism or as the site of a new spaceport or some form of industry. For example, the local office of the Ministry of Tourism has recently taken to conducting tours to an abandoned boom–town where tourists get to experience the life of miners by digging for their own tasar crystals. (Ministry workers "salt" a played–out mining tunnel with small, single–colored crystals.)

The Empire is involved with the extraction of tasar crystals in more ways than through the Ministry of Tourism. Shortly after the Emperor's rise to power, he declared that the Tasariq would remain a free people as long as they paid taxes to the Empire. An Imperial governor was appointed, and he was given a small Army garrison to maintain order, and a Guardian–class light cruiser, a pair Skipray blastboats, four Z–95 Headhunters, and half a wing of TIE starfighters to patrol the space around the planet.

The current governor is a Chandrilese named Dem Keval, and with the increasing activity on Tasariq, he is finding his military resources stretched to the limit. The garrison only able to control key installations and the lack of law enforcement in the mining camps is of great concern to the governor. His request for additional troops has been denied repeatedly by the sector moff, so he has entered into a contract with a clan of Iotrans who patrol the outlying regions of Tasariq under the guise of the Tasariq Rangers. The Iotrans more than adequately pick up the slack for the Imperial Army forces stationed on Tasariq. Governor Keval permits the Tasari to police themselves so long it is understood that the Tasari laws do not cover non–Tasari.

The governor and the Tasari are still accountable for the taxes to Coruscant, despite the extra money spent on the Tasariq Rangers. Governor Keval's sense of honor and personal pride will not allow him to let Imperial Advisors and other bureaucrat declare the Tasari a slave race, so he has ordered additional taxes leveled against all new tasar crystal finds. A stiff tariff is also added to all imports, thus forcing up the price of off–world products. The natural result has been a marked increase in smuggling and a thriving black market. The Imperial custom force on Tasariq is too small to be very effective against smugglers, but large enough that it still poses enough of a threat that amateurs are discouraged from conducting runs to Tasariq.

Native Lifeforms of Tasariq

There is a saying that is popular among anthropologists, biologists, and xenobiologists: there is no place where lifeforms cannot exist, and if survival is possible, life will adapt.

The world of Tasariq is a perfect example of this. Although this temperate world's climate and eco–sphere was fundamentally altered, the world's sentient species survived, as did innumerable forms of plant, fungus, insect, and mammalian lifeforms. The Tasari themselves were responsible for saving some species—for example, they continued to grow various kinds of grain in the habitable craters while also cultivating plants that were highly efficient in converting carbon dioxide to oxygen in order to keep their air in the craters breathable. Many other creatures and plants survived through sheer tenacity and an ability to mutate to survive under the new conditions.

It is not possible to cover all the lifeforms that exist on Tasariq. In this article, we limit ourselves to a look at the Tasari and three of the world's most dangerous beasts. Gamemasters who use Tasariq as the location for an extended campaign may wish to expand the selection of creatures. Those in need of inspiration for what kind of alien creatures might be found on Tasariq can turn to *Creatures of the Galaxy*, a supplement for the *Star Wars Roleplaying Game*. If reader demand is strong enough, additional details on Tasariq may even be presented here in the *Star Wars Adventure Journal*.

The Tasari

Appearance and Biology: Tasari are hairless humanoids with scaly skin. They have large beaked noses and feathery crests that give their faces a superficial resemblance to those of birds. They tend to be shorter and of lighter build than the average human. Their natural lifespan is about 120 standard years.

Tasari mate for life, and rarely does one of their species take a second mate after the first one passes away. The females lay three to five eggs at a time, and they do not lay a second clutch until the young from the first batch have been raised. Both parents take part in raising the young. Tasari mature into adulthood in 15 standard years.

Temperament: Tasari are typically inquisitive, creative, and open–minded. They are also quick–witted, with sharp senses of humor and an innate ability to evaluate situations and arrive at decisions swiftly while taking into account potential long–term impacts of their actions. They have a love for creating and discovering new things and rarely pass up the opportunity to learn something new about a person or a piece of technology they encounter.

History and Culture: Tasari history and culture both have been shaped by the disaster that altered their world and destroyed their ancient hi–tech civilization. Their history is a chronicle of ingenuity as they adapted to life in the deep craters and underground and struggled to rebuild their lost technology and civilization.

The foundation of Tasari culture is the family. Individual family units are united in clans, each of which claims to trace their roots back to one or more legendary Tasari who are credited with playing a role in saving the race from destruction after the meteor strikes millennia ago. The clans are each led by a Council of Elders, the heads of which meet twice a year in Barimoq Crater, the Tasari ceremonial capitol. Here, the Elders set policies for dealing with off–worlders and make revisions or additions to the Tasari legal codes to reflect changes in their rapidly evolving society.

The Tasari—from the individual families through to the Council of Tribal Elders—defer to the eldest among them. As a people, they have great respect for the wisdom that age and experience bestows in a being. They do not consider one sex superior to the other, but only use age as a guideline. The Elders, in turn, recognize that the advice and opinions of younger Tasariq is important for the ongoing evolution of their society, particularly if the advice offered by Tasari who have experienced the galaxy at large.

The Council of Elders generally guide the Tasari in such a way that they remain open to friendly interaction with off–worlders. As Tasari technological and scientific know–how increases, the Elders are also increasingly encouraging Tasari, particularly those who graduate from the university, to journey into the rest of the galaxy and increase their knowledge of the beings and cultures that exist out there and then return to Tasariq to start teaching courses of their own.

A dark subcurrent of Tasari culture is a resurgence of primitive blood cults. In the centuries after the meteor shower struck Tasariq, the Tasari reverted to barbaric practices. Among these were blood sacrifices to the tasar crystals, as the Tasari believed only by spilling blood could they unlock the mystical potential of the colorful stones. They also believed the sacrifices would appease the dark gods that had sent destruction from the sky.

Although the Tasari outgrew these beliefs as a culture long ago, a few communities of Tasari still hold to them. In recent years, a growing number of Tasari have traveled off–world and have seen the treatment the human–dominated Empire has given other alien races, like the Wookiees and Mon Calamari. This in turn has caused many Tasari to grow fearful for the future of *their* species and world and they have turned to the old ways in an attempt to make the galaxy safe for themselves; after all, blood sacrifices to the tasar crystals prevented any further meteor strikes.

Technology Level: The Tasari were on the threshold of rediscovering Atomic–level technology when the Republic established contact with their world. They had not developed blaster technology but instead relied on slug–throwing firearms. At present, the Tasari culture uses an odd mixture of their own fairly primitive equipment and off–world devices, partly due to the heavy tariffs imposed by the Empire on imports.

The Tasari founded a university on their world some years ago, hoping to attract off–world teachers to their planet in order to gain the know–how to construct their own starships, fusion plants, and other hallmarks of a Space Age culture and thus fully join the Galactic civilization. Although they managed to attract top instructors initially, their university has suffered in recent years. COMPNOR has placed the university on a list of "unreliable" institutions because it is operated primarily for the benefit of an alien society, and many of the best academians and instructors are fearful of being blacklisted. Others, however, join the faculty at Tasariq University as a way of protesting the racist policies of the New Order, so the Tasari efforts have not come to a complete standstill.

Trade and Technology: The tasar crystal trade dominates the Tasari economy. While they operate hundreds of highly efficient factories producing everything from footwear to aircraft, Tasari technology is too primitive to interest other worlds.

The Tasari Council of Elders oversees the ever–expanding efforts to mine tasar crystals, with the blessing of the Imperial governor. They impose no limits on who can mine where, but insist that all claims be registered with the Imperial authorities in Tasariq City. (This is partly at the insistence of Governor Keval, but the

Elders also understand the importance of Tasariq meeting its tax obligations to the Empire.)

Tasari in the Galaxy: Tasari are only rarely encountered off of Tasariq; they are still developing a complete understanding of the intricacies of space travel. Those who are encountered are frequently rootless travelers working their way from system to system in temporary jobs as technicians or as low–level lab assistants. Other Tasari fall in with free–traders, smugglers or other beings on the fringes of respectable society. No matter where they are encountered, though, they are on a quest for knowledge about the galaxy at large and rarely remain in one place for long. The Tasari have yet to venture much further than the Inner Rim worlds.

The Tasari

Attribute Dice: 12D
DEXTERITY 1D/4D
KNOWLEDGE 1D/4D
MECHANICAL 1D/3D
PERCEPTION 2D/5D
STRENGTH 1D/3D+2
TECHNICAL 1D/2D+2
Special Abilities:
Inheritance: Tasari can inherit Tasar crystals which will give them special Force powers. Only important characters will have such crystals. For examples of powers, and determining inheritance at random, see Tasar crystals.
Story Factors:
Force-sensitive: Because of their proximity to Tasar crystals, more Tasari are Force–sensitive than is usual. See the tasar crystal rules later in this article.
Move: 10/12
Size: 1.4–1.7 meters tall

Personality Notes: The Tasari as a species are friendly, outgoing, open–minded, and always willing to try something new, or venture to some as–of–yet unexplored territory. They have a virtually insatiable curiosity about all things. They are not capricious, however. They typically weigh potential outcomes of their actions before deciding on a course. Once a course has been chosen, they are not afraid to reverse themselves or admit mistakes once new knowledge comes to light.

Suggested Skills: The Tasari are a peaceful people, so most of their skills are focused around *Knowledge, Mechanical, Perception*, and *Technical*. They frequently conform to the templates of Armchair Historian, Curious Explorer (both presented in the sourcebook included with the *Star Wars Gamemaster Screen Revised*) or the Tasari Student on the next page.

Tasari Student

Character Name: ______________________

Player: ______________________

Species: Human

Sex: ____________ **Age:** ____________

Height: ____________ **Weight:** ____________

Physical Description: ______________________

Background: Your people need help to develop Tasariq to its fullest potential. Knowledge is important and off–worlders hold the keys to that knowledge. You have already studied as many off-world skills as you can on Tasariq and now the time has come to leave your world. You bid farewell to your family and friends, and begin your adventure into the unknown.

Personality: You are driven by curiosity. You are intelligent and learn quickly. You're idealistic, but practical. You want to learn all you can, but have to survive in the meantime.

Objectives: To see the universe, learn useful skills and improve the ones you already have. Eventually, you will return home and teach what you have learned to other Tasari.

A Quote: "How does that work? Show me, please."

Connection With Other Characters: You could serve as guide or interpreter for the other characters while on Tasariq in return for passage off the planet.

DEXTERITY 3D
- Firearms ____

MECHANICAL 2D+1
- Ground vehicle operation ____
- First aid ____
- Ground vehicle repair ____

STRENGTH 2D+1
- Climbing/Jumping ____
- Stamina ____

KNOWLEDGE 4D
- Alien Species ____
- Cultures ____
- Languages ____
- Planetary Systems ____
- Survival ____
- Value ____

PERCEPTION 3D+2
- Bargain ____
- Investigation ____
- Persuasion ____
- Search ____

TECHNICAL 2D+2
- Communications ____
- Computer programming/repair ____
- Ground vehicle repair ____

Special Abilities: *Inheritance*: The character inherits one tasar crystal with a power as play begins. The power of the crystal is determined using the rules on page XX.

Move: 10

Force Points: 2

Force Sensitive?: Yes

Dark Side Points:

Character Points:

❑ Wounded
❑ Incapacitated
❑ Mortally Wounded

Equipment: Breath mask, 2 personal oxygen tanks, comlink, datapad, medpac, recording rod, knife, 5-shot revolver, 100 rounds of extra ammunition, 250 credits

Tom Moldvay and Steve Miller

Dangerous Creatures of Tasariq

Spidercat

Type: Temple guardian
DEXTERITY 4D
PERCEPTION 3D
STRENGTH 3D
Special Abilities:
Claws: Spidercats strike victims with barbed claws on their legs for STR +2.
Poisonous bite: The bite attack of a spidercat does 1D damage. Additionally, the victim must roll a moderate or better result against his Strength attribute or be paralyzed for for 1–6 hours.
Move: 12
Size: 2 meters long

Capsule: Spidercats are fur–covered insects that look like a cross between a spider and a cat. In the dark times after the destruction of their society, the Tasari bred spidercats for use as guardians in the temples devoted to the tasar crystals. Even now, more ferocious spidercats (*Dexterity* and *Strength* of 5D each) are found in the areas surrounding the forgotten temples.

Sting–Snake

Type: Ground snake
DEXTERITY 3D
PERCEPTION 3D
STRENGTH 2D
Special Abilities:
Electrical discharge: Sting–Snakes attack by discharging electricity from the stinger in their tail. The sting inflicts 3D damage upon the victim. After an attack, it takes an hour for the snake to build up enough charge for another attack.
Move: 9
Size: 1 meter long

Capsule: Sting–snakes are found in all the habitable craters of Tasariq. They rarely attack humanoids, but can be dangerous if startled or cornered. They are found in greater–than–normal concentrations around the ancient temples because trained sting–snakes were used along with spidercats as temple guardians. (Off–worlders have also discovered that sting–snakes can be trained as attack beasts, and an increasing number of miners are using them to guard their tents and vehicles.)

Tunnel Worm

Type: Earth–burrowing carnivore
DEXTERITY 3D
PERCEPTION 2D
STRENGTH 4D
Special Abilities:
Bite attack: STR +2D damage.
Move: 8
Size: 4 meters long

Capsule: Tunnel Worms are large segmented worms that live in tunnels they burrow in the earth. They can hunt on the surface for hours, living off stored oxygen. They tend to cluster around habitable craters where the most food is available, but concerted efforts are made to keep their numbers down near inhabited craters.

Equipment and Vehicles

All vehicles, weapons and gear from the *Star Wars Roleplaying Game* rulebook and the *Star Wars Sourcebook* is available on Tasariq. In addition, the natives have an array of technologies of their own. While not as advanced, and frequently not as versatile or reliable as that manufactured and used across the galaxy, Tasari weapons and gear do have the benefit of being much cheaper, thanks to the tariffs imposed by the Imperial governor in order to pay the salaries of the Iotran police force he has secured. Those off–worlders either not able to afford black-market prices or simply too honest to turn to such shady characters have been relying on Tasari technology.

Tasari–made equipment can be purchased for the normal price

listed in the rule book, while imports cost three times the normal price if bought in Tasariq City or Elikann Crater, and four times normal if bought in a mining camp such as Roaring Crater. Thus, the characters could buy a Tasari–made knife or breath mask at the normal price, but a pair of macrobinoculars would cost 300 credits. Gamemasters should also keep in mind that the technology level of the native Tasari is substantially lower than the galactic norm. The items manufactured on Tasari are roughly equivalent to what a person might have been able to purchase on Earth in an industrialized nation of the early 20th century. There are a some differences, but this is a good guideline for the gamemaster trying to decide wether an item might be locally manufactured or imported.

For shady characters, imports are offered on the black market for twice the normal cost—a pair of black–market macrobinoculars costs 200 credits, for example. The black market can also provide goods normally illegal on Tasariq (category X) or goods that require a special local or Imperial license to buy or sell (categories F and R). Category R goods, however, cost three times normal while category X goods cost four times normal. To determine the category for an item on Tasariq when there are two possible ratings, choose the higher rating. If there are three possible ratings, take the average rating.

Here is a selection of native–made vehicles and equipment that is widely used by off–worlders and Tasari both.

General Equipment

Blaststicks and Blaststick Detonators

A blaststick is a mining explosive used by Tasari in construction of their underground tunnels. Many offworld crystal miners have also found blaststicks useful in their hunt for crystals—although some crystals are destroyed in the explosion, many survive, and miners who are in a hurry to make a profit are happier picking through rubble than digging into the hard ground or cliff walls.

While blaststicks were once generally available, the unsafe practices of many off–worlders (and the stern suggestions of the Imperial government) has recently caused the Tasari Council of Elders to place limitations on the sale and purchase of blaststicks. Licences issued by the Council are now required for all who would buy or sell the items.

Blaststicks are typically sold in packages of ten, along with a detonator. The blaststicks are generally harmless until they are connected with the detonator through electrical wires. While the blaststicks are naturally destroyed on detonation, the detonator can be used again and again, as long as the detonator is set up outside the blast area. A single detonator can trigger up to five blaststicks at one time, and each can be programmed with as much as a one-minute time delay. They are all triggered by the push of a single button, however.

Blaststicks are inert until coupled with a detonator, but they can be triggered by the stunbolts fired by most blasters.

Blaststick

Model: TasCorp Blaststick
Type: Explosive
Scale: Speeder
Skill: Demolitions
Cost: 50 (per stick)
Availability: F
Blast Radius: 0–2/4/6/8
Damage: 3D/2D+2/2D/1D
Game Notes: A blaststick is treated like a grenade for purposes of determining damage, except they cannot be thrown. Damage is cumulative if more than one blaststick is used.

Blaststick Detonator

Model: TasCorp Detonator Model 3E
Type: Electric explosives detonator
Skill: Demolitions
Cost: 200
Availability: F

Breath Masks

Tasari breath masks function along the same line as the breath masks manufactured across the galaxy. (See pages 225–226 of the *Star Wars Roleplaying Game, Revised and Expanded* rulebook.) The Tasari masks are bulkier and their oxygen supply consists of an airtank that weighs two kilograms. They have an advantage over other breath masks in that the Tasari have developed a way to compress the oxygen (or any other gases a being might need to survive) so that each tank supplies the wearer with an average of six days worth of breathable gases, depending on how much physical exertion the being experiences.

Breath masks and oxygen tanks are sold separately.

Tasari Breath Mask

Model: Bavar Breathing Systems Portable Environmental Support Unit
Type: Breath mask

Tom Moldvay and Steve Miller

Cost: 40 credits
Availability: 3
Game Notes: Tasari breath masks cover the face and nose of humanoid beings. Oxygen is supplied through a hose, from a detachable tank. See the "Oxygen Tanks" entry for additional information.

Mining Kit

The Tasari offer mining kits for sale. A complete kit provides all non–power equipment needed for successful mining, and these are widely used by the native Tasari in their search for tasar crystals. Many cash–poor and ill–prepared off–worlders often start their quest for tasar crystals with these native mining kits.

They include basic tools for manual excavation of tasar crystals or debris resulting from blaststick detonations, a week's worth of military–style dried rations, a breath mask and two personal oxygen tanks. The entire kit is fitted into a sturdy backpack which is designed in such a way that miners can use it to carry tasar crystals once they start eating their rations.

Tasari Mining Kit

Model: TasCorp Essential Miner's Gear
Type: Utility kit for miners
Cost: 200
Availability: 3
Game Notes: A mining kit provides characters excavating tasar crystal with +1D to their *Search* or *mining* skill rolls.

Oxygen Tanks

For those who travel the inhospitable surface of Tasariq, oxygen is a valuable and important commodity. The standard breath masks available throughout the galaxy only work for approximately one standard hour at a time before the filters need to be replaced and the power pack recharged. Tasari oxygen tanks, when used in conjunction with Tasari breath masks or attached to proper valves on vehicles or pressure tents, supply breathable atmosphere gases for an average of six days. Each tank is fitted with a gauge so the user can keep track of how much tine remains before the air supply runs out.

The oxygen tanks come in two different sizes, one for personal use and one for use on vehicles and temporary shelters. The personal oxygen tanks weigh two kilograms, while the vehicle tanks weigh ten kilograms. Both kind of tank is readily available in any major settlement on Tasariq.

The oxygen tanks are intended to be reused, although many off–worlders treat them as disposable due to their relatively low cost. The Tasari virtually always reuse them, and every settlement has at least one Filling Station where the tanks can be pumped full of oxygen again. It costs 1 credit to have a personal tank refilled, and 5 credits for a vehicle tank.

The manufacture of oxygen tanks is a community project for the Tasari, which is one reason why they are very low priced. Tasari who commit minor infractions of tribal law are sentenced to manufacture oxygen tanks for anywhere from one day to six weeks, depending on the crime. Quality control is very strict, and should a criminal produce an oxygen tank that fails the safety inspection, his sentence is extended by an additional week.

Tasari Oxygen Tank

Model: Tasari Elder Council Oxygen Tank
Type: Element of portable life support units, available in personal and vehicle models
Cost: 10 credits (personal) or 55 credits (vehicle)
Availability: 3

Game Notes: Tasari oxygen tanks have armor values of 1D (personal model) and 3D (vehicle model). Should a personal tank be punctured, the carrier is subjected to 2D damage from the explosion and shrapnel generated by the sudden release of the compressed gases. When vehicle tanks are punctured, all beings within 2 meters suffer 2D damage.

Pressure Tents

Pressure tents provide inexpensive shelters on the surface of Tasariq. The light–weight domed tents come unassembled, are easy to set up, and can be packed away when not in use. The tents are constructed from hollow poles covered with a plastic skin. A special entrance forms an airlock. Large tents have two airlocks and can be joined together to make many–roomed buildings. A gas regulator maintains the atmosphere.

■ Pressure Tent (small, medium, and large)

Model: TasCorp Enviro–Tent 2A (small), 9B (medium), 30C (large)
Type: Survival tent
Skill: Survival
Cost: 100 (small), 350 (medium), 1200 (large)
Availability: 3
Game Notes: A pressure tents provides a safe habitat on the surface of Tasariq. A small pressure tent uses 2 individual oxygen tanks; a medium pressure tent uses 2 vehicle oxygen tank; a large pressure tent uses 4 vehicle oxygen tanks. The tanks provide one week of use. A pressure tent can be set up in about an hour. A small tent holds 1–3 people; a medium tent holds 6–12 people; a large tent holds 20–40 people.

Pressure tents only protect the inhabitants from weather conditions, even severe storms. It provides no protection from blaster fire, explosions, or projectile or melee weapons.

Weapons

Tasariq manufactured weapons range from daggers to slug–throwers. They do not have blaster technology, although thanks the off–world instructors at their university they are gaining an understanding of these more advanced weapons.

A generally peaceful people, Tasari weapons are usually designed for hunting or defense against dangerous predators. They rarely have the punch of slug–throwers manufactured by worlds who have been in contact with the galactic civilization at large.

Tasari Crossbow

This simple missile weapon is popular among the Tasari blood cultists, as it, along with the dagger and the sword, is a traditional weapon of a warrior. Crossbows are never mass–produced, but instead are built by individual Tasari as dictated by tradition. (At one time, building a crossbow was a major rite of passage from childhood into adulthood.)

Crossbow

Model: Tasari Crossbow
Type: Custom–made projectile weapon
Scale: Character
Skill: Projectile weapon: Crossbow
Ammo: 1
Cost: Not available for sale
Availability: 3
Fire Rate: 1
Range: 10/20/40
Damage: 3D
Game Notes: Crossbows do only 1D damage to targets wearing Space–Age bodyarmor (such as stormtrooper armor or blast vests). It takes ten rounds (one minute) to reload a crossbow.

Tasari Slugthrowers

The slugthrowers of Tasariq are crude and unrefined. They have severely limited ammo capacity, and it is very difficult to fit them with muzzle flash suppressors, silencers, and other such devices that make slugthrowers attractive to most off–worlders. (Slugthrowers are viewed as an assassin's weapon by many other cultures in the Galaxy; unlike blaster bolts, the projectile in invisible to the eyes of most beings until impact.)

Tasari slugthrowers, however, are made for self–defense (the revolver) or for hunting (the rifle), neither of which needs the kind of modifications that many off–worlders might feel they need.

Nonetheless, due to the tariffs leveled by the Imperial Governor on imported goods, many off–worlders have been turning to Tasari weapons when their blasters begin to run low on gas charges.

Revolver

Model: Barimoq Industries Protector
Type: Slugthrower revolver
Scale: Character
Skill: Firearms: Slugthrower
Ammo: 5
Cost: 200
Availability: 3
Fire Rate: 1
Range: 3–10/30/55
Damage: 3D+1
Game Notes: 2D+1 damage when used against targets wearing Space–Age body armor

Rifle

Model: Barimoq Industries Provider
Type: Slugthrower Rifle

Scale: Character
Skill: Firearms: Slugthrower
Ammo: 4
Cost: 450
Availability: 3
Fire Rate: 1
Range: 5–15/50/150
Damage: 5D
Game Notes: 3D damage when used against targets wearing Space–Age body armor

Vehicles

Surface vehicles for Tasariq are all self–enclosed with replaceable oxygen tanks to maintain a safe breathing atmosphere. While most military–grade vehicles can typically be sealed to maintain an atmospheric integrity, most civilian craft must undergo some modifications. The normal cost for such modifications is +50%. The cost is in addition to higher price on Tasariq. The cost of surface vehicles is thus 250% normal at Tasariq City and Elikann Crater and 350% normal in surface mining camps.

Tasari vehicles, such as the steam rover detailed below, are constructed to be airtight and do not require additional modifications.

MechMiner

A MechMiner is a small machine vehicle with tracks. The driver sits in the control seat and can operate a variety of useful mechani-

Public Transportation

Not everyone on Tasariq can afford their own steam rovers, and even fewer can afford to own shuttles or other flying vehicles. The natives and many off–worlders rely on the tube transit systems to travel from crater to crater.

Tube Transit Fares

Tasariq City to/from Elikann Crater	**2 credits**
Tasariq City to/from Barimoq Crater	**4 credits**
Elikann Crater to/from Barimoq Crater	**5 credits**

The listed fares are one way. The price is the same for either way. High-speed shuttles run every half-hour during the day and every two hours at night. Journeys to and from Tasariq City take about 15 minutes, but it takes half an hour to travel between Elikann Crater and Barimoq Crater.

cal mining tools. With a MechMiner, a single person can do the work of a dozen men by hand. They are gaining popularity on Tasariq, for although each and every crystal in a claim might not be found using a MechMiner as opposed to when the mining is done by hand, the speed with which crystals are excavated more than makes up for the shortfall.

MechMiners are 3 meters long but built low to the ground to better fit into mine shafts. On Tasariq, an operator needs to wear a breath mask.

MechMiner

Model: Akin–Dower Mechanized Autominer Mk IV
Type: Mining machine
Skill: Machine operation: mining machines
Crew: 1 operator
Cost: 12,000 (new), 3,000 (used)
Availability: 1
Game Notes: If successfully operated, MechMiners provide characters excavating tasar crystals with +2D to their *Search* or *mining* skill rolls.

Steam Rover

Steam rovers are half–tracked ground cars of Tasari design that are powered by steam turbines. Their engines run on compressed hydrogen and helium which heats steam in a boiler to power the pistons. The fuel is replaceable. A large airscoop separates, compresses, then replaces gas lost during operation. At the optimum cruising speed of 40 KMH, the fuel is largely self–replacing. The rovers can obtain speeds of 80 KMH, but the fuel is burned quicker than it is replaced in these cases. Steam rovers carry a hundred gallon water tank at the back. Under normal conditions the water tanks need to be refilled every 2,000 kilometers. The cab of the steam rover is completely self–enclosed. One tank carries sufficient oxygen for three days under normal usage. Steam rovers are built to be solid and dependable. They can climb steep grades and can travel most anywhere on the planetary surface of Tasariq.

Steam Rover

Craft: Barimoq Industries All Terrain Cruiser K–111
Type: Ground half–track
Scale: Speeder
Length: 8 meters
Skill: Ground vehicle operation: ground car
Crew: 1 driver
Passengers: 6
Cargo Capacity: 5 metric tons, 10 cubic meters
Cover: Full

Cost: 11,000 (new), 3,000 (used)
Maneuverability: 1D
Move: 22, 80 KMH
Availability: 3
Body Strength: 3D

Secrets of the Tasar Crystals

Those who deal in the tasar crystal trade, be they miners or merchants, know the values of a tasar crystal—the range is 2Dx1000 credits. Although the Tasari claim there are rare "magical" crystals that are worth far more than that, most off–worlders view this as empty superstitions of a primitive people.

The truth, however, is that there are indeed rare tasar crystals that hold a variety of powers. These crystals somehow became charged with a high concentration of Force energy during the devastation that caused their formation. Beings who carry such power crystals on their person for 2D months gradually become attuned to the crystal, and the result is that they become Force–sensitive and gain specific Force power–like abilities as dictated by the type of crystal they carry. The level at which the Force–like power functions is dependent on the character attuned to the crystal.

A power crystal is theoretically worth 10 times the normal price, but power crystals are seldom sold by those who recognize them for what they are.

If the characters are mining on Tasariq, the Gamemaster should roll 3D for every seven total days they spend working an area rich in crystals. For each 6 rolled, the characters have discovered a power crystal. (The number of normal crystals mined is equal to the number rolled divided by 2.)

Crystal Power Value	Type of Character
4D	Native Tasari
3D	Jedi
2D	Force–sensitive (prior to attunement)
1D	Other

Characters who own more than one tasar crystal may find that they function at different levels. For example, if a character who isn't Force–sensitive becomes attuned to a power crystal, then it functions at 1D, However, if he later becomes attuned to a second power crystal, it will then function at 2D, because he has became Force–sensitive in the process of growing attuned to the first one.

The Power Crystals

Eighteen power crystals are listed below. Should the characters acquire powered tasar crystals, the Gamemaster can either pick types of crystals from this list and arbitrarily decide what kind of crystals they are, or he can roll randomly using the following generation system and tables.

First, the Gamemaster rolls a die to determine which tables to consult. A second roll determines the exact crystal under each table.

The powers are not cumulative with Force powers a character may already possess; instead, the character must use the power with the highest rating.

Amethyst Crystal

Color: Deep purple
Power: Ion Generation
Effect: Ions have a soothing effect upon most beings Ion generation will help calm lost tempers and promote a feeling of good will. The power will add +1D (+2D for Tasari) to interpersonal skills such as *willpower, bargain, command, con*, and *persuasion*.
Difficulty: Easy used within 2 meters. Raise the difficulty level by one for every additional 2 meters of range.

Aquamarine Crystal

Color: Pale blue green
Power: Psychometry
Effect: *Psychometry* is the ability to handle a non–animate object and discover information about the past of that object.
Difficulty: Easy to receive simple information (mood and physical condition of the person who last handled the object); Difficult to receive complex information (name, race, and other personal information).

Tasari Crystal Random Generation Tables

Table 1 (1–3)	Table 2 (4–5)	Table 3 (6)
1. Amethyst	1. Azurite	1. Bloodstone
2. Aquamarine	2. Carnelian	2. Chalcite
3. Citrine	3. Jasper	3. Garnet
4. Peridot	4. Malachite	4. Opal
5. Spinel	5. Tourmaline	5. Sardonyx
6. Topaz	6. Turquoise	6. Tiger's Eye

Azurite Crystal

Color: Mottled blue
Power: Remain Conscious (as per the Force rules, except no required power is needed).

Bloodstone Crystal

Color: Dark gray with flecks of red
Power: Wound Reduction
Effect: If the *Wound reduction* power works then the user has his wound level healed by one. The power can only be used once per day.
Difficulty: Easy for wounded; Moderate for incapacitated; Difficult for mortally wounded.

Carnelian Crystal

Color: Orange shading to red
Power: Animal Telepathy
Effect: *Animal telepathy* allows the user to read the thoughts of an animal and other creatures. The more intelligent the animal, the more complex the thoughts. Simple animals have thought processes based strongly on instinct. The power does not work on sapient species.
Difficulty: Easy.

Chalcite Crystal

Color: Green mixed with swirling golden lines
Power: Receptive Telepathy (as per the Force rules, except that no required power is needed).

Citrine Crystal

Color: Yellow brown
Power: Accelerate Healing (as per the Force rules)

Garnet Crystal

Color: Red, brown, and green
Power: Control Another's Pain (as per Force the rules)

Jasper Crystal

Color: Brown shading to blue–black
Power: Magnify Senses (as per the Force rules)

Malachite Crystal

Color: Bands of light and dark green
Power: Poison Sense
Effect: Poison sense allows the user to sense, in advance, any contaminants or other factors that could make a substance dangerous to ingest.
Difficulty: Easy

Opal Crystal

Color: A rainbow spectrum of colors
Power: Battle Sense
Effect: If the *Battle sense* sense power works then the user receives +1D for initiative on the first round of combat only.
Difficulty: Average

Peridot Crystal

Color: Olive green
Power: Control Pain (as per the Force rules).

Sardonyx Crystal

Color: Red and white
Power: Accelerate Another's Healing (as per the Force rules).

Spinel Crystal

Color: Red brown
Power: Hyperthermia
Effect: *Hyperthermia* is the ability to see minute temperature differences in animate objects, allowing rolls against a character's Perception or search ratings to detect the changes. The range is 15 meters. Hyperthermia also allows a character to see animate objects in the dark. It also acts as a diagnostic aid in healing, giving a bonus to the *first aid* skill equal to the number before the "D."
Difficulty: Easy.

Tiger's Eye Crystal

Color: Dark brown with a central yellow eye
Power: Telekinesis (as per the Force rules).

Topaz Crystal

Color: Golden yellow
Power: Life Detection (as per the Force rules).

Turquoise Crystal

Color: Light blue shading to green
Power: Natural Navigation
Effect: *Natural navigation* prevents the user from getting lost, as long as the person has a map or some sense of the appropriate direction. If the individual has no idea of the surroundings, the person can still discern the magnetic north.
Difficulty: Very Easy.

Tourmaline Crystal

Color: The blue spectrum, from pale azure to deep indigo
Power: Empathy
Effect: *Empathy* allows the user to experience the emotions of a sapient individual. No actual thoughts can be read.
Difficulty: Easy for own species; Moderate for other species.

Tom Moldvay and Steve Miller

Characters of Tasariq

Ansan Talam

Ansan is a human male of interminable age. A life spent living and working under the harshest of conditions while staking and mining claims has left him looking weathered; he could be anywhere from 40 to 70 years of age. His general appearance is "old," with graying hair and beard, but if someone asks his age, Ansan replies that he can still outwork nearly every other miner—and will proceed to prove it. So far, no one has ever gotten his actual age out of him... perhaps he doesn't even know it himself.

Ansan was one of the first miners to arrive on Tasariq and he has been mining there for more than 20 years. He is a fiercely independent trailblazer who is typically found scouting unexplored craters and combing the barren surface of Tasariq for tasar crystal deposits. He rarely finds the richest deposits, but when he does strike it rich he typically sells his claim by the time a large mining camp has grown in the region. Ansan likes open spaces and solitude, and this always keeps him moving and ahead of the congestion of civilization.

Despite his many years of working on Tasariq, Ansan has very little wealth. For all his love of personal independence, Ansan is a fervent supporter of the New Order. The miner is a diehard racist who donates the vast majority of his earnings to the Committee of the Preservation of the New Order, COMPNOR. He's been a member since the group was first founded by a core of enthusiastic supporters of Palpatine's agenda, and continues to view COMPNOR as a grassroots organization run by the people of the Empire, for the people of the Empire, even if the truth is that COMPNOR has long since become part of the Imperial bureaucracy. A fair percentage of the money he has left goes to buying equipment he is certain was designed and built by humans, frequently costing far more than the average price of the already expensive offworld goods on Tasariq. The only piece of alien equipment he owns is a steam rover which he was forced to purchase when his landspeeder was damaged beyond repair in a tunnel worm attack.

When dealing with humans, Ansan is friendly in a reserved way. He is willing to help newcomers to Tasariq—as long as they are heading nowhere near regions he is currently staking claims. He is coldly hostile toward aliens, with the exception of Bersin Sekolah for whom he has developed a grudging respect. Ansan admires Bersin's dedication to Tasariq.

Ansan Talam

Type: Grizzled Miner
DEXTERITY 2D+2
Blaster 4D, brawling parry 3D+2, dodge 4D
KNOWLEDGE 3D+1
Mining 5D, survival 5D, value 4D+1, willpower 4D
MECHANICAL 3D
Communications 3D+2, ground vehicle operation 4D, machine operation: mining machines 5D, repulsorlift operation 3D+1
PERCEPTION 3D+2
Bargain 4D+1, investigation 4D+2, search 5D, sneak 4D+1
STRENGTH 2D+2
Brawling 3D+2, stamina 3D+1
TECHNICAL 2D+2
Demolition 4D+2, ground vehicle repair 3D+1, repulsorlift repair 3D+2
Special Abilities:
Tasar crystal: Ansan discovered a Citrine crystal which gives him the *Accelerate healing* power with 2D worth of control.
This character is Force-sensitive.
Force Points: 2
Dark Side Points: 1
Character Points: 6
Move: 10
Equipment: Breath mask, extra oxygen supply, small pressure tent, comlink, macrobinoculars, medpac, 10 blaststicks, complete mining outfit, Corellian Mk IV MechMiner, Barimoq K-111 steam rover, blaster (4D), sporting blaster rifle (4D+1), location finder plus 3 homing transmitters, 1,100 credits

Bersin Sekolah

Bersin is a Ithorian male who is well into middle-age. He served as a Republic Scout, but he retired shortly after the Empire was declared. By observing his new superiors, the wise Ithorian felt certain that the Scout Service would soon become a tool of military expansion and oppression, and he did not want any part of such ventures. Sadly, his instincts proved right.

Bersin decided to spend his retired life on Tasariq, a world that fascinated him from the moment he first laid eyes on it as a greenhorn scout during the Clone Wars. He is dedicated to spending his remaining years finding a way to restore life to the surface of Tasariq.

Bersin has lived on more than twenty years on Tasariq, studying the ecology of the planet while attempting to create strains of plant life that might turn the poisonous gases on the surface into breathable oxygen. While the technology exists to create artificial atmospheres, Bersin rightfully believes that the Empire would never invest that kind of money in making Tasariq's surface liveable again. Further, he would rather identify a natural, permanent solution rather than leave the world at the whim of atmosphere generators that might break down at any time.

Bersin maintains dwellings in virtually every inhabited crater on Tasariq. He is rarely found in any of them, however. He spends most of his time conducting research either in one of his many greenhouses or on the planet's surface. Few native Tasari know the planetary surface as well as Bersin.

Bersin's dedication to restoring Tasariq to a liveable state has made him a hero to all native Tasari. He is so revered that he has been adopted by a leading family and thus has Tasari "relatives." The natives have also gifted him with a special signaller that he can trigger in an emergency. If the signal goes off, an immediate planet–wide search will begin, starting at the spot where the signal was last recorded.

Bersin's secretly favors the Rebel Alliance and stays in contact with Jhorag Corconnan. However, the Ithorian does not openly encourage Rebel activity on Tasariq as he does not want to invite the brutal reprisals he knows the Empire is capable of leveling against rebellious planets.

Bersin Sekolah

Type: Ithorian Ecologist
DEXTERITY 2D+2
Blaster 3D+2, dodge 3D+2
KNOWLEDGE 5D
Alien species 6D, alien species: Tasari 7D, agriculture 6D, agriculture: Tasariq 7D, ecology 7D ecology: Tasariq 8D, languages 6D, planetary systems 6D, planetary systems: Tasariq 7D, survival 6D
MECHANICAL 2D
Communications 3D, ground vehicle operations 3D, ground vehicle operations: ground car 4D, starship piloting 2D+2
PERCEPTION 3D
Investigation 4D, persuasion 4D
STRENGTH 2D+2
Stamina 4D
TECHNICAL 2D+2
Computer programming/repair 4D+2, ecological machines 4D+2
Special Abilities:
Tasar crystals: Bersin has been rewarded with a topaz crystal which gives him the power of *Life detection*, and a turquoise crystal which gives him the power of *Natural navigation*. Both have a power value of 3D.
This character is Force–sensitive
Force Points: 4
Character Points: 11
Move: 10
Equipment: Breath mask, extra oxygen tanks, small pressure tent, comlink, datapad, macrobinoculars, medpac, recording rod, Barimoq K–111 steam rover with built–in ecology computer, miscellaneous ecological machines, sporting blaster rifle (4D+1), blaster pistol (4D), knife, 1,400 credits emergency signal system

Dunclair Gostegion

Dunclair is a middle–aged, handsome, charismatic human with unruly brown hair, a trimmed mustache, and piercing blue eyes. He was born in the Corporate Sector. From the time he was very young, he knew he wasn't going to follow in his parents' footsteps to become just another minor cog in the machines of the galactic megacorps. As a teenager, he drifted from swoop gang to swoop gang in his home system. Eventually, his father decided to send the young man away to a strict boarding school located on an airless asteroid. Young Dunclair stowed away on a freighter and he hasn't been back to his homeworld since.

Dunclair drifted through the Corporate Sector for a few years, even traveling with the famous gunslinger Gallandro for a while. He spent time in the Centrality and eventually wandered across the

Inner Rim systems until he found himself on Tasariq. Along the way, he became one of the galaxy's premiere professional gamblers, as well as establishing a reputation as a dangerous gunslinger.

Dunclair has been on Tasariq for the last seven months. Although he'd never admit it, he is laying low. Roughly a year ago, Dunclair played a high–stakes sabacc game with a pair of young sharks and the Baron Administrator of Besbin's Cloud City. During the course of the game, Dunclair caught one of the kids cheating. He called him on it. The kid went for his gun, and a split–second later Dunclair had shot him dead. The gambler soon learned that the young man was the only son of a powerful Vigo of the Dark Sun criminal syndicate—and he knew he was trouble. Unable to know how the Vigo would react to the loss of his son, but not willing to risk death to find out, Dunclair decided that what he really wanted from life was an extended vacation on Tasariq.

Dunclair is willing to take any risk if the odds are right. He easily loses his temper but during times of danger he remains icy cold. Dunclair's word is his bond, but he is otherwise willing to con trusting marks out of their credits. Dunclair has killed several opponents in fair fights and acquired a reputation. Dunclair usually avoids politics but he favors the Rebels and has aided them in the past.

■ Dunclair Gostegion

Type: Gambler and Gunfighter
DEXTERITY 4D
Blaster 6D, blaster: hold–out 7D, brawling parry 5D, dodge 6D+2, melee combat 5D, melee combat: vibroblade 6D, melee parry 5D
KNOWLEDGE 3D
Streetwise 4D, survival 4D, value 4D

MECHANICAL 2D
Repulsorlift operation 3D, space transports 3D
PERCEPTION 4D
Bargain 5D, con 6D, gambling 7D, persuasion 5D+1
STRENGTH 3D
Brawling 5D, stamina 4D
TECHNICAL 2D
First aid 4D, repulsorlift repair 3D
Force Points: 4
Dark Side Points: 2
Character Points: 14
Move: 10
Equipment: Deck of sabacc cards, game–rule datapad, expensive clothing in black, breath mask, 2 medpacs, modified vibroblade (6D+2) modified holdout blaster (4D), modified heavy blaster (5D+2), "quick–draw" holsters for all weapons (+1 on draw initiative), 5,700 credits

Garuk

Garuk is a native Tasari male who leads an evil secret cult that worships Tasar crystals. He was raised in the cult, and his father led it before him. His family has secretly maintained the ancient rites and blood rituals that many Tasari once believed protected their world from another disaster from space. The family and their cult professes to shun all off–wold influence and believes that the Tasari should never leave their homeworld.

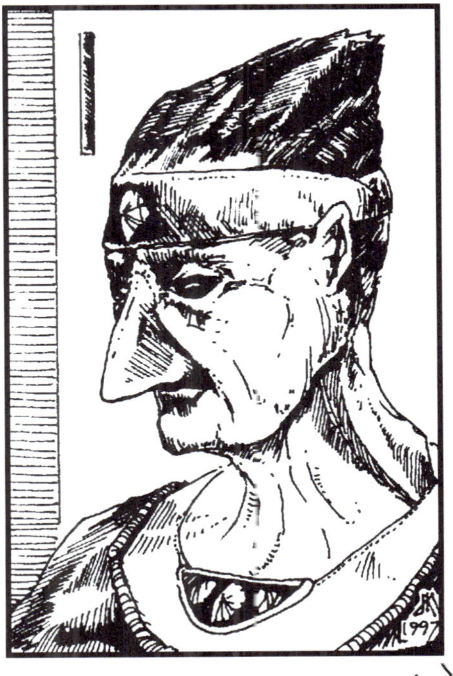

Although Garuk pays lip service to the cults beliefs, he does not actually follow them himself. He has a taste for the luxury and easy living provided by the advanced technologies that off–worlders bring to Tasariq. For several years, Garuk has been leading a double life, presiding over services and then telling his followers that he must go into the wilderness to commune. The truth is that he journeys to Tasariq City where he maintains a suite in the Imperial Hotel. In order to pay for his lavish dwelling, he has been secretly selling off the cult's tasar crystals. (Only the cult leader is allowed to enter the inner sanctum where the crystals are kept, so the cultists have not discovered the loss of their precious treasure.)

■ Garuk

Type: Tasari Cult Leader
DEXTERITY 3D+1
Bows: crossbow 5D+1, dodge 5D+1, firearms 4D, melee combat 4D+1
KNOWLEDGE 3D+2
Ancient Tasari rituals 5D+2, alien species 4D+2, Tasari culture 4D+2, survival 4D+2, value: Tasar crystals 5D+2, willpower 4D+2
MECHANICAL 2D
Ground vehicle operation: steam rover 3D+2
PERCEPTION 4D
Bargain 5D, command 5D, con 5D, forgery: tasar crystals 5D, sneak 5D
STRENGTH 3D
Stamina 4D
TECHNICAL 2D
First aid 3D
Special Abilities:
Tasar crystals: Garuk wears a golden amulet with three tasar crystals—citrine, peridot, and bloodstone, which give him the Force powers of *Accelerate healing, Control pain,* and *Wound reduction*. On his ceremonial headband is a Jasper crystal that gives him the power of *Magnify senses*. On his left arm bracelet is a Tiger's Eye crystal that gives him the power of *Telekinesis*. All the powers have a rating of 5D.
This character is Force–sensitive.
Force Points: 1
Dark Side Points: 6
Character Points: 13
Move: 10
Equipment: Ten–shot pistol (3D+2) with two spare clips, ceremonial axe (5D), crossbow (3D), sacrificial knife (4D+1), breath mask, extra oxygen tanks, small pressure tent, Barimoq K–111 steam rover, comlink, medpac

Jhorag Corconnan

Jhorag is known on Tasariq as a purchasing agent for a Corulag gem dealer. He is a friendly, outgoing, human male who is well–liked among the small corporate culture on the world as well as by the miners who sell their crystals to him. He has a reputation of being a fair, if dull and thoroughly forgettable, man. Jhorag is average in size, weight and looks. A suspicious being might actually think that Jhorag's bland appearance is purposefully cultivated. The suspicious being would be right.

Jhorag is in fact an Alliance Intelligence operative who has been sent to Tasariq to organize local Rebel Alliance cells. Despite his successes on other planets in the sector, and despite concerted efforts, the Rebel presence on Tasariq is virtually non–existent.

Even though many of the Tasari Elders are dissatisfied with Imperial rule, and increasingly wary of what the future might hold, they have thus far refused to join or support the Rebel Alliance—the Tasari aren't sure who is actually on the "right" side in the ever–expanding galactic civil war. The off–worlders on Tasariq are similarly disinterested in joining the Alliance's fight for freedom—for the most part, they want to avoid politics, make their fortune and return home.

Jhorag is never seen in public without his A2 Accounting Droid, obstensibly so he is always ready to do business. The truth of the matter is that the droid has been modified to function as a security droid—the droid's programming has been upgraded to include several of the functions attributed to security droids and it functions more or less as Jhorag's bodyguard. The holographic recorder and projector that the model is normally equipped with has been replaced with an onboard blaster. (Casual inspection of the droid does not reveal this modification until the weapon is fired; the muzzle appears to be the lense of the holorecorder.) The droid's designation is A2–ZP, but it is typically known as "Zip."

■ Jhorag Corconnan

Type: Rebel Cell Network Organizer
DEXTERITY 3D
Blaster 5D, dodge 5D, grenade 4D, melee combat 4D, melee parry 4D
KNOWLEDGE 3D
Bureaucracy 4D, business 5D, intimidation 4D, law enforcement 4D, streetwise 4D, value 5D, willpower 4D
MECHANICAL 3D
Communications 4D, repulsorlift operations 4D, space transports 4D, starfighter piloting 4D, starship gunnery 4D, starship shields 4D

PERCEPTION 3D
Bargain 5D, command 5D, investigation 4D, persuasion 6D, sneak 4D
STRENGTH 3D
Brawling 4D, stamina 4D, swimming 4D
TECHNICAL 3D
Blaster repair 4D, computer programming/repair 4D, demolition 5D, droid programming 4D, first aid 4D, security 5D
Special Abilities:
Tasar crystal: Jhorag has a Peridot crystal in a ring that gives him the *Control pain* power with a value of 2D.
This character is Force–sensitive.
Force Points: 5
Character Points: 12
Move: 10
Equipment: Breath mask, small pressure tent, comlink, datapad, 2 medpacs, macrobinoculars, recording rod, 2 frag. grenades, thermal detonator, vibroblade (6D), blast vest (+1 energy, +1D physical), enclosed Nightfalcon speeder bike, hold–out blaster (3D), heavy blast pistol (5D), AZ accounting droid, 3,300 credits

■ Zip

Type: Modified Genetech A2 Accounting/Business Unit
DEXTERITY 1D
Blaster 6D, dodge 2D
KNOWLEDGE 3D
Bureaucracy 8D, business, 8D, value 7D
MECHANICAL 1D
PERCEPTION 1D
Bargain 3D, search 6D
STRENGTH 1D
TECHNICAL 1D
Computer programming/repair 3D+2, security 5D
Equipped With:
• Hemispherical body with two fine manipulators
• Repulsorlift unit (2 meters ceiling)
• Speech synthesizer
• Onboard light blaster (3D damage, 3–10/30/100)
Move: 10
Size: 1 meter wide, 0.6 meters tall
Cost: Not for sale

Kullan Velerinden

Captain Kullan Velerinden embodies both the best and the worst of the Imperial Army Officer Corps. On the one hand, he is a brave, resourceful warrior who pilots an AT–ST as though it is an extension of his own body. When under fire in the field, Velerinden is always in the lead of his walker unit. He never issues an order he himself is not willing to execute. On the other hand, Captain Velerinden abuses his authority for personal gain in every conceivable way, ranging from blackmail and protection rackets to out–and–out murder. If there is something Velerinden wants, Velerinden gets it, sooner or later, whether the owner wants to part with it or not. The only line he draws is that he never forces himself on a female; although he is somewhat rough around the edges, Captain Velerinden is a perfect gentleman. While he is never shy about expressing his desires, once he has been rebuffed, he leaves the woman alone.

Kullan Velerinden was the son of a petty thief on Elrood, and was laying the foundation for a career as an ally basher when one day he picked the wrong victim—an Imperial Army major in civilian clothing. After giving the youth a severe beating, the major gave him a choice of poisons: He could either sign up with the Army as a recruit or he could take his chances with Elrood's harsh legal system. Young Velerinden chose the Army.

Velerinden thrived in the Imperial Army, despite his own expectations. As he completed basic training, his impressed drill sergeant recommended him as a candidate for the Academy. Velerinden was accepted, and he had found his calling... service to the Empire.

Kullan Velerinden, however, was anything but an honorable officer; his roguish nature still prevailed over all the training he received. Assigned to a small support unit of AT–STs, he became his own "procurement officer," taking it upon himself to get the best supplies for his unit, turning around and selling them to black marketeers for some cash and second–grade supplies.

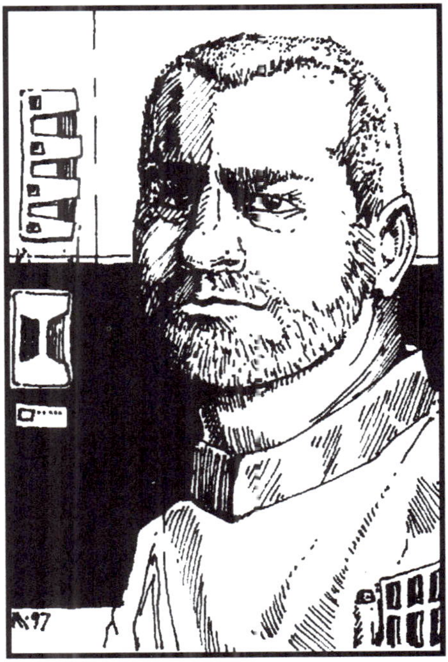

As he rose through the ranks, Velerinden excelled on the battlefield through bravery and skill as an AT–ST pilot. Off the battlefield, he raked in thousands of credits through a variety of illegal activities. He has very little to show for all his years of crookedness, however. Velerinden loves high–stakes sabacc games, but unfortunately for him his love for the game outstrips his talent for it.

As Velerinden stood on the threshold of a promotion to major, a more honorable officer who had uncovered his illegal activities threatened to expose him. By calling in some favors among his criminal contacts, Velerinden managed to destroy his rival with only minor damage to his own career; instead of a promotion, the High Command awarded him with his own command. He was placed in charge of the small garrison on Tasariq, second only in authority to the governor.

Velerinden is making a fortune from his posting on Tasariq, finally making money faster than he loses it at the sabacc table. He has assembled an impressive array of thugs and leg–breakers around him. He gets a cut of virtually every illegal activity on Tasariq, and a network of informers allows him to crack down on criminals who do not pay him. In addition, the captain has a number of avenues through which he extorts protection money from legitimate business people, miners, and independent freighter captains. Under Captain Velerinden's watchful eye, any criminal and fugitive—even known Rebel Alliance operatives—can find safety on Tasariq... as long as they have the credits to pay for the privilege.

Velerinden is a large muscular man with brown hair and eyes. He wears a full beard which he keeps meticulously trimmed. Although his command position exempts him from needing to go into the field, he often chooses to pilot AT–STs during raids designed to clean out wilderness smuggler hide–outs.

Kullan Velerinden

Type: Imperial Army Captain
DEXTERITY 3D+2
Blaster 5D, brawling parry 5D, dodge 5D, grenade 4D+1, heavy weapons 4D+1, melee combat 3D, melee parry 2D+2
KNOWLEDGE 3D
Bureaucracy 4D+1, intimidation 4D+1, law enforcement 4D, streetwise 4D, survival 3D+1, value 4D
MECHANICAL 2D+1
Starship gunnery 2D+2, starship shields 3D, walker operation: AT–ST 5D+2
PERCEPTION 3D
Command 5D, gambling 5D, investigation 4D, search 4D, sneak 3D+2
STRENGTH 4D
Brawling 5D, climbing/jumping 4D+2, lifting 5D, stamina 5D
TECHNICAL 2D
Blaster repair 3D, demolition 3D, first aid 3D, walker repair: AT–ST 3D+2
Force Points: 2
Dark Side Points: 4
Character Points: 8
Move: 10
Equipment: Blast helmet and blast vest (+1 energy, +1D physical), modified blaster pistol (4D+2), breath mask, 2 grenades (4D), comlink, datapad, macrobinoculars, medpac, 2,700 credits

Mendegar

Mendegar is a slightly built, tall human woman in her early thirties. She has a slender, angular face that is almost always set in a sneer. On those rare occasions a smile crosses her faces, it's a sight that either inspires joy or fear in those who witness it. She wears her blonde hair in a crewcut, and her blue eyes look like chips of ice. She is rarely seen in public unarmed or unarmored.

The woman now known as Mendegar used to be called Nell Wenn. As a young girl, she admired constables, Sector Rangers and other law enforcers, beacons of security in the harsh and over-crowded cities of her homeworld, Deysum III. There was nothing she wanted more than to join the ranks of those who devote their lives to the law and the protection of innocents. As soon as she turned sixteen, Nell entered the Police Academy on her home-world, ultimately hoping to some day join the Sector Rangers. But the young woman never got that far.

When Nell joined the police force, she did not find it to be the fellowship of selfless, brave public servants she had dreamt it was. Instead, she found that the constables with whom she served were self–serving, greedy beings who were themselves not much better than the criminals they fought. Many of her colleagues extorted protection money from businessmen and criminals alike and in many cases only those who could afford to pay gained the full benefit of police protection.

Naively, Nell thought the corruption was limited to her unit. She went to her superiors, only to be lectured on how she needed to realize that she was an adult now and that she needed to learn the difference between reality and public relations. Outraged, Nell next went to the planetary governor's office with her evidence of corruption. The governor's people promised they would launch an investigation. That night the apartment she shared with her boyfriend was firebombed. She barely survived. He was less fortunate.

As soon as Nell was released from the hospital, she tendered her resignation from the constabulary. She wasn't finished with police work, however. Nell carefully and surreptitiously investigated the circumstances surrounding the firebombing of her apartment and in the process uncovered a ring of corruption that reached from rank–and–file constables all the way to the governor's top aide. While gathering this evidence, she discovered that several corporate interests had placed bounties on unknown saboteurs that Nell knew to be some of her former colleagues. Assuming the "professional" name of Mendegar, she received accreditation from the Empire as a bounty hunter and took on all contracts related to the activities of the corrupt law enforcers who had killed her boyfriend and shown her that in the real world money was more important than honor and justice; now she was showing them that money and justice *could* go hand–in–hand.

Once her mission of vengeance was over, Nell continued working as a bounty hunter under her assumed name. She has been on the hunt now for almost 15 years now, plying her trade from the Outer to Inner Rim. For the last three years, Tasariq has served as her homebase, although she spends at least half her days away from the system. Rumors link her romantically to Captain Velerinden, although the truth is that he is merely her primary employer on the planet.

Mendegar has developed a reputation of being willing to take on any commission as long as the price is right. She is cunning and ruthless, but conducts herself with a rigid sense of honor. She remains true to pledges made to client and prey alike, but otherwise will use any ruse or trick to capture her prey. Mendegar prefers bringing in her captures alive—even if they oftentimes are severely injured.

Mendegar

Type: Bounty Hunter
DEXTERITY 4D
Blaster 5D, blaster: heavy blaster 6D, dodge 5D, dodge: energy weapons 6D, melee combat 5D, melee parry 5D
KNOWLEDGE 2D+2
Intimidation 3D, law enforcement 5D, streetwise 3D+2, survival 3D+2, survival: Tasariq surface 4D+2, willpower 6D

MECHANICAL 2D+2
Ground vehicle operation 3D, repulsorlift operation 4D, space transports 3D+1
PERCEPTION 3D
Investigation 5D, persuasion 3D+1, search 3D+2, sneak 4D, sneak: urban 5D
STRENGTH 3D+2
Brawling 4D+2, stamina 4D+2
TECHNICAL 2D
Security 3D
Force Points: 1
Dark Side Points: 2
Character Points: 18
Move: 10
Equipment: Jet pack, protective vest (+2 to resist damage), 2 medpacs, modified heavy blaster pistol (5D+2), light repeating blaster (6D), hold-out blaster (3D), vibroblade (6D+2), breath mask, extra oxygen tanks, comlink, macrobinoculars, Barimoq K–111 steam rover, medium pressure tent, 2,200 credits

Suraya

Suraya is an average sized human, large in the shoulders and in the belly, with short black hair and brown eyes. Originally a minor smuggler on the Outer Rim, Suraya relocated Coreward after offending Jabba the Hutt. (Suraya spoke highly of one of Jabba's lieutenants, not knowing that said lieutenant had been fed to the rancor only minutes before Suraya entered the throne room.) Fearing Jabba's wrath, he picked the most out–of–the–way world he could find where he thought he would still be able to make a living. That world was Tasariq.

Suraya made planetfall the very day Governor Keval instituted the new tariffs on off–world goods. Suraya had cash and contacts, and virtually overnight he went from a small–time smuggler on the run to the premiere black market operator on Tasariq.

Suraya kept an extremely low profile, hoping to avoid both Imperial authorities as well as any roving agents of

Jabba the Hutt, and to this day he remains cautious to the point of paranoia. Nonetheless, Suraya believes that a few months ago, *someone* notified Jabba because, despite his monthly "insurance" payments to Captain Velerinden, a cargo shipment from the spaceport to Suraya's warehouse was hijacked. When Velerinden heard that Suraya thought he had been attacked by Jabba's hired thugs, he threatened to withdraw all protection from the black marketeer. Suraya convinced the captain to continue his protection, but it now costs him 200 credits a week instead of the 100 he had been paying.

Shortly thereafter, Suraya bought his security droid, K4X4. Between the droid and the extra money he is paying Velerinden, he has since had no trouble. The black marketeer still lives in fear, however, constantly expecting Jabba to strike again. (The truth is that Jabba has long since forgotten about Suraya's ill–timed remark. The attack was actually staged by Velerinden who was looking to scare Suraya into paying him more protection money. The captain had no idea how successful the attempt would be.)

■ Suraya

Type: Black Marketeer
DEXTERITY 3D
Blaster 4D, dodge 4D, melee combat 3D+2, melee parry 3D+2
KNOWLEDGE 3D+1
Intimidation 4D+1, law enforcement 4D, streetwise 4D+1, value 5D, willpower 4D
MECHANICAL 2D+2
Ground vehicle operation 3D, repulsorlift operation 3D+2
PERCEPTION 3D+2
Bargain 5D, hide 4D+2, persuasion 4D+1, sneak 4D+1
STRENGTH 2D+2
Brawling 3D+2, stamina 3D
TECHNICAL 2D+2
Computer programming/repair 3D+2, droid programming 3D+1, droid repair 3D, repulsorlift repair 3D+1, security 3D+2
Force Points: 1
Dark Side Points: 1
Character Points: 7
Move: 10
Equipment: Battered Ubrikkian SuperHaul cargo skiff, breath mask, comlink, datapad, medpac, vibroblade (5D+2), hold–out blaster (3D), blaster pistol (4D), K4 security droid, 3,800 credits.

Valjak

Valjak is a tall, strong Tasari who has dedicated his life to fighting evil. He belongs to a secret order known as *Kiana*, the "warriors of light." Through the centuries the Kiana have fought against the evil cults that worship tasar crystals with bloody sacrifices. Today there are so few Kiana left that the order is considered a myth by most Tasari. To earn his living, Valjak hires out as a guide to off–worlders. The excursions into the wilderness afford Valjak a cover for his searches for evidence of blood cult activity.

Although Valjak has never left Tasariq, he was educated at Tasariq University and has a basic understanding of the cultures of a number of off–world species and humans. Still, like most other Tasari, he doesn't fully understand the conflicts that are fueling the galactic civil war. For this reason, he tends to be slightly more pro–Imperial, since he views the Imperial authorities as potential allies against the blood cults should he need them.

Valjak

Type: Tasari Warrior of Light
DEXTERITY 4D
Brawling parry 5D, brawling parry: martial arts 6D, dodge 6D, firearms 5D, melee combat 5D, melee combat: sword 6D, melee parry 5D
KNOWLEDGE 3D
Alien species 4D, cultures 4D, cultures: Tasari 5D, planetary systems: Tasariq 5D, survival: Tasariq surface 5D, willpower 4D
MECHANICAL 1D+2
Ground vehicle operation: ground car 3D+2
PERCEPTION 4D
Command 5D, investigation 5D, persuasion 5D, search 5D, sneak 6D
STRENGTH 3D+2
Brawling 5D, brawling: martial arts 6D, climbing/jumping 5D, stamina 5D
TECHNICAL 1D+2
First aid 3D+2
Special Abilities:
Tasar crystals: A citrine crystal on Valjak's right bracer gives him the accelerate healing power. An azurite crystal on his left bracer gives him the remain conscious power. A jasper crystal on Valjak's headband gives him the magnify senses power. A bloodstone crystal in the pommel of Valjak's sword gives him the wound reduction power. All the powers have a value of 5D.
This character is Force–sensitive.

Force Points: 6
Character Points: 14
Move: 10
Equipment: Five–shot revolver (3D+2) with 100 rounds of extra ammunition, Four–shot rifle with 100 rounds of extra ammunition, sword (5D+2), knife (4D+2), breath mask, extra oxygen tanks, small pressure tent, Barimoq K–111 steam rover, comlink, macrobinoculars, 2 medpacs, 700 credits

Yasinda Bardak

Yasinda is well known among many of Tasariq City's social layers. She is the youngest daughter of the owner of TranStar Construction, a Mid–Rim company that operates in a half–dozen systems, and is the Senior Executive of the Tasariq branch, so she is welcomed in the inner circle of the corporate executives on Tasariq. She was educated on Coruscant, so her well–polished manners make her a favorite at functions in the Governor's Palace. She has a taste for holovids, cantina bands, and other pursuits of the "common being," so she spends many free evenings in Tasariq City's entertainment district, Paradise Square, more often than not arm–in–arm with a recently arrived spacer.

Yasinda is a tall, good–looking woman in her mid-twenties with coppery red hair and a biting sense of humor. Gossip holds that she was shuttled off to Tasariq because her parents were mortified because the wild streak exhibited by their Coruscant–educated daughter wasn't fading as she matured but instead was seemingly growing wider. Indeed, those who get to know Yasinda discover that she is a woman who does as she pleases, when she pleases. They also discover that as the Empire increasingly restricts freedoms on Tasariq, Yasinda is seeming to make an increasing number of disparaging remarks about the Empire, Imperial policies and even the Em-

peror himself. She recently brought all conversations to a screeching halt at a dinner held by the governor when she questioned the wisdom behind the Tarkin Doctrine just a little bit too loudly.

The truth about this charming, willful young woman is that she is an Imperial Intelligence solo agent. She was recruited into a special Intelligence program secretly overseen by the Emperor himself. She was recruited due to her sensitivity to the Force, and was to one day joint the ranks of the Emperor's Hand, but unfortunately her strong will got in the way. Her upbringing was so steeped in New Order propaganda that she firmly believed the Force was nothing but the figment of outdated superstitions. When the Force entered into the training program she was undergoing, she marched straight into the office of the officer she believed to be in charge and demanded to be released from the program. The Emperor, knowing that she would be of use elsewhere, ordered her wish granted.

Yasinda entered the field as a solo agent and spent her first year subtly rooting out Rebel sympathizers among the uppercrust of Mid–Rim society by projecting a carefully cultivated image of free–spiritedness. She was never overtly involved with their arrests, but instead carefully and secretly leaked information told in confidence to the appropriate authorities.

Two years ago, she was transferred to Tasariq under the cover of having offended her parents through her continued associations with "questionable individuals." She has been told her mission on Tasariq is the same as it was in her home system—to locate and quietly neutralize Rebel sympathizers. The truth about her mission is far more sinister.

The Emperor has long been aware of the properties of tasar crystals, and has been curious about what impact they might have on beings who are Force–sensitive but not Force–active before they travel to Tasariq. Yasinda, Force–sensitive yet so close–minded she refuses to accept the Force as real, presented herself as the perfect subject for observation. Before she went to Tasariq, her lover, who unknown to her, is a fellow Intelligence operative, presented her with a gift—an amulet containing a Tasar crystal that had been modified to look like a more mundane gem as a token of his "undying love." The man, himself a graduate of the Emperor's secret Force–training program, now visits Yasinda every few months to secretly evaluate any impact the Tasar crystals may have had on her.

Yasinda has spontaneously become Force–active. At first, once she became attuned to the Tasar crystal she always wears around her neck, she suddenly found herself with abnormally keen senses when she tried to eavesdrop on conversations or make out what two people were surreptitiously exchanging. As she tried to figure out what was causing these flashes of superhuman abilities, something far more frightening starting to happen; she started hearing voices in her head, voices that seemed to be the thoughts of those around her. The thoughts ranged from the mundane equivalent of "mental humming" by her secretary during corporate meetings, to obscene fantasies when she walked by workmen at construction sites. As far as Yasinda knows only a few select alien species have telepathic powers, so she is growing increasingly fearful that her strange "powers" are actually the delusions of a diseased mind. She has received several physicals from various doctors on Tasariq, and all have told her that she is in condition. She has made requests to her controlling agent that she be reassigned to another world, assuming that the rustic nature of Tasariq has been wearing on her nerves in some fashion that only her subconscious is aware of. But so far, all her requests have been refused... because the Emperor is not done with his experiment.

The constant mental stress caused by Yasinda's uncontrolled Force powers is threatening to truly drive her insane. So far, her exceptional willpower and years of training has allowed her to put up a front of calm, but it's growing increasingly difficult for her. The visits from the man she loves—and who she, tragically, believes loves her back—relieve some of the pressure she is under, but it's not enough. With each passing week, the voices in her head grow more frequent....

Unless Yasinda uncovers the nature of the rarest of tasar crystals or is somehow convinced that the Force is real and that she needs help mastering her untrained powers, she will eventually crack under the mental strain. She is growing increasingly paranoid, and she will probably murder the next Rebel she uncovers rather than setting him up for capture—it might seem perfectly reasonable to her that the Rebel scum in question has been using some experimental device to drive her insane!

Yasinda Bardak

Type: Imperial Intelligence Solo Agent
DEXTERITY 3D+1
Archaic guns $D+2, blaster 5D+2, brawling parry 5D, dodge 7D+1, firearms 6D, melee combat 4D+1, melee parry 6D+1, pick pocket 5D+2, thrown weapons 6D, vehicle blaster 4D

KNOWLEDGE 3D
Alien species 5D, bureaucracy 6D, business 4D+2, cultures 4D, languages 5D, planetary systems 5D, streetwise 5D, survival 4D, willpower 7D
MECHANICAL 2D+2
Archaic starship piloting 3D, astrogation 4D, beast riding 5D, communications 4D+1, ground vehicle operation 4D, machine operation: construction machines 4D+2, repulsorlift operation 3D+1
PERCEPTION 3D+1
Bargain 4D+2, command 5D+2, con 6D, investigation 5D+2, forgery 4D, persuasion 4D+1, search 6D, sneak 6D
STRENGTH 3D
Brawling 4D, climbing/jumping 4D+2, stamina 4D, swimming 3D
TECHNICAL 2D+2
Computer programming/repair 5D, demolition 3D+2, droid programming 4D, first aid 3D+2, security 5D
Special Abilities:
Tasar crystal: Yasinda wears an amulet with a tasar crystal that grants her the equivalent of the force power *magnify senses*. She can currently use this ability at a rating of 4D, but Yasinda has no control over her force abilities; they activate at random.
Force skills: Sense 2D
Sense: Life detection, life sense, receptive telepathy
This character is Force-sensitive.
Force Points: 2
Dark Side Points: 5
Character Points: 17
Move: 10
Equipment: Breath mask, comlink, assorted illegal listening devices and homing "bugs," datapad, medpac, recording rod, modified vibroblade (6D), Incom T–47 airspeeder, modified hold–out blaster (4D), heavy blaster pistol (5D), amulet with inset tasar crystal, C5D construction droid, 2000 credits plus access to a secret fund holding 20,000 credits.

Encounter Statistics

In order to make this description of Tasariq as comprehensive and useful for Gamemasters as space allows, the following section presents a selection of generic characters for use during adventures on Tasariq.

Many other characters inhabit Tasariq of course, including those presented in the "Gamemaster Characters" chapter of the *Star Wars Roleplaying Game* rulebook and in the *Star Wars Gamemaster's Screen*.

Claimjumpers: All stats are 2D except: *blaster 3D+1, dodge 3D+2, melee combat 3D, melee parry 3D, survival 3D, and brawling 3D.* Move 10. Heavy blaster pistol (5D), knife (3D), breath mask, complete mining outfit.

Imperial Officer: All stats are 3D except: *blaster 5D, brawling parry, 4D+1, dodge 5D, grenade 4D, command 5D, and brawling 4D+1.*

Move 10. Blast vest and helmet (+1 energy, +1D physical), heavy blaster pistol (5D), 2 grenades (4D), comlink.

Miners: All stats are 2D except: *blaster 3D, dodge 3D+1, survival 3D, machine operation 3D, and brawling 3D+2*. Move 10. Blaster pistol (4D), breath mask, complete mining kit.

Outlaw Leader: All stats are 3D except: *blaster 5D, dodge 5D, melee combat 4D+1, melee parry 4D+1, vehicle blaster 4D+1, survival 4D, repulsorlift operation 4D+1, and command 4D*. Move 10. Heavy blaster pistol (5D), knife (4D), comlink, breath mask, speederbike.

Outlaws: All stats are 2D except: *blaster 3D+2, dodge 4D, melee combat 3D+1, melee parry 3D+1, vehicle blaster 3D, survival 3D+1, and repulsorlift operation 3D*. Move 10. Heavy blaster pistol (5D), knife (3D), comlink, breath mask, one speederbike per 2 outlaws.

Tasari Blood Cultist: *Dexterity 2D+2, crossbow 4D, dodge 3D+2, Knowledge 2D, survival 3D, Mechanical 1D, Perception 3D, Strength 2D+1, axe 4D, Technical 1D*. Move 10. Crossbow (3D, takes ten rounds to reload), axe (4D).

Tasariq Ranger: All stats are 2D except: *Strength 3D, blaster 4D, dodge 4D, grenade 3D, and brawling 4D*. Move 10. Blast vest (+1 energy, +1D physical), blaster pistol (4D), grenade (4D), comlink. These characters are all Iotran.

Workers: All stats are 2D except: *dodge 3D, machine operation 4D, and brawling 3D+1*. Move 10.

Adventure Ideas

The planet Tasariq has been conceived as a setting for adventures involving virtually any type of *Star Wars* player character. Rebels, Imperials, smugglers, gamblers, explorers, scouts, corporate troubleshooters or executives, scientists, historians... there is a little something for everyone on Tasariq.

The following suggested adventures and encounters may help gamemasters jump–start the process of creating adventures and campaigns on the Planet of Crystal.

Arrival in Tasariq City

The characters land at Tasariq City. They are met by four customs inspectors, three Army troopers and Captain Kullan Velerinden. The inspection is nominal (3D skill).

Captain Velerinden warns the characters there has been a rash of vandalism at the spaceport but, for only 200 credits per week, he will assign troopers to guard the ship. If the characters do not pay, Kullan will send off-duty troopers to vandalize the ship. The price of "protection" will then be raised to 400 credits per week. Kullan will also charge for F, R and X items brought onto Tasariq. An F-rated item has a permit fee of 10 credits. An R-rated item requires a special license of 50 credits. An X-rated item requires an outright bribe of 200 credits.

Tasariq City

1. Tasariq Control: The spaceport communications center.

2. Docking Bay: For regular spacecraft, 100 credits fee.

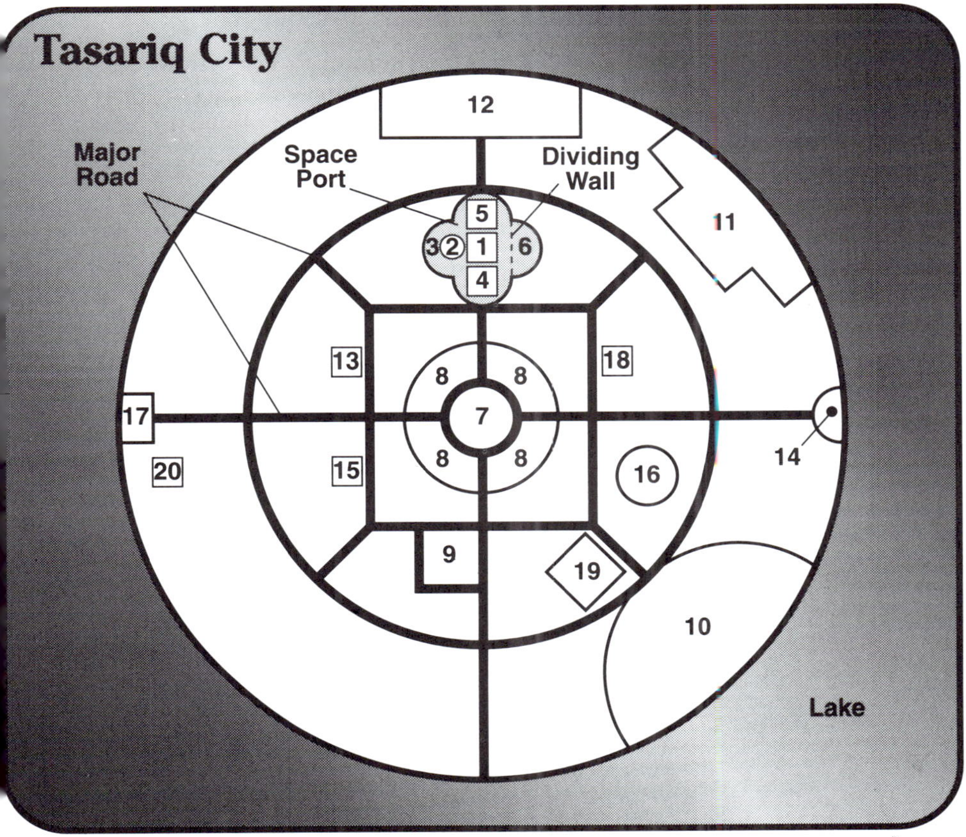

3. Berths: For regular spacecraft, 200 credits per week, repairs by special order.

4. Customs: Administration center and check point, 3 companies of Tasariq Rangers consisting of Iotran troopers and human officers.

5. Port Authority Building: The spaceport command center.

6. Imperial Navy Yard: Army and Navy fighters, transports, and patrol craft dock and receive maintenance here.

7. Circle Park: The city park, open to the public.

8. Shopper's Round: Offers a wide variety of stores, including an open–air bazaar.

9. Paradise Square: The entertainment district with bars, holo–theaters, gambling clubs, and assorted entertainments.

10. Lakeview: The hotel district, with luxury shops.

11. Administration Building: This building houses both the Imperial command center and the offices for interstellar corporations active on Tasariq. It serves as the planetary headquarters for most non–military bureaus and departments.

12. Military HQ: Three companies of Imperial Army troopers are stationed here, along with a detached unit of IntSec troopers.

13. Constabulary: Command center and jail. It also serves as the headquarters for the Imperial police force: Two companies of Tasariq Rangers plus one detached company of Army troopers.

14. Governor's Mansion. The Imperial Governor and his family live here. A unit of storm troopers in posted here, and offices for the governor's top aids are located on the bottom floor.

15. Claims Office: Claims registry and assaying, managed jointly by the Empire and the Tasari Council of Elders.

16. Cultural Center: Includes a library, a museum and the Tasari Hall of Culture. The Tasariq office of the Imperial Board of Culture is also located here.

17. Tube Shuttle: Regular shuttles to tube station located in the crater wall.

18. Utilities: The control center for power, light and communications in the city.

19. Tasariq University: Off–world teachers, Tasari students.

20. Tourist Center: Operated by the Imperial Ministry of Tourism, these offices are here to supply general information about Tasariq to visitors. A variety of tours and vacation activities can be arranged here.

Street Urchin

The characters encounter a 12–year old human girl, Niosa Bliana, peddling treasure maps. She offers her services as "expert" city guide. Niosa will try to get 40 credits a day, but will settle for 20. Niosa has contacts with the black marketeer Suraya and the native guide Valjak. Niosa has a 4D+2 bargain skill and a 5D con skill. If the characters do not hire her, Niosa will choose one character at random and try to pick his pocket. She has a 5D pick pocket skill and a 4D+1 running skill.

Wrong Place at the Wrong Time?

The characters have a need to buy some supplies on the black market, and they are hooked up with Suraya. During the negotiations, a gang of hijackers try to steal Suraya's goods. The hijackers are six disguised Army troopers led by an officer. They work for Captain Velerinden who plans to use the attack as an excuse to raise the price of "protection."

If the characters defend Suraya and his goods from the hijackers, they get an extremely good deal on their purchases. However, they are later taken into custody by Army troopers and brought before Captain Velerinden. The corrupt officer demands a "fine" of 100 credits from each character who was involved in the altercation. If they refuse to pay, they are placed under arrest.

If the characters avoid detention, or refuse to pay the bribes and escape, Velerinden hires the bounty hunter Mendegar to capture them.

High Stakes Game

The characters have a chance to join a special sabacc game. Dunclair Gostegion and Kullan Velerinden are playing. Two other players are a team of cheats. Halfway through the game, Dunclair catches them cheating. Dunclair, Velerinden and the two cheats draw their blasters. Each cheat has *blaster* 5D and *dodge* 5D and uses a modified hold–out blaster (3D+2).

Femmes Fatale

Yasinda Bardak befriends the characters and tries to learn their secrets. She will secretly follow the characters and eavesdrop on conversations. She will search any rented quarters they may have and then their ship. If Yasinda finds out anything incriminating, she will do her best to set up the characters to be arrested for whatever crimes they've committed. If she finds evidence the characters have connections with the Rebel Alliance, she will set them up for the murder of a customs official, a murder she actually commits.

If the characters evade arrest, Captain Velerinden hires Mendegar to capture them. Additionally, if Yasinda discovered connections with the Alliance, it is possible that her paranoia runs wild and she begins to stalk the characters herself. While Mendegar is the overt threat, the hunter has been hired to bring them in alive. On the other hand, Yasinda, who, is perhaps still believed to be a friend by the characters, is dedicated to seeing them dead. (This adventure seed might work work well in combination with "Blackmail," featured below.)

Shootout

Mendegar has been hired to hunt Dunclair Gostegion by a family whose son was killed by Dunclair in a fair fight. The characters might be caught in the middle when the bounty hunter shoots it out with the gunfighter, or they might become targets themselves if Mendegar has trouble tracking Dunclair but comes to suspect the characters might know where her quarry is hiding.

Blackmail

If any character is on the Imperial wanted list, Kullan Velerinden finds out. Kullan is willing to "bury" the list for only 500 credits. Unfortunately, he makes a new blackmail demand every several days. The second demand will be for 1,000 credits. Each demand thereafter will be for 2,000 credits. If the individual does not pay then Kullan will issue an arrest warrant, sending six Tasariq Rangers plus an Imperial officer. If the individual still eludes arrest, Kullan will take out a contract with the bounty hunter Mendegar.

Rich Strike

Dunclair Gostegion offers to sell the characters a rich claim he won in a Sabacc game for 15,000 credits. The characters try out the claim and find 3,000 credits worth of Tasar crystals in a single day. The sale is actually a con. The site has been "salted" with small crystals in easy to find places (which the characters have already found). Except for the salted crystals, the claim is worthless.

Wilderness Journey

The characters travel from Tasariq City to Roaring Crater, a distance of 2,300 kilometers. For each day of travel roll 1D, on a roll of 1 there will be a random wilderness encounter. Roll 1D for the time of the encounter, 1–4 = day; 5–6 = night. Roll 1D for encounter type, 1–2 = creature, 3–4 = outlaws, 5 = cultists, and 6 = storm. A creature encounter can be with either 1–3 spidercats, sting–snakes or tunnel worms (gamemaster's choice, or random). An outlaw encounter consists of one outlaw per character plus an outlaw leader. The outlaws will be on enclosed speederbikes. Normally, two outlaws ride each bike, one to drive and one to fire the laser. A cultist encounter will be with 2D worth of Tasari cultists. A storm encounter means the characters have to stop travel for an entire day. Use the wilderness random encounters any time the characters venture into the surface wilderness.

Roaring Crater

Roaring Crater is the largest active boom–town on Tasariq. Several rich tasar crystal veins have been found in and around the crater, and the settlement is growing larger with each passing day. Law enforcement here is lax and frequently the best shot is the one who is right.

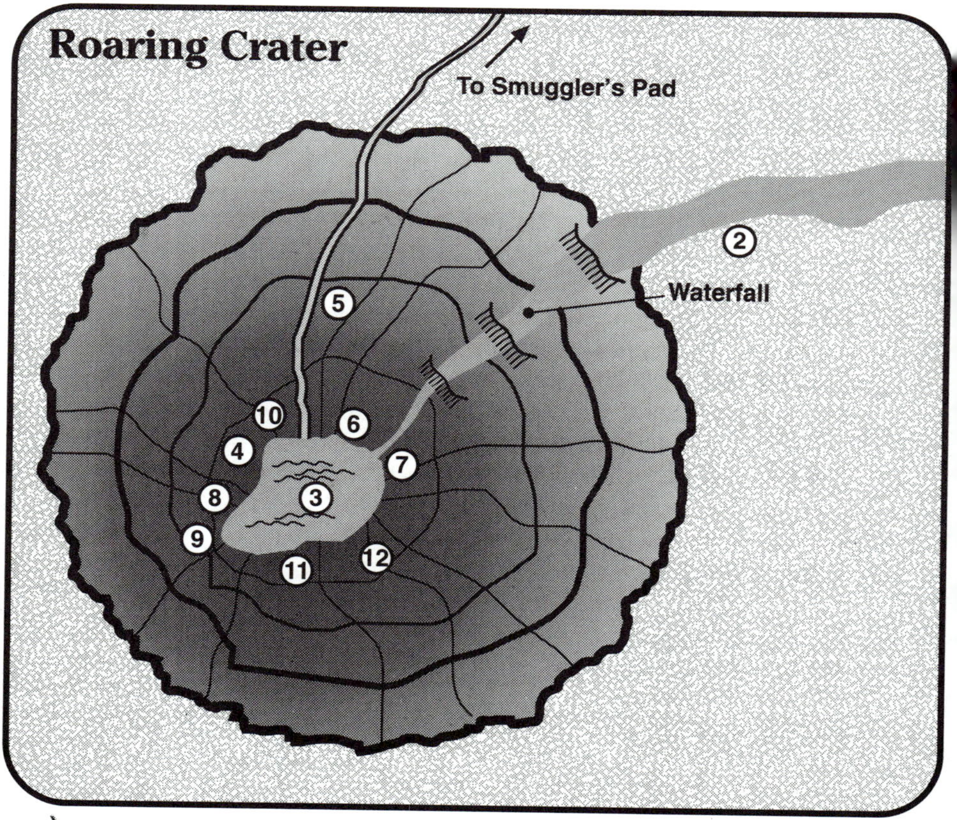

The traffic to and from Roaring Crater includes both ground vehicles and starships. A crude landing pad that is capable of handling light freighters and smaller ships has been constructed near the lip of the crater, and the area is rapidly becoming "smuggler central" as well. The spaceport has virtually no traffic control, and is unsafe by most standards. The Imperial authorities have yet to crack down on it, but many suspect it's going to happen any day.

1. Waterfall: Roaring Crater got its name because the peculiar acoustics of the crater let the waterfall be heard from anywhere within the crater.

2. Roaring River: Diverted into the crater seven months ago.

3. Echo Lake: Provides oxygen for the crater, and has been stocked with fish by the owner of the Lakefresh Restaurant. (Fishing is generally forbidden, although licenses can be purchased from the Lake Fresh (#9). The owner has hired some thugs to patrol the lake shore. (Use Outlaw stats.)

4. Assay Office: Includes claims registration. It is manned both by Imperial bureaucrats and Tasari natives.

5. Wilderness Road: A crude road that makes exit and entry easier and leads to the smuggler's landing pad a few miles from the top of the crater.

6. Bersin Sekolah's Tent: One of the Ithorian's many dwellings. It is guarded by two Tasari natives.

7. Roaring River Cantina: The most popular drinking tent.

8. The Lady Luck: The largest gambling tent.

9. Lakefresh Restaurant: Features fresh fish from the lake.

10. Rich Strike Hotel: A large hotel tent that offers reasonable rates for individuals who do not have their own tents.

11. Kelbarone's Mercantile: Handles most normal equipment, though at triple the normal cost.

12. Variety Theater: A restaurant during the day, it features holo–movies and live entertainment at night.

Smuggling Run

As an alternative to landing at the spaceport in Tasariq City, the characters get the coordinates for the Roaring Crater pad from off-world contacts. The gamemaster should roll 2D (no wild die). On any roll of 4 or higher, the characters land safely. On a roll of 3 they encounter a headhunter patrol ship. On a roll of 2 they encounter a light cruiser patrol ship. Once on the planet, the characters can sell their smuggled cargo.

Claimjumpers

Ansan Talam has made a rich strike, but is having trouble with masked claimjumpers. He hires the characters as guards because, as newcomers, they cannot be part of the plot. He will offer them 100 credits a day each, or 10% of his finds. When Ansan journeys to his latest claim he is attacked by the claimjumpers. There will be one claimjumper per character, including Ansan. After a month's work, Ansan's claim yields 6D worth of tasar crystals.

Wilderness Sweep

The Empire sends a strike force to clean out the smugglers at Roaring Crater. The ground forces consist of 20 troopers and one officer plus Kullan Velerinden, who personally pilots an AT–ST walker. Two TIE fighters lead the attack with a strafing run that damages smuggling craft on the ground so badly none can lift off. The characters will personally only have to deal with one trooper apiece. If the characters have no other escape from camp, Ansan Talam will offer them a lift as he flees in his steam rover.

The Search for Bersin Sekolah

Bersin Sekolah's emergency signaler goes off. A planet–wide search begins for the noted ecologist. The characters can join the search either at the urging of Jhorag Corconnan, because they already know Bersin Sekolah because of the 10,000 credit reward being offered by the Tasari Council of Elders.

Bersin's signal was triggered in the high desert near Roaring Crater. During their search, the characters discover that Bersin has been kidnapped by Tasari cultists who hate his efforts to "modernize" the planet. They have not killed the ecologist because he is an adopted Tasari. The search is complicated by several factors. Kullan Velerinden believes the ecologist has hidden a cache of crystals. He leads six trusted troopers in the search and is likely to shoot other searchers on sight. Mendegar has hired five ex-rangers to help her search. The Iotrans do not want to split the reward with anyone. Garuk plans to sell Bersin for random to the highest bidder. He contacts the Imperials, the mercenaries, and the rebels. The three search parties enter the cultist temple from different doors and meet at the alter room. A four-way showdown results, with Garuk leading 20 cultists.

TWO for ONE

By Paul Danner

Illustrations by David Day

"You want me to help you steal a Star Destroyer?" Sconn said, a bit too loudly.

After a reproachful stare at his nephew, Cavv quickly scanned the crowd at Stock Lights. Most of the scruffy–looking bunch were busy with their own shady dealings and paid the duo no mind. A particularly ugly Rodian at the next table glanced over for a moment, then resumed his own conversation. However the Rodian's companion, a tiny Mixtwirk, had slyly turned his antennae in their direction.

Cavv reached over and closed his hand firmly around the Mixtwirk's aural appendages. "If you want to keep these attached, friend, I advise you point them somewhere else."

The small alien squawked in fury at Cavv, who responded by squeezing harder.

The Rodian leaned back in his chair, apparently removing himself from the conflict. In actuality, the alien's hand was sliding over to his holster.

Sconn flashed the Rodian a grin and slowly shook his head 'no'. The alien's bulging eyes followed Sconn's hand as it brushed back his sleeve. The wrist laser concealed underneath was pointing directly at the Rodian's chest.

Cavv chuckled. "I think it's time you boys were leaving."

The small alien chirped indignantly.

"Because I own the place," Cavv replied, releasing his grip. "And since that was your last meal here, it's on the house. I suggest you catch the heel–and–toe express before my supply of altruism runs out."

The Mixtwirk seemed to consider making a retort, thought better of it, then motioned for the Rodian to leave.

Cavv settled back in his chair. "So, where was I?"

"One step away from the Old Spacer's Home," Sconn said.

"Hilarious, nephew. I often wondered if I was the only one in our family with a sense of humor. Now I know for sure...I am."

"Well there's one thing that I never find the least bit funny... death." Sconn waved his hand dismissively. "And what you're proposing is suicide."

"You said you'd help."

"That's because when you asked me to assist you in 'acquiring' a ship for the Republic, you neglected to mention it was going to be an Imperial Star Destroyer."

Cavv seemed to have found something very interesting to look at on the floor.

"Either the ghost of the Emperor just materialized under our table, or there's another point of interest you haven't told me about."

Cavv looked back up at his nephew. "Well, technically, this ship isn't a Star Destroyer."

"Thank the Force for small favors."

"It's really more of a Super Star Destroyer."

Sconn didn't say a word. His mouth opened ever so slightly, but no sound emerged.

"You did promise," Cavv said with his best spotluma smile. "And from what I've heard, Sienn Sconn always keeps his promises, doesn't he? As the old Devaronian saying goes, *Even a fool can find that the—*"

Sconn quickly stuck an interrupting finger in the air. "Fine. You win. We'll go get ourselves killed. Just don't start with those blasted platitudes."

Sconn shifted uncomfortably in his seat. One problem with newly installed governments is that their leaders still thought like the revolutionaries they once were. In the Alliance, no one wasted material on creature comforts, so not even a distingushed general had plush chairs in his office. Sienn Sconn liked such amenities—the good life as it were. Unfortunately, from the way General Airen Cracken was talking, Sconn's life was about to turn bad. Very bad.

"...estimate the remaining crew complement of the Super Star Destroyer *Guardian* at about 250,000 of which 40,000 or so are trained combatants." The General stated this as if he was merely ordering roast pormork at the nearest space diner. That made Sconn extremely nervous.

Cryle Cavv glanced over and could tell by his nephew's expression that Sconn was drifting into hyperspace. He delivered a subtle, yet sharp, nudge to Sconn's ribs.

The General continued: "We can only estimate the weapon and shield strength of the ship, but are confident the hyperdrive is temporarily out of commission."

Cavv nodded. "As I recall, the *Guardian* took quite a pounding at Tantive V before it finally escaped."

"We believe that was the last jump it made." The General's voice lowered. "The *Guardian* is still out there, somewhere, battered and broken. Just waiting for us."

Sconn raised a finger into the air. "When you say 'us,' whom exactly are you referring to?"

"Nephew!"

Cracken grinned. "A valid question, Cavv. I am speaking metaphorically of the Republic and more specifically the New Republic Special Acquisitions Unit."

Sconn brightened a bit. The SAU. Now that was very professional–sounding. Then the thief realized something. "Never heard of them."

"Er." Cracken glanced at the far wall. "They're a recent development."

Sconn's nose crinkled. "How recent?"

"Just a few minutes ago."

"Oh well, as my uncle always says," Sconn glanced meaningfully at Cavv, "*Never look a gift garral in the mouth; it's likely to bite your head clean off.*"

Cavv cleared his throat noisily.

"Who exactly heads up this unit?" Sconn asked.

Cracken paused a moment, then gestured theatrically. At Cavv. "A legendary acquisitions specialist."

"And his team?"

"A veteran unit consisting of," there was another pause before the general finally said, "you."

"Me," Sconn echoed. He added hopefully, "Anybody else?"

"No."

Sconn inhaled a long breath of air through his nostrils, and settled down in his chair. He tried to, anyway. It was like sitting on a blasted rock.

Cavv steepled his fingers. "After all these years, how did you come across this find?"

"Luck actually. Some of our probe droids have run across a number of *Lambda*–class shuttles appearing in Imperial–controlled systems requesting parts to repair the hyperdrive of a large capital ship. It took a little digging and a lot of time, but further investigation revealed that the shuttles were part of the complement of the *Guardian*." Cracken's eyes flashed as he seemed to be reliving the moment. "The ship is extremely vulnerable to attack and potential capture. Taking a Super Star Destroyer intact would be one of the greatest coups in New Republic history. I know it won't be an easy task."

"There's a shock," Sconn muttered.

"Unfortunately, because of NRI's efforts to find who's behind the mysterious terrorist bombings throughout the Core sectors, I don't have much in the way of personnel or ships to spare. And of course, the *Guardian* must first be located."

"Easier done than said," Cavv said with a dismissive wave of his hand.

"I think you have that one backwards, uncle."

Cavv's eyes were nearly twinkling now. Sconn recognized the look. "My sources, and they are quite reliable, have uncovered a clandestine meeting to take place less than a week from now on the planet Vohai in the Parmel Sector. A *Lambda*–class shuttle is scheduled to rendezvous with the famed Vohai Unirail at Sensyno Station."

Sconn wasn't liking this at all. Cracken's face had erupted into a smile frighteningly similar to the one his uncle was wearing.

"Burgo Teage, a nefarious black market dealer, is meeting up with the shuttle's occupants to close a certain deal in which hyperdrive components for a capital ship play a rather key role." Cavv waggled his eyebrows and leaned back with utterly dramatic flair.

Cracken was already pressing the inter–comlink panel on his desk. "Gerind, I'm going to need two tickets for the Vohai Unirail's next excursion."

Cavv clamped a hand on Sconn's shoulder, jovially shaking his nephew. "Good news, boy. You're going on vacation. With your favorite uncle no less."

"You're my only uncle," Sconn reminded him.

"Funny you should mention it. See, the Rodians have an old saying about family and favoritism..."

General Cracken tried valiantly to maintain a straight face as Sconn managed to sink even lower in his chair.

"Welcome aboard Corellian Translines SV–45 express transport to Vohai," came a voice tinged with a carefully cultivated, cultured accent. "I'm Duran Har, your captain. Sit back, relax and enjoy the journey. If there's anything we can do to make the trip more pleasant or you, use the call button to your right, and one of our attendants will be with you momentarily." The captain then launched into an abbreviated travelogue for Vohai and the rest of the planets in the Parmel Sector.

Sconn rolled his eyes in annoyance as the sturdy StarSpeeder 3000 lurched into hyperspace. "You'd think Cracken's people could have arranged something less touristy."

Cavv looked up from his datapad. "We don't want to arouse any suspicion. And don't forget, from here on in the name's Burgo Teage."

"Let me guess, I'm your lovely assistant."

"Correct. Except for the lovely part." Cavv looked back at his datapad and said: "Gronk."

"Pardon?"

"Gronk." Cavv started laughing. "That's your name. Gronk."

Sconn was not amused.

Sconn glanced up through the transparisteel skylight to thin unirail track.

"Something wrong?" Cavv asked.

"The fact that we're about two kilometers above the ground hanging on a super–conductive wire that doesn't look it could support the weight of a Wookiee much less 46 rail cars."

"Relax. To date the Vohai has a perfect safety record."

"Yeah, well, to date *we* hadn't ridden on it."

They sat in the upper level of the dining/casino car, nursing fluted glasses of Renan wine. Their table, nestled in the corner offered an excellent view of the turbolifts down to the casino portion of the car.

Sconn checked his chronometer.

"Relax, neph—" Cavv pressed his lips together. "I mean, Gronk. Our guest still has some time before his nightly foray to the gambling tables. And we're not scheduled to reach Sensyno Station for another hour." He let his gaze travel to the viewport nearby. The clouds had thinned somewhat and the night sky unfolded around them. Brightly twinkling congregations of light on the horizon marked the location of some of Vohai's cityscapes. "Take a moment to enjoy the spectacular view, savor your wine, delight in the simple pleasures of the moment." Cavv raised his glass in a toast.

"I thought you retired to do just that."

"I did. But this was one mission I couldn't turn down. So I made myself un–retired." Cavv's voice took on a distant quality. "It's a very strange business we're in, nephew. You steal a wallet and you get tossed in jail. You steal a man's wife and you get a bloody nose. But you steal something large enough, you get famous. A Super Star Destroyer! This will make us the greatest thieves who ever lived."

"Or we'll die trying," Sconn said flatly, swirling the remains of his wine around in the glass and then taking a mouthful.

"You know, you've been nothing but negative since we started this trip."

"Maybe because I don't want to die."

"We all die, nephew. It's the way of things."

"I have no desire to help things along. And at the moment I seem to be in the express lane to the Great Beyond."

"Actually, I think this little adventure will be good for you. You've turned into quite the sourpuss. Some of those faces you make could curdle lum." Cavv gestured. "There! That's exactly what I'm talking about!"

"You invited me along."

"You didn't have to accept."

"Now you tell me."

There was a long silence.

"Is everything okay, nephew?"

Sconn remained silent, staring out the viewport at the passing clouds.

"You know," Cavv stopped at the brink for a microsecond, then went ahead and jumped off the edge. "Ever since Shandria dumped you, your attitude has made Barabels look positively even–tempered by comparison."

Sconn's face flushed. "Shandria did not dump me. It was a mutual decision. Considering you seem to know everything, I'm surprised you got that little bit of data wrong."

"Nobody's perfect, nephew. We all make mistakes." Cavv's voice softened. "Shame to let a nice girl like that get away, though. You two made a lovely couple, when you weren't trying to kill each other."

"That's all over now," Sconn said through clenched teeth. "Much like this conversation."

"There he goes," Cavv said quietly.

Sconn looked up as a Herglic in a finely tailored, expensive silk suit waddled toward the turbolifts.

"Looks like Burgo's listing a bit already," Cavv noted. "That's good."

Sconn made a face. "How can you tell with all that jiggling?"

"Actually he's in decent shape."

"Only if your definition of exercise includes deep elbow bends as he lifts a mug to his lips, or the Herglic equivalent of lips."

Cavv and Sconn watched Teage enter the turbolift, occupying nearly all of the available space in the process. The only other passenger, an unfortunate Ithorian, found himself on intimate terms with the side wall of the car.

Cavv turned to Sconn. "I have an idea."

"Obviously the dark side of the Force at work."

"I'm going to make friends with Burgo, let him win a hand or two of sabacc, Tatooine Sunburn him into unconsciousness, and make sure he gets safely stuffed into an out–of–the–way storage area."

"Are you sure these Imps don't know Burgo's not human? Even with the silk wrappings I'm not sure you could pass for Herglic," Sconn said. "Well, not without adding at least a few more pounds."

"As much as I'm sure I'll miss your lightsaber–sharp wit, why don't you make yourself useful and go check on Burgo's precious cargo." Cavv stood up, adjusting his clothing. "Think you can handle that?"

"A little basic break–and–enter?" Sconn's voice took on a sarcastic tone. "Oooh. I don't know, that's kind of tough." Sconn downed the rest of his wine in one gulp. "I'm sure I'll manage just fine, Master Burgo. But thanks for asking."

Sconn was surprised at how easily the door swung open. Even as the question popped into his mind, the answer hit him.

More accurately, two huge muscular fists shot forward and grabbed him by the shoulders. The next moment, he was yanked into the suite and he found himself airborne, soaring past the luxurious furnishings until he slammed against the far wall.

Sconn's mind raced to catch up with current events but was still stuck on *Ow. Ow. Ow. Ow.*

Across the room, a hulking Reigat closed the door to the hallway. He detached an extremely nasty–looking vibroaxe from the harness across his broad back as he turned toward Sconn and began crossing the room. Reigats were quite a large species, but they really loomed when a body happened to be staring up at them from a prone position on the floor.

"You must be Gronk," Sconn guessed.

The Reigat smiled in the affirmative, displaying a row of teeth filed into long fangs. "You must be ready to die, little humanoid. I will dance on your corpse."

Sconn stumbled to his feet and slowly reached for the silver haft tucked in his belt. "You wanna dance, big boy?"

The handle slid into the thief's palm with the familiarity of an old lover. A quick twist extended it in both directions, completing the sudden transformation into a meter–long staff. Sconn flicked his finger, and the tips crackled with azure stun energy. "Okay, I'll lead."

"...so the Hutt thinks about it for about a microsecond and," Burgo unleashed a bone–rattling burb, "says, 'I don't know if I like it but I'll take two more anyway!'"

Cavv threw back his head and roared at Burgo's joke, spilling a good portion of his drink on the floor.

The Herglic was positively quivering in amusement at his own joke. Burgo took a sip of his Tatooine Sunburn and with some effort managed not to fall of his barstool.

"That's a good one," Cavv said wiping his eyes.

The Herglic finished off the Sunburn with one mighty gulp and patted Cavv on the back with an unsteady fin. "I like you... not only do you stink at sabacc, you enjoy good Herglic jokes."

Actually, Cavv had missed the humor completely, but he wasn't about to argue that point. There was an old Quarren saying: *When you have the glowfish on the hook, don't talk it to death. Just beat*

it over the head with a big club.

Cavv motioned to the server droid behind the bar, ordering another round of Sunburns. He was amazed Burgo could still talk after a half–dozen of the potent drinks. With a little minor sleight–of–hand, Cavv had managed to covertly spill the contents of his glasses into nearby plants. Then again, a drunk Herglic was not the hardest audience in the world to misdirect.

Burgo wrapped a fin around the glass and checked his chronometer squinting and shaking his head as he tried to clear his vision.

"Got a date?" Cavv inquired innocently.

"Can't quite remember," Burgo said, then erupted into gales of laughter. "So I hope she does!"

Cavv joined in whole–heartedly, then made a show of unsteadily getting to his feet. "Come on, I'll make sure you get back to your room with all my money intact." He lowered his voice to a conspiratorial whisper. "I hear a lot of thieves take these trips just to prey on poor, innocent folks."

Burgo stood and attempted a knowing wink in return, but succeeded only in closing both eyes and nearly fell down. Cavv locked an arm around the big Herglic, and the duo wobbled their way toward the turbolifts.

As they staggered inside, Cavv smiled to himself. This mission was easy credits, so far. And he was the one who had the difficult assignment.

Sconn was probably making himself comfortable in Burgo's suite. Typical. Lately, his good–for–nothing nephew was always lying down on the job.

Sconn was indeed fully horizontal, but not by choice, as his body slammed against the wall. Suddenly the thief's world went vertical again and his head hit the carpeted floor of the passenger car. Before he knew it, he was oriented horizontally again. His body was having a hard time keeping up with the rapid changes in position, already occupied as it was with an overflow of information from various pain receptors.

As Sconn struggled to his hands and knees, Gronk closed in to finish the job. The vibroaxe arced overhead, flashing as the wicked blade began its descent.

From his prone position on the floor, Sconn rolled forward, right between the thick trunks that passed for the Reigat's legs. There was ample clearance for the balled–up thief, however his extended stun staff slammed against the alien's groin and mid–section.

Gronk roared in pain. The axe bit into the floor and lodged there as the Reigat's nerveless fingers twitched right off the handle.

Sconn finished his tuck–and–roll and came up in a battle stance. "Come on!" the thief roared in challenge. He flicked the small switch, shifting the staff's full charge to a single pulsing tip.

The Reigat bruiser turned, eyes pulsing like overloaded turbolasers about to blow. Gronk left the axe where it was and just drove his powerful legs forward in a furious charge.

The thief was ready and swinging the stun staff with both hands. The crackling tip of the weapon met the Reigat's hard head. Irresistable force met with an immovable object.

A sizzling flash preceded a blinding surge of stored energy being released and Sconn's staff broke into two jagged pieces. The confused thief looked down at the remains of his beloved weapon and then back up at the Reigat.

A wide smile split Gronk's ugly face in two. He took a threatening step forward... and collapsed to the floor. He groaned once and then lay perfectly quiet.

Sconn exhaled audibly and slumped back against the wall adjacent to Burgo's suite. His eyes fluttered closed.

When he finally opened them, Cavv was standing over his nephew, hands on his hips. "I knew it," he mumbled.

"Well, don't just sit there, nephew. We're not here on vacation, remember?"

Sconn continued to stare straight ahead.

"Drag your little friend into the closet so we can straighten this place up and get ready for our meeting."

Sconn slowly held up the broken half of his stun staff and began some whimsical calculations regarding width, length and depth.

"Attention, gentlebeings. We're about to reach Sensyno Unirail Station. There will be a minor layover for resupply. Passengers are encouraged to take this opportunity and stretch those weary appendages. Feel free to explore the gift shop and other wonders of the newly refurbished—"

"Oh, put a spanner in it," Sconn grumbled at the comm–unit. The thief stretched out on the couch and stared at his chronometer. "They're late, uncle. I don't like it."

Cavv finished checking the trio of large crates piled against the far wall and took a seat at the thick repliwood table. He absently wiped at the surface, sending imaginary dust motes scattering. "You need to calm down, Sconn. At this rate you won't live to see a hundred."

Sconn rubbed his shoulders, still sore from his encounter with the Reigat and laughed without humor. "Hah! At this rate I won't live to see these bruises heal."

Before Cavv could respond, there was a sharp rapping on the door. Two knocks. Very crisp. Very Imperial.

The two thieves exchanged a meaningful glance. "Showtime," they said in unison.

Burgo was just regaining consienceness. He was tired, confused, and more than anything else really, really cold. With a shrug of his immense weight, the lock on the seafood freezer compartment gave way and the lid swung wide. The Herglic stood up, sending more than a few terrified cooks scrambling from the dining car kitchen.

Burgo didn't recall much of the last few hours. His head currently felt like it was tops on the travel itinerary for a rampaging herd of bantha. In fact, all he knew was that he needed to get back to his suite and go to sleep for a long time. (Or at least until the bantha herd finished their vacation in his skull.) Now if only he could remember where his room was.

He fished around his pockets with a flipper and felt a small rectangular square of plas. Burgo withdrew the key card, imprinted as it was with his suite number. The Herglic smiled and climbed out of the storage unit.

The first Imperial, a beady–eyed specimen of humanity, slid the credit voucher across the table. Cavv noted the man's fingers twitched slightly; it was, after all, a lot of money.

Cavv silently checked the amount and nodded in satisfaction. He motioned over his shoulder, and Sconn dutifully opened the first cargo crate for inspection. The second Imperial stuck his broad nose, obviously broken more than once, into the container and examined the contents.

After a few tense moments, the second Imperial was satisfied and nodded curtly his partner.

Cavv could barely restrain himself as he reached for the stun pistol in his pocket. *This is almost too easy*, he thought.

The door to the suite swung open and for the briefest of moments, time froze.

Burgo stood there looking a bit muddled, the key card still wedged in his flipper.

Cavv cursed curse Herglic fortitude.

The Imps gawked.

Sconn wondered why his uncle hadn't just lifted Burgo's key card in the first place?

Then with a dramatic groan, the closet where they had stashed Gronk collapsed from the dead weight and the Reigat henchman spilled to the floor.

"Burgo!" Cavv yelled without realizing it.

"Gronk!" said the Herglic.

"Burgo?" cried the Imperials in unison.

"Urrrr," groaned Gronk.

Then everybody started shooting.

"Well," Cavv said as he wiped the sweat from his forehead, "that certainly could have gone better."

"That's one way of putting it." Sconn surveyed the carnage in the room and shook his head. "That's just great! Without the Imps, we have no one to fly us back to the *Guardian*."

Cavv harrumphed and crossed his arms. "I am a fair pilot, you know."

"The way things are going, more than likely you'll pilot us into a black hole." Sconn set his exhausted wrist laser to recharge mode and leaned heavily on one of the crates, now complete with blaster–scoring. "I say we call off this idiotic mission, go home and get drunk on Corellian whisky."

"There's always the 'Endor Run,' nephew."

"No thanks. I'm allergic to Ewok fur."

"We're not actually going to Endor—sometimes I wonder what laser facility you got your brains shipped from—we're going to follow in the footsteps of some of the greatest Heroes of the Rebellion and— "

"Die horrible deaths?"

"No. Sneak into the vornskr's den by dressing up as a vornskr."

Sconn folded his arms across his chest. "I refuse to be the rear end again."

"Listen, if you just listened to my directions instead of being so headstrong, you never would have fallen into Lady Jalaka's pool."

"I couldn't hear a thing in that ridiculous costume. If you weren't so sloshed on Savareen Brandy to give me coherent directions it never would have happened. And no matter how wonderful the party, it's no fun spending an entire evening staring at your—"

"Back to the task at hand," Cavv interrupted. "The fact is we've got an important job to do and we're going to get it done. No matter the cost."

"Speaking of costs, you never told me how much we're going to be paid for this idiotic endeavor."

"How much?"

"Yes. As in 'credits.' As in 'it better be a lot.' As in 'more than I can imagine.'"

Cavv was silent for several heartbeats. Then he said, "Nothing."

"Why am I not surprised?"

"Well, there is your regular salary as a member of the SAU. Plus hazard pay."

"What? I'm not part of any New Republic operations!"

"Technically—"

"No," Sconn said flatly. "I've been handed the membership speech before, so you can save your breath."

"Then you won't be compensated at all." Cavv shrugged. "Think about it, nephew. We do this right and you could be a ranking officer."

"I don't care about rank or money. I don't want one and I already have more than I need of the other. I'm a thief who has outlived his usefulness. The galaxy has played an ironic joke on Sienn Sconn. I've stolen enough to be happy in this life, but my life still isn't happy."

"That's why when I steal now there's a purpose. Acquiring things for a cause. A good cause."

"It's still just a means to an end. I wasted my life for something I realize now that I never even wanted. I've turned into the stinking idle rich that I used to steal from."

"Is that what you really think? That it was all for nothing."

"Nothing of real value."

"Funny thing about that. Value is a subjective measurement. The Galactic Regulatory Commission may set the exchange rate for credits, but what's really important to us can only be decided by us." Cavv smiled softly. "That's why I intend to finish this mission."

"Then you'll die."

"Perhaps I will. But at least I'll have died trying."

"There's nothing worth dying for."

Cavv's eyes grew distant. "Maybe I shouldn't have brought you along."

"One man can't make a difference."

"Maybe not, but without that first man to stand up, you would never have a second, or a third, or a fourth. Everyone starts off alone."

"Some of us end up alone."

"We're trapped only in the prisons of our own minds."

"And which legendary philosopher spouted that nonsense?" Sconn asked sarcastically.

"Me." Cavv sighed. "Go home, nephew. I thought this mission would do you good, but I see I was wrong. I wish you the best of luck with whatever path you decide to travel."

Cavv removed the shuttle control code from the dead Imp and quietly left the suite. "May the Force be with you, Sienn."

Sconn stood there alone among the silent dead.

Cavv paused to watch the Unirail depart Sensyno Station and then walked toward the *Lambda*–class Imperial shuttle. The old thief paused in the shadow of the massive dorsal fin. He used the control code to lower the access ramp and entered the craft. He step was heavy and his shoulders were slumped.

He knew something was wrong as soon as he stepped into the cockpit. Even before the figure in the co–pilot chair swung around, a blur of Imperial gray.

Cavv went for his hold–out blaster though it was probably too late. *There were only supposed to be two of them*, his mind wailed.

"No one should have to die alone," Sconn said, looking up at him from the command chair. His nephew was wearing an Imperial uniform and looked halfway respectable for once. "Even a stubborn old bantha like you."

Cavv was still grinning when Sconn turned the chair back around and muttered: "Instead of standing there like a slack–jawed Gotal, why don't you make yourself useful and access the nav computer? That way when we jump to lightspeed we might actually end this trip at a certain Super Star Destroyer instead of in the middle of a sun. Although truthfully, I'm not quite sure which one would be worse."

The *Guardian* loomed large in the shuttle's main viewport. Even in its current dilapidated condition the Super Star Destroyer was an impressive sight. In fact, the battle–scarred superstructure seemed all the more menacing for its ability to survive such extensive wounds.

The mighty Imperial warship moved in limping orbit around a large blue–green world.

"Where are we?" Cavv whispered.

"Back end of the Outer Rim. How appropriate." Sconn gestured at the screen. "That's the planet Soullex over there." He checked the sensor readouts. "There are three prefabricated garrisons on the surface. Well, that should cut down on the ship's compliment a bit—10,000 down, only about 100,000 more to go."

The comlink buzzed, echoing through the cabin.

"I think that's for you," Sconn said. "You know, they're going to recognize their buddies. And we're not them."

"Send them a text message. We're having a problem with our communications system."

The answer came quickly.

"They say there's no malfunction," Sconn reported.

Cavv put a pair of blaster bolts into the shuttle's comm unit. "There is now."

Sconn read the screen. "Acknowledged. They want us to stand by and they'll tow the shuttle inside."

"We're in, nephew."

"Unfortunately," Sconn replied. The shuttle rocked softly beneath them as it was caught in the grip of the *Guardian*'s tractor beam. "Now what?"

"The shuttle has arrived, Admiral," the deck officer reported over the comm. "But there's been a slight problem."

Gaen Drommel looked up from his novel and favored the major—Drommel couldn't quite recall the man's name at the moment—with a dark glare.

The Admiral calmly placed the ancient book on his desk, the heavy leather volume creaking to rest on the shiny plasteel. "Is my memory slipping, Major, or did I specifically give orders that I was not to be disturbed?"

The image of the dumbfounded major on the viewscreen flickered for a moment and then disappeared entirely. The Admiral moved a gloved finger from the control panel and quietly left his quarters.

The command deck of the *Guardian* was silent, quite a feat considering the amount of personnel occupying the cavernous space. Drommel crossed the deck in his usual long, measured strides until he was face–to–face with the junior officer.

"You disobeyed my order."

"My apologies, Admiral. I merely assumed you'd want—"

"*Never* assume, Major. You know what happens to those who assume, don't you?"

"Yes, sir," the major answered quickly, but didn't sound sure if that was the correct response.

There was a sizzling blast. The major fell to the polished floor. Dead.

"You see, you assumed again. And I had just told you not to." Drommel slid the smoking blaster back into its holster and swept his gaze over the rest of the assembled bridge crew. "Did everyone learn their lesson for the day?"

No one spoke.

"Good," Drommel nodded, casually stepping over the corpse. "Now, about that shuttle."

Cavv grunted as he attempted to squeeze himself into the stormtrooper armor.

Sconn cocked an eyebrow. The younger thief was already suited up, except for the helmet which promptly got stuck as soon as he slid it into place. Sconn had nearly yanked his own head off trying to remove the thing and he wasn't eager to repeat the claustrophobic incident. "Is the body glove supposed to bulge out between the armor pieces like that?"

"Nephew?"

"Yes, uncle?"

"Do shut up."

After a string of Corellian curses and some help from Sconn,

Cavv managed to get into the armor.

Cavv looked himself over and shook his head. "How do these guys ever use the refresher?"

"Maybe they don't. It would explain why they're always so ornery." Sconn handed over one of the blaster carbines.

Cavv checked the charge on the weapon's power pack and gestured to his nephew to proceed. Both men reached for their helmets...

Just then the heavy blast door suddenly slid back and a shiny, silver droid stared into the supply room.

There was a moment of silence, then the droid cried out in alarm. "Intruders! Spies! Impostors! Malcont—"

The rest of it was muffled as Sconn slapped a hand over the shrieking vocabulator and yanked the astonished droid inside.

Drommel watched as the tech team combed over the shuttlecraft. His expression remained neutral, though after what happened to the major, no one wanted to stand too close.

The Admiral focused his attention on one of the junior techs, struggling with a ventral compartment. The wiry officer was trying to pry open the access hatch. A series of sharp tugs later and the obstinate compartment opened, spilling two bodies onto the hapless tech. Both individuals were dressed only in their gray undergarments. A clutter of civilian clothing and a discarded Imperial uniform was tangled around them.

Medical personnel, standing diligently by until needed, suddenly rushed in to make a pronouncement. "They're alive, but heavily stunned."

Drommel nodded then turned his attention to the senior tech. The man gestured at three containers being loaded onto a repulsorsled. "It appears the cargo is all here, sir."

The Admiral gave him a look.

"But I'll just double–check to be absolutely sure," the senior tech added very hastily.

Drommel couldn't suppress a slight grin. Fear was extremely effective at keeping order; that was a lesson he'd learned from Tarkin. The Admiral considered himself more than a mere student of humanity. True he learned from great men, but more importantly, Drommel would learn from their mistakes. And he certainly would not repeat such foolish errors.

Niovi, the ranking colonel, began barking out orders to the assembled squad of naval troopers. "The intruders must be found. Alert all stations to begin a deck–by–deck search. We have a lot of ship to cover—"

"Belay that order." Drommel motioned to the overzealous man. "We're merely looking for the first two stormtroopers which had contact with that shuttle. They'll be our impostors, so find and detain them. Immediately."

"Stormtroopers, sir?" asked the Colonel.

The Admiral lifted a single eyebrow. "Unless someone happens to see two naked beings running around the ship. In which case, detain them as well."

Sconn held the business end of the blaster carbine pointed directly at the droid's face. "Let's start over. Shall we?"

"Greetings. I am CT–EX human/cyborg relationships."

"How about we just call you Teex?" Cavv asked.

"As you wish. Can I be of assistance?"

"That depends," Cavv said. "How well do you know this ship?"

"Which ship would that be?"

"How about the one we're standing on?" Sconn snapped. "In. Whatever."

"It may not my place to say, sir, but you are mistaken. This is no ship."

"Then exactly where are we?"

"Here." The droid tilted its head ever–so–slightly. "Would you like me to provide you the exact spatial coordinates?"

"So you admit we are in space."

"Of course not. You would have imploded by now if that were true." There was a slight pause and then the droid added, "Vacuum–for–brains."

Sconn blinked once. Twice. "What did he just say?"

"I'm not quite sure I heard him correctly," Cavv said, trying not to smile.

"Repeat yourself," Sconn ordered the droid.

"Yourself."

Sconn began to squeeze the trigger. Cavv pushed away the barrel and studied their mechanical captive. "Wait. I think I have an idea."

"Does it involve a thermal detonator?" Sconn asked, staring angrily at the silver droid.

Before Cavv could answer, Teex chimed in, "Of course not. That would blow a large hole in this ship." Pause. "Nerfherder."

Sconn was still struggling to get at the droid even as Cavv shoved him toward the door. "Maybe you should just stand guard until we're done in here."

Sconn nodded to a passing stormtrooper patrol, then eased his stance from rigid attention. The armor was hot, the helmet was heavy and he didn't feel like playing toy soldier. The thief longed for the good old days at the Binary Bar, drinking, swapping tall tales, and staring at beautiful women. That was where he met Shandria; she was an Alliance operative on the run from Imperials. He had always been a sucker for a pretty face, but she was so much more.

Sconn shook his head, recalling one of his uncle's adages. *Spend too much time looking backwards and you may just miss the big, gaping hole ahead of you.*

The blast door slid back, interrupting his thoughts. Teex exited and wandered off without a word. Cavv emerged right behind him, patting Sconn's armored shoulder. "We need to talk."

Cavv led them to a bank of turbolifts. The duo stepped into the first car and descended further into the bowels of the *Guardian*.

"Where we going?"

Cavv's helmet stared straight ahead.

"Oh, I'm really not going to like this am I?"

"Detention Block 220."

"When Tatooine freezes over!" Sconn halted their descent and faced his uncle. "Have you completely lost your mind?"

"Teex told me there are New Republic prisoners aboard. We're going to rescue them."

"What? That's ridiculous. If by some bit of sheer luck we actually manage to steal this blasted ship they'll be free anyway. Whereas going to the detention block to orchestrate a jailbreak would seriously hamper our efforts. Especially if we get caught!"

"We have a duty—"

"Don't start with that again. Listen, uncle, a thief with a conscience is like, like a rude protocol droid. Useless. Ineffective."

"You have a lot to learn about life, Sconn. I was hoping this assignment would open your eyes to that. There is a larger world around you."

Sconn jabbed a gloved finger at Cavv's armored chest. "You are not Obi-Wan Kenobi. I certainly am not Luke Skywalker—I'm much more handsome—and I don't care if the Queen Princess of the Galaxy is being held prisoner here, we are not going to a detention block under any circumstances." Sconn paused for a moment, catching the look on Cavv's face. "Don't say it."

"Then I'll do it alone."

Sconn groaned. "I really, really don't like you. You know that, right?"

The senior tech offered a stiff salute. "The parts check out, sir."

"Begin repairing the hyperdrive immediately. Triple your work force if need be, but no one sleeps until the job is finished." Drommel stared out the transparisteel viewport at the planet below. "Send word to the garrison commanders. With any luck we'll be leaving this backwater system very shortly." His eyes flickered back to the tech. "How long until we can test the hyperdrive?"

"Best estimate would be at least 48 hours, Admiral."

"Then we shall be underway in 36. Do I make myself clear?"

"Yes, sir." The tech spun on his heels, barking out the Admiral's orders to his team.

Drommel joined Colonel Niovi, who was hovering at the nearby comm-station. "Any word on our fugitives?"

"No contact as of yet, sir."

"I want them found."

"Colonel Eijul is optimistic."

"He will be among the first things I will retrofit on this ship when we return to Imperial space," Drommel said as he strode toward the turbolift. Niovi struggled to keep up. "Eijul would have difficulty locating the intruders if they pranced right into a detention block and turned themselves in."

The doors to Detention Block 220 slid open, drawing a disinterested glance from the duty officer. The black-uniformed man continued entering data into his console, figuring the two stormtroopers were part of the group searching for the two stormtroopers... who were impostors!

The duty officer snapped his head back up just the butt of a blaster carbine completed its downward arc. The man's field of vision suddenly jumped to hyperspace, and he slid to the floor beneath the console.

"Anyone else?" Sconn asked.

Cavv checked the display. "The rest of the guards are busy looking for us." The old thief grinned. "They must have figured this is the last place a fugitive would go."

"Sure. Nobody could be that stupid."

Cavv ignored that comment and unlocked the blast door leading to the cells. He gestured grandly down the cramped corridor. "After you."

Sconn unceremoniously pushed his uncle ahead. "Age before beauty. Take the right. I got the left."

"Sabacc!" cried Cavv.

He was at the last cell on his side when he found them: Half a dozen Republic soldiers who unwittingly found themselves trapped by the *Guardian* when they exited hyperspace. They were a scraggly group and hesitant to trust Cavv until his code phrases and short anecdotes convinced them he was no Imperial.

"Any luck over there?" Cavv asked.

Sconn peered into the next chamber. A single prisoner sat there in a soot–stained jumpsuit. His breath suddenly caught. Before his mind could catch up with his body, one hand was slapped against the control panel. The door slid back and he practically stumbled into the cell.

The dark–haired beauty looked up in confusion and Sconn gazed into a face he'd never thought he'd see again.

"What are you doing here?" he blurted out.

"I'm a prisoner," the woman answered, then narrowed her eyes. "What do you *think* I'm doing here?"

Sconn tugged dramatically at his helmet, fully expecting to rip it off with a grand flourish. It didn't so much as budge.

"What's taking so long, nephew?" Cavv entered the cell sans headgear. His eyes grew wide as he saw the woman.

"Cavv!" she cried, running over to hug him. She girl released Cavv from the embrace and turned just as Sconn managed to remove his stubborn helmet.

Their eyes met and held. Time held its breath.

Sconn spoke first, his voice soft yet charged with a spectrum of emotions. "Shandria."

Her mouth opened, but before she could speak the other prisoners swarmed into the cell to greet their old comrade. Sconn stepped backwards to the door, though his eyes remained locked with Shandria's for another heartbeat. He then looked away from the reunion and stepped out alone into the empty corridor.

"I have an idea, but it's a bit risky." Cavv looked up from the security console, pausing to allow Sconn one of his obligatory slanderous comments, but none were forthcoming. The younger thief stood quietly against the wall, his eyes staring off into space.

"Anything is better than remaining captive here." Shandria said. A rumble of agreement rippled through the assembled prisoners.

"Here's the plan," Cavv said. "My nephew and I will venture to the *Guardian's* engineering room and attempt to gain manual control of the hyperdrive systems. This will hopefully allow us to program a quick jump to friendly space without having to take the command deck."

Sconn remained silent through Cavv's recitation of the details, offering no comment at all.

When it was over, Shandria began handing out blasters to her group. Cavv and Sconn readied themselves for yet another stormtrooper impersonation.

As the two groups separated, Shandria and Sconn lingered behind. They both started talking in unison, resulting in a stop–and–start garble of unintelligible conversation.

The thief held up a hand. "Let me go first. There's something I have to tell you."

"Sconn, I... there's been so much that... I guess what I'm trying to say, is that it's been so long and... I just can't do this right now." Her eyes lingered on the floor. Her voice became a whisper. "I'm sorry."

Sconn nodded, moving to rejoin his uncle. Cavv was busy adjusting his comlink to a particular frequency. "Teex, are you ready?"

The droid's filtered voice crackled to life. "Affirmative, sir. The Jawa rides at midnight."

"The Jawa rides alone." Cavv glanced over at his unusually quiet nephew. "Let's go."

"Sconn?" Shandria's voice wavered slightly.

He glanced over his shoulder.

"Take care of yourself."

"We certainly will," Cavv said, feigning indignation.

The senior tech was sweating profusely as he made the final adjustments to the *Guardian*'s newly–repaired hyperdrive. The perspiration was not only a result of the difficult labor, but the incessant tapping of Admiral Drommel's boot against the deck.

"How much longer?"

"We can make our first jump in ten minutes, sir." The tech used the neck of his coveralls to wipe some grime from his forehead.

Drommel glanced over at the dozen crewmen toiling around him, many of whom had not slept in 24 hours or more. "Carry on, then. I have other matters to attend." Drommel spun sharply and exited. Two stormtroopers entering the room separated to allow him passage.

The senior tech sighed at the new interruption and waved his arms at the troopers as one closed the security door behind them. "This is a restricted area. You're not allowed in here."

A blaster bolt knocked the man right off his feet.

Sconn swung his blaster from side–to–side, training the barrel on each of the remaining techs. "Anybody else want to ask us to leave?"

No one did.

As they stripped off their helmets, Cavv glanced at his nephew in horror.

"You look like a bantha just stepped on your foot," Sconn said, that familiar half–smile playing at the corner of his lips. His voice lowered. "Relax. It was set to stun."

Cavv shook his head in amazement.

"So, you going to get to work or do you need an engraved invitation from Mon Mothma?"

"Good to have you back." Cavv patted his nephew's shoulder as he passed.

Sconn herded the techs into a huddle in the corner of the room. Cavv searched through the abandoned toolkits, picking up a pair of hydrospanners and approaching the main hyperdrive control with a hesitant gait.

"You do know what you're doing?" Sconn asked.

"Of course," Cavv said with a derisive chuckle. "How hard could it be to override a hyperdrive?" He went to work with a hydrospanner and almost immediately several lights on a nearby panel started to flash bright crimson.

"What is that?" Sconn started forward, though still keeping his weapon trained on the techs. "Some sort of tamper alarm?"

"Don't be silly, nephew. These systems don't have alarms." Cavv returned to work.

Warning klaxons began to wail, the deafening clamor forcing everyone to cover their ears.

Sconn flashed his uncle a look then aimed his blaster at the hyperdrive systems, trying to figure out what looked unimportant. "When in doubt, blast it."

"Well said." The new voice came from behind Cavv and Sconn, who immediately spun around, weapons at the ready. The security door had opened again. Admiral Drommel stood calmly at the entrance, hands folded behind his back. He was surrounded by a phalanx of stormtroopers and navy troopers. "And quite ironic, don't you think?"

"'*Don't be silly, nephew,*" Sconn said in a mocking tone. "'*These systems don't have alarms.*'"

Cavv gave him a sour look.

They had been stripped of their armor and weapons and were now sharing a table in an interrogation room. The next few minutes were spent in silence.

Drommel entered with a flourish, followed by two stormtroopers who obediently took up position at the door.

The Admiral pulled up a chair. "I have subjugated entire systems, including this backwater locale," he said. "Now I will subjugate you. So it would be in your best interest to tell me the truth and save yourselves some pain. How does that sound?"

Neither man answered.

Drommel slammed both hands on the table, causing Sconn to jump. Cavv continued to glare at the Admiral.

"You will answer my next question or I will have my men bring in laser cutters and remove a limb of their choosing. Do I make myself clear?"

"Sure," Cavv said.

"Very good." The Admiral leaned back in his chair. "What are you doing here?"

Cavv remained silent. Sconn pursed his lips.

"Did you not hear me?"

"I heard you," Cavv said. "You told me to answer your next question and I believe it was '*Do I make myself clear?*' to which I responded in the affirmative."

"That wasn't a question."

"Well, I'm not quite sure about the actual punctuation that appeared in your mind, but the inquisitory inflection was definitely there."

Sconn watched, fascinated, as a vein on the Admiral's forehead began to dance.

Cavv pressed on valiantly. "So I did, in fact, answer your next question. You should be more careful with your semantic accuracy."

"Sorry nobody's allowed inside." The naval trooper held out his hand to halt the silver droid ambling his way.

"I have orders from Admiral Drommel himself."

"So do I. Hyperdrive auxiliary control is off limits, even to the tech staff."

"We are about to effect a test of the hyperdrive system," the droid said. "My task is to monitor the results of the experiment and confirm the readouts received on the bridge."

"Why didn't they send an astromech then?"

"It is not my place to question the Admiral's orders." Teex lifted a comlink in the direction of the trooper. "I'll contact him so you can ask him that question yourself."

The guard anxiously placed a hand over the device. He was present on the command deck when the last person who had disturbed Drommel had been punished. "There's no need for that. I'm sure, uh, the Admiral wouldn't want to be bothered."

He stepped aside to allow Teex entrance.

The trooper knew it was impossible but could have sworn he heard the protocol droid mutter something as he passed and it sounded a lot like, "Nerfherder."

Drommel was growing more irritated by the microsecond. The younger captive wouldn't say a word and the old one would not shut up.

Cavv checked his chronometer, stifling a yawn. "Frankly, this little chat has about worn me out, so I don't think I'll be much help to you anymore. Perhaps we could continue this later. I know I could use a good meal and a sonic shower. Plus it'll give you some more time to read up on High Inquisitor Tremayne's *Basic Interrogations*."

Drommel's voice seemed very distant. "Take them away. Into a cell. Now."

As the stormtroopers led the prisoners away from the him out Cavv treated the Admiral to his warmest smile. "I enjoyed this little chat, Admiral. I hope we can do it again soon. Although you might want to prepare some thoughtful questions beforehand. I could put together a reading list of relevant materials if you'd like. And listen, don't be afraid to refer to your notes if—" Cavv's voice continued to drone on even as he was escorted down the hall.

Drommel's lower jaw had shifted to the side, his eyes never leaving the ceiling.

"Admiral," came Colonel Niovi's voice from the doorway. There was no response, but he bravely ventured ahead anyway. "We're clear for a test jump to hyperspace, sir. All systems at your command."

"Very good, Colonel. I'll join you on the command deck momentarily."

Niovi nodded and quickly backed out of the room as the distinct sounds of furniture being badly mistreated echoed from inside.

The procession leading Sconn and Cavv to detention cells suddenly gained another member.

"This way," ordered the attractive female major who bore a striking resemblance to Shandria. "Block 220 is where we're keeping the Rebel scum."

"All systems are nominal, sir," Niovi reported. "Lightspeed test at your command."

Drommel nodded with a thin-lipped smile. Not even the antics of those idiotic intruders could spoil this moment. "On my mark."

The entire command deck was silent as Drommel began the countdown. "Three. Two. One." He raised a gloved hand and snapped it into a fist as he cried out in victory. "Mark!"

There was a burst of palpable acceleration and the crew held its collective breath. The monstrous ship shuddered once as the viewports became a streak of starlines, then a twisting blue cyclone.

Then the process reversed itself as the ship dropped back out of hyperspace. The stars had changed, and the planet Soullex was no longer visible, drawing an impromptu cheer from the crew. Drommel beamed, delighting in his triumph.

Then the great ship suddenly shuddered beneath his feet, sending more than a few officers crashing to the deck.

"Report!" The Admiral grabbed hold of a nearby console to steady himself.

"We are under attack, sir! The coordinates for our test jump were altered. Someone must have bypassed the navcomputer." Colonel Niovi's hands flew across the console, pulling up more tactical information. "Sensors are detecting one New Republic Star Cruiser, two Corvettes, and an Escort Frigate. They're recharging the ion batteries!"

"Intensify all shields," Drommel roared. "Scramble all fighter wings!"

Another barrage of ion cannons rocked the *Guardian* and a strange, filtered voice crackled over the ship's comm.

"Attention Super Star Destroyer. This is Captain Volahn of the New Republic cruiser *Equity*. Power down your weapons and surrender immediately."

All eyes were focused on Drommel. "Even in our current state we're more than a match for that pitiful fleet," he snarled. "And they dare ask us to surrender? We'll burn our response into their hulls!"

"That's always your answer isn't it, Drommel?" The Admiral

whirled toward the sound of the annoying old man's voice. Intruders stormed the command deck. "You!"

Cavv and Sconn were in the lead. Shandria was right behind, directing the rest of the Republic prisoners to fan out into cover positions.

The Imperial officers and naval troopers drew their weapons and likewise took cover behind duty stations. The standoff had begun.

Drommel remained in the open, standing at the top of the command walkway with his fists clenched in rage. "Fools. You'll never leave here alive."

"That's where you're wrong, Admiral," Cavv said, coming out from cover and joining Drommel in the open. "Everyone can make it out of this just fine if you do the intelligent thing and surrender." Cavv eyed the Imperial crew. "I'm not going to bother making any long–winded speeches about freedom and honor and courage to you. I won't even lie and promise full amnesty, but a peaceful resolution wouldn't hurt your chances."

"Enough of this," Drommel roared "Kill them all!"

The tension on the command deck was electric. Both sides took aim.

Sconn began talking. "A wise man once told me: *A good warrior knows when a battle should begin, but a great warrior knows when it must end.*"

Silence fell again over the command deck. One by one, the Imperials lowered their weapons.

Drommel gave a strangled cry of rage and frustration. A blaster suddenly appeared in his gloved hand, pointed at Cavv. The thief flinched and closed his eyes, certain that he and the Admiral were about to be caught in the crossfire as both sides began to shoot. He heard the first shot, but instead of feeling superheated plasma burn through his chest, he heard a body fall to the deck.

Cavv opened his eyes and looked with surprise from the fallen body of Admiral Drommel to the weapon held in the hands of Colonel Niovi.

"As acting commander of the *Guardian*, I officially surrender her and all aboard to the benevolent sovereignty of the New Republic."

"Well, I don't know how we did it, but we did it," Sconn said, raising his drink.

Three glasses of fine Cassandran Choholl clinked together in a toast.

Cavv took a long sip and sighed in contentment. "Now that I'm retired, I suppose you'll be taking command of the SAU."

"Not on your life, uncle. My resignation is sitting on General Cracken's desk."

"I knew you'd join us sooner or later, even if it was just for one mission." Shandria smiled at him. "I especially liked your proverb. Very eloquent."

"It should be. I'm the one who taught it to him," Cavv said. He noticed the way Sconn and Shandria were looking at each other and rose to his feet with a slight smile. "Dessert should be ready by now. I'll just go and check." Cavv disappeared into the kitchen.

Shandria gave the apartment another appraising glance. "Your taste has improved, Sconn."

"Enough credits can get you anything. Well, almost anything." Sconn stared into his glass. "Something has been missing here. For far too long."

Her eyes finally found his. "Is that a simple lamentation or a veiled question?"

"Both." Sconn took a deep breath. "I love you."

"She knows."

Sconn and Shandria both turned to stare at Cavv, who was peeking out from the kitchen. He put a hand to his lips, which had twisted into a blushing grin. "Sorry."

Shandria smiled, laying her hand over Sconn's and saying: "I missed you."

Cavv beamed. "There's an old saying about true love."

"What?" Sconn and Shandria asked in unison.

Cavv opened his mouth to answer, then closed it. "You know, I don't recall. Nobody's ever actually let me finish that one before."

Roleplaying Game Statistics

Cryle Cavv

Type: Acquisitions Specialist
DEXTERITY 3D+2
Blaster 6D, brawling parry 4D+2, dodge 7D, grenade 5D, pick pocket 8D, running 4D
KNOWLEDGE 3D
Alien species 8D+1, cultures 7D+1, languages 7D+2, streetwise 10D+1, value 11D, willpower 9D+2

MECHANICAL 3D+1
Astrogation 7D+1, sensors 6D+2, space transports: Arakyd Helix 7D, starship gunnery 7D, starship shields 5D
PERCEPTION 4D
Con 11D+2, hide 10D, investigation 9D+1, search 9D, sneak 8D
STRENGTH 2D
Brawling 3D
TECHNICAL 2D
Computer programming/repair 6D+1, demolition 5D+2, droid programming 5D, droid repair 7D, security 9D+2
Force Points: 5
Character Points: 22
Move: 10
Equipment: Chronometer, comlink, hold-out blaster (3D+2)

Capsule: Cryle Cavv is a man who relies more on brains than blasters. He's always ready with a platitude, obscure axiom, or instant word of wisdom. As he's fond of saying, "There's always somebody waiting with a bigger, better blaster, but it's a lot harder to upgrade wits. And wits never run out of energy."

It's hard to argue with success. Cavv has survived over 65 years, keeping one step ahead of the Empire for most of them. Though much of his past is a well-guarded (and sometimes classified) secret, it is known that he spent a good amount of time on the planet Contruum, birthplace of Alliance General Airen Cracken. Cavv was part of "Cracken's Crew," the infamous guerrilla force that terrorized the Imperial occupation forces on Contruum.

The best description of Cavv was offered by General Cracken, who said, "For somebody who talks so much, it's amazing how very little actually gets said."

Paul Danner

Sienn Sconn

Type: Master Thief
DEXTERITY 4D
Blaster 5D+2, blaster: wrist lasers 9D, brawling parry 6D, dodge 9D, melee combat: stun staff 10D, melee parry: stun staff 8D+1, pick pocket 7D, running 6D, vehicle blasters 5D
KNOWLEDGE 3D
Alien species 5D, cultures 6D+1, languages 7D, law enforcement 7D, streetwise 9D, value 10D, willpower 7D+1
MECHANICAL 2D
Repulsorlift operation 5D, repulsorlift operation: speeder bike 5D+2
PERCEPTION 4D
Bargain 8D+1, con 9D, gambling 5D+2, hide 8D+1, search 10D, sneak 11D
STRENGTH 3D
Brawling 5D+2, climbing/jumping 8D
TECHNICAL 2D
Computer programming/repair 7D, demolition 5D, security 8D
Force Points: 4
Character Points: 20
Move: 10
Equipment: Stun staff (STR+3D+2 includes stun charge; STR+2D without stun charge), wrist laser gauntlets (5D)

Capsule: Sienn Sconn is an intergalactic thief who has reached the top of his profession and found himself wanting. Usually quick-witted, spontaneous, and mischievous, Sconn is experiencing a crisis of conscience and has come to fear that he has become little more than one of the idle rich he used to prey upon. In many ways he is a different man than the carefree thief of a decade ago.

Of course, some things never change. He still considers himself 'one-of-a-kind'. He refuses to follow prescribed rules, and often times, common sense. This independent streak was what ultimately doomed the love affair between himself and Shandria L'hnnar, a New Republic Intelligence field operative with whom he had shared many adventures over the years.

Sconn refuses to steal from anyone except Imperials, crime lords and the obnoxiously rich. He's known for his ferocious tenacity, technological skill and daring feats of escape. Another key element of his personality is a strong streak of morality. It is a side he has always tried to conceal, due to the negative effects it could have on his reputation as a notorious brigand.

Like many in his chosen profession, Sconn has a penchant for getting into trouble, but unlike others, also excels at getting back out again. Considering he's still alive after many encounters with bounty hunters, dealings with the scum of the galaxy, and escaping the collective wrath of a wide assortment of Imperials, it truly seems that Lady Luck has embraced Sienn Sconn.

Admiral Gaen Drommel

Type: Imperial Admiral
DEXTERITY 2D
Blaster 6D, dodge 7D+1
KNOWLEDGE 3D
Alien species 6D, bureaucracy 6D, cultures 7D+2, intimidation 8D+1, languages 5D+2, planetary systems 6D+2, planetary systems Soullex 8D, tactics: capital ships 10D, tactics: fleets 10D+2, tactics: starfighters 8D+1
MECHANICAL 3D
Astrogation 6D, capital ship gunnery 7D, capital ship piloting 5D+2, capital ship shields 6D, starship gunnery 5D, starship shields 5D
PERCEPTION 4D
Bargain 8D, command 9D, command: Imperial Navy officers 11D, con 6D+2, investigation 4D+1, persuasion 4D+2,
STRENGTH 3D
Brawling 5D+2
TECHNICAL 3D
Capital starship repair 7D, security 6D+2
Force Points: 5
Dark Side Points: 20
Character Points: 18
Move: 9
Equipment: Blaster pistol (4D), comlink, rank cylinders, datapad

Capsule: Admiral Gaen Drommel was commander of one of the Empire's precious few Super Star Destroyers. His ship, the *Guardian*, was stationed near the Imperial capital of Coruscant during the Battle of Endor. With word of the defeat of the Imperial fleet and the death of the Emperor, Drommel fled Coruscant to his home region, hoping to use the fleet to consolidate power into a personal empire.

Soon after, Drommel and a group of three Imperial Star Destroyers launched a short but devastating campaign against Alliance safe worlds and bases.

During the last battle of Drommel's campaign, the Battle of Tantive V, two of the three *Imperial*-class Star Destroyers were destroyed, while the third, the *Wolf's Claw*, was captured by Alliance forces. Drommel managed to escape with the *Guardian,* though the ship was heavily damaged before it managed to make the jump to light speed.

The *Guardian* has spent over a decade in orbit around the obscure Outer Rim world, Soullex with its hyperdrives inoperative. Drommel had intended to effect repairs as quickly as possible, but the parts needed became hard to come by as the Empire disintegrated into civil war and then became mostly absorbed by the New Republic.

Drommel's search for spare parts and technical assistance had to be slow and covert in order to avoid discovery. He has no intention of serving the enemies he has sworn to crush and hopes that the *Guardian* will become the center of a successful attempt to crush the Rebels once and for all. Drommel knows of the failed campaigns launched by Zsinj, Daala and Thrawn, but feels confident that with the right troops supporting him, he will be successful. After all, Drommel believes, Zsinj was a lunatic, Daala was a woman, and Thrawn was a non–human alien—they were all inherentily inferior to him and his genius.

Shandria L'hnnar

Type: New Republic Operative
DEXTERITY 3D
Blaster 6D+1, dodge 6D, melee combat 5D, melee parry 4D, vehicle blasters 5D
KNOWLEDGE 4D+1
Alien species 8D, cultures 8D, languages 9D+2, planetary systems 9D, willpower 7D
MECHANICAL 3D
Astrogation 7D, sensors 5D, starfighter piloting 7D, starship gunnery 5D+2, starship shields 4D+2
PERCEPTION 3D+2
Bargain 6D, hide 5D, persuasion 8D, search 5D, sneak 5D
STRENGTH 2D+1
Brawling 4D, climbing/jumping 5D, stamina 5D
TECHNICAL 2D+2
Computer programming/repair 7D, demolition 5D, security 7D
Force Points: 3
Character Points: 18
Move: 10
Equipment: Unadorned jumpsuit, chronometer

Capsule: Shandria L'hnnar is a long-time New Republic Intelligence operative. Though her intellectual ability outshines her physical skills, her sheer willpower, tenacity and determination are enough to keep her superiors from suggesting that she stay out of the field and remain behind an analyst's desk. She is, in fact, one of the few New Republic Intelligence operatives to not be forced behind a desk after completing twenty field missions.

A native of Corellia, Shandria dreamed of entering the Imperial Academy and graduating at the top of her class. She had always been an excellent student, with a natural ability to quickly learn and retain information. Her dreams were short-lived however, as she discovered the truth about the Empire when her best friend was arrested for little more than holding anti–Imperial opinions. The incident served to open Shandria's eyes. She never saw her friend again, but soon after joined the Rebel Alliance herself.

Shandria met Sconn while on a mission to Venaari and a mutual attraction bloomed immediately. As their paths crossed again, the attraction grew into to love.

Their relationship eventually soured. As Sconn became increasingly disenchanted with the emptiness he felt at the top of his profession, Shandria became increasingly insistent that he face the fact he's no longer the dashing young thief he once was and put his talents to use as an official operative for the New Republic. Sconn, on the other hand, began insisting that Shandria give up field work to spend more time with him; she wasn't getting any younger either, he was fond of reminding her. After one particularly nasty argument, Shandria left Sconn again—this time for good, she said. She took on the most dangerous, longest-term mission available... yet another attempt at tracking down the *Guardian*.

For the first time in her career, everything that could go wrong for Shandria *did* go wrong, and she found herself imprisoned along with a group of Republic troopers in the *Guardian*'s detention block.

Game information created by Paul Danner, Steve Miller, and Louis J. Prosperi.

the Draw

By Angela Phillips

Illustrations by Brandon McKinney
Map by Tim Bobko

"All right, *Blue Boy*, bring it on home."

Starlines resolved into a blue–green planet as Mair Koda dropped her freighter out of hyperspace over Vernet. "Lockin' good," she murmured, smiling at the first sight of her homeworld in over six months. The *Blue Boy* dropped through the cloud cover; Mair followed the familiar coastline into the grain belts of Vernet's southeastern continent. She nudged her ship over the mountains of the continental spine and Maz–Verlin came into view, the city's lights still glimmering in the minutes before dawn. Mair aimed for the starport's red and blue lights.

What's that? Mair wondered as she caught sight of an unfamiliar pattern of ground lights. It looked as if a cluster of buildings had been erected in the north of the city, but the sky was too dark and *Blue Boy* moving too fast for her to make out any details. She made a mental note to ask about it later.

The farming colonies on Vernet were small enough that the locals considered a star freighter's arrival a major event. As Mair strode down the ramp onto the packed clay field that served as Maz-Verlin's spaceport, she saw a ring of spectators waiting to see what "good ol' Mair" had brought for them this time. Even in the gray light of dawn she could recognize individuals and knew what each person wanted. Her foster–parents, Arn and Emmi Stonelaw, had ordered a new strain of crop seed, a calibrator for their laser plow and twenty meters of duranex to make new coveralls for their sons. Lorne Turvey, local barkeeper as well as part–time operator of the spaceport, had requested as many recent holofeatures from the Core as Mair could bring him. Pursey Vermilla, local character, waited for disks of the latest fashions and (ever in vain) for a bolt of vine–silk.

"By thunder," Mair swore, grinning broadly, "don't ya'll have anything better to do, that you're waiting for me at oh–dark–thirty in the morning?"

"Welcome home, Mair," said Pursey, pushing to the front of the crowd. "Did you find my silk?"

With her clients' assistance, Mair had most of her cargo off–loaded by mid–day. Only a few bulky pieces of farm machinery remained on board as she handed the bolt of duranex over to fifteen–year–old Yuri Stonelaw and smiled as the fair–haired boy staggered under its weight.

"Hey, why didn't your brother show up, kid?" Mair asked, helping the boy get a grip on the bolt. Yuri scowled, the expression seeming out of place on his round, rosy–cheeked face. "What's the matter?" Mair continued, "is Kristoff sick or something? I haven't seen him all morning—usually he's first in line when I come in—after Pursey, of course."

"Kristoff," said Arn Stonelaw, taking the duranex from his son, "has more important concerns now than waiting around the spaceport."

"What, he married?" Mair hooted. She stopped laughing; Arn's expression was grim and Yuri's was downright venomous. "All right, I put my foot in it, I'm sorry—what's wrong?"

"Everything," Yuri began, but his father cut him off.

"Nothing's wrong—just different, that's all. Folks gotta adjust. Now help me, Yuri, this cloth's heavy. Mair—you come out to the farm tonight, have supper."

Mair nodded agreement as the Stonelaws moved off, then shook her head in wonder at whatever mysterious changes had befallen her friends as she went back into her ship to clean up.

Twisting her wet, black hair into a knot at the nape of her neck, Mair stood on the *Blue Boy's* ramp looking out across the landing pad into town. Center Street seemed empty for that time of day. Most afternoons there would be a group of boys, led by Kris Stonelaw, playing an impromptu game of no–rules quambah while anyone else with time on their hands watched. Now there was no one about but three pastel–furred pittins chasing leaves and one short, stocky figure walking toward the ship.

"Hey, Yuri!" Mair called. "Your parents think they need to send you to fetch me to dinner? Ya'll think I'm going to pass up home–cooking after weeks of space grunge?"

Yuri smiled as she put an arm around him. "I'm so glad you're home, Mair," he said, "it's so good to have somebody to talk to again."

"What, Kristoff suddenly too grown–up to listen to a little spud like you?"

Yuri stopped, looked Mair dead in the face. "They took him," he said. His blue eyes, which for as long as Mair could remember had held nothing but laughter, were full of loss as he repeated, "They took him. They took all the boys."

"Who?" Mair asked, stunned.

Yuri looked down the empty street, then began tugging Mair's arm, leading her back to the ship. "You don't know?" He said. "No one's told you?"

The spacer shook her head. "I'm a fungus, and they keep me in the dark. What's wrong? How bad can it be if your folks didn't contact me—and don't yank my arm off!" she protested as Yuri pulled her into the *Blue Boy*.

"The Empire," Yuri said, as if that explained everything. "They ripped up a bunch of forest, built a base, and drafted all the young men to be soldiers."

Mair collapsed into a battered conform–lounger in shock. "There goes the neighborhood," she groaned. "All the young men?"

"Everybody between eighteen and twenty–five," Yuri said, "everybody able–bodied that is. They didn't take Daoud Vari—even though the Empire could afford to fit him with prosthetics."

"If the Empire wanted recruits without legs, they'd cut'em off themselves," said Mair. "I suppose, when they came in, they gave ya'll a load of tripe about 'preparedness' and 'ensuring Vernet's security' and 'working together to combat galactic instability,' right?"

"Yeah—how'd you know?"

"Same load of tripe they always start out with. I got friends—same thing's happening on worlds all over. The Imps come on all truth and justice, and next think you know they're pawing through every cargo shipment and trying to stuff homing beacons up your nose."

Yuri leaned toward the spacer, his earnest look incongruous on his childish features. "Then you understand, Mair, why we've got to get Kris out of there."

"Whoa, cool your ion drives, boy!" said Mair, blinking. "How did we get from 'Imps make sorry neighbors' to 'we've gotta get Kris out'?"

"Well, we can't let him become like them, can we?" said Yuri as if stating a self–evident fact.

Mair sighed. "You don't know what you're asking me, boy."

"I know a way into the camp, if you just hold lookout for me."

"And if I got spotted I'd have to leave Vernet and never come back. Never mind what'd happen if I got caught."

"We won't get caught," the boy insisted. "We can't just give Kris up!"

"And what do you think will happen to him after if we get him out—the Empire ain't too kind to deserters. He'd have to leave too."

"He could ship out with you," Yuri suggested.

"How would your parents feel about that?"

"Better than they do now—at least he'd be free. He might as well be gone already, or dead, for all we see of him. If he gets off–world at least we'll know he's got a chance to lead his own life. Please help us, Mair."

Mair dropped her head into her hands, sighing. "I can think of about a hundred good reasons to go on as if we'd never had this talk—but I love you and Kristoff like brothers. I'll be taking off again in a few days, and by thunder Kris'll be with me. Tell me how we're going to get into the camp."

Yuri climbed out of the creek and shook water from his clothes. Drawing the waterproof pouch from his tunic, he removed the blaster he'd taken from his father's cupboard and checked again to ensure the selector was set to "stun." The wind whipped through the tree tops. A nightscreeg called mournfully to its mate as they hunted by the light of Vernet's three moons. Yuri willed himself to be brave. He stood as tall as he was able and tried to suck in his belly, but the large stack of chor–cakes he'd eaten to fortify himself for this midnight commando run made it difficult. He felt as if he'd swallowed a lump of ferrocrete.

A splash from the creek caught his ear. He ducked behind a clump of underbrush and waited; it should be Mair, swimming beneath the camp's perimeter field as he had, but it wouldn't hurt to be careful. A dark object was flung out of the water onto the grassy bank: a blaster rifle. A figure clambered from the creek and Yuri tensed in fear; instead of the familiar silhouette of Mair Koda, he saw the glossy armored form of an Imperial scout. Swallowing back both his fear and his chor–cakes, Yuri leapt out of the bushes and opened fire on the interloper. "Thunder and lightning, Yuri! It's me!" came the trooper's modulated voice, as the armored figure dove to the ground. "Put that thing away—you want to wake up

everyone on the night–side of the planet?"

Yuri lowered his weapon. "Mair?"

She pulled off her scout trooper helmet. "You spud!" she exclaimed. "I told you I'd be disguised!"

"But as one of t*hem*?"

Mair snorted. "How else is a woman supposed to get around an Imperial Army training post?" She jammed the helmet back on. "Ugly as it is, I still can't show my face—besides, I have a backup plan in case we get spotted." She got to he feet, shaking water from her armor. "The classic 'you're my prisoner' routine. Give me your gun, Yuri, and put your hands on your head."

Yuri complied. "I'm sorry I shot at you."

"Forget about it—with your aim, you couldn't hit a Hutt."

"Where'd you get that armor?" Yuri asked.

"From a friend."

"Where'd your friend get it?"

Mair paused. "Yuri, there are some questions you're off not asking. Just start marching, and we'll get your brother out of that camp before the Imps even know we were here. Don't worry."

They moved out of the woods across the training fields, heading toward the central complex. Yuri, hands still on his head, walked ahead of Mair, who held her rifle level with his back. They traveled in silence for a long while. Finally, Yuri spoke: "Mair?"

"Keep it down," Mair hissed. "We're getting close, and if anyone hears us talking, we're busted."

"But I was wondering...."

"What?"

"I've heard Imperials use brainwashing—what if Kristoff doesn't want to be rescued?"

Mair said nothing; the same fear had been preying on her mind, but there was no way she was going to share that with Yuri. "Of course he'll want to be rescued," she said, as much to reassure herself as the boy, "if only because army chow is nasty. By the way," she said, changing the subject, "stroke of genius, swimming under the security field like that."

Yuri shrugged. "I saw fish swim back and forth under it, and figured anything they could do, I could do. I spend a lot of time there, sitting by the creek." He sighed. "I can't believe it was only this summer when Kris and I were swimming there. The last day—'course I didn't know then it was the last day—we caught mud crabs and built little pens out of dirt to hold 'em, but they kept getting away."

"Just like we're gonna get away," said Mair. "Now hush up, we're getting close to the barracks."

Security problems were apparently far from the commander's mind at the Vernet training camp; Mair and Yuri were able to make their silent way among the buildings undetected. The door to trainees' barracks was locked from the outside, but Mair sliced it open easily with a few strokes of her electro–pick. Yuri slipped quietly inside while Mair stood by the door in her scout's armor and tried to look like she belonged there.

Yuri paused while his eyes became accustomed to the darkness of the windowless barrack and then began searching for his brother among the bunks. All the sons of Vernet lay sleeping in identical rows, each in identical drab underclothes, each with his hair shorn away. Some slept so quietly they could have been dead, and Yuri shivered at the thought that he was creeping through a morgue filled with all the companions of his childhood.

He found Kristoff on a lower bunk halfway down the line. He paused to look at his brother. Kristoff Stonelaw was tall, muscular, strong–featured, and handsome: everything young Yuri hoped to become in a few years' time. Yuri reached out to tap his brother's shoulder gently.

"Kris?" he whispered.

Kristoff's eyes flew open immediately. "Yuri? What're you doing here?"

"Come on," Yuri whispered eagerly, "Mair's waiting outside."

"What?" Kristoff's eyes were full of bewilderment.

"She's going to take you off–world. Come on, Kris, before the others wake up."

"Off–world?" Kristoff sat up in his bunk. "Yuri, what are you talking about?"

"We're getting you out of here. We're rescuing you."

"Rescuing me?" Kristoff asked in an incredulous tone of voice. "I don't need any rescuing. What kind of garbage has Mair been telling you?"

What is taking so long? Mair wondered; she feared she knew. *Come on, Kris, listen to your brother, the spud's got sense. Come on, think with your own brain....*

As she stood there, the event Mair had feared the most happened: a lone night patrol guard walked around the corner of the barrack, nearly bumping into her.

"Hey!" said the guard, "what are you doing here? What's your operating number?"

Mair stared silently at the guard and fingered the safety on her gun.

"I'm talking to *you*, kid," the guard continued, "do you even know tonight's pass phrase?"

Pass phrase? Mair wondered. *Oh, well...* "Darth Vader wears frilly underclothes?" she suggested cheerfully as she whipped out her blaster, stunned the guard and ran.

The shot outside their door woke the recruits; instantly the quiet of the barracks was replaced by the grunting, shouting, and other sounds of 100 young men tumbling out of their bunks. Yuri gave Kristoff one last agonized glance; Kristoff snatched at his brother but missed. Yuri shoved his way through the dark confusion and darted out the door.

Mair was nowhere to be seen, so Yuri just kept running, away from the buildings and out through the woods toward the main gate of the camp, while lights and sirens came on and the sounds of pursuit grew louder and more organized behind him.

Luckily, Yuri found a huge nole tree not far into the woods. He flung himself up the branches and was a good four meters off the ground before the pack of drowsy, half–naked recruits blundered past, waving infra–red scanners haphazardly through the underbrush and shouting. He waited until the ruckus had passed him by, then slipped down the tree. He quietly doubled back towards the creek, skirting the compound and its lights.

Yuri paused at the edge of the water, wondering: stay or go? His heart pounded in fear at what the Imperials might do if they caught him, but how could he ever abandon Kristoff?

"Yuri," said a familiar voice behind him. The boy turned to face his brother. Unlike his comrades, Kristoff had put on trousers, boots, and gun belt before leaving the barrack. He stared intently at Yuri. "I knew you'd be here," he said with the ghost of a smile. "I knew this was how you had to have gotten in."

"Kris, come with us," said Yuri. "It's still not too late."

Kristoff shook his head. "I belong here," he said. "This is where I want to be."

"You didn't think that way when they came to draft you."

"That's because I didn't know better," said Kristoff. His eyes shone glassily in the light of the setting moons. "Yuri, I don't know what kind of lies that Mair is telling you, but—"

"She hasn't told me anything."

Kristoff held up his hand for silence. "Yuri, you have to understand. The galaxy is in a very fragile state right now. We live in dangerous times. Threats to our planet are everywhere—smugglers, pirates, anarchist rebel terrorists. Vernet has to be prepared to defend herself, and I'm proud to be a part of her defense. Can't you see I'm this for you?"

"They won't let you come and visit us," said Yuri. "And they won't even let us send you messages!"

"Sacrifices must be made," said Kristoff. "Now come with me, Yuri."

"What?"

"I have to turn you in to my commanding officer. He'll want to question you about how you got in here."

"Why don't you tell him?"

"Standard procedures, Yuri. I have to turn you in. And he'll need to discipline you."

"Huh?" Yuri's eyes grew wide with fear.

"He won't harm you, Yuri, not permanently," said Kristoff, his voice eerily calm. "It'll be painful, but we have to make an example of you." He raised his blaster.

Yuri backed up to the brink of the water. "Kris, what are you doing with that gun?"

"If you won't come willingly, I'll have to—"

"Kris, look at what you're doing!" Yuri cried. "They're making you shoot me, they're messing up your mind!"

Something grabbed Yuri's legs from behind and yanked him into the creek before Kristoff could fire on him. He struggled, but strong arms pulled him beneath the force barrier and hauled him from the water outside the camp.

"Come on," said Mair, now stripped of her armor, as she hustled the boy onto her swoop bike. "We can't help him!"

"Kris!" Yuri cried one last time. He looked over his shoulder as the swoop took off, to see his brother standing just inside the force field, his gun hanging limp in his hand, a puzzled look on his face.

Maz–Verlin was in chaos when the bike roared down Center Street: lights were on all over, and people were milling aimlessly in the road.

"You can't get to your ship, Mair," said Lorne Turvey, standing at the entrance to the spaceport. "They're having some kind of problem out at the base, called and said I had to close the port."

Mair gave him a withering look. "Do you think that included keeping me away from my own property?"

"Well, um...."

"Didn't think so," she said, pulling the bike around him.

"What about the Stonelaw boy?" Turvey called after her.

"I need his help," Mair said as she drove up the ramp into the Blue Boy.

They were in hyperspace before anyone could stop them.

"Hey, spud, buck up," said Mair, as she sat down on the bunk beside Yuri and put her arm around his shoulders.

"I can't go home now, can I?" he asked.

Mair shook her head. "You heard what Kris said—by the time they were done 'disciplining' you on that base, they would have tortured you until your brains were mashed chorba. They would do the same to me, if they caught me. There's no going back for either of us."

Yuri sighed and leaned his head against Mair's shoulder. "I can't believe they turned my own brother against me." His voice hitched and tears began to run down his cheeks. "I can't believe Kris was going to shoot me. I've lost him forever."

"Hey, hey," said Mair, hugging the boy and blinking away tears her own. "He didn't shoot you, did he? He could've jumped in the creek after us and caught us, but he didn't."

Yuri nodded silently.

"Deep down inside, some part of him didn't want to turn you in, didn't want to hurt you. Yuri, we may not've won Kristoff back from the Empire, but I don't think we've lost him all the way yet, either." She smiled at Yuri through her tears. "Consider this round a draw."

Roleplaying Game Statistics

Mair Koda

Type: Independent Freighter Captain
DEXTERITY 2D+2
Blaster 3D+1, brawling parry 4D, dodge 3D
KNOWLEDGE 2D
Business 4D, planetary systems 3D+2, intimidation 3D, value 4D+1
MECHANICAL 4D
Astrogation 6D, space transports 4D+2, space transports: Ghtroc freighter 7D, starship gunnery 4D+2, swoop operation 5D+1
PERCEPTION 2D+1
Bargain 5D
STRENGTH 3D
Brawling 4D+1, lifting 3D+2, stamina 5D, swimming 3D+1
TECHNICAL 4D
Blaster repair 4D+2, first aid: humans 6D, space transports repair 4D+2, space transports repair: Ghtroc freighter 7D, starship weapon repair: laser cannon, 5D+2
Force Points: 3
Character Points: 7
Move: 10
Equipment: Blaster (4D), multi–tool and hydrospanner (in pockets)

Capsule: Mair Koda's friends jokingly refer to her as being "as subtle as a thermal detonator in a bowl of breakfast cereal, and almost as pretty." Though this statement is something of an exaggeration, the outspoken spacer prefers to survive by a combination of hard work and humor, since she's sure she'll never make it on good looks or charm.

Angela Phillips

Born the only child of independent spacers, Mair spent her early childhood onboard the *Blue Boy*—until her mother ran off with a Wroonian smuggler. Her father didn't feel up to the challenge of simultaneously making a living and keeping his overly adventurous daughter from an early death, so he entrusted Mair to friends. Arn and Emmi Stonelaw, chorba–farmers on the backwater agricultural colony of Vernet, already had two sons, and they were perfectly happy to take Mair in as a "big sister." Mair worked on the Stonelaw farm until the age of eighteen, when she returned to the *Blue Boy* . Her father groomed Mair to take over the ship; when the old man died, she inherited the *Blue Boy* and her father's regular shipping route.

Honest and honorable, twenty–two year old Mair makes her living transporting goods between the inhabited planets of the Zuni cluster. It's lonely, unglamorous work for the most part, but it's what she feels she was born to do. She's been offered more "exciting" jobs, of course—smuggling for assorted petty crime rings—but has always refused. She has enough common sense to know that a crime boss would gladly make a meal of a small–time operator like her (in some cases, literally!).

She's also been approached by the Rebel Alliance. Though she approves of their goals, she's so far remained neutral. Her strongest loyalty in life is to her foster–family; now that her attempt to free Kristoff has made her a criminal in the eyes of the Empire, it remains to be seen how long her neutral stance will last.

Yuri Stonelaw

Type: Idealistic farm boy
DEXTERITY 1D+2
Running: short sprint 3D
KNOWLEDGE 2D+1
Survival: temperate forest 3D, willpower 4D
MECHANICAL 1D+2
repulsorlift operation: landspeeder 2D
PERCEPTION 3D
Search 3D+2, sneak 3D+1, sneak: in forests 5D
STRENGTH 2D
Climbing 2D+2, swimming 3D+1
TECHNICAL 1D+1
Force Points: 1
Character Points: 3
Move: 10
Equipment: Blaster pistol (4D)

Capsule: Fifteen–year–old Yuri Stonelaw is at that awkward age between boy and man; his thoughts are at times surprisingly mature, but his body hasn't caught up with them yet. He worships his older siblings. He longs to have the qualities he admires in them: Mair's easy humor and quiet competence; Kristoff's strength, good looks and magnetic personality.

His world was shattered with the arrival of the Empire on Vernet: they took his brother. Convinced that Kris would never willingly submit to domination, Yuri began planning a rescue. He knew Mair loved Kris as much as he did, and would help him any way she could. The one thing he didn't plan on was the strength of Imperial indoctrination techniques.

Kristoff's refusal to defect was the cruelest blow Yuri had yet received. Forced to flee his homeworld with Mair, Yuri still holds hope of liberating his brother from the Empire. He'll likely encourage Mair to join the Rebellion as well.

Kristoff Stonelaw

Type: Imperial Recruit
DEXTERITY 2D+2
Blaster 3D+2, dodge 4D, grenade 3D+2, vehicle blasters 3D+1
KNOWLEDGE 1D+1
Bureaucracy: Imperial Army 2D+2, survival 2D
MECHANICAL 2D
Hover vehicle operation 2D+1, repulsorlift operation 2D+1
PERCEPTION 2D
Search 3D
STRENGTH 3D
Brawling 4D, stamina 3D+1, swimming 3D+1
TECHNICAL 1D
Blaster repair 1D+2, demolition 2D
Force Points: 1
Character Points: 2
Move: 10
Equipment: (When armored) blaster rifle (5D), field armor and helmet (+1D physical, +2 energy), grenades (5D), helmet comlink, survival gear, utility belt with supplies

Capsule: Kristoff Stonelaw is one of those tragic figures of his era—honorable men who believe the New Order is just. He had no personal experience with either the Empire or the Rebellion before he was drafted. The horrifying training holos of riot and revolt which his trainers showed him seared indelible impressions in his innocent mind; how was he to know that the Rebels he saw were acting in desperation, struggling to the death against slavery and genocide? All he knows is what the Empire tells him. Add to their propaganda the drugs they slip into his food and water and the subliminal messages played while he sleeps, and Kris Stonelaw can't truly be held responsible for turning on his brother.

Kris' intelligence and charisma will likely put him on the fast track for promotion when he's out of training. Once he has the chance for a little freedom of thought, as well as real experience of the galaxy beyond his homeworld, he will likely see the truth behind the lies the Empire tells him. Time will tell if he has the strength to face what he sees.

The Blue Boy

Craft: Ghtroc Industries class 720 freighter
Type: Light freighter
Scale: Starfighter
Length: 35 meters
Skill: Space transport: G.I. class 720 freighter
Crew: 1, gunners: 1
Crew Skill: See Mair Koda
Passengers: 10
Cargo Capacity: 135 metric tons
Consumables: Two months
Cost: Not available for sale
Hyperdrive Multiplier: x2
Hyperdrive Backup: x15
Nav Computer: Yes
Maneuverability: 1D
Space: 3
Atmosphere: 260; 750 kmh
Hull: 3D+2
Shields: 1D
Sensors:
Passive: 15/0D
Scan: 30/1D
Search: 50/3D
Focus: 2/4D
Weapons:
1 Double Laser Cannon
Fire Arc: Front
Crew: 1
Skill: Starship Gunnery
Fire Control: 1D+2
Space Range: 1–3/12/25
Atmosphere Range: 100–300/1.2/2.5km
Damage: 4D

Capsule: Mair Koda inherited the *Blue Boy* from her father; the Ghtroc freighter was old even when he bought it, but the family's careful maintenance has kept the ship reliable. They haven't done much modification of the original design—monster engines and bristling weapons racks are for smugglers and pirates, not honest freight–haulers.

Now that Mair has run afoul of the Imperial authorities, she may change her mind about her ship's needs.

Vernet

Type: Terrestrial
Temperature: Temperate
Atmosphere: Type I (breathable)
Hydrosphere: Moderate
Gravity: Standard
Terrain: Plains, forest, mountains
Length of Day: 25 standard hours
Length of Year: 335.2 local days
Sapient Species: Humans
Starport: One limited service (Maz–Verlin)
Population: 4000 humans (approximately)
Planet Function: Agricultural
Government: Farmer's Co–op Council
Tech level: Space
Major Exports: Grains, chorba roots
Major Imports: Technology, esp. farm equipment and droids
System: Vernet
Star: Unnamed (yellow)
Orbital Bodies:

Name	**Planet Type**	**Moons**
Danar	searing ball	0
Vernet	temperate forest	2
Terana	asteroid belt	0
Welarn	gas giant	23

System Summary

The Vernet system is located near the heart of the Expansion Region. It is part of a cluster of stars located far enough away from any major trade routes to have remained relatively undeveloped and rustic.

Vernet is the only world in the system capable of supporting human life, and it is the location of the only permanent communities there. Over the centuries, pirate bands and smuggler rings have operated out of the system's wide asteroid belt or from bases on moons orbiting the gas giant, but none have seriously threatened Vernet or its trading partners in nearby planetary systems; the Vernet system was their hide–out, not their hunting ground.

The wide, fertile grasslands of Vernet make it a perfect planet for intensive agriculture. Relatively few humans inhabit Vernet; most of the actual farm labor is done by huge cultivator/harvester droids. The primary crops in the plains are barma beans and assorted grains; farming continues into the mountainous regions with tracts of Corellian chorba–root, as well as herds of nerfs and barves.

Vernet's only city, Maz–Verlin, is surrounded by huge storage silos. All farm produce is brought to the silos at Maz–Verlin and flown out from there to nearby systems by various independent shippers. The silos are owned by the planetary government, a council elected by farm owners to negotiate crop prices and import rates with off–worlders. The Co–op Council insures fair and equal treatment of all citizens; Vernet's farms are prosperous, and thanks to the Council, everyone shares this prosperity.

The Empire's primary interest in Vernet is gaining control of its produce—as expendable as the Emperor considers his troops, he still has to feed them. Stormtroopers eat a lot of barma beans. The training base outside Maz–Verlin is, as Mair Koda suspected, only the beginning. The Empire plans to insinuate itself into Vernet government, ultimately placing the planet under the control of an Imperial governor. The governor will sell all of Vernet's crops directly to the Imperial Quartermaster–General, at a vastly reduced price, of course. At that point, the farmers can say good–bye to prosperity.

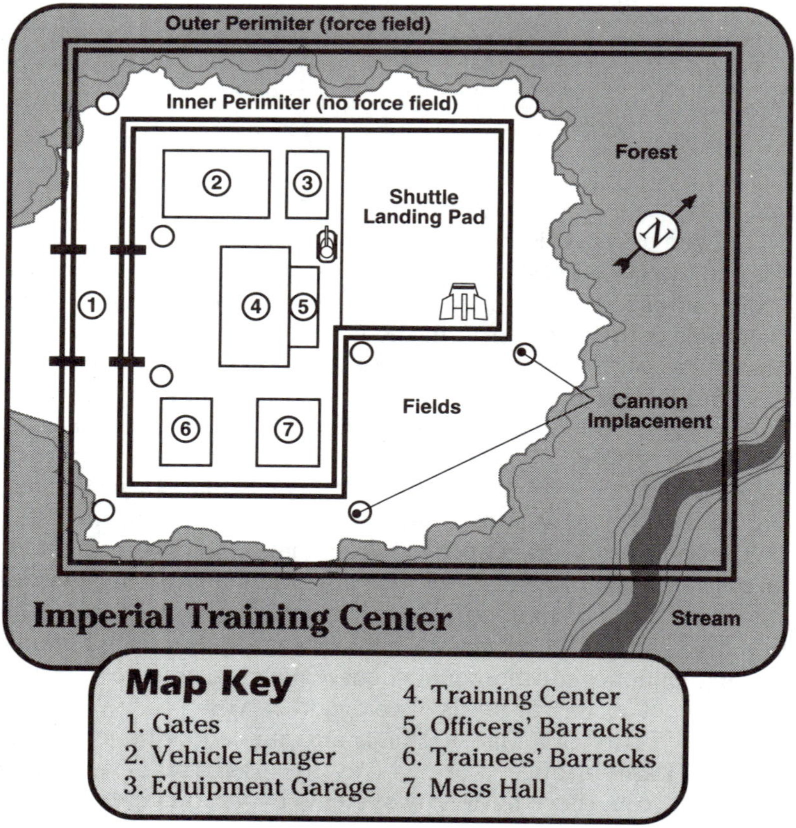

Map Key

1. Gates
2. Vehicle Hanger
3. Equipment Garage
4. Training Center
5. Officers' Barracks
6. Trainees' Barracks
7. Mess Hall

Drafting Vernet's young men serves two purposes: providing the Emperor with more cannon–fodder, and removing those natives from the population most likely to actively oppose their planet's gradual enslavement. Sadly, this sort of quiet oppression is going on all over the galaxy.

Vernet Imperial Army Training Camp

Contrary to popular legend, the Empire generally sees no point in slaughtering people it can draft—the New Order would never have become so powerful if all its leaders were so shockingly wasteful. The establishment of a small training post on Vernet allows the Empire to exploit the human as well as agricultural resources of the planet.

The officers of the Vernet post transform the planet's farm boys into loyal soldiers of the Emperor through a combination of physical and academic drills, weapons and vehicle training, and, of course, intensive psychological reprogramming Special emphasis is placed in training the troops to fight in forested, uneven, and otherwise unpredictable wild terrain, since wilderness ambushes are the favorite tactic of cowardly rebel terrorists.

Once their training is complete, the soldiers of Vernet will be ordered off–world to defend the New Order. They will be replaced by new draftees from other systems—draftees with no emotional ties to Vernet, who won't hesitate to participate in its subjugation.

■ Vernet Imperial Army Training Camp

Purpose: Indoctrination of indigenous personnel
Area: 1.5 square km (outer perimeter), .15 square km (inner perimeter)
Infrastrure: Training center/officer quarters, trainees barracks, mess hall, vehicle hangar, equipment storage garage, shuttle landing field
Personnel:
Officers: 3 commissioned, 10 non–com
Trainees: 100
Droids: 25 standard support, 6 E2–16 instruction
Vehicles: 20 speeder bikes, 5 landspeeders, 3 AT–STs, 1 medium *Imperial*–class repulsortank
Armaments: (not including vehicle–mounted weapons)
Stationary: 10 medium laser cannons, mounted at gates and perimeter corners
Mobile: 150 heavy blasters, 150 repeating blaster rifles, 25 grenade launchers w/ ammo, 25 light laser cannons, 6 cases of thermal detonators. Except for blasters, all the ordinance locked in the equipment garage when not in use for training.

Scoundrels

"Look, I think it's best of we split up here! The Imps got a good look at me, so I'll be more of a hindrance than a help to you. I guess I shouldn't have made it a point to rearrange that loud-mouthed lieutenant's face.

"I'm sure the offer still stands. Noone is a good guy, and he's as trustworthy a thief as you'll ever find. He'd never leave a partner high and dry.

"If you make it to Tasariq, look for us somewhere near Paradise Square. If you beat us there, you can start the stake–out of Velerinden. Or you can perhaps make your fortune mining tasar crystals. Ha!

"Oops. Here come the stormtroopers. I'll go over the roof and make sure they catch sight of me again. That should draw them away, and you. And don't worry. I've outrun Espo troopers on their home turf before, so stormtroopers are barely a challenge.

"Good luck! And I hope to see you on Tasariq!"

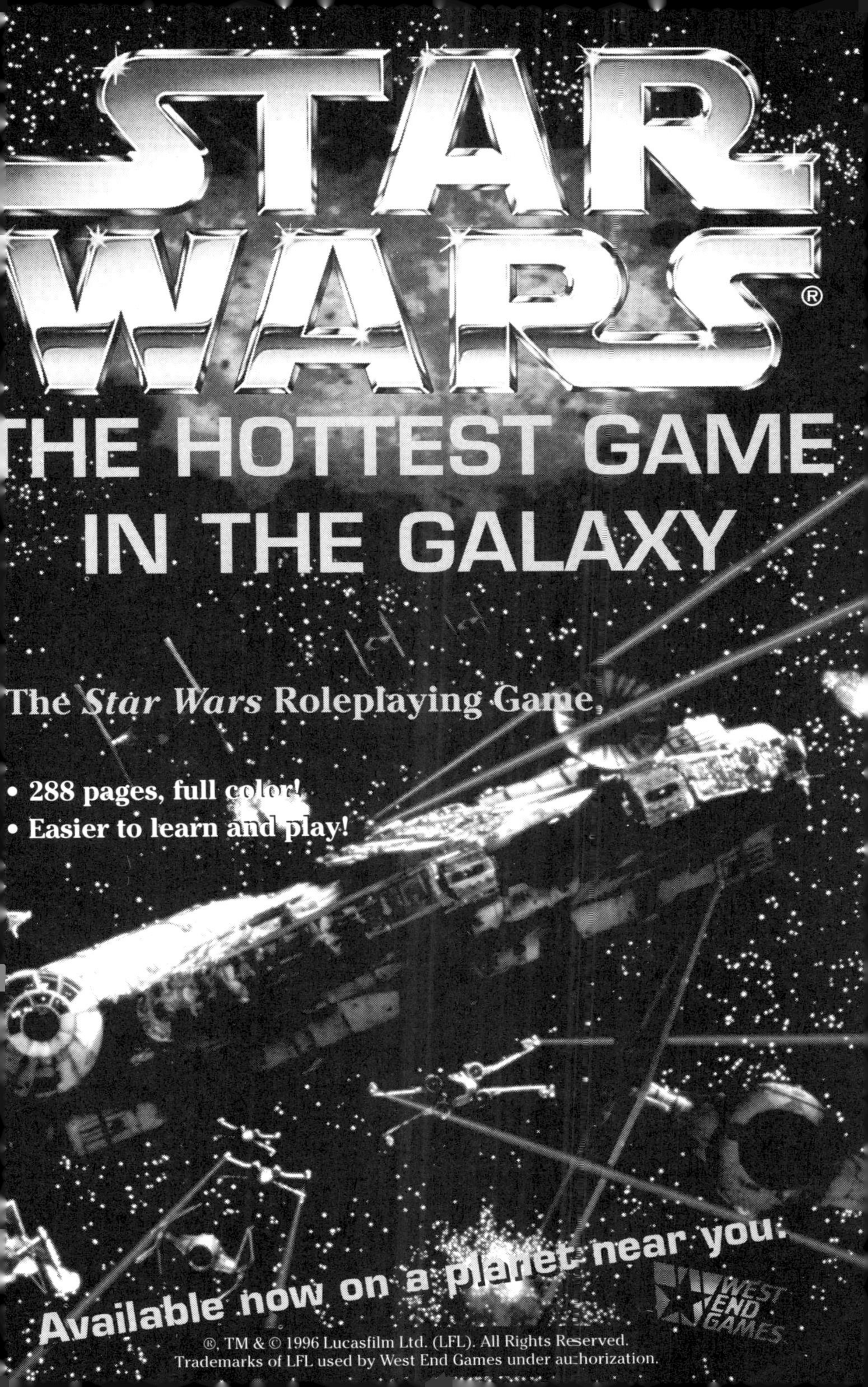
STAR WARS®
THE HOTTEST GAME IN THE GALAXY
The Star Wars Roleplaying Game.
• 288 pages, full color!
• Easier to learn and play!
Available now on a planet near you.
WEST END GAMES
®, TM & © 1996 Lucasfilm Ltd. (LFL). All Rights Reserved.
Trademarks of LFL used by West End Games under authorization.

About the Authors

Kevin J. Anderson is the author of the *New York Times* best-selling "Jedi Academy" trilogy, and more than a dozen other novels, including the Nebula Award Nominee *Assemblers of Infinity* (with Doug Beason). His other *Star Wars* projects include three anthologies of short stories, *The Illustrated Guide to the Star Wars Universe* with artist Ralph McQuarrie, several entries in the "Young Jedi Knights" series with Rebecca Moesta, and the script for a forthcoming "Tales of the Jedi" comic book mini-series. This is his first short story for the *Star Wars Adventure Journal*.

Paul Danner is a Florida–based freelance writer who has contributed several works of fiction to the *Star Wars Adventure Journal*. Among these are "One of A Kind" in *Journal* #5, which features the first meeting of Sienn Sconn and Shandria L'hnnar; "Easy Credits" in *Journal* #9, which sees Sconn trapped between a Mystral Shadowguard's burning wrath and a corporate princess's scheming affections; and "Small Favors" in *Journal* #12, which tells of the time Cryle Cavv had to extract a Rebel spy from under the nose of Darth Vader himself.

Patricia A. Jackson is an administrative assistant at Jackson Elementary School in York, Pennsylvania. Between her duties of school disciplinarian and spontaneous kickball games, she speaks with children about the joys of writing—all with the hopes of reaffirming their commitment to get a good education by excelling in academics. Patricia has contributed many short stories to the *Journal*, including "The Final Exit" in issue #4, which pits Thaddeus Ross against the flamboyant dark Jedi Aldaric Brandl.

Steve Miller has been active in the roleplaying game field as a designer and editor since 1993 and can be held accountable for releases from TSR, White Wolf, Imperium Games and Archangel Entertainment. Steve joined the staff of West End Games in May of 1997 to assume the editorial reins of the *Star Wars Adventure Journal*.

Tom Moldvay is a veteran game designer who contributed heavily to TSR's *Star Frontiers* and *Gangbusters* roleplaying games. He has worked on games from several of the industry's leading publishers over the years, including Avalon Hill's *Lords of Creation*. "Tasariq: The Crystal Planet" has been used as the setting for adventures run by Tom at roleplaying game conventions, and he has now provided the world for use by *Star Wars* Gamemasters everywhere as his first contribution to the *Journal*.

Timothy Squire O'Brien was born to a life of wealth and comfort, educated in the finest schools, and raised to inherit a vast financial empire. Instead, he turned his back on his life of privilege and entered a career as a freelance game writer and designer. He lives in a small, one-room shack in the Pennsylvania hills, and walks 15 miles to work, uphill both ways. Timothy is one of the *Journal's* most prolific contributors. Among his many articles are "Repulsortank Battlefield," a survey of Imperial Army armored units and ground tactics in *Journal* #9; and "Alliance Intelligence Reports: TIE Fighters," a history of the development and strategic use of this mainstay of the Imperial Navy in issue #10.

Angela Phillips, a teacher from Virginia and regular contributor to the *Journal*, started "The Draw" at Sci–Con in Virginia Beach, in a writing workshop run by former *Journal* editor Peter Schweighofer. "Kristoff" is named after a young gamer at the workshop who said he wanted to be a stormtrooper and to "contribute to the *Star Wars* universe." Angela thinks fen should stick together—have fun being a stormtrooper, kid! Among Angela's previously published works is "The Most Dangerous Foe" in *Journal* #11, the story of a young Jedi trainee during the "Tales of the Jedi" era.

Eric S. Trautmann is entering his third year as a full-time editor/designer for West End Games. Eric began his freelance writing career with the adventure "Easy Money" in the *Star Wars* supplement, *The Politics of Contraband*. He has contributed to such projects as *The Star Wars Roleplaying Game, Revised and Expanded*, the *DarkStryder Campaign*, *The Truce at Bakura Sourcebook*, *The Last Command Sourcebook* and a host of other *Star Wars* and *Indiana Jones* supplements. Eric hopes he will one day be referred to as a "*Star Wars* guru," and with his recent promotion to *Star Wars* Line Editor that wish may come true. Currently, Eric resides in the Greater Honesdale Metroplex—a massive urban sprawl that puts Coruscant to shame—with his fiancé and a moderately psychotic feline.

Daniel Wallace is the author of the forthcoming *Essential Guide to Planets & Moons* and *Essential Guide to Droids*. He inhabits the planet of Detroit in the remote Michigan system. "The Great Herdship Heist" is Daniel's first contribution to the *Star Wars Adventure Journal*.

About the Artists

New Jersey native **Tim Bobko** has drawn hundreds of illustrations for all of West End Games' lines during his four years as an on-staff graphic artist.

Kathy Burdette is a Virginia-based editor and freelance artist. In her spare time, she writes short fiction and smuggles nerfs onto Wroona.

Mike Chen is a veteran cartoonist and illustrator whose work has appeared in DC Comics, Marvel Comics, Valiant Comics, Archie Comics and several other publications. Mike also works as an instructor and the Special Projects Coordinator at the Joe Kubert School of Cartoon & Graphics Art.

Joe Corroney is the art and design coordinator for an educational textbook publisher in Columbus, Ohio, and a freelance artist whose work has appeared in publications from DC Comics, ICE, West End Games, and other publishers.

David Day has been publishing in the comic book field since 1986 on titles such as *Spiderman, Doctor Strange, Nightmare on Elm Street*, and numerous movie merchandizing projects. He recently completed a cover for a novel published by Harper-Collins, and has illustrated game products from Chaosium, TSR, and West End Games. David lives in Lansdale, Ontario, and enjoys playing hockey.

Brandon McKinney is a California based illustrator who recently completed work on illustrations for the *Essential Guide to Planets & Moons*. Among Brandon's other credits is work for Warp Graphics' popular *Elfquest* comic book line.

Jeff Menges has been working in the field of fantasy illustration since 1987. His work has appeared all over the American gaming market. Jeff lives on the northern shore of Long Island with his wife Lynne, son Matthew, and their rampant dachshund, Buddy. When not shackled to his drawing table, he likes to roam the shore or park looking for scenes for his next piece.

Doug Shuler has been a freelance artist for nearly a decade and has done work for many game companies, including GDW, Steve Jackson Games, ICE, White Wolf, FASA, and West End Games. His illustrations continue to appear on cards for *Magic: The Gathering* and *Vampire: The Eternal Struggle* from Wizards of the Coast. A *Star Wars* fanatic, he lives in Boulder, Colorado, with his wife, Jordi, their infant daughter, Brianna, and five maniac cats. Doug is the only artist who's work has appeared in every issue of the *Journal* to date.

Will Warren is a freelance artist who recently graduated from the Joe Kubert School of Cartoon and Graphic Arts. He's originally from Connecticut, but now finds himself living and working in New Jersey. When Will is not hard at work at his drawing table, he's usually busy catching some "Z's."